ORIGINS OF CATHLEEN

Origins of Cathleen

A Diversion

R. C. HUTCHINSON

LONDON

MICHAEL JOSEPH

First published in Great Britain by
MICHAEL JOSEPH LTD
52 Bedford Square,
London W.C.1
1971

7181 0910 4

Printed in Great Britain by
Northumberland Press Limited, Gateshead,
and bound by Dorstel Press, Harlow

FOR
ALL MY GRANDCHILDREN

1
Helma

In my earliest recollection of Helma O'Kneale she sits, bare to the waist, on the old piano stool in Howard's study, or 'studio' as he often liked vaingloriously to call it. Behind her are the home-made bookshelves and the messy picture which he attributed (against all the evidence) to Jan van Goyen. I remember exactly the way in which Howard said from one side of his mouth—the other being occupied by brushes—

'Ryan, come and say how-do-you-do to Mrs O'Kneale. She's your sister's new governess.'

Obediently, I went up to the woman and shook her hand; assuming from her foreign look that she was Russian I mechanically wished her good morning in that language, to which she responded in acceptable English:

'You are well, Ryan, yes?'

I did not trouble to pursue those vacant courtesies. My object in visiting Howard was to get his help with a plan loosely made that morning: I meant to construct a glider on which I should launch myself from the fields below Wycliffe Avenue, to sail high over the river Brent and land, admired by all, on one of the greens of the Hendon golf links.

'Howard,' I said, 'I've got to get four struts about three yards long, very strong but very light. Do you think they'd have that sort of thing in Belson's yard?'

'Very likely,' he replied. 'There'd be no harm in asking.'

'And do you think it would come to more than three and eightpence?'

7

'Look, do stand back—you're right in my light!' was all he answered to that.

Though by no means a perceptive child, I realized then that I had chosen a bad moment to approach him. One of my father's weaknesses was a belief that he could paint the human face and form; few people stayed in our house for any length of time without being impressed as models. In truth his only gift—apart from teaching—was that of an engraver, chiefly of urban scenes, but one was expected to take his lubberly excursions in the field of portraiture as seriously as he himself did. For a while I stood where I was on the slender chance of getting some attention, but my cause became hopeless when Sonya Mihailovna arrived with a heap of linen on one arm and a broken ewer in the other hand.

'I will take this back to those Selfridges,' she announced. 'It's not legal, to sell a vase so thin it break the first time it knock on the wall.'

'Indeed, no—I'd take no nonsense from these London shopkeepers,' Howard said.

'And Semyon,' she continued, as if enlarging on the same topic, 'would prefer not to pay for his room till after Christmas.'

She had advanced into the line of sight between Howard and his model. With some impatience he motioned her to stand clear.

'Semyon is nothing but a skulking parasite,' he announced, with such vehemence that two brushes fell to the floor. 'The very day after Christmas, in come the police force and out goes that idle scallywag. Tell him that.'

'I have tell him already,' Sonya said.

Her expression then was one I recognized—artificially smug. As a rule my parents' business with each other was transacted at chance meetings on the stairs or in the passages, occasionally they settled things by shouting through the hubbub at family meals. Here, in salient contrast, was a meeting which my mother had organized tactically, knowing that when Howard was astride his hobby-horse he was likely

8

to accept her decision with the minimum of fuss. Old Semyon had long been a strain on Howard's tolerance; no doubt
on Sonya's too, but some sort of maternal feeling, or just
the obduracy of wives, compelled her always to be on the
side of the extinct firebrand whose yellowing manuscripts
and horrid underclothes had for years been filling one of
our largest bedrooms. At this encounter she had swiftly
scored another victory: till Christmas, at any rate, Semyon
was safe. She was about to go when the presence of the new
governess seemed suddenly to glance her consciousness.

'Helma will catch cold,' she said abruptly.

'Certainly she will,' Howard retorted, 'if platoons of people
keep coming in to gossip and leaving the door open. We
might as well be in the middle of Hyde Park Corner.'

My mother's response was to turn to Helma herself, saying
wisely, 'Listen, chérie—when you are become a block of ice
you will need to stand up and walk abroad. It is the only
thing, with these painting men—that is something I know.'

That image of ice in auto-motion revived for a moment
my own interest in Howard's model, and instead of following Sonya downstairs to see if I could engage her in the
problem of long, light struts, I edged to a position from which
I could compare my father's hopeful daubing with the object
it was meant to represent. The former was worth a moment's
attention because of the green and violet shades which—
following his current theory of portraiture—he had introduced in the hair. In contrast, the woman herself had
nothing remarkable to show: in her pale brown chignon I
could detect no trace of violet or any other engaging colour.
She was every inch a governess, sitting so stiffly that she
might have been a window-dresser's dummy, and on a pallid
face where I observed not one distinctive feature she wore the
expression of vacuous devotion to duty which one associates
with private soldiers of long service.

In a recent article on the O'Kneale affair (in the *Irish
Quarterly Review*) Dr Stuart McMeikle speaks of 'the tragic
face of Mrs O'Kneale'. At the time of that first meeting with

9

Helma I believe I discerned some sadness in her face, but even that impression may come from later knowledge posing as memory. And so backward was I in education that for me the word 'tragedy', if I had heard it then, would probably have had no meaning.

No doubt a more intelligent small boy would have wondered why a new governess for Anastasia had been installed only a few hours after her departure for three weeks' holiday with our cousins in County Donegal, especially when (according to friends of mine) my sister was more than likely to be torpedoed and drowned on one or other crossing of the Irish Channel. But in our home the tutorial programme was always exceptionally fluid, and often it seemed to be fitted less to our educational lacunae than to Sonya's need of some cover for her intemperate hospitality. For some time before the October Revolution the more nervous—or shrewder— of my mother's relations were contriving to leave Russia; many came to England; and if my father wished to know why an ancient woman from Vologda was inhabiting his former dressing-room it was easiest to say that she had come to repair Anastasia's manifest weakness in the French language, or needlework, or the geography of Kandalaksha Bay. That system, which had some resemblance to episcopal patronage, is exemplified by its use with Semyon: at a time when I was academically adrift, having been dislodged from Miss Judson's school in Bear Lane for correcting with my fists the presumption of a child called Archibald Tremayne, the redundant Semyon was beneficed as my tutor in history; not wholly conscienceless, he had me in his noisome room for an hour every day, to read me *Das Kapital* in Solovyov's translation and to inveigh against his former friends in Hampstead Garden Suburb as 'betrayers of the Revolution of 1905'. So in a broad sense there was nothing strange in Helma's appointment: apparently she was one of those people whose features Howard imagined he could put on canvas—he spotted them, as often as not, among the students at his lectures—and I presumed that he had brought her home for that purpose; whereupon Sonya, an inveterate snapper-up of unconsidered trifles, seeing her at once as a possible replacement for the Danish girl whom Anastasia had defeated a few weeks earlier, would have discovered in the new arrival's mental baggage some branch of learning in which my sister was deficient—this was never hard to find—and signed her on as a governess before the woman herself had realized what was afoot. Howes Croft, the lank Victorian house we lived in, was often populous with long-term visitors who had been absorbed as casually as that.

For the time being my own interest in Anastasia was financial. Our Donegal cousins were generous, and without exerting the smallest charm (she had none that I knew of at her disposal) my sister at the end of her stay might easily pick up tips to the tune of a pound or two. This had happened on earlier occasions. I hoped, then, that a little flattery would win me a long-term loan, large enough to meet the cost of wood and canvas for my glider; and with this in mind I resolved to pray every night that the German submarine commander, aiming his torpedoes at the Fleet-wood steamer with Anastasia aboard, would fire them slightly askew.

As to Anastasia's newly appointed governess, she provoked so little curiosity in me that although her surname, O'Kneale, was one I knew well in other connections it simply rang no bell. She would not last long, I fancied—in so far as I thought about her at all.

In writing of Anastasia's education I am determined not to be uncharitable either to her or to Sonya: it is fairest to say that the subject had become a large anxiety in which they were both involved and both helpless. True, there were times when my elder sister seemed to face with cold indiffer-ence the prospect of finally leaving the world as ignorant a creature as she had entered it. When one governess—a woman of conspicuous intelligence with a teaching diploma from Montpellier—had surrendered the appointment after forty exasperating minutes (creating, I think, the low record for duration) Anastasia had only said, 'Well, who in the world would want to get like her!' On the other hand, the resignation of Zinaida Dygasinska, most pathetic of Sonya's protégées, did appear to cause her some hours of moral discomfort.

In that occurrence there was an element of drama which left a vivid impression on my mind. In the coach house, where she often fled to escape the importunities of visitors and servants, Sonya was seated in the decrepit landaulet, painfully composing a letter to recommend the services of some compatriot to the Duke of Rutland, with whom she claimed acquaintance. (The acquaintance existed, I suspect, only in her fecund imagination, though she may have bowed to him at some reception. I think she felt that the duke, being himself of reputable stock, must see that her friends were of a sort deserving dignified employment.) I sat beside her as adviser on orthography, for she had never mastered such English pedantries as the distinction between *their* and *there*, or realized that those minutiae were just as baffling to a pseudo-English boy of eleven years; I can still hear the note of weary indignation in her incurably foreign voice as she demanded,

'For the love of God, Ryan, tell me how you spell that ridiculous "emolument".'

'Why have you got to use such silly words?' I countered.

'Because an English letter has to be "in good form". Howard always says I should write "dibs", but I think that's only an Irish word.'

'All right: E-M-O- double L-E-W-M-E-N-T.'

'There must be two L's? You know for sure?'

'Well, of course! One L would look very uneducated.'

I always found Sonya adorable in her moods of wistful dependence, and I was much enjoying our symposium when

12

the sound of staccato footsteps made me look up, to see Anastasia marching towards us across the cobbled yard. Her rugged face was the colour of Gruyère, and when she came sharply to a halt, as an army runner does, it looked as if someone had her by the neck.

'Sonya, I'm sorry,' she said breathlessly, 'but it won't work and that's the end of it.'

I was fascinated. I had never before heard her use the word "sorry" and it faintly surprised me that she knew it.

My mother added a few words to her letter, rehearsing them aloud: '"My uncle was himself hitherto possessing a great estate in Kazan Government."' Then she turned to give Anastasia her tentative, maternal smile.

'What is it, petite? Today you make holiday?'

'It's her face,' Anastasia said. 'It's like the way Pavel does junket. And she keeps blubbing.'

Sonya's eyebrows evinced a delicate concern. 'Which face, chérie?'

'She's only got one. That woman, I mean.'

'Zinaida Dygasinska? Oh, but Zinaida has been at every sort of trouble. Before the War the strikers of Saratov killed her old father, just below her eyes.'

'Well, that isn't what she's blubbing about now.'

'And her beautiful place in Tchernogov, she lost that too. And all her servants.'

'Zinaida would lose the Crystal Palace. She's an absolute ninny.'

'But her grandfather Evgeni Solovyev was a member of the Imperial Household.'

'Well, people like Emperors are trained to put up with boring grandfathers.'

This exchange of views was the more interesting to me because Zinaida herself was already hovering at the other side of the yard, like a nervous actress awaiting her cue. Just then I could see exactly how her face, appealing as that of a dead fish does, would impinge on Anastasia, who in those days was as sensitive to adult distress as a professional

13

matador to the sufferings of bulls. Coming nearer, with her damp chicken-eyes aimed obliquely at my mother's chest, she spoke as if Anastasia's far from ethereal body were quite invisible to her.

'Sonya Mihailovna, I have to tell you your daughter has no interest at all in Batu Khan.'

My mother hastily put on her disciplinary expression, much as a modest woman will seize a dressing gown before she answers a knock on her bedroom door.

'Ah, but that is foolish of you, Anastasia.'

'Or in either of the Kipchak Hordes,' Zinaida said.

'Sonya, I'm fearfully sorry,' Anastasia said again. 'I suppose there are people who like Mme Dygasinska's voice, I expect they adore her going on and on about that stupid Bet-you-can.'

'Batu Khan,' Zinaida corrected.

'Bet-you-can't and his chipmuck herd. But frankly the whole business just makes me vomit.'

'Batu Khan was not stupid,' Zinaida announced. 'He was wicked, yes, but not stupid at all. It is English girls who are stupid when they will not listen to their teacher.'

'Actually Anastasia is more pig-headed than stupid,' I said, feeling I ought to give my sister some comradely support.

'You shut your gab!' Anastasia said. 'No one wants to listen to dribbling little spotty-faced boys.'

'What Ryan means,' my mother said for Zinaida's guidance, 'is that she will be less stupid when she arrives at a better mood.'

I was ready to overlook Anastasia's rudeness because I was engrossed in the shape the debate had assumed: each of the contestants was speaking as if her rival were not present, while Sonya, turning her beautiful eyes from one to another like a Wimbledon umpire, seemed to uphold this dignified alienation. All the same I was uneasy, as children often are when they feel that their elders are reaching flash-point. The look of self-indulgent martyrdom in Zinaida's crumpled

14

face, the combination of murderous fury with despair in Anastasia's, were together drawing too heavily on my mother's moral reserves; the corners of her mouth had begun to work in the way they did when people grumbled to her about my own peccadilloes; soon, I thought, she would be in tears—a thing I hated in a woman so civilized, so *sympathique*, as she—or the genes derived from some distant Tatar forbear might cause her first to go rigid and then, like a prophetess provoked, to release a torrent of searing rhetoric. Happily the conflict was interrupted: with his settled inconsequence Howard had come among us, he was standing just behind Zinaida with the air of a man arrived by accident on an unfamiliar planet, and now, in the Tipperary voice which returned to him whenever the harshness of life was beyond endurance, he said,

'My socks have gone again. The green ones. The ones which go with my Edinburgh suit. I can't imagine what happens to things in this house.'

An attack of that kind often served as a goad to my mother's mental processes, causing her brain to move, as it were, into a higher gear. On this occasion she settled Howard's business with two trenchant strokes: 'They were too old, I gave them to Semyon.' Then she swiftly returned to the tearful Zinaida.

'*Zinaida, toute la nuit passée je ne songeais qu'à tes talents extraordinaires*! I remember so vividly your beautiful house, how skilfully you ordered the decoration, the furnishings. It's just a tomfoolery that all such genius should go to waste.'

'It would be a convenience to me,' Howard was saying, 'if now and then you'd have the courtesy to consult me before disposing of my property to the rag, tag and bobtail of Petrozavodsk.'

But Sonya was not to be deflected. 'Just so,' she said briskly. 'After now I shall give you some news of your ruinous stockings every day.' And she turned to Zinaida once more. '*Ecoute, ma chère*: I've been making a plan for Natasha

15

Pisensky and her husband to have a *magasin de modes* in the Holland Park—evening gowns, very dear, for only a high clientèle—we have simply to get some money from my Uncle Nikolai who has all the money in the world locked up in his stupid bank at Lausanne. Soon they will need to employ a new designer, an artist of first-form talent. That is a situation for nobody, my love, but you.'

This vertiginous flight of Sonya's fancy had the sort of effect I had learnt to count on: if in her rhapsodic vision the Pisensky pair (as devoid of business sense as any I have known) were already established in their shop and making fabulous profits, the brainless Zinaida can hardly have been less bemused than she. So! With the future secure—the Pisenskys prosperous, the War over, the fashionable world entranced by Zinaida's sartorial confections—what need to worry about an 'English' girl who stubbornly refused to see the relevance of Ivan Berladnik or the Golden Horde to London suburban life in the reign of George the Fifth?

Only to Anastasia herself was this retreat into fantasy something less than a sound solution. The trouble, I suppose, was one of temperament: Zinaida was not the kind of fool she suffered gladly, and in her view, as I could see, the woman whom Sonya had adroitly pacified should rather have been made to answer for her gross incompetence. Later I found her as near to weeping as a girl of her granite composition could ever come. She said,

'I just wish Howard or somebody would put some sense into Sonya's head about her drivelling refugees. Just because they've been booted out of their own homes it doesn't mean they've turned into saints and heroes. I don't see why they've got to be treated like holy blessed martyrs and let off everything for the rest of their lives.'

I said—wishing to defend Sonya—'Perhaps with an ordinary girl Zinaida would have been all right.'

'What do you mean—"an ordinary girl"?'

'Well, to start with, one with a girl's sort of face, if you see what I mean. When Zinaida sees a craggy sort of thing

16

like a bit of the Carpathians it naturally sets her wheezing on about Batu Khan and all that bilk.'

'Yes, Rin-Bin, and when I see a thing like a frog that's had its bath in a jerry it sets me wanting to wring its scraggy little neck.'

This concept she went on to illustrate with so much physical violence that for an hour afterwards I wished I had not squandered my patience listening to her grumbles. But in truth I had largely shared her point of view. In her unfriendly attitude towards Zinaida Dygasinska there may have been some xenophobia of a special kind, for in a subtle way she and I were sick of visitors from abroad. Coffee-housing in the harness room where we spent much of our time together, we enjoyed at least one area of sympathy—a fitful but unanimous contempt for the country which had seen our birth; yet secretly, as I discovered long afterwards, we both cherished the same daydream, that we should one day turn into English children; for English children were respectable, and in our hearts we yearned for the trappings of respectability. We should have valued a mother who spoke the English language in the flat, hard voice, with a faintly metropolitan inflexion, of the mothers of our friends; a father who, like other people's fathers, went up to town in a dark suit and even a silk hat rather than jacket and breeches of shaggy tweed; who if he had to wear a beard would at least cut it to the neat shape of Commander Macdonald's across the road and, when a friend in the No. 13 bus whispered that half his flies were undone, would quietly rectify this lapse instead of smiling seraphically and crying out for the benefit of all his fellow passengers, 'Ah, now, there never was an invention so bothersome as those wee buttons and all!' Yes, and because we longed to be indistinguishable from the rest of Hendon's juveniles we obscurely resented the miscellaneous persons who, arriving at Howes Croft for food and lodging, for re-direction, or just the heartening warmth that flowed from Sonya's absurd benevolence, could never be confused with the citizens of Holders Hill.

So the Zinaida episode was more than once in what counted as my mind when the time approached for Anastasia's return from Kilmacrenan. Childish intuition told me that she and this Helma O'Kneale, destined by my parents for a sort of double harness, had not been so designed by nature. By then I had learnt from observation a little more of the new duenna; enough to suggest that what lay ahead was not one drastic battle on the Zinaida pattern but a war of attrition which might last for days.

Being so well used to aliens, I should have given no thought to the nationality of this Helma had I not chanced to find, beside a chair where she had been sitting, a book with the sinister title *Deutschland, ein Wintermärchen*. This revelation I felt it my duty to report to my father.

'Howard,' I said, finding him in the matrimonial bedroom, red and swearing as he worked himself into his Volunteer uniform, 'I think you ought to know something I've found out about that woman Mrs O'Kneale—or, as I should call her, Frau O'Kneale. I'm pretty certain she's a German spy.'

'Well, you'd better tell the police,' he said rather absently. 'Only first go and find Sonya and see if she can put her hands on a bootlace—black.'

'All right. And can I have twopence to use the Strouds' telephone?'

'Yes. No. Certainly not. At any rate get under the bed and see if you can find the belt thing which goes with this damned fancy-dress. What? Good—give it me. Now what is all this? Helma O'Kneale spying? Spying what on?'

'Well, us, I suppose.'

'Listen—is it sunstroke you have, or were you just cracked at birth?'

I could have made a sharp riposte to that tasteless attack, but I chose to ignore it.

'Besides,' I said, 'there's the aerodrome. She might be spying on that.'

'And what would a spy observe in a field as flat and bare as a pauper's plate?'

'Well, the Germans are always trying to bomb it, you said that yourself when Pavel was making such a fuss about the noise of the guns. And they keep getting closer. There was the one they dropped in the Express Dairy fields, and last week they got a dud one nearly into Commander Macdonald's garden.'

'Serve him right—silly old bore. I hope they get him in the solar plexus next time, with a live one.'

In youth one has simply to bear with adult evasions. 'They probably will,' I said, 'if this governess person we've got now sits up all night tapping messages in morse to tell the Taubes just exactly where the old man lives.'

We were in the early autumn of 1917, and there I felt I had shrewdly scored a point of some importance, since Macdonald was known to work in the Admiralty and was busy—one assumed—with secret plans for the final destruction of Scheer's High Fleet. But Howard was in one of his unreceptive moods, and instead of attending to my logic he chose to lecture me.

'Listen, Ryan,' he said with unusual pomposity, 'I will not have allegations brought against people living under my roof—or what counts as my roof, though God knows it wouldn't stay mine for a week if it wasn't for the loving-kindness and charity of your mother's pot-bellied relations in Lausanne. Least of all will I have nonsensical accusations brought against a poor unhappy widow woman who comes to me for succour and support and plain ordinary decent bowels of mercy.'

As this would obviously develop into a long oration I edged towards the door, and when he momentarily broke off to curse a brace-buckle which had nicked his thumb I seized the chance to interrupt:

'All right,' I said coldly. 'If you don't mind Sonya and me and all the rest of us getting blown sky-high because you choose to turn my mother's relations' roof into a hidey-hole for any dirty German spies who like to ooze in here disguised as widows—'

'Ryan,' he thundered, 'I will not have you saying insulting and un-Christian things about the Germans. God knows, the Germans are the greatest pestilential plague of all time, with their contempt for other people's rights and their infernal arrogance—they're all the same as that goose-stepping, cheating bully of a Kaiser William they have lording it over them. But if ever you find your way to pick up a scrap of education you'll know that even a godforsaken dirty crew like them can have decent folk among them—there was Lucas Cranach for one, and Altdorfer, and one or two more I can't at this moment put a name to. And what's more, if you'll trouble to acquaint yourself with what the British have done to my country from the time of the blackguard fitzGilbert on till now you'll observe the Germans are not the only gang of murderous thieves in Europe. I'll thank you to remember that!'

So often had my father advertised his breadth of mind in terms like those that I paid him little attention. But it interests me now to speculate on the syncretic character of his racial sympathies. Only to his most intimate friends would he confess, in a whisper, that he had in his veins (from some generations back) one small smear of English blood. Yet the second week of August 1914 had found him in the Artists' Rifles, burning with British zeal, and I have little doubt that he would have fought as sturdily as the man beside him could he have stayed the course. (In the event, his service as a paid soldier had lasted barely a month when it was judged superfluous to the national requirement— ostensibly because of his poor health. Years later I learnt from Owen Pitt-Lacey that the health which had caused concern was his platoon sergeant's: Howard had made himself an intolerable pest by arguing, day in, day out, that the method recommended by the drill book for presenting arms was aesthetically and physiologically absurd.) It is, I believe, the simple truth that few men or women in those demoralizing years had as little animus against the people we were fighting. I still see clearly the flame of sincerity which burned unflickering in his large brown eyes that day, when, his excitement all at once subsiding, he turned from protest to persuasion.

'Listen,' he said again, 'even if there was no connection, I would want everyone in this household to show a proper courtesy and kindness to Mrs O'Kneale, with her man lost, and cut off as she is from her own people. And I will beg you, Ryan, on my own rheumatic knees if you require so, to treat the poor creature as if she was no German at all but a proper human being.'

Such earnestness was rare in the man, and as all children are impressionable it strongly affected me. I resolved there and then that if a column of soldiers came to our house, the commander shouting, 'Deliver the spy O'Kneale, in the King's name!' I would stand with my arms spread, holding them at bay. 'There is another law,' I would say, 'that of hospitality! Spy or no spy, the frail O'Kneale is the stranger within our gates. You shall touch no hair of her head, you and your rabble, until your brutal bayonets have carved their way through my own quivering breast.' But whether Anastasia would support me in this courageous role was an open question; or rather, a question which had hardly opened before it firmly closed again.

'Even if there was no connection': those words, pronounced with the bravura which flares so readily in Celtic intercourse, made an aural impression on my mind but nothing more. Recalling them, I see that Howard must have supposed I knew what the connection was: probably he took it for granted that Sonya had explained the reason for Helma entering our household (while Sonya, for her part, must have thought that he had done so). Was it through my exceptional dullness that the reference failed to stir my curiosity? Here I am ready to defend my earlier self. Grown-ups are seldom consistent in their communication with children: they officiously defend them from the real or imaginary dangers

of much adult knowledge, they complain when the fledg-
lings invade their conversation with artless and distracting
questions, and then they are equally vexed when the creatures
profess a total ignorance of plans which have been discussed
in their presence all morning. In this instance I lay the
blame for my apparent impercipience on the failure of my
parents to confer attentively with each other. Sometimes I
have felt that they both regarded human speech as an
instrument not so much for exchanging information as for
laryngeal exercise and refreshing rivalry, like a public competition for town criers.

That talk with Howard left me committed to a double-sided
duty. I had to serve as bodyguard to Helma, since my father
had so bidden me; but because I saw dangers to which he
was oblivious I felt it equally my business to protect my
own kin—and especially Sonya—from the German woman's
machinations. I resolved to keep watch on her movements day
and night.

In practice, a night watch proved infeasible: I had to be
content with fixing strands of cotton across her door and
so discovering whether she left her room during the hours
when I was not in action. But in daytime she was seldom
difficult to locate as she moved about the house with a
baggage train of mops and brooms, of steaming pails, great
slabs of Monkey Brand, an aged Ewbank sweeper which
squealed like a farrow of sucking pigs. The woman was
right-minded to the point of lunacy. Because she was on our
strength as governess and had no one yet to govern she
deemed it necessary to earn her oats by frenzied domestic
labour. For three whole days, while Pavel was enjoying his
bi-weekly Bacchanalia in the wood shed, she cooked for the
entire household, and thereafter she sought and attacked
the dirt which ordinary housemaids wisely overlook with
the raging zeal of a Savonarola in pursuit of sin. So dismal
a routine soon overtaxed my patience in observation; but

I continued to make periodic forays for reconnaissance, and to record my findings in an exercise book which I still possess. The relevant page is headed *Anti Espinage Dairy*, and among the entries I find:

'Thurs. AM. H.O. cleaned upstair windows, some on airerdrome side. PM. H.O. in top passage on knees pretending to wash floor could have been looking for clews.
'Mond. 10.30—11.40 (about) in Howards study (Howard not their). Saw her through door crack rubbing desk where he keeps Volunteers papers. I snezed and she startled gultily, she said What are you doing Ryan with a strong axent. I said O nothing at all I always sneze once or twice on vewing a lovly woman. She loked bafled.'

Moreover, I was sufficiently conscientious to spend most of one chilly morning squatting among the cleaning tools in a cupboard below the kitchen stairs which Helma often visited; hidden under sheets of the *Daily Telegraph*, with a carefully cut embrasure, I thought I might observe her in the very act of installing and wiring an infernal engine. There, once more, my vigilance ended in failure: in the near-darkness my quarry, before she had time to pass from the role of working housewife to that of enemy agent, trod heavily on my protruding left foot, making me squeak with pain. But the loud scream she uttered in answer to that negligible protest served me as proof that I had not been on a false trail. Once more I had to find, impromptu, some excuse for what she might regard as irrational behaviour, and being a child of sadly circumscribed imagination I said I was looking for moles.

'Pavel told me there were moles in here,' I said, 'just after his last drunk. I thought I'd better shoo them out in case they frighten the char.'

I could see she did not believe me: we became entangled rather painfully in mutual suspicion.

'You have such funny games,' she said, 'you English boys!'

23

That remark, too, struck me as insidious. She had seen, I thought, that I was a danger to her plans, and she meant to spike my guns by a subtle attack on British patriotism which should lower my morale.

At that period I was inclined, as a rule, to note the appearance of adults with about as much attention as the citizens of New York or Chicago give to lofty buildings; but the broom-cupboard encounter, bringing sudden pressure to bear on a slovenly intelligence, caused me for the first time to make a concentrated study of Helma's face and person.

I had previously met no specimen of the people we were at war with, and the gossip of our Russians had made me picture them as creatures of enormous size with heads like great cubes of sandstone where the snarling features had been cut as if with a woodman's axe. Such mythology does not yield readily to the evidence of one's senses. This Helma was by no means large, but I realized that an endemically martial race would select—or even breed—individuals below the normal dimensions to suit the feline business of spying, and there was in her grimly serviceable dress, in the puritanical severity with which her yellow hair impaled by an armoury of pins was stooked in the nape of her neck, at least an aura of discipline which vaguely corresponded with my preconceptions. Again, though I had at that time little interest in women's shapes I could see that hers, so much less fluent than Sonya's but so economically forged when compared with Anastasia's accretion of bunts and bulges, was perfectly adapted for such pursuits as sliding along a trench at dusk and stabbing the backs of English soldiers as they stood on the fire-step. Only her face failed, under this closer scrutiny, to match the Valkyrian part for which I naturally cast her. It was not, after all, featureless, but even to my callow observation the spare sculpture of her cheeks and temples presented an austerity more reminiscent of monks than of soldiers, and her sombre, curiously tenacious eyes spoke to the small boy staring foolishly towards them of endurance rather than any bellicose intention. Someone in the Swiss connection had given me for my birthday a child's life of St Joan with Vuillermet's mezzotint illustrations; and even at that early encounter I think I caught some faint affinity between the face I saw and one of those marvellous engravings—not the most famous one, of the Maid marching towards Orleans, but that of her watching the flames as they leap towards her breast.

Was I burning with patriotic rage against this dangerous intruder? Simply, I had no feeling of that kind. For me Helma O'Kneale was still too negative a person to be execrated: she and I had each a national responsibility, and I saw her merely as my opponent in a battle of wits where we were fairly matched, for while I belonged to the more astute of the two sexes she had all the advantage which comes with the middle years. Forty-five or so was what I then judged to be her age. Now I can give it with greater accuracy: she had just turned twenty-three.

Indeed, there may be a morsel of scientific truth within the romantic notion that a bond of understanding unites the hunter and the hunted. Determined as I was to frustrate this woman's Hunnish designs, I was yet ready to exchange civilities when she and I met on a purely social plane; and because the absence even of such crude companionship as Anastasia's left a gap in my daily life I saw no harm in using my enemy to fill it. Meeting her at breakfast I would click my heels and bark out, 'Hutchinson!'—for a boy called Arvid Lowenhjelm had told me that this was the recognized form of greeting on her side of the firing line; and to complete my devoirs I would execute the marionettish bow I had learnt at a dancing class, and put on my effulgent social smile, murmuring, 'I trust, gnädige Frau, I see you well.' To that emetic exhibition she would respond with a grave, unvarying politeness which curiously refreshed me; dimly suspecting that I was weak in anti-espionage, I found some consolation in this evidence that at least I could handle women with an innate sense of style.

'Today I am glad,' she said one morning in her solemn but not unfriendly way. 'My Cathleen is nearly well, tomorrow she will be out of bed again.'

This was on a day when, through my inefficiency in stalking, we kept coming face to face at turns in the upstairs passage, and though I felt no interest in her remark I found it convenient to pretend one. Till then it had not occurred to me that a widow might possess an infant, and I said,

'Oh, have you got a sister?'

'Cathleen is my child—my little girl,' she said.

'Oh. And you've had her for some time?' I asked urbanely.

'Soon she will be three years old.'

'Oh, I see.' The topic seemed to be exhausted, but since my strategy was to gain the woman's confidence I made an effort to keep it alive. 'You like it?' I inquired.

' "Like it"?'

'This child—having it about. I suppose you have to feed it and all that.'

'But everybody likes having a child,' she said.

It took me some moments to find a gloss on that implausible statement. Then I said, 'Well of course Sonya does, when she's not all tied up with her beastly relations and things. She keeps having them. I mean, she had Anastasia, and then me—and I was hell to have, Howard's told me. And even now she has one or two occasionally. I think she really rather enjoys getting these eternity gowns and things, she used to think they camouflaged her absolutely till that gassy old Andrey Aksakov gave the game away—he said, "*Sonya, ma chère, quand tu es enceinte tu as le corps d'Aphrodite et le visage d'un ange.*" Of course Andrey was in the Imperial Navy, I suppose that makes you rather quick-witted. Only Howard says he can't have ever spent much time looking at Aphrodite.'

'That is interesting,' Helma said.

26

I could see I was boring her, and on that occasion I made no further effort to put her at her ease with friendly conversation. The reason why that exchange stands out in my memory is that the child she spoke of came to serve—surprisingly—as a *liaison d'intérêt* between her and me.

It was a day or two later that, keeping Helma in view as she made her regular purgative progress from the front door towards the kitchen stairs, I saw she was being followed by a tiny creature with another broom. That was a striking spectacle. The broom was full-sized, an impossible tool for the infant trying to wield it, yet as far as the encumbrance allowed the little thing was studiously copying every one of her leader's movements: with her head bent she advanced steadily, always with the left foot forward, and with a tolerably rhythmic motion of her shoulders she kept the broom-head in play, though only in random contact with the floor. Engrossed in this quaint performance I forgot about security; emerging from the linen press which I had used as a secret observation post, I descended forthrightly from the landing to the hall. There my antagonist, suppressing every symptom of surprise, greeted me in a manner hardly distinct from cordiality.

'Here is Cathleen,' she said.

'Oh—hullo,' I said to the child.

It crossed my mind that the creature might be part of a shrewd cover-plan; her colouring was as far as possible from that of the woman claiming to be her mother—her hair, mostly pinioned in two short tails, was black as a labrador's—and I saw not the slightest similarity in their features. They had in common, however, a distinctive look of purpose, a spareness of body and taut economy in movement which did something to corroborate Helma's story; and however un-Teutonic her face, only a German child, I had to allow, would set itself to domestic labour so soon after leaving the womb. Such were my serpentine reflections while Cathleen and I methodically scanned each other's appearance. Then, startlingly, the child said, 'Allo!' and smiled; the smile

27

employed the whole of her face, her cheeks drawing far apart, her black pupils almost disappearing as the flesh about her eyes was screwed into quilted coverlets. *'Bub!'* she said. That could only be a German word, and I remember a moment when I thought resentfully, 'How could anyone entice this infant to be one of that tribe—the brutes who trampled on brave Belgium and only just failed to bomb our own Express Dairy!' But the wave of indignation yielded instantly to one of marvelling at the creature's merriment; I had never imagined that so new a human being could manifest such gaiety and such delight.

The fact is that until that day I had concerned myself very little with younger fry. Conveniently, a former owner of our amorphous house had extended its hinder part to embody what had once been a gardener's cottage; that annexe served as an infantarium, practically self-contained, where under the rule of an aged *nyanya* my belated siblings lived their rudimentary lives in minimal contact with mine. In later years I came to like them; but at that time I found it best to ignore, as far as I could, the existence of these hominids who seemed to have less *raison d'être* than domestic animals and who could not follow the rules of the simplest game. At that stage in life one's poverty in experience leads to false assumptions: I had taken it as universal truth that the young, like root crops, are better out of sight until they reach a serviceable size (at the age of, say, ten), so it was no small shock to me to come on an infant hardly out of the play-pen who was unmistakably a person; who—as I divined —possessed within her tiny frame a grasp of life and its enjoyments more suited to someone aged eleven. In those first moments of our acquaintance I knew for certain that this child, for all that her linguistic range might be limited to 'Allo' and *'Bub'*, would never irritate or bore me, even if she and I chanced to find ourselves spending some years together on a desert island. Then, having decided that the miniature person who had abruptly entered my life was one of extraordinary interest, I went about my own business, cheerfully forgetting her existence.

My next meeting with the young thing was equally unexpected. It took place on—I think—the next evening.

I had fished out of the Brent two planks which I fancied
could be sawn lengthwise and then nailed together to form
the main wing-member for my projected glider. As they
were coated with mud and tar my first concern was to clean
them, and for that purpose I took them after tea to the
kitchen. There I found Pavel shaving Semyon, as he did about
twice a week—he had begun his working life as a barber
at Baku. Had he been alone he would have made no fuss
about my using his sink, but he liked showing off to Semyon
at my expense, and I had hardly begun to shift the china
which was stacked there when he turned on me as if I were
threatening to steal his wages.

'You leave my crocks alone! You touch my crocks and
out comes your insides, off comes your tiddlies and I put
them on the grill—there, see?—all on one big skewer for
Semyon's supper.'

Doubtless those words went farther than his intentions—
Pavel had always a taste for the picturesque—but as they
reached me in a gastric cloud which stank of Hollands,
with Pavel himself brandishing the soapy razor as he
advanced in its wake, I fled the room with no pretence of
defiance. I was not a valorous child. After all, I thought, the
superior facilities offered by the bathroom would easily com-
pensate for the fag of carting my planks upstairs.

The bathroom at Howes Croft, as I remember it, was hardly
a recognizable precursor of the neat hygeian shrines which
builders of today insert in every suburban villa; it had
started as a double bedroom, and the great iron bath, its
buxom curves unscreened, stood out from the wall in the
mainstream of cold air which flowed between the ill-fitting
door and the tall north window, as if the workmen had
simply been too lazy to carry it another yard. I always enjoyed
that room: the smell of steam from rusted pipes—one only
to be savoured now in the city of Bath, among the Roman

cisterns—was to me delicious; with so much space to run about in you were saved, in a clement season, from the fatigue of drying; and a frugal plumber had fixed the cold pipe so far from walls and ceiling that, having filled the bath to the brim, you could leap from the box which entombed the pedestal, swing, and land on your behind in the water. In the course of years Anastasia and I had discovered many new ways of extracting pleasure from that portion of our home.

What I had forgotten, in my headlong flight from the kitchen, was that this was the nursery bath-time. On opening the door I was met by clouds of steam filled with such a caterwauling as I should have thought excessive in the parrot house at Regent's Park, and it greatly vexed me to find that the bath was occupied by my twin sisters Brigid and Polina, unsightly blobs of whitey-pink which looked (in a phrase of Howard's) like something knocked off by Rubens on a sterile day; in the manic fashion of infants they were hitting the water and laughing hysterically, imbibing each other's splashings like the figures of the Moro Fountain in reverse action. I told them to move to one end. Lost in their juvenile diversions they did not hear me. When, of necessity, I had seized and pushed them into a less obstructive position, a few drops falling from the hot tap on Polina's shoulder set her screaming like a soul in torment, and Brigid, following the tedious laws of twinship, had to howl as well.

I could see that Polina was not really being scalded, and, depressing as it was, that uproar need not have interfered with my own modest purpose—to clean a small quantity of timber. But now came a further hindrance. In the old rocking chair which, rather oddly, was the room's only mobile furniture, the nurse Mavrusha was seated with my brother Vladimir, nude and glistening, on her knees. Flexibility in mental process was never the hallmark of the Russian *nyanya;* those indomitable women had, on the other hand, an extravagant sense of loyalty towards their charges. In

30

the previous century Mavrusha had defended my mother from the several ferocities of the Russian climate, from bacilli, perhaps from wolves; she was ready now to guard my sisters from what appeared to her unicellular mind a simple case of attempted fratricide. Transferring poor Vladimir to the floor, the fanatic carline rose, rushed and gripped me from behind.

'You wicked boy!' she squeaked in her own tongue, shaking me by the arms. 'You leave Polina alone! Don't you touch her with that dirty wood—take it out of here this minute!'

The indignity of the situation was heightened now by a fresh contribution. My brother was a notably quiet baby, and has in fact retained through life his pacific temperament—later on he was found to be too torpid even for the Diplomatic Service, and after a crammer had jockeyed him into Woolwich he became in due course a Sapper colonel of the most silent and innocuous kind; but the least aggressive nursling can resent being dumped in half-dried nakedness on wet linoleum, and he may have inferred from the *nyanya's* response to our sisters' ludicrous behaviour that to make a hideous noise is the surest way of calling attention to one's early grievances: by the time I had broken free from Mavrusha's grasp and turned to face her he was wildly kicking the air, flaunting the male accessories in a way which struck me as socially incorrect, and yelling at least as lustily as Polina and Brigid combined.

I almost cried myself. This was my home, where even in the kitchen I was surely entitled to civil treatment, while here in the bathroom my seniority gave me rights unquestionably superior to those of Mavrusha's squealing herd. I had come quite peaceably to carry out the first stage of a modest engineering project, a work which called for no one's patience but mine; only to be met by as frantic a resistance as if I had broken in at the head of a Mohock gang. Those truths I should have made plain to Mavrusha in a few caustic sentences, but my brain was so bludgeoned by the pandemonium that I could not find the Russian words

31

I needed (and her grasp of English was roughly equal to that of a budgerigar). As I stood glaring at the rabid old woman my attention was again diverted: yet another individual— a lay figure in the lamentable drama—was now visible through the steam.

Close to the farther wall the tiny Cathleen stood with her back towards us, stooping to dry her knees with what looked to me like a professional carefulness and calm. At our earlier meeting I had remarked the athletic neatness of her physique; now, with the fullest opportunity to compare her form with the roseate, fubsy bodies of my own kin, I was arrested by its lithe slenderness and its rare colouring—all her skin was that pale shade of olive which I associate now with the most beautiful of Indian women. The least learned eye can, in my belief, recognize absolute perfection; and in that slight, sinewed, bending form I—at the age of eleven years—witnessed a perfect thing. As I looked she turned and saw me. At once her face showed a delighted recognition, she dropped the towel and came forward with (as it appeared to me) the easy grace of an accomplished hostess. Standing with her feet apart, straight-legged, looking up at me with all her features stretched in a lavish smile, she uttered once more the exotic greeting 'Bub!' And had she expressed herself with the craft of Sappho and the passion of La Duse her speech would not have stirred me more than that one word did.

The strange rapture of this occurrence would have cancelled all the previous frustrations. But Mavrusha in her officious mood must needs interfere once more. The attitude of the *nyanya* towards the human body defies analysis; enough to say it suddenly occurred to her that Cathleen and I were in conversation, that we were unrelated, that one of us lacked clothes. As if I had been caught red-handed in what the tabloids call a 'grave offence', she went into a fresh attack with every gun blazing:

'Ryan, how dare you—a great boy like you! You ought to be ashamed—such rudeness to a little girl with no papa to protect her. Be off with you! I'll tell your little mother. I'll tell your great father, he'll thrash you till the skin falls off your shoulders.'

Poor Howard—how ill at ease he would have felt in such a mettlesome undertaking! But the threat to Sonya was one I could not disregard: reports on my conduct were always the more embarrassing to her because she could never make head or tail of other people's rules for behaviour. In any case I had no thought of defying this pocket-size Nemesis, this shrivelled creature wrapped in bombasine who had placed herself, quivering with pious rage, between me and my exquisite new friend. Habit is perhaps the least resistible of moral forces. While Sonya in my earlier years had stood for life's deliciousness, Mavrusha had represented its grim compulsions, and to me she remained—like the statue which surmounts the Old Bailey—a symbol of righteousness, its boundless power and constant inconvenience. At this time I must have been almost as tall as she, yet I still saw her as one who towered over me. I could have pushed her out of my way without undue exertion; instead—and without another glance at Cathleen—I quickly left the room as she commanded.

Emotion thus obstructed will soon seek another outlet; mine found one in the sort of day-dreams which I suppose are almost universal among young males of the human species. Mavrusha in her tirade had talked of Cathleen having no father to protect her. I needed no more prompting. By the time I was back in my own room I had dedicated the rest of my life to Cathleen's tutelar service.

From what did she need protection? Even to one of my meagre experience it was clear that the constrictions of middle-class life in the twentieth century excluded many traditional hazards: ready as I was to thrust my bare arm between the jaws of any tiger which might pounce upon my charge, I realized that the London suburbs were now monotonously free from raids by the more dramatic carnivores. There remained a decent chance of fire, and the fact that I had lately fled—in the space of ten minutes—from the hollow threats of a Transcaucasian barber and the moral fury of a senile nursemaid was not enough to disturb my belief that the challenge of a blazing house would find me unafraid. I visualized the face of my young friend, deadly white, in one of the attic windows as a band of flame climbed hungrily towards her; I saw the fire brigade defeated as their ladder, which had twice caught alight, could be held with its highest rung no nearer than ten feet from the weeping child—a gap which no man dared to leap; I pictured myself taking the leading fireman's place, jumping, clawing the burning window-sill and hauling myself inside, wrapping the grateful girl in the wet sheet I had intelligently thought to tie about my waist and, as I leapt again with her trembling body held close to mine, hearing from the crowd far below one voice (that of Commander Macdonald) murmuring 'God, that fellow has pluck!' More reasonably, in those days of amateurish but persistent air raids, I was presently assuming that sooner or later my dear one would need to be rescued from a German bomb.

The bomb, in my chimerical anticipation, was one which came through our roof, penetrated the upper floors and landed in the drawing-room without exploding; it happened that Cathleen was in that room at the time, and being too young to realize her danger continued to play with her dolls on the carpet while the dreadful thing smoked and sizzled beside her. Here it was Howard who first came on the scene, crying, 'Lie still, child, with your face to the floor!' But for me, arriving at his heels, such prudent words were no substitute for action: in an instant I had gathered the bomb to my stomach—turning so that the dear one had my body as immediate fender between her and the deadly weapon—and in another I had run with it out to the road; there were still three seconds to go (as I knew from an older boy's dissertation on the Mills grenade), and I had

34

run some sixty yards in the direction of the golf course before—crack, woomph!—the bomb went off. There were various endings to this attractive episode. In the most conventional I simply woke in the Hendon Cottage Hospital surrounded by admiring nurses, Helma arrived to thank me for saving her child, I made a modest reply and then expired with a moving dignity while a Welsh choir sang *Rock of Ages* or, at my own request, something from *The Bing Boys on Broadway*. In a later version, one I came to prefer, my body was blown into many small pieces, which in due course were reverently collected by wolf cubs of the 9th Hendon Pack (the pack from which, in real life, I had lately been asked to resign because of 'irresponsible and uncublike behaviour') and borne on a gun carriage to Golders Green for cremation; the tearful cortège included many school teachers who had once been rude to me, as well as such illustrious people as Mr Gordon Bottomley and Mr Grahame-White.

I have never exactly understood how those chivalric trains of thought led me towards a vision of marriage with Cathleen as the supreme happiness, the goal of my existence. No matter: our times do not lack schoolmen panting to illuminate the twisting roads of mental causation. Enough—for me—that tableaux of our courtship and nuptials, ever firmer in colour and outline, came to be constantly entwined with the more dynamic scenes of peril and deliverance.

In one of those projections my darling (now fifteen) is half-reclining on a couch of the sort enjoyed by Mme Récamier, while her dress remarkably resembles the one in which that paragon was draped for David to render her immortal. I kneel at her feet, or rather—for acoustic reasons —near her hips; and I murmur breathlessly (for I have just been stroking the winning crew in the Boat Race),

'Cathleen, my dear, I have something to confide to you: I have loved you passionately for thirteen years. Having rescued you from many dangers I am now twenty-four and today I got my Blue. Will you—for now and evermore—

consent to share my bed and board?'

Tears fill her eyes as she answers, 'Alas, dear Ryan, it may not be. I cannot conceal any longer the stain on my escutcheon. *I am the daughter of a German spy.*'

To that confession there was no response which satisfied me as both sensible and shapely. In the end I generally fell back on Dickens (a new discovery), from whom I borrowed shamelessly: 'Dear girl, it is a far, far better thing that I do, proposing to a spy's daughter, than I have ever done before.'

In my congenial fabrications those generous words soon overcame her womanly scruples: we were married on the following Sunday in Claridge's foyer, which I took to be the recognized venue for such affairs, in the presence of Lloyd George and others. The officiant was always the exarch of Bulgaria—I no longer remember why.

The new direction which my thoughts had taken was injurious to my work in anti-espionage (which, it must be confessed, had begun to bore me). I reasoned that if I caught Helma in the very act of transmitting messages to Luden- dorff's headquarters I should be bound to report the offence, and an arrest would certainly follow; then, since a child of three could hardly be left to look after herself while her mother was under lock and key in Wormwood Scrubs, Cath- leen would be taken into custody as well. That prospect was unbearable. I began to trim my sails, arguing that if by a cir- cumspect complaisance I could arrive at friendly relations with Cathleen's mother I might lead her by degrees to a healthier outlook, one which at length would bring her anti- British activities to an end.

Already (as I now believe) I faintly sensed a strain in her which would not be unresponsive to amicable overtures. But in developing my new strategy I should be faced with a major obstacle: it was impossible to imagine Anastasia behaving sympathetically—indeed, I could not think of con- fiding my views or plans to a person so insensitive as she. Nor would it be easy to steer the delicate course I had mapped if Anastasia were bent on some deviant tactic of her own.

And yet I was conscious of some impatience for my elder sister's return. In the first decade of life one perceives the necessity of conversation, early in the second one comes to realize that what passes for converse with one's seniors is illusion—something in the mechanics of the adult mind makes it incapable of serious application to any views that a less staled intelligence has to offer. My parents, for example, exercised a general benevolence towards me, but whenever I sought their interest in ideas which I felt to be important their reception was so half-hearted that I soon lapsed into despondent silence. So it was that Anastasia had a place in my social life. Were I to say that I found her conversation stimulating I should be guilty of hyperbole: if she had any original thoughts she lacked the means to express them, and the dullness of the ones she uttered was somewhat magnified by the monotony of her elocution. All the same I had missed her, as one misses on its decease a dog which for years has growled and snuffled by the fireplace and shed its hairs all over the house. I should have thought it shameful to let anyone know about this tidal wave of brotherly affection; but within my heart I acknowledged there was something to be said for getting my ponderous playmate home.

The day of her return stays vividly in my mind as an instance of the curiously complex way in which my parents would organize what one had supposed to be the simplest sorts of business.

From Ireland one of our Thornley cousins was to accompany Anastasia to Fleetwood and there, having herself to catch a northbound train, was to hand her over to another of Howard's relatives (who littered the Lancashire seaboard); he—a failed Dublin poet keeping an equally unsuccessful harness shop in Blackpool—was to put her on the London express, bribing the guard with half a sovereign to defend her maidenhood. The train was due in London at 3.15. Sonya had an engagement for that afternoon—she was to disentangle the affairs of an aunt at Shepherds Bush who in ignorance of local custom had threatened a rent-collector with a dog-whip—but it was understood that Howard, in an interval between his classes, would meet Anastasia at Euston and embark her in a second-class carriage for Finchley (Sonya having the unshakable belief that the Great Northern suburban line, its trains equipped with communication cords, afforded safer passage for young females than the Hampstead and Highgate tube); understood, that is, by everyone except Howard himself. Asked at breakfast what time he would be starting for town, he surfaced very slowly from the *Cork Weekly Examiner* to say,

'Starting what? Where? I don't go up today.'

'But you said you'd meet Anastasia at Euston,' my mother shouted from her end of the table.

'Anastasia? I thought she was at Kilmacrenan. No, I never said anything so inconvenient. What makes you think that way?'

'We talked about it in bed, more than a week ago.'

'Then I can't have been concentrating. Why didn't you remind me!'

'You will have to go, all the same.'

'I'll have to do nothing of the sort. Did you not know, mavourneen, I've only today to worry out the Forbes Oration I have to give at Aberdeen on Tuesday? And anyhow the child can find her own way out—she'll come to no harm.'

There I was able to put him right, with some information from a boy called Cyril Eldersfield who had gained top marks at Miss Judson's for General Knowledge. 'There's the white slave-dealers,' I said.

Howard looked at me as if I'd spoken in some language he didn't understand, so I explained:

'When girls come to London by themselves they're caught by lewd men who undress them and stuff them as tight as sardines into wooden crates, to go to South America in what's

38

called The Middle Package. And England gets tons of tinned beef in return.'

'Ryan, will you hold your brainless, gibbering tongue,' Howard said. (Though tolerant in many ways, he could never bear discovering that in some departments of life his son was better informed than he.)

'But of course Anastasia might like that,' I continued, shrewdly pretending to be a little on his side. 'She's always saying she finds London life so boring.'

Now it was Sonya's turn to interrupt me: *'Tais-toi, Ryan, tu m'agaces!'* From her tone of voice I could tell that Howard had got on her nerves, so I made no further effort to enlighten them.

While all this committee work was in progress Semyon was leaning right across the table to lecture Helma, as he did at every opportunity, explaining in his singular pasticcio of hobbling English and putative German that Marx's doctrine had been perverted by 'that rabble in Moskva', so that only he, Plekhanov and a Mrs Tibb who lived at Kensal Rise were left as curators of the true gospel of Dialectical Materialism. It was obvious even to me that Helma, jammed between two transient refugees, nodding bravely with eyes like frosted window panes, had allowed her thoughts to stray from Semyon's pulpitry; when he came to one of his rare pauses she deftly turned to Sonya, saying,

'Mrs Hutchinson, I may go, please, to meet your little girl?'

('Little girl': I looked forward to telling Anastasia of that designation.)

It was patent that Sonya did not welcome Helma's suggestion, and I was not surprised to hear her answer, 'Oh, but you would not possibly find her in such a crowd of other passengers!' At the time I guessed that she was afraid of the German woman kidnapping Anastasia and smuggling her away to Berlin, to be used as a hostage; but since then I have come to accept an alternative explanation—that, as she recalled the disheartening imbroglio with Zinaida Dygasinska, she

39

thought it needful to imbue the wilful girl with some notion of tolerance before facing her with so daunting an image of Teutonic sobriety as her new teacher.

'It's a most genteel offer, Helma,' she concluded, 'but I have another design which appears more easy.'

Had she? Within a fraction of a second (most likely), yes. In emergency the speed of Sonya's brain and hands amazed me—I have known her to seize one of the study curtains and run up a pair of knickers for an absent-minded guest between Mass and Sunday luncheon. I am sure the grateful smile she gave to Helma had not reached its highest, melting brilliance before she thought of another member of her protectorate, one Princess Vobedenostev, a dwarfish, beak-nosed woman with shoulders like those of an ox, inhabiting a moribund hotel in some sad street behind St Pancras. Here was the sort of chance my mother loved, to kill—or at least maim—two birds with the same blithely catapulted stone.

'Howard, listen!' she called, surmounting the voice of Semyon, which had returned to relentless operation. 'It's a shameful time we have no visit from Irina Nikolayevna. In April I promised we will invite her as soon as we have a room open.'

'Well, we haven't,' Howard said bleakly, 'a room—as you call it—open.'

She rode this frivolous objection into the rails. 'Ryan,' she said, 'you can move your things for a few nights into Pavel's storeroom. And then Helma, my love, perhaps you will have the great goodness—instead of voyaging to Euston—to make a new bed for Irina Nikolayevna in Ryan's room. (Semyon, dear, will you either lock your mouth or take your dessert out in the garden—and I've told you twenty thousand times you need to wear a collar and cravat in the dining saloon.) Now listen, Helma: Ryan's *vase de nuit* can stay where it is—it comes from the Civil Stores and it's quite robust, it will do for Irina just as good. And Mavrusha will show you to find the visiting sheets—when you lay the bed it's nice to put them with the holes at the bottom, where nobody will meet them.' Here my mother laughed, in sudden and joyous recollection. 'Most of the holes come from poor Natasha,' she said gaily. 'Her grandmother who finished herself in a nun-house have told her the smoothing iron will do no use if it isn't quite red-hot—nothing I say will change her mind. So, it's a lovely kindess, Helma *chérie*, that you're doing to Irina. She also is a woman of great distress—her futile father drowns himself in the Neva and she must live in one of these English *pensions* which are suited for only pillow-bugs and mice.'

Here my mother's face took on a look, at once melancholy and faintly, regretfully, amused, which for me had a strange fascination and which, many years afterwards, I saw her wearing only an hour or so before she died. It told me ever and again of the vast landscape which had come to crowd her mental vision, a countryside of many aspects, of snow-bound steppes and frozen rivers, shabby streets and florid drawing-rooms alive with the myriad faces of her friends. One had thought that when her mind was flooded with the plenitude and brilliance of that panorama its practical side would cease to function. Never so! On this occasion she was still dilating upon Irina's misfortunes when her eyes returned to me, and without even a change of tone she went on from reminiscence to direction:

'You, Ryan, you will have to construct a telegraph for Irina, in English—if you make it in French the postal clerks will only turn it into a shepherd's pie. You must tell her I'm sorry I have not written for a long time—I've been so engaged with my war work, also there are these aerial bombs arriving and so on. So now it will be a great pleasure for Howard and me if she will arrive this afternoon for a visit of four or five days. (I expect if I speak to the butcher myself he will give me a great portion of meat to fit us all.) And perhaps she will have the kindness while she is coming to call at Euston Station to gather Anastasia from *Irlande* at a quarter after three.'

'Then he might put in something about the weather,' Howard suggested.

'No no, it must be extremely short, because telegraphs cost so much money, also Irina will not have much time to read it—she is a woman of such stupidity and laziness she will never learn, poor love, to read in English.'

'I think—if it won't permanently damage Ryan's self-esteem—I'll write the telegram myself,' Howard said.

Only one as familiar as I with the general course of Sonya's contrivances could have hoped for this one to succeed. It was, in fact, entirely a success.

In the late afternoon I was in Anastasia's room, disposing in her bed the rusty tins and other metallic trifles which I had collected as a symbol of welcome—our humdrum lives were constantly refreshed by such festive ritual—when the sound of wheels and creaking springs drew me to the window. The dingiest of the station cabs was standing in the small arc of gravel which we magniloquently called 'the drive'; Irina Nikolayevna had alighted and was starting up the usual row over the fare while the horse, left to itself, was snatching generous helpings from the *viburnum carlesii* which Howard had irresponsibly planted within convenient equine reach. Irina's notions of *haute couture* were very much her own; today the internal structure of her toilette was so arranged that her afterpart, draped with many yards of olive gros-de-Naples, resembled in shape the tabernacle which telephone engineers erect over holes in the road, and I was so entranced by the lively movements of this miniature pavilion as she leant forward to emphasize her arguments against the cabby with her arms and shoulders that I did not immediately notice Anastasia, who had emerged on the other side and was lugging an old holdall of Sonya's towards the steps. The holdall, over-stuffed, looked as if it were about to fall to pieces, and Anastasia herself presented an appearance of similar dislocation—her coat was laughably mis-buttoned and her face the colour of puff-balls, reminding me that girls were not really designed for sea travel. All the same

42

I was much excited at seeing my only elder sister again.

'Hullo—are you back?' I called.

'Oh no!' she shouted in reply. 'I'm just a ghost of myself which Irina Nikolayevna ran into at the station.'

That struck me as a remark of superlative ineptitude: in her present guise she might have been a body dredged from the Thames, but the part of ghost was conspicuously one for which nature had not cast her. Putting this view gently, I said,

'You can't run into a ghost. You go straight through them.'

'Oh, shut your silly mouth!' she bellowed back.

I saw then that she was in one of her difficult moods, so I changed the subject, asking, 'Did you get torpedoed?'

'Do I look as if I'd been torpedoed!'

'Well, you do rather,' I said. Then, wishing to be tactful, I added, 'But of course I've rather forgotten what you looked like before you went away.'

I had noticed comparatively early in life that women are apt to jump from one thing to another when you try to involve them in rational conversation: it was no surprise, therefore, that instead of following my lead and expanding on the hazards of wartime travel she said irrelevantly,

'This thing is beastly heavy.'

By then she had dragged the holdall as far as the steps, and I could see she was right. I said sympathetically,

'Yes, it looks it. Did you go collecting boulders or something at Kilmacrenan?'

'Any decently brought-up boy,' she pursued, 'would come and give me a hand with it. Anyone except a bone-lazy little skulking scab.'

That observation was in questionable taste, but I knew it was often best to meet ungracious manners with a tranquil courtesy. I answered, 'That's what I should like to do, but I've been a bit worried lately about my heart.' Then, being as helpful as I could, I said, 'Pavel's drunk today but I don't think Semyon is. If I was you I'd get Semyon to take one end.'

43

'Well, will you go and get him!'

Her request was inconvenient—I had still a few more bibelots to arrange in her bed. 'At the moment,' I told her truthfully, 'I'm rather busy.'

'Busy?' she exclaimed. 'You little pimply scrimshanking blot, you've never done one hand's turn in all your life! *You* haven't changed! Just the same snot-nosed, stuck-up, little whimpering mumsy-blubbing brat! Why Sonya didn't strangle you at birth I can't think, you lazy good-for-nothing niffy little bulgy-bottomed toad!'

Hearing her speak in that emotional way was like old times, and I was starting to enjoy our talk when Howard, with his genius for ill-timed entrances, interrupted us with a scarcely civilized cry from the window above the one where I was standing:

'Ryan, you clod, will you stop your infernal shindy!' From that salvo he broke off to address Irina Nikolayevna's poop in the laundered voice he always used when attempting the part of English Gentleman: 'Good day, Mme Vobede-nostev! How delightful to have you here once more. I greatly regret that my wife is not at home to greet you—she's away to Shepherds Bush, trying to get some perishing old aunt of hers out of the clink.' Then he continued to blackguard me in his ordinary tone: 'How in the name of all the holy powers d'you think I can tinker up a forty-minute spiel on Sant' Apollinare Nuovo for these damned Scotchmen with you squealing and gibbering like a whole monkey-house right underneath my chin!'

Even at an early age I possessed a certain sense of justice, and I could not allow that inculpation to pass unchallenged. I called back,

'That isn't true, sir.' (The 'sir' was a piece of flattery which I had sometimes found to be worth its cost as a lubricant.) 'The person gibbering and squealing like a monkey-house isn't me.'

'Will you pipe down!' he roared.

For me, leaning far out and twisting my neck to turn my

44

face skyward, this was a comfortless interview, but I was so much vexed by Howard's unfairness—not understanding then that the academic life is repressive and engenders moods of petulance—that I went on trying to reason with him.

'When I reach puberty,' I said, 'my voice will be more like yours and less like someone else's. But until then you can always tell hers from mine because it's more wobbly and screechy.'

'*Shut up, you blockhead!*'

I had yet one card to play—a remark by one of Howard's own colleagues, a professor of psychology, which I had stored for use on some appropriate occasion. 'In the elocution of the young human female,' I told him, 'a note of incipient hysteria may often be discerned.'

That *coup-de-maître* brought our discussions to an end— my father could parry it only by naked violence. With greater benevolence than wisdom my mother always had a big vase of flowers standing on his desk; this, now, he seized by its base to shake it as one shakes a thermometer, aiming the contents at my head. Naturally he missed: he was a man devoid of athletic skills, and such simple, practical achievements were always far outside his reach.

It was in every sense a thoughtless gesture, which could have done much harm: he might easily have soused Irina, who had turned to reply to his speech of welcome, or the cabman, whose forbearance had already been put to stringent test by his client's abstruse harangue on roubles, versts and shameless extortion. Providentially the water missed them both. It missed the horse as well, but the flowers fell within inches of its nose. Sated with viburnum, the animal had probably sunk into a daydream; its nerves may have been ragged as a result of air raids, and one sees how the sudden descent of flowers as if from heaven might mystify a creature without the power of reason, but I should not have expected so sharp a reaction: as though shot in the breast it impetuously reared and stood for a long moment on its hind legs, in the way that horses as a rule do only in films—and be it remembered that the more athletic film horses are normally without the embarrassment of a growler's shafts attached to their sides. That performance may have been more disturbing when viewed from ground level than as I saw it from above; and while I was shouting 'Encore!' Irina was justified, I suppose, in screaming, '*Isvoshtchik!* Stand on your horse, for the love of God!' But her cryptic injunction went unheeded. The cabby, no doubt long convinced that his horse was the saner of the two creatures he had to deal with, stayed dumb and motionless, while the horse itself attended to no voice but mine: to my wonder and delight it did its circus trick again.

It was disappointing that Anastasia played so unimpressive a part in these proceedings. While I had always kept at some distance from the larger quadrupeds, preferring their aesthetic aspect to any other, my sister belonged to that class of girls which seems more at home with horses than with its own species—the main purpose of her stay at Kilmacrenan had been to use the long slim legs of the Thornleys' hunters for locomotion instead of her own fat ones and, when not being bounced about on the backs of those creatures, to serve as their maid. I looked, then, for her to run and soothe the poor beast which had been alarmed by my father's indiscipline. In fact she made no movement. It should in fairness be noticed that she may have been tired from travel; certainly she failed to see the danger in a new development which began and ended with the speed of events in dreams.

Helma must have been taking her child for a walk. The first I knew of this was the sudden appearance of the tiny Cathleen—whose movements in real life seemed always to take me by surprise—emerging from a short cut through a clump of rhododendrons. Another infant, finding itself almost under the fore-hooves of a rearing horse, would surely have uttered a scream as loud as Irina's and run for its life. Not so this one: as greatly charmed as I was by so unusual a display, she stood gazing up at what must have been to her a beast of gigantic size, and when it returned to its

46

normal stance—the hooves passing within a foot or two of her forehead—she remained waiting hopefully for the spectacle to occur once more. It would please me to record that, instantly realizing her peril, I slid down a drainpipe, dashed at full tilt and caught the horse's bridle; but in actuality I viewed the scene—from, as it were, the dress circle—with the restful detachment of unimaginative children at a Punch and Judy show. How strange—I vaguely thought—that this young thing should choose to loiter underneath a rampant horse! With the same remoteness I observed her mother's behaviour. If Helma showed any sign of horror that detail failed to plant itself in my memory; the voice in which she cried out, '*Ruhe, Pferdchen!*' was, as I recall it, perfectly steady. But her movement was as swift as if a powerful gust of wind came suddenly to carry her to Cathleen's side; in an instant—and without apparent effort—she had lifted the child astride her hip and borne her to safety. One had said, from the skill and insouciance of the operation, that she performed it every day; and just as casually, catching sight of Anastasia's derelict luggage, she picked it up with her free hand and carried it into the house.

The sum of those events was so arresting that I nearly failed to complete my welcome for Anastasia—I had only just placed the last piece of barbed wire when she arrived in the bedroom.

'Who was that woman with the child?' she demanded. 'Another of Sonya's wandering sheep, I suppose!'

Her combative expression made me disinclined to give her a full answer.

'She's a sort of government person,' I said; and as that information evidently failed to satisfy her feminine curiosity I added a few details as they came to my mind: 'Her name's Iphigenia Ballcock, she's an unmitigated daughter of General Kitchener—or was, till he got drowned in the Black Sea. She takes her child round to climb up and inspect the inside of people's chimneys—if the kid doesn't do it properly they light a fire underneath and scorch her feet.'

Yes, the homely adage that absence makes the heart grow fonder was perfectly illustrated by my feelings on recovering my sister. As we gossiped that evening in the congenial privacy of the harness room I realized (perhaps no more than subconsciously) how good it was to have as companion a person who would never change. The queerly inflated body on which clothes of every kind lost their shape and cohesion, the raucous laugh, the cumbrous movement of arms, legs and mind, these had for me the subtle charm, the warmth, of all reliable, familiar things. But with that flood-tide of fondness for Anastasia my anxiety regarding Helma grew more acute. It was clear by now that the feelings I had for Cathleen involved me in giving at least some moral support to her mother. Meeting afresh the impregnable stolidity of my sister's countenance, I lost all hope that she would understand or endorse my new, ambiguous loyalties.

The holiday seemed to have left her in a pugnacious mood, 'What did you mean,' she demanded, sprawling over the saddle bench and angrily darning her yellow jersey, 'telling me that female was called Ballcock? She isn't. Her name's O'Kneale—Sonya says so.'

I had to admit that I often confused those two names.

'But they're not in the least alike,' she said.

I could see we were in for a pointless argument, and my only course was to wear her down. 'The two names go together.' I said firmly. 'You see them on all the hoardings —"O'Kneale and Ballcock, Old-established Family Solicitors, Purveyors of Fried Fish to the Nobility and Gentry".'

That was effective—girls, I knew, could never concentrate for long when confronted by thoughtful exegesis. With her mind wandering all over the place, as it always did, she said suddenly,

'O'Kneale—I suppose she might be something to do with Kevin O'Kneale. The one that's dead now.'

48

'Don't be a fool!' I said. 'Kevin was Irish. This person's no more Irish than Mavrusha.'

There—as I now recognize—my own logic was a little at fault; and if Anastasia had been attending carefully to what I said she might have won the rally by pointing out that Sonya wasn't Irish either, but had turned into Mrs Hutchinson simply because Howard, at a loose end in St Petersburg, had happened to look in and marry her. Characteristically, my sister missed that chance to score; with her mind still moving in zigzags she said,

'Apparently she's my governess—Sonya gets governesses like Pavel gets fleas. This one's a German and she's got a broken heart like all the others—it's because as usual she's lost her mother or husband or someone—and I've got to be responsive and docile and all the rest of it, like I was supposed to be with that Dygasinska excrescence.'

'Oh, so you've had Sonya's pi-jaw already?' I said. 'Was she in bounding form?'

'Not awfully. Semyon came wandering in and she suddenly remembered she had a pi-jaw up her sleeve for him too, so she tried to get us both done together. She was on at Semyon about not airing his views on Angles or someone in front of Irina Nikolayevna.'

'But he hasn't got any other views to air, poor juggins.'

'At any rate he's not to keep telling her that all her ancestors were fornographic bloodsuckers, because Irina's supposed to be sensitive about all sorts of little criticisms on account of her loony papa getting himself drowned and all that. Sensitive! If you ask me, that old plough-horse wouldn't feel it if you banged a six-inch nail into her sit-upon. And then Sonya got back on to me, and I've got to turn myself into a slop-faced little English lady.'

There was a note of despair in her voice which I could readily understand.

'I did read a story,' I told her, 'where an ace magician turned a fierce hyena into a dormouse.'

But by now she had worked herself into a state of simmer-

49

ing indignation where such encouragement was of no avail.

'It was all so stupid,' she said, 'with Semyon there. Of course he didn't know what in the world Sonya was talking about—she kept drifting out of her awful English into her mangy Russian and back again—he thought she was telling him *he'd* got to turn himself into a nice little English lady so he could get lessons from this O'Kneale specimen.'

'While you give your time to not telling Irina Nikolayevna her potty papa was a bloodsucking fornographist?'

'There's nothing funny about it. I don't see why I've got to have a governess at all. Isn't there some place like Harrow, only for girls, where you get educated miles and miles away from one's mother?'

'Not for girls,' I told her. 'If you take girls away from their parents they merely get rounded up in batches by the white slavers. No, if you're a girl you've simply got to be stuffed with education one at a time, like those poor geese at Strasbourg.'

'But why has it always got to be one of these ghastly refugees, or some other filthy foreign person! And when it comes to having a *German*—well, what are we doing this war for!'

Here was the issue I had been nervously waiting. As a first recourse I tried to give her thoughts a new direction, asking in a friendly tone, 'Did you get any chink off the Thornleys?'

'Not for lending,' she said rather sharply. 'And anyway you owe me three and six already.'

'Three and four,' I corrected.

'Plus a bob interest—you've had it for centuries. I cannot see,' she went on, with that attachment to barren topics which marks the simple mind, 'why Sonya has to scour the whole world to rope in these forsaken women to be my governesses. I mean, haven't the Germans got any sort of Dr Barnardo's where they can keep their own widows and that sort of thing?'

I said, 'Well, one thing I can tell you—this Helma isn't in the least pro-German.'

'How do you know?'

'Because I put a Union Jack where she'd suddenly see it when she went into Sonya's room, and I hid to see what she'd do.' (This happened to be true.) 'If she was pro-German she'd have done a great golloping spit, or at any rate she'd have shouted out, *"Donner und Blitzen!"* '

'Oh, bunkum!' Anastasia said, in the flat, I-am-older-and-wiser tone which drains all colour and warmth from conversation. 'And another thing, I don't see how she can governess me at all decently if she's got that ghastly brat hanging on to her all day long.'

'She hasn't,' I said. 'Mavrusha looks after it a lot of the time—it's herded in with Brigid and that crowd. And the brat isn't as ghastly as all that, either.'

'All brats up to the age of twelve are just stinkingly ghastly,' Anastasia said.

The remark was symptomatic. My sister had long been notorious for her lack of maternal instinct—the dolls which unbriefed aunts produced for her birthdays had always looked, by nightfall, as if they had stood in the way of Timur the Lame. Later, it is true, she assembled enough maternal sentiment (as far as I could judge) to sate the needs of the five infants resulting from her union with Henry St Auberlin. But at this time—she was in her fifteenth year—it was a thankless exercise trying to inspire her with more womanly feelings towards the younger generation.

I made one effort to temper her bigotry with reason. 'What you mean,' I said, 'is that Brigid and Polina are nothing but a plague, and completely revolting—especially when you get them cluttering up the whole bathroom. Well of course you're absolutely right—Mavrusha ought to be sent abroad with them somewhere, some place like the Canadian prairies where there's a bit more room. Only this infant of Helma's—who's called Cathleen—she's really quite a different sort of thing. She doesn't bulge, and she doesn't go bawling and squeaking all over the shop. Most of the time you just don't notice she's there at all.'

Anastasia nodded. 'In fact,' she said, in the caustic voice she used when she had run out of arguments, 'she's your idea of the ideal girl!'

Sarcasm is an ugly device, especially when used by girls. For Sonya's sake—and perhaps a little for my own—I had done my best to smooth my sister's passage into a new educational phase by presenting a view of the human race more tolerant than hers. Failing in this brotherly office, I could only leave the affair to take its course.

I did persuade her to go to bed early, hoping that a long night's rest might make her more magnanimous towards Helma, but here my thoughtfulness was rendered sterile by a tiresome mischance. Finding the barbed wire and other tokens, the simple creature took some pains to move them into what she thought was my bed, not knowing I had lent it to Irina Nikolayevna. Irina, never familiar with the symbols of English affection, chose to regard this garnishing as calculated insolence; always histrionic, chronically lachrymose, she debouched to the landing in her empire nightgown and, meeting Howard there, created a preposterous scene. When my own total innocence had been established Anastasia was awarded another pi-jaw—an unhappy prelude to the new campaign to turn her into a woman of refinement and learning.

Not without self-reproach I recall that while Helma, next morning, was helping to clear away the breakfast things Anastasia and I continued to loll by the table, so deeply absorbed in arguing whether the horse or the glider was the sounder means of locomotion that we were startled when the German-sounding voice intruded. Changing abruptly from domestic servant to official, Helma had taken up an unmistakably military stance at Anastasia's shoulder; her smile was magisterial, faintly sinister, as she delivered her directive:

'Your mother has told me, Anastasia, that this room is also for our schoolwork. Today we commence our studies here at half-past nine.'

Even then the word 'commence' made me shudder; and at 'studies' I glanced nervously at Anastasia's face to see how she was taking that unseductive announcement. Approximately, her response was that of a camel to a light slap from its sowar: she turned her head for an instant, her eyebrows raised disdainfully, then went on talking to me.

Here was the shape of things I had long and gloomily foreseen: the wretched girl had already armed herself for resistance, her latest teacher would last no longer than the others and in consequence the orbit of the bewitching Cathleen would cease for ever to intersect with mine. I had, however, made counter-preparations of my own. Drifting as she always did from the subject of our discussion, Anastasia began to wax eloquent on the superiority of the Thornleys' horses in appearance and behaviour to the Thornleys themselves—one of her favourite themes; I waited till she paused, choked by her own verbosity, and then I opened up with a speech I had roughly rehearsed the night before:

'Look, Stasey, this jumfumble about education—I've been thinking, it strikes me you're lucky, really. Sooner or later I'll be made to join one of those swish boarding kennels for English boys—Howard says it's the simplest way to get a decent character and all that fush. Then I'll have to take cold baths and play manly games like football—it all comes in Talbot Baines Reed. Now you, by simply being a girl, get off all that. Girls don't have to fight the Germans or build the Empire or anything, so they don't need to have any character, or team spirit or anything, so they're not made to have cold baths and sleep in filthy freezing dormitories.'

'Well, I wouldn't mind cold baths,' she said with her usual perversity. 'And I don't see anything against football, though I suppose it's not much fun for timid little knock-kneed boys who can't even ride.'

There I was tempted to point out that fat girls who needed horses to get them from one spot to the next would be nothing but a blockage and a blight on any football field; but experience warned me that such statements of fact inhibit the smooth flow of a discussion. Instead, I went on patiently to develop my case.

'Another thing,' I said, '—with any luck you can get your education over and done with in quite a short time, then you can be a débutante, or a stable girl, or whatever you want to. I've been reconnoitring this new woman, and I can see she's pretty slick at teaching. I should think if you just sit tight and lap up what she says you'll have soaked up all the education a girl's got any room for in about a year.'

The way in which I spoke those sensible words impressed me, at the time, with its quiet conviction. It cannot be inferred that Anastasia received the same impression.

'I suppose Sonya's talked you into saying all that,' she answered frigidly. 'Isn't he mumsy's good little boy, bless his precious heart! Or did she give you sixpence for the job?'

'Now listen, Ananias-and-Sapphira,' I said (preserving a dignified and courteous tone), 'I'm simply putting forward some ideas for you to consider—'

'Yes, and I consider them the most boring ideas I ever heard.'

'If you'd only keep an open mind—'

'If you'd only keep your mouth tight shut!'

(Not long ago I attended some public function—the opening of an exhibition? the closing of a town-hall?—at which Anastasia was the centrepiece, and on waking from a short doze I heard her say, in the voice which has disabled microphones from Dover to Dunvegan, *'Whatever our differences, we in this country are universally agreed that freedom of speech is the most precious of all our traditions.'* And how much of that freedom, my dear Stasie, did you ever vouchsafe to me?)

From that point our discussion (as commonly happens where there is a fundamental lack of sympathy) tended to take a circular course. Once more I tried to establish the point first made to me by Howard that Helma, though a German, might yet be acceptable as a human being. Rebutting this view, Anastasia evolved a theory that I was currying favour with the enemy in case they should win the War. I said it was all very well for girls, who didn't have to fight, to display their patriotism by being nasty to defenceless members of the other side. She answered that as far as she knew I had done no fighting either up till now—nor was it likely that a mewly puky boy who was terrified of horses and football would ever get as far towards the Front Line as the Girl Guides. Soon, flagging in debate, we fell back on a pattern of versicle and smooth response so familiar to us both that our voices discharged it without much need for mental support:

'You'd be frightened of an earwig.'

'You'd run away from a clockwork mouse.'

'You're the sort of boy who'd do so-and-so on the drawing-room carpet.'

(I refrain from quoting precisely the coarse expression my sister used).

'You'd do so-and-so on the carpet in Buckingham Palace,' I replied.

These exchanges had continued peacefully for some time when a light remark of mine concerning Anastasia's intellectual limitations—a truth which perhaps I should have phrased more euphemistically—appeared to touch some tender nerve in her somewhat primitive mentality. With a feline movement she pounced and tipped my chair so that I found myself with my back on the floor; then, before I had time to take defensive action, she knelt on my stomach and with a pincer grip on both my ears fastened my head against the floor.

'Just try repeating that!' she said.

'Repeating what?'

'You know! About me being balmy.'

Few sensations I know of are so demoralizing as that

of being sandwiched between a well-worn dining-room carpet and something like a hundredweight of peevish girlhood. At the risk of insincerity I had to temporize.

'I didn't say you were specially balmy. What I was *going* to say was that you were comparatively un-balmy as girls go.'

That seemed to me a generous reparation, but she lacked the grace to accept it.

'And what you're going to say *now*,' she answered, using my head to emphasize her words rather in the way an auctioneer wields his gavel, 'is—"*I am a rude and balmy little boy.*"'

'I am a barred and rheumy little boy.'

'Say it properly!'

'I am a rude and balmy boy.'

'And I stink like a dead water-rat,' she prompted.

'And you stink like a dead water-rat,' I said.

Still unappeased, she lowered her head to bite me; I seized the heaven-sent chance to spit at her forehead, with such precision and force that the shock made her loose her hold. With a twisting movement, then, I dislodged the bulk of her, we rolled together underneath the table and finished at its other side, where I, taking my turn, held her head captive with a skill and resolution which a Rugby player would not have been ashamed of, while she kicked out so wildly that a Shield Back chair which her foot encountered travelled two or three yards to shatter the glass front of a bookcase. Naturally I found this phase in our dispute more palatable than the one before it, and I must have been—for the moment —at least as vexed as she when a chillingly pedantic voice came from the outer world to invade our privacy:

'Now, Anastasia, you will sit here, please. Today we first attempt a conspectus of our mathematical knowledge.'

It was laced, that alien voice, with a surprising authority. I stood up quickly, edging away from Anastasia's reach as the seer Daniel may have edged from the lions' after his night in session with them. Helma herself was already seated, in the chair which Howard occupied at mealtimes. Two or three places away, in patent independence, Cathleen was perched on another of the Hepplewhite chairs, and though her chin was only just level with the table she seemed to be absorbed in a book which lay open there—her face was a study in sagacious calm.

'See,' Helma said, addressing the sprawl of ill-darned stockings and suspenders which was still the only part of Anastasia on public view, 'my little Cathleen has commenced her studies already.'

I still think that was an unwise thing to say.

I myself was tempted now to linger for the enjoyment of Cathleen's society, but for the time being I had had my fill of Anastasia's; so, with a deferential nod to Helma and a smile to her daughter, I was about to retire, leaving the distaff side to achieve what harmony it could, when the bleating of my name informed me that a fourth female was present. At the little davenport which Sonya used for paying bills and answering invitations Irina Nikolayevna sat with the anguished patience of one who awaits the pains of childbirth or suttee.

'Ryan,' she warbled, in the voice that always seemed to force its passage through artificial tears, 'if you have finished your jollity with Anastasia perhaps you will spare me just a little portion of your busy time.'

At that age I entirely lacked the gift of objectivity. Orpen, who had painted her, once told my father that Irina's complexion was as perfect as any he had known; to me her face was as much worth study as that of a wax figure in the window of Bon Marché, while her eruptive bosom, harshly caparisoned with cameos and clustered pearls, presented to a small boy of exceptionally simple outlook the image of all that was baneful in the adult and feminine. Now I should certainly have fled, but as other dreadful creatures do this woman exercised some sort of hypnotic compulsion. I wavered, like a bird fastened by a serpent's eyes, and she quickly completed my arrest.

57

'Your kind mother said she was sure you would give me a little help with something I try to write—she says you're so clever with the English words and phrases.'

Yes, she had all the trump cards in her hand—the show of womanly weakness, an appeal to filial loyalty, ingenuous flattery of the sort which never fails with a male child. I went, moving one of the chairs, to sit at her side.

She had understated her requirement. Like every Russian émigré she was writing her memoirs, and doubtless in the hope of large American sales she had decided to render them in English, a language she had chiefly learnt (I imagine) in casual exchanges with bus conductors, shop girls and the like. In her oil-cloth bag she had two or three books like small ledgers filled already, as far as I could see, with her regular and curiously childish hand. What the artless product had cost her—how many laborious hours in her cold and meanly lighted bedroom at the Duntisbourne Hotel—I do not know and did not then consider: I presumed that Russians reminisced as dogs barked and ravens cawed, from a senseless *joie de vivre* which nature had implanted. The important fact, that morning, was that with my extensive scholarship at her command this pestilential woman meant to overhaul a great part of her manuscript.

'I will first read to you some pieces from my portrayal of the life of Novozersk... *"Each evening while the sun descended we surveyed our peasants at their homeward promenade with the croppings of the day."* Is that nice English, Ryan?'

'Indeed, madame, I find it beautiful.'

I gave her, I'm afraid, only the smaller part of my attention. A slight shift of the eyes was all I needed to get from a Venetian wall-glass an oblique, absorbing picture of the dining-table, where the small face of Cathleen showed itself —a portrait not so much of charming infancy as of complex intelligence: she looked to be at once engrossed in the book before her and aware that she was under observation, to be playing conscientiously the part of student and deliciously

58

amused by her own performance. How could the eager, troubled, china face of Irina compete with a spectacle so endearing, so serene, as that!

'Yes,' I kept repeating, 'that is most interesting, and very well expressed.'

'You think so truly, Ryan? Now here is a passage which composed itself with some hardship. *"In December my dear father and I have made the sledge-journey of eleven days to the marriage of my cousin Tatiana Vassilyevna with a young landowner of her province. Many more cousins are also at their side, there comes a great hunt for the wolves with balls etcetera and often the merrymaking has continued loud and long until the dawn."* Do you think that is quite nice for composition?'

'It's very exciting. Perhaps it would be still better English to say, "The merrymaking was as broad as it was long." '

She pencilled the correction.

'And now,' she said, 'there are lists of all the people at the hunt party and the balls. Those names perhaps will not be very interesting for you?'

'Oh, but I should like to hear them.'

In truth I had long been case-hardened to the stupefying sameness of Russian life as annalists of Irina's sort exposed it: those hunts, those festivals, the endless concentrations and dispersals of people whose names were all alike. And I found some entertainment of a simple kind in the contrast between the two voices claiming my attention, the cloudy verbiage effusing from poor Irina, the patient but incisive diction with which the resolute Helma sought to make a dent in my sister's impenetrable mind. My image of Helma was at least enlarged that morning. Somehow she had persuaded Anastasia to sit in the appointed place and to look—however leaden-eyed—in the direction of an open text-book. Now, firm but not unfriendly, tireless but never strident, she was trying to find some corridor between the mental desert where her pupil lived and the fertile country of her own intellect and learning.

59

'But listen, please, Anastasia: we use such a symbol as a letter from the alphabet because it is something we can manage. It would be not so easy to say, "the number of men and women the ship could hold" over and over again.'

'It would give me no trouble at all,' Anastasia said.

'There I must correct you. It is not at all an easy exercise to say, "the number of men and women the ship could hold multiplied by two and divided by eleven." Such sentences would soon be impossible to manipulate.'

'But then I never have the smallest wish to multiply and divide people.'

'And you cannot picture yourself a tourist manager who must move his customers from London Bridge to Windsor Castle, with two ships for his use and afterwards eleven carriages?'

For me the duel had a fascination resembling that of sheepdog trials; I found it increasingly hard to pretend that I was wholly absorbed in the chronicle which flowed from Irina's narrow mouth as water from a worn faucet. Now and then, however, the very dullness of her manner was curiously piquant; as when she read: ' "*My two elder brothers were serving in the Preobrazenski Regiment when the War began. Each of them was killed during a few weeks. My younger brother was an artillery officer. He by chance was quickly killed also.*" ' And when, pausing, she asked me, 'In that I have the syntax not so exact, perhaps?' I had just sufficient decency to answer, 'I don't think syntax really matters when you've things like that to write about.' Her reference to the War brought some discomfort of another kind; for all my ignorance, I did remember that Russia was on our side, so the two women dividing my attention had reason to detest each other. With my special interest in one of them I found this thought disturbing.

There was no sign that Helma herself was troubled by anything she may have heard from my end of the room; now and then she threw an encouraging smile to Cathleen, or stretched to supply her with paper and crayons, but chiefly she was intent on guiding her less tractable charge, step by step, through a problem so elementary that I had solved it in my head while Anastasia was painfully constructing the original equation. While all this gave me some entertainment, my prime anxiety was constantly increasing. If this morning ended without open trouble it would be reasonable to think of this achievement as confirming Helma in her appointment. So far Anastasia seemed relatively docile, but I did not trust the omens. Children, generally denied full knowledge of what is happening around them, are perhaps hypersensitive to those currents of emotion which reveal themselves through momentary changes in the weather of the eyes, words left half-spoken, pendent silences; as a square of sunlight crept along the crimson table-cloth, in turn illuminating Cathleen's lovely head, a hand of Anastasia's fiddling with a ruler, the dedicated face of Helma focussed on her pupil's work, I felt as a mountaineer might feel if he had to surmount a notorious couloir with a known epileptic on the rope.

'You are satisfied, Ryan, the composition I have used for that passage is "all-right"?'

I beckoned my thoughts back to the path of duty. 'It sounded,' I said, 'very smooth and easy to understand.' She smiled contentedly. '*Ah, tu es un critique trop indulgent, à mon sens!*' 'The next pages I need not read, they have been corrected already by my friend Professor Katamenkov, who made a particular study of the English language. But here there is a portion I have composed a little after the professor's examination: "*My father wrote it will be safer for me to stay at Veltiskoye, as there is much restlessness in Petrograd. I wrote then to Masha to send my white fox coat, but she is so extremely stupid she sends my sable coat which is not so warm and has a most unfashionable shape. Mme Sabodin agrees with me that even at Veltiskoye a woman must look unsuitable in a coat which was fashioned in 1910, so it is entirely a troublesome situation.*" That is correct—"a troublesome situation"?'

'It might be slightly better to write, "A time for weeping and gnashing of teeth"—that's the more usual thing to say in English.'

'"Gnashing of teeth"—*bien*! And here is a piece where I write of deserting soldiers. *"In the near village there was a bizarre man with the name of Luka who made himself the chief of almost thirty uncontented soldiers and led them to illegal actions. A message came that at Mme Sabodin's house those men had stolen many things, also violated two of the young women and then cruelly killed them. To be safe from such behaviour I and the rest of our household went in the night to the house of the stationmaster for refuge. From there I saw my old house burning till it was finally destroyed, for me that was a great sadness and through all the next day I was weeping."* There also must I say again, "and gnashing teeth"?'

I shook my head. Sometimes the least sensitive of children may be impressed by naked statements: suddenly I had seen this brainless woman turned into one who stood at the stationmaster's window, watching the flames consume her home, doubtless wondering whether the crazed soldiers who had 'cruelly killed' two women would propose adding to their score.

'I don't think,' I said, 'there's anything which needs changing there.'

It must have been in the short interval when Irina actually held my attention that a page was turned in the academic programme at the other end of the room. I know it surprised me to hear Helma dilating on a topic which seemed to have no mathematical reference:

' ... So I have obtained a copy of his *Sartor Resartus* in the shortened form, which I should like you to study with me. It is an easier work—it gives you better entertainment —than some of his historic books, like the history of the French Rebellion. We may commence, I think, with Mr Barrett's introduction.'

Anastasia's face was so turned that, in the glass, I saw it

only in profile, but this view was enough to warn me of impending trouble: that rigid mouth, those cataleptic eyes, belonged to a character I had long before named Pig-head Popsy. It was no more unexpected than the striking of a church clock when she said abruptly,

'Well, frankly, Mrs O'Kneale, I don't want to read anything that dreary Scotchman wrote at all. Someone else made me read a thing he wrote about heroes, it was really the most utter bosh I ever came across.'

That voice of my sister's, level and cold as a Norfolk wind, put an end to my pretence of being engaged with Irina. I turned flagrantly to watch the dreadful play, and saw that Helma had stiffened as nervous patients do at the prick of a hypodermic needle.

'It is quite wrong,' she said, 'to employ such a word as "bosh" for the writing of Thomas Carlyle. Carlyle is one of the most famous names of English literature, he was the friend of Goethe, he is known to all Europe.'

Anastasia nodded. 'Yes, what they seem to like in Europe is all the most boring people they can find over here—Ruskin and Byron and people like that. And Carlyle was the worst of the lot, book after book after book about dreary ideas and stupid people like Frederick the Great.'

'Frederick the Great was not a stupid man. He had many faults, yes. But he was a great monarch and a philosopher also.'

'Yes, I suppose that's how every German looks at him. They admire that bossing and booting sort of person.'

At those words Helma stood up, and for a moment I thought she might slap Anastasia's face. I rather hoped she would, for although I knew nothing about catharsis intuition told me that the miasma resulting from Anastasia's boorish conduct could be dissipated only by an act of violence. (Perhaps Irina hoped so too; I sensed the fact that behind my shoulder even that dim-witted creature was trembling from the excitement of the drama.) But in life the *coup de théâtre* does not occur; even the furious retort which I

63

could almost see on Helma's lips remained unspoken. Instead, she said in a voice just under control,

'It is time now for Cathleen to have her rest; I leave you for a little while. When I return I should like to hear, please, what course of literature-study you have to propose to me.'

With that she marched out of the room; and my beloved Cathleen, as if on a short lead, sedately followed her.

In the moral shambles she left behind there was no acceptable part for me to play. I was enough a creature of the suburbs to realize that in Irina's presence I could not tell Anastasia what I thought of her: however ignorant of common English phrases, such as 'swollen-headed bitch' and 'bellyaching skunk', Irina might guess from my tone of voice that I addressed my sister without exaggerated suavity. On the other hand I could not quietly resume the office of Irina's literary adviser as if nothing had happened. In such a predicament it is best, I think, to let instinct take command. I did so then. 'If you will excuse me, madame,' I said, 'I'd like to be sick for a short while in the garden.' And with no further care for protocol I went the way that Helma and Cathleen had gone.

Sailing, as it were, before a strong wind of shame and indignation I made my way at once to Helma's room. My knock was not audibly answered, but presently the outside handle turned and the door was pulled far enough open to reveal the face of Cathleen, her expression changing in a moment from that of a punctilious parlourmaid to one of joyful welcome.

'Bub!' she cried; and then, deploying the whole of her linguistic achievement, 'Allo, Bub! Allo!'

Just then I was not in a state of mind for dalliance; I said portentously, 'I'd like to see your mother, please,' and as those words seemed to be outside my darling's range of understanding I squeezed gently past her into the room.

This was the first time I had been inside it during Helma's tenancy, and the experience was like finding a part of one's native country under foreign occupation: the basic furniture was, I suppose, the same, but an extra bed had been introduced for Cathleen, giving it the crammed appearance one associates with provincial antique shops, while the accretion of such things as paper-bound books, pictures of waterfalls and forest glades, climbing boots, alpenstocks, Bavarian patchwork counterpanes, had so transformed its looks and smells that the rest of Howes Croft might have been a hundred miles away. Those alien flavours were sufficiently disconcerting, and the spectacle of Helma herself, standing motionless beside the larger bed and staring at the wall, did nothing to encourage me: a child even less perceptive than I would have known from her white face, the trembling of her hands and chin, that except for the proud repression of tears she was weeping. If I had paused to compose a suitable speech I should not have spoken at all.

'Stasey's a silly old sow,' I muttered spontaneously; and then, having once been kicked at school for priggish utterance, I added with respectable humility, 'It's really my fault she's like that today. I got her just above the eyes with a load of my gob—that always makes her touchy.'

Helma's eyes turned slowly in my direction, but only as if she had been disturbed by some noisy creature too far off for her to identify. She said nothing. I laboured on, trying to make the whole position plain.

'I don't think we've been brought up quite enough, not so far, Stasey and me. I don't think Russians are awfully good at bringing people up, really, and Howard's always too busy. Look, gnädige Frau, I think if you'll only stay here for a time you'll find our characters getting slightly less repulsive—I mean, not quite so lewd and consumacious—as time goes on.'

It looked as if she would make some answer then, but it's difficult, I suppose, to talk to children in a language not your own, and I could see she was still having trouble with her tear-glands, as women do at the least convenient times.

For both our sakes I turned away and started goggling at her knick-knacks.

'Crikey,' I said, 'you *have* turned this room upside-down!'

Above the smaller bed she had hung the photograph of a soldier in British uniform. It was the work of an Aldershot photographer—I speak exactly, since it stands before me now —and I should call it a fair example of a style in portraiture still honoured in thousands of humble homes; that *genre* which by denying all the sitter's personality, all that would speak of flesh, blood and a third dimension, reduces him to a diagram embedded in khaki serge and metal trimmings. Yes: and yet when I first glanced at that banal production, that travesty of photographic art, it recalled to me entirely a man who in life could never have been mistaken for any other—a tall fellow, preternaturally thin, on whose long head the soldier's cap was here shown to perch as irrelevantly as the headgear of a snowman; one whose supple mouth appeared in a peculiar way to mock the learning of the forehead and the gentleness of the wide-lashed, lambent eyes.

'But where,' I asked in fatuous innocence, 'did that photo come from? It's Kevin.'

Now her eyes came slowly to rest on my face, but she still failed, I think, to get me in focus. When she spoke her voice sounded impersonal, betraying no emotion.

'That,' she said, 'is the best man who has ever been.'

It was not a statement which I felt like contradicting.

66

2
Kevin

A simple calculation shows me it was Brigid and Polina with whom Sonya was pregnant at the time of my grandfather's first fatal illness. And that, I suppose, would account for the preternatural enlargement of her person which rather frightened an infant as ignorant, timid and adoring as I was then.

'Some days I think the poor girl may explode any minute, and wreck the whole property.'

I did not see my father's face when he spoke those dreadful words, since I was lying on my belly behind the small sitting-room sofa, drawing a fight between the Archangel Michael and a mad giraffe; but his voice, earnest and husky with gloom, was enough to alarm me.

At the age of seven one's native curiosity is in going order, and I was always trying to find solutions to things which puzzled me by picking up threads of adult conversation; already I had realized that the talk of men, being less concerned with frills and furbelows, was more informative than that of women, and since my opportunites for hearing Howard in converse with other males were scarce I took care not to miss them. On this occasion he was entertaining an old friend called Mr Shaw, a shaggily breeched and bearded Irishman not unlike a leaner version of himself, who was known to Anastasia and me as a tireless producer of enigmatic jokes. I had little use for this man, who took no notice of me except to say at our first meeting, 'Howard, I implore you now not to rear this poor creature as a third-rate artist. Let you be true to your Protestant profession and make him into a fat stockbroker, with a gold watch-chain and a motor car.' All the same, he had some value as catalyst: Howard talked more lavishly with him than with the polyglot rabble he normally encountered at our dining-table.

'I've sad news, G.B. My aunt Theresa writes that my old father is going downhill very fast now.'

Naturally those words incised themselves deeply in my mind. I am not sure if I had previously grasped the fact that Howard possessed a father of his own. Now I pictured a person of prodigious antiquity—white locks and cascading beard, translucent flesh, hideously protrusive eyes—mounted on a decrepit bicycle and recklessly descending a road as steep as the one between Hendon Church and the aerodrome.

'Have they put him in hospital?' Mr Shaw asked, and in a flash I saw the ancient man in bed, all tangled up with wheels and handlebars.

My father must have shaken his head. 'They tried him in a hospital at Waterford,' he said mournfully, 'but it wasn't practical. He raised the subject of theology and threw a medicine bottle at a woman who couldn't follow his opinions. By bad luck that was the Matron. They had him labelled "convalescent" before you could say "Gavan Duffy" and he was out the very next day.'

'What, back to his farm?'

'No, he was too sick for that. But Theresa herself took pity on him. Mike Kearney—that stupid ox she married, you remember?—Mike bought up that great old pub in Castlemagonagh to run it as a business proposition, and she has it on her hands still. Forty-six bedrooms—God alone knows what any woman could hope to do with such a contraption in Castlemagonagh! So in the goodness of her heart the old bitch has thought to install her obsolescent brother in what they call the Bridal Suite.'

My father's voice had become so woeful that I was glad his friend was there to offer sympathy. Mr Shaw was quick to turn sorrow into indignation: doctors and their nostrums, hospitals and the fiends in petticoats who kept them going, all alike were instruments of Satan. I had long ceased to swim in this flood of rhetoric when Howard, seizing the quarter-second in which the orator paused to clear his throat, began a speech of his own which filled me with misgivings:

'Well, I do my last Wölfflin lecture on Friday, and then I'll run over and see the old fellow I'd like to wish him well before he starts on his last journey. I shall take the wee boy with me—he ought to have one sight of his grandad, and with Sonya in her present state it'll do her good to have him out of her way for a while.'

Those dramatic announcements came so fast that my astonished brain could not keep level. In my overdriven fancy the weird old man whom Howard spoke of, just out of bed and still festooned with bits of twisted bicycle, was racing off again—to the North Pole? to Darkest Africa?— when the sentence fell which I have already recorded: 'Some days, G.B., I think the poor girl may explode and wreck the property.'

In the tangle of sentiments promoted by those words fear had its place: if in truth my mother was going to burst, bringing our home about her ears as Samson brought the house of the Philistines, the coward in me actually preferred the thought of being elsewhere, waving farewell to my peripatetic grandsire. And then, since nothing had been said about Anastasia travelling with Howard and me, the prospect of even transient release from my elder sister's patronage and bullying was more than grateful. That expectation had, none the less, its darker side: Anastasia might come in for treats which I should miss; at the least she would have Sonya for some days to herself, and I could not feel that her influence on our susceptible mother would be entirely wholesome. Beyond these apprehensions was the dim, unformulated knowledge that Sonya counted on my support. If, with a sound like thunder, she was going to disintegrate, my place was surely at her side; duty might call my father to cheer his own crumbling parent at the start of one more senseless excursion, but he should be able to perform that office without assistance from me.

I had learnt, however, that where major policy was being settled people of my age had no *locus standi*. It never occurred to me to tell my parents I should rather stay at home than take part in Howard's recondite mission. As soon should I have asked them to reconsider my outlandish name.

It must have been the archaic *Duchess of Ormond* ('Mother Butler's Floating Flea-House') which took us to Rosslare. I think of that unlovely steamer mainly as a mobile cantonment for Howard's relations—we were only half-way up the gangway when there were joyful cries from red-faced men and jaunty girls in travelling veils on the deck above us: 'Why, if it isn't Howard himself, the old galoot! Mabs —Noreen—come and take a peep at your uncle Howard, the great professor from London College!' But in truth I cannot remember a time when I did not know my father as one to whom a substantial part of the population was apparently related; even in London he was often hailed by smallish, hungry men who were able to establish some tribal connection, and in any westward journey the number of chance acquaintances who proved to be his cousins seemed to increase with every degree of longitude. This phenomenon by no means embarrassed him. Broadly, he seemed to find every encounter with a member of the human race agreeable, and whenever it turned out that one of these was distantly derived from the same loins as he the pleasure became an intoxication. For me it was no surprise, then, to discover that a steam-packet was simply another place for Howard to be greeted and encompassed by his kin; only with a certain weariness of spirit did I hear the familiar kind of slogans breaking out again:

'Why, yes, Sheelagh O'Donovan—God bless the child— she would be Liam O'Donovan's daughter by his second wife, who was first cousin to my own Aunt Sadie Lehane...'

No wonder that my father, enveloped in these social joys, had little mind to spare for the continuous yawns of the small boy leaning against a ventilator at his side. It was a female cousin, a megalithic image of boisterous maternity, who noticed my paling cheeks, swooped, and carried me as if I had been a baby to some bleak depository where at least I could lie on a cushioned bench with an appropriate vessel beside me.

Strangely, the worst pangs attending that prostration came from a sense of sin. Longing for Sonya, I thought I must have committed some hideous crime for which this exile was the punishment; now I remembered how I had once thrown a much-praised drawing of Anastasia's on the nursery fire, once I had bitten the fleshy part of her arm, and once told Mavrusha she was a beastly muzhik who ought to be made into potted meat. Perhaps it was no more than justice that a person with so dark a moral record as mine should be made to lie, surrounded by groaning bodies, in a kind of charnel-house through whose pin-hole windows a watery horizon was seen remorselessly to rise and fall. The ship was palpably out of control. I knew (from a story Sonya had read me called *A Young Hero of the Baltic Sea*) that my proper business was to report to the captain, offering myself for some courageous undertaking, but the noxious winds coursing in my stomach and forehead told me just as plainly that I could not walk to the door four yards away. I was to perish, then, ingloriously; without the chance of explaining to Sonya why I had failed to do her credit; without telling her of my burning devotion, or even pointing out that before I had bitten Anastasia she had used my own pencil-box to hit me on the side of my neck.

Those cheerless meditations were not much relieved by the advent of what appeared to be some kind of nursery-maid.

'Are you after vomiting?' this person asked me, in the hearty tone of a fair-ground gipsy offering a turn at hoop-la; and when I failed to answer that oracular question she went

71

on: 'We're short of wee pails this trip. If you don't mean to take advantage of the one beside you it'll do for the lady over there—and it's my opinion she hasn't all day to wait.'

At that time I had not heard of Sir Philip Sidney's altruistic conduct after Zutphen, but I must instinctively have recognized the immediate situation as one of the same order. I gave my bowl a feeble push towards the nurse; simultaneously the ship reared like a circus horse, and the bowl described a large half-circle on the floor.

'These English boys!' the girl cried enthusiastically. 'They'll have their football game, if they've neither foot nor ball to play with!'

Thereafter she and a colleague in the same uniform settled to the task of entertaining me. A thousand tales and ballads present us with the charm of the Irish girl—her lovely skin, the laughing mouth, the eyes put in with a sooty finger. I will champion that tradition so long as I have breath or biro. But in every generation there must be a few individuals deviant from the norm; at the time I write of, it may have been the accepted practice to cull from the flock the rare young woman who failed to reach the Irish standard and appoint her stewardess aboard the *Duchess of Ormond*. These two who set themselves to raise my spirits on that voyage were doubtless golden-hearted girls; but the first had teeth designed for a larger woman (or one at a slightly earlier stage of evolution), the voices of them both recalled the skidding of knives on china plates and their laughter was like the cry of macaws gathering to feast.

'And where would you be visiting?' the one with the dog's teeth asked me. 'What? Now that's a shame—they've not much love for English boys at Castlemagonagh.'

'Ah, it's a pack of lies that Rosie's telling you!' the older woman—Nora—said. 'It's more than a month now since an English boy was killed there.'

'Killed?' I said.

'Ah, you should have heard the screams he made—they

had him dangling thirteen hours from the castle tower with his neck in a turkey-halter.'

'And who's telling the fibs now!' Rosie cried. 'Listen, laddie, there's not one living soul been hung in Castle-magonagh for a twelve-month or more. If there's any foreigner they don't care for they simply cut his throat in a quiet way at the back of the Town Hall, with no loss of dignity on either side.'

The fusillade of laughter which broke from both women as an epilogue to that announcement was not enough to cancel its effect. I asked in grave anxiety:

'But do they hate all foreigners?'

'Ah, bless you, no!' Nora said. 'Only the English kind.'

I wanted to explain to these women that I was not English at all but a mainly Russian boy who for obscure reasons had been domiciled at the edge of London; perhaps they would then goodnaturedly advise me how to make my ethnic status clear to those who would otherwise be inclined to cut my throat or put it in a turkey-halter. But at that age I was singularly weak at explanations.

'Shall I tell him about the goblins?' Rosie asked, and Nora nodded: 'It might be best.'

'Well now, if a wee small man with great green ears will come and ask you to play with him in the orchard, you'd best tell him in a civil way you have other things to occupy your time.'

'Och, the green men will do him little harm,' Nora said. 'What he needs to keep away from is the leprechauns.'

'Leprechauns?'

'Whist—they take a grudge against you if you speak their name too loud. Yes, Castlemagonagh's famous for its lepre-chauns, and it's terrible creatures they are, with their serpent's eyes and their long twisting horns.'

'Ah, the cruel claws they have!' Rosie said. 'They'll jump on a strong man and tear the liver from his stomach before his very eyes.'

'Ay, and drain the blood from every vein in his body.

That's the way they use their long tongues—a yard or more a leprechaun can shoot his squirmy tongue, with a spike at its end like a fisherman's gaff. That's the worst part when they get you, the spike boring into a big blue vein. After that the agony's not so bad, you just get fainter and fainter as the creature goes on sucking.'

Rosie was nodding sombrely. 'Sure, it's not a dainty death,' she said.

Those friendly warnings were at the forefront of my mind throughout the train journey which followed. Howard had always been tolerant of my reasonable requests, and I thought if I begged him to get us a lodging in some quarter known to be free from leprechauns he would surely oblige me. My difficulty was to find the words and the opportunity for arranging this business. At Rosslare we had parted from the main body of Howard's relations, but one of them, a woman whose kindly features were almost lost in the surrounding massif of bonnet and bosom, came to sit facing him in the railway carriage; she was palpably a sympathetic listener, and her presence led him to talk of feelings I should never have suspected in a grown person. Simmering with impatience, I yet hung upon my father's words as the crowds at the Français once hung upon the voice of Rachel.

'Yes,' I remember him saying, 'it's more than a year since I last saw the old tiger. And yet I find it hard to think of a world with him not in it. I've friends enough to fill my days, but I tell you, Hanna, I love that man.'

'That's only right,' the old woman said emphatically. 'It's a good and true thing for a son to love the man that begot him.'

'Ay, but there's more to it than filial affection. He thrashed me for my small misdeeds, that's true enough, but when I was most of all a disappointment to him he let me go my own way, with no harsh word spoken. He'd always hoped I would one day take over Connaheen—which he'd made the finest dairy farm in the Province—despite my handicap of a college education. My own ideas were the purest nonsense as he saw them—pictures were all outside his comprehension, and he thought only a poor spineless fellow would fall back on teaching. Yes, it needed all my small store of courage to tell him of the lecturing post I meant to have in London —I thought the sound of his displeasure would agitate the Wicklow Mountains. But in truth he said nothing when I told him—it must have been a whole minute or more he was dumb as a slaughtered ox. After that he said, "You'll be needing cash to set you up in a high-priced place like London. There's a small piece of property I have in County Longford, I'd better turn it into cash for your present convenience." That was all. I tell you, Hanna, as soon as I was out of the old man's sight I cried like any babe.'

If most of that account was meaningless to me, the final words so shook my embryonic brain that for a while I almost forgot my private troubles. Cried? My father? I simply could not picture this great bearded man in tears. But before the journey was over I received some evidence that he had not been indulging in romance. I had spent a few minutes asleep, hearing the conversation only as a rhythmic droning interwoven with the plod of the bogies below me, when one of the sudden checks to which Irish trains were in those days subject brought me to frightened wakefulness. At that moment I did see drops of moisture on Howard's cheeks; and as weeping is an experience intimately known to the youngest children I could almost feel the painful effort it cost him to suppress the tears when he spoke again.

'You'll believe me, Hanna, I cannot bear to think of him weak and helpless—the great, proud, self-willed old tartar he's always been!'

How could I ask this shaken (but still enormous) man to concern himself with my malaise—with the terrors which, having no place in his important world, were ravaging the tiny one I lived in?

A chance did come at length through one of those derangements which were almost inseparable from travel in that period and region. After running placidly for perhaps a

75

quarter of an hour the train stopped with a jerk so violent that our kinswoman exclaimed, 'Ah, that's a collision, now! There'll be corpses on the line all over again.' She spoke with the sort of authority one connects with Deborah the wife of Lapidoth, and it caused another of our fellow-passengers to get up and lean far out of the window. He reported presently: 'Ah, 'tis only the old river bridge is bending. They're shoring it up the best they can.' At which a friend of his, without looking up from his paper, said, 'They'd do best to scrap it altogether. It was never much of a bridge.' These technicalities, catching my father's attention, drew him swiftly from the flood of melancholy which had hitherto submerged him—he was by nature incapable of standing aside from any dramatic or inconvenient occurrence—and as he moved to take his turn at the window I found the boldness to pluck at his coat.

'Howard!'

'Yes, gosling?'

'I won't be left alone where we're going, will I?'

'I don't see why you should be. Why?'

'I wouldn't like to be alone if I met a leprechaun.'

'A leprechaun? Ah, you don't want to vex yourself about those creatures—there are worse bodies in the town than them. A leprechaun will do you not much harm if you just stand up to him. If the very worst happens, you've only to drop a pinch of salt on the rascal's tail.'

It seemed to me that I needed more explicit directions for executing that tactic, but because I had been nursed with a smattering of two of three languages I was absurdly slow in my use of any. The report on the bridge proved over-pessimistic; if it was indeed in a parlous state our driver soon decided to chance his arm, and did so with success. The spasm with which we set off again recalled my father to his own burdens, and there was no more opportunity for investigating mine.

* * *

76

Lately, from curiosity, I went a little out of my way to take a fresh look at Castlemagonagh. In half a century the Conor Maguire Hotel had become smaller, as such buildings do, and notably smarter, with its name displayed in neon tubes, geraniums on its window-sills, its newly cream-washed walls ennobled by the *nihil obstat* of the English motoring clubs. For the rest, the town did little to recall a fragment of my infancy. In Henry Grattan Street, where the hotel stands, there were a few features I recognized— the wistfully Ionic porch of St Columban's Church, the frowning Mechanics' Institute—and it was refreshing to see between a supermarket and an Esso garage the sign *Mrs Malachy o'Luing's Refined Underwear* surmounting a narrow shop which defiantly retained the shabbiness of earlier days; moreover, though it looked a good deal shorter, the street had still the generous width that I remembered, and the motor cars which thronged both sides had not been placed, as in English towns, in slavish alignment with the kerbs. But otherwise this main artery of Castlemagonagh had largely acquired those modern trappings which impose a dismal uniformity on a thousand High Streets, whether in Norfolk or Nebraska: I could see it only as a hazy, artificial reconstruction of the place whose enormous size and strangeness had once so overwhelmed a bewildered pseudo-English child.

In deference to the opposed wishes of two noblemen, Castlemagonagh Station was sited where it would afford the minimum convenience to either; as a late result, that peaky, fearful, perhaps abnormally simple infant had travelled four or five miles in an outside-car before it brought him and his father into Henry Grattan Street, early in an April evening, just as the gas lamps were being lit to supplement the greenish light which a few naphtha flares were already casting on the chapmen's stalls. By then the business of the cattle market must have been over, but while the drovers loitered in Doheny's or the Queen of Spain their beasts were still in the pens, except for a small proportion of the sheep and poultry which, apparently on parole, were perambulating the carriageway and footpaths with the air of impoverished gentlefolk taking part in a public holiday. The Bannengarry meeting is in early April; I suppose it was the patrons of that event who made up the larger part of the crowd which filtered between the wheeled traffic and sometimes, coagulating in loquacious bunches, brought it practically to a halt. With the roving animals these nomads made a quaint fraternity; I remember vividly a bowler-hatted man with a crab-like walk who came up to embrace our horse, addressing it in terms of decorous gallantry, and how a squawking hen which rose suddenly from almost underneath the shafts alarmed me by perching on my knees. No doubt that incident amused my father: our ambling passage through a familiar countryside, the sight of tinkers' vans and unkempt hedges, had gone some way to restore his spirits. But to me the foreign scene which gathered about us in the dwindling daylight was unreal and sinister; in a vague way I felt that the decrepit buildings flanking the street belonged to an earlier world than mine, that the sea of raffish caps and dented billycocks which lapped against our wheels, the incoherent chatter from a pungent stratus of tobacco smoke, were the outworks of a hellish barricade planned to divide me finally from Sonya, from everything I understood, from the only atmosphere I had so far learnt to breathe.

According to my mental record it was in the lobby of the Conor Maguire that our horse was finally pulled up and an aproned man smelling of beer lifted me down. That picture reveals a flaw in my memory: no carriage of any sort could have been driven between the pillars supporting the hotel's porch, let alone through the doorway. I can only suppose that at that date and hour the *va-et-vient* between the lobby and the footpath was such that the two were practically merged into one piazza. But in any case a tired small boy thinks less of his surroundings than of his personal security.

Security? All I had to rely on was Howard's legs, happily

sheathed in such barbarously patterned trousers as a Hungarian Count might buy to join a Scottish shooting party. To these I literally clung, as a shipwrecked sailor will cling to any piece of wreckage which has proved its buoyancy.

Again I had a dog's-eye view. The place we had reached was a shifting jungle of trouser-legs, with a skirt now and then scudding between them; the web of alien voices which had stretched below was now above me, I caught occasionally a name which sounded like 'Oshannahan', spoken with evident distaste, and once the observation, 'Och, he rode her like she might have been my grandma's sofa.' There were frequent shouts of 'Another the same for Mr MacCarthy!' salvoes of blaring laughter, much clinking of coins and glasses. From that fabric of extraneous sounds there emerged a few voices which by degrees I could distinguish and identify with the visible portions of their owners; one in particular had the gentle music which I learnt later in life to associate with County Mayo.

'Dr Caheen is with him now,' it said. 'You'll have a full report the moment he comes down ... Yes, he's come to be past eighty himself, the poor old doc, but he still delivers as neat a baby as you'll find in this town. Now and then he falls asleep across a patient's bed, but he does them no harm at all.'

There was a pair of humbler voices, man's and woman's, which always came in partnership. The man had muddy boots, laced with string and emitting a richly stercoral smell; his way of speaking, as I recall it, makes me think of messengers in Attic drama:

'A great man, the maister's been—you'd travel far to find the like of him. He'd take no foolishness from duke or stable lad.'

At that the woman's voice came in, low and mournful: 'I sat with him a while last night. He was calling out for his Janet Aruba, the way it fairly broke my heart—and she dead and buried these thirty years.'

'Ah, it would not be his wife he had in mind,' the man

79

said. 'It's the Dexter calf he gave her name to—he loved that creature like you'd love a terrier hound. There was never a day, when the maister was up and roving, that he didn't pay a call at the new byre, just for the gratification of wishing a fine morning to that wee heifer.'

'Take it either way,' the woman answered, 'it's a sorrowful thing he'll not see the one or the other again.'

'Faix, I could have Janet Aruba here and beside him within the hour.'

'It's no use, Thomas Morrissey. A grand establishment like this, they wouldn't let her pass the door.'

Talk of that kind seemed to go on for an eternity, while my father—as a rule far from taciturn—made only the smallest contribution. I suspect that his normal ebullience was stifled partly by filial anxiety, partly by the hypnotic effect of an aural barrage which must have brought back his early, impressionable days. But in truth he was allowed few openings; whenever the chorus of concern and veneration for my grandfather subsided, a sad voice palpitant with nerves and husky with deference would start afresh, much as the moan of tramcars comes to bridge the spells of quietness in a busy street:

'I give you my plighted word, Mr Hutchinson, with my right hand upon my heart, you could not do better than order Eamonn O'Callaghan to make the Arrangements. It's the Dignity he gives to the entire transaction. He has a pair of blacks that step together like fairies in a playhouse.'

'Ay, O'Callaghan does well enough,' a sharper voice would comment, 'at putting a Catholic below the ground.'

That remark, I suppose, implied a challenge, and the man with a boot brush in his throat would be quick to answer it: 'Now you know as well as myself, Mr Haughey, Mr O'Callaghan will take no less pains and trouble to inter a Protestant than he would with a believing Christian. Did he not have the contract for Sir Reginald from Dunnisleigh, with not less than twenty carriages, and gentlefolk from as far as Dublin City weeping like water from a tap, and flowers enough to start a forest...'

Time drags for an infant with nothing to occupy his hands or mind, and the tedious prattle of grown-ups brings it almost to a standstill. That interval when Howard and I, encompassed by static advisers, were becalmed in the Conor Maguire lobby seemed to extend towards eternity, but in reality it may have lasted no more than five or ten minutes when, as a south-west monsoon comes to end the hot dry season, a new presence broke upon us.

'So this is the Russian woman's child!'

Those words, in a voice regal though not unfriendly, turned my gaze upward. Beyond a glacis of magenta velvet it reached a riot of decoration, row upon row of pearls three times the size of Sonya's, then a crinkly face coated with white powder, then a pagoda of mahogany-coloured hair. On this aged and manifestly wicked figure I fastened eyes which must have been stretched wide with awe.

My father was answering: 'In a technical sense, Aunt Theresa, you might say I had a hand in him myself,' and that modest statement was enough to provoke the passion for argument which seems to run in the female side of his family. (I have noticed it in Anastasia.)

'Och, there's nothing of the Hutchinsons in that face, God be praised,' Theresa said. 'He's more of a MacLoughlin —that's his great-grandmother's indignant nose he has. Put him up on the counter there—we'll get a bit more of the gas on him. Yes, I can see the eyes come from his mother's side,' she added graciously, '—you could think they might belong to a bashi-bazouk.'

If I had hated being submerged beneath that concourse of orators I was no better pleased to be raised above it. Dumped on the high reception desk, appraised like a poodle at Cruft's, I should have cried from shame had I not felt it still more discreditable to be seen crying. Fortunately Theresa soon lost interest in the misanthropic face of her great-nephew. She was, after all, a person not desperate for mental occupa-

81

tion; an intelligence slightly more advanced than mine would have guessed from a certain restlessness in her speech and aspect that she suffered from too many years, too much activity, too little sleep.

'And is that your baggage, Howard? Well, of course it is —no one outside our family would openly perambulate with such tinker's trappings. And why the servants have left it there for all the world to stare and shudder at is more than I can fathom.' With that she raised her chin, to shout above the general hubbub like a trainer of lions: 'Finlay! Kevin! Mrs Quevedo!' Her imperious cries had as much effect as the supplications of the priests of Baal in their match with Elijah. She turned to my father again.

'Those people, they think I pay them to look beautiful! And that's a notion will make you smile, if ever you get a glance at one of them.' Her own face suddenly relaxed in a smile of surprising cordiality. 'Well now, Howard, it's a sad cause which brings you back, but just the same it's good to see you. Is it not time you kissed me?' She presented a cheek for this operation, which Howard performed with appropriate panache. 'Now listen, dear boy, I'm putting you and the wee lad at the back there, in the Auction Room. Any other time you'd have had the best room in the whole gymnasium—except the one your father has while he lasts out. But you see how it has to be, this week we have people coming for the races from as far as Cork and Sligo, and needing somewhere to lay their foolish heads, and tonight the Sons of Probity must needs be holding their Easter Ball in the old shippon across the yard, to loosen the monotony.'

'Aunt Theresa, will you stop fretting!' Howard said heartily. 'If it was just the coal store you had to offer us it would make no odds at all. The wee boy has no more taste for foolish luxuries than I have.' (That remark, as I reflect upon it now, strikes me as an interesting example of *suggestio falsi* hiding in the shadow of a gigantic falsehood.) 'But listen, now, it's my father I've come to see on this visit and my heart's breaking for a sight of the poor old man. If I can just slip aloft—'

'Ah, it needn't break,' Theresa said reasonably. 'There'll be hours yet, after that old fumbling doctor man comes off him. I've known your father longer than you have, Howard, and I tell you he's no ordinary man, God bless him—he's not the sort that dies and has done with it in some odd moment, as if they'd never thought that much of living, anyhow. No, James'll fight it out all the way, he'll settle for dying at some inconvenient hour of the early morning. Now as I was saying, you're in the Auction Room, and you'll find some bits and pieces there that Dungal Ritchie has to sell on Tuesday—they won't interfere with you at all. There's the one bed for you both but you won't be crowded, you could put a Chinese family in that contraption and run a field-rake up and down between them—it's the old four-poster your uncle Michael bought from the sale at Castle Weavey, the day he was so unwise from his refreshments he thought the thing was a Baptist chapel.'

'Why, that's perfect,' Howard answered politely. Even I could see he was miserable with longing to get to his father's bedside, but the man could display, under pressure, manners of remarkable forbearance. 'Now don't you trouble any more about Ryan and me, we'll be fine and cosy.'

Theresa, however, persisted: 'Wait, I ought to tell you—there'll be one other sleeping with you, but that's only General Almore, and he has his own wee bed which did for his campaigning. That and his canvas bucket and all the gear—he likes to remind himself of the pleasures he had from the North West Frontier. He's English, poor creature, with no more sense than a Galway gander, but he does no kind of harm to man or maiden.'

I think my great-aunt would have liked to continue till breakfast time her sketch of the auction room's amenities: for people of her sort, harnessed to busy lives and large responsibilities, there is much refreshment in intervals given to copious delineation. But a hairless man who wore a corduroy coat over breeches and gaiters had been making a slow descent through the crowd on the broad central staircase; he now appeared at Theresa's side, to address her with the graceful negligence of a superannuated gnome:

'Well, Mrs Kearney, I've fixed up poor Jimmie the best I can—he has enough nostrums to keep him philosophical for a while to come. And now there's a physic I could do with for my own digestion.'

'Indeed, doctor, you deserve that dose exactly,' my great-aunt said, flashing a signal to the man behind the entrance bar. 'But look now, did you ever meet young Howard here, Jimmie's boy?'

The doctor turned to inspect my father's face, then he nodded. 'Why, did I not snick out the tonsils from this wee man just thirty years ago, the very day of that unpleasantness they had in the Phoenix park—the two operations stay in my mind together. And some years before then I had relieved him of another natural piece he had no use for.' He grasped my father by the arms. 'Well, Master Humphreys, it lifts my heart to see you! If this had been your day for shaving I'd have picked you from a thousand at the Dublin Horse Show—even now I see at the farther side of this great shrubbery the elegant small face I used to know. Here's wishing you a long life, dear boy, and as many loving wives as you may need to see you through! I heard your pappy say some time ago you'd gone to seek employment as a drawing master—in England, did he tell me? Ah, from what I hear, you need some fur about the face to guard you from the bitter cold they have in that country.'

It would, I think, have been evident to anyone but the senile nincompoop addressing him that my father was suppressing an impatience by now perilously close to flash-point. The arrival of a 'ball o' malt' squired by a fat cigar just saved the situation: the besotted doctor paused to take over the management of those articles, and Howard seized his opportunity:

84

'Will you tell me, doctor, is there any hope at all for my father?'

The doctor screwed his face, as if he had never before been so uncouthly questioned. He unearthed a box of matches and very slowly contrived, without spilling a drop of the whiskey, to light the cigar. Then he said, 'Well now, you have to remember your father's getting on in life, and an old heart won't take the load as a young one will.'

'Yes, but—'

'A younger man, as I was saying, might have come through the present visitation, and none the worse for it at the farther end. But there it is, there comes a time for all of us. We can only turn round and be thankful for all the good years that are gone behind.'

'You mean, my father's near his end?'

The doctor took out the cigar and examined critically the neb of ash. At length, as if deciding to accept a poor business offer, he ponderously nodded.

'He'll not last through tonight.'

The striking changes in Howard's bearing during the train journey had shown me he was something besides the trousered person who was vaguely supplementary to Sonya: had I not found him open to infirmity which could actually betray itself in weeping! None the less I was startled by the effect which the doctor's last words produced in him. For an instant he looked as if he were passing through a flame; then, trying to speak and failing, he put his wrist against his mouth in a defensive, hopeless way which was pitiful to see. I think the clearest of all the impressions left in my mind by that kaleidoscopic hour was the curious stillness his emotion imposed on the people—not of conspicuous sensibility—grouped about him: as if he had uttered an anguished cry they froze into silence, their eyes avoiding his face. That stillness held when he turned to walk as if in his sleep towards the stairs; and it was curious, again, how the knots of racing men and farmers, apparently engrossed in their own clamorous concerns, yet moved a little way to clear his passage—as when royalty moves through a crowded ante-room.

Yes, recalling that strange scene after many years I can report it with a decent objectivity; at the time, I was not so far detached, and I made a troublesome situation more difficult by bursting loudly into tears. Plainly there was some excuse for this: for one so little used to travel the journey had been tiring, and in strange surroundings it is alarming for an infant to see the only person he knows apparently deserting him. Yet as I voyage backward through time, picking up the lucid fragments of sensation as well as I can, I am persuaded that what chiefly caused those intempestive and humiliating tears was a callow sympathy with Howard in his distress. Myself drenched with sorrow at being parted from Sonya, and knowing now that my father could be afflicted by emotions of the same kind as mine, I supposed that in a person of his enormous size and age the misery might be many times as great. It was probably my earliest experience of feeling pain at second-hand, and in the first seven years of life I had not acquired a skin thick enough to withstand such an infliction.

My outburst must have been vexatious to Theresa, who though not without goodnature was deficient in that primal instinct which enables so many women to tolerate the limitless absurdities of children. She stared at me aghast, and I thought for a moment that she would apply a widely accepted remedy for juvenile disorders—a hearty cuff on the side of my head. She refrained, however; and, wisely detaching herself from the immediate problem, asked in a general way,

'Where in the world is Kevin O'Kneale? Has anyone seen him?'

Some sort of bush-telegraph must have operated then, for—as I remember the episode—a new figure appeared on the scene as swiftly, unaccountably, as the fairy godmother in a pantomime. This, I should add, was no fairy to look at, but a young man grotesquely overgrown, thin and slightly

86

stooped like a prize dandelion. His height was emphasized by a white monkey-jacket which had evidently been cut for a far smaller man; I say 'white', but it was so much stained and spotted that a patch of pure whiteness would have been hard to find. At that period I had little interest in fastidious grooming, but the disarray of this fellow's ginger hair, the limpness of the sham bow-tie dangling from a wing collar which might have been made of paper, the ragged cuffs which linked the yellow sleeves of the jacket to his thin, furred wrists, suggested even to me a difference between his standards and those of what in those days was called 'good service'. Sonya would have applied to him one of her genial laconisms: 'In my father's household such people were not much taken for domestic use.'

'Ah, Kevin, this is Ryan Hutchinson,' Theresa said, with the understandable detachment of one calling attention to the result of a dog's sickness. 'I've put him and his father in the Auction Room. Will you take him and show him where it is.'

At that point the shabbiness of Kevin's attire may have worked to advantage—a figure of any grandeur would have aggravated my alarm and distress. I know that when this elongated yokel grinned at me, calling, 'Well, Ryan, shall you and I be facing life in company!' I at once slipped down from the desk and with irrational confidence went to take his hand.

The Conor Maguire was never over-staffed in Theresa Kearney's day, and when I think of the business it had to handle in the course of that evening I marvel that one of the servants should have given so much time, such gentleness, to a single customer—a lonely and distraught small boy. Kevin was not content to show me where I had to sleep; while I was undressing he stayed and chatted much as an old friend would.

'And you belong to London City? A remarkable outfit,

that must be! Have you brothers and sisters? A big sister—well, that's fine to be getting on with. I have four of them myself, and six brothers (would you believe it!) all of them older than me—I come at the end of all the family, like a rusty saucepan tied to the cat's tail.'

It is a measure of the man's appeal that it almost neutralized the initial gloom of the overloaded room to which he had brought me: he sold it, as they say, with gestures of possessive pride and affection which seemed to engage his whole personality.

'Yes, the old lady has more elegant apartments, but this is the one I'd always choose for myself—it has not the mortifying tidiness of some of the rooms upstairs. This bed, it's a bit old-fashioned, and larger than need be—you could fit four wheels and it would do for a tinker family to spend their lives in—but it will give you as sweet a night as any of the eight-and-sixpennies. Most of this clobber will be gone on Tuesday—there are parties in this neighbourhood who'll buy a stone-dead donkey to ride him in the Kenmare hurdles —and not before it's time; that female resting on the hat-stand, she's hardly decent, to my way of thinking. If you're wondering about the wee tent over there, that one belongs to the English General. He'll be in later on and putting himself to sleep in that small private habitation, but he'll not be vexing you at all—he has such a sweetness in him, if the fairies changed him to a Persian kitten you would likely take him for a nun.'

Much of his talk was too fluent for me to follow, but the subjects of his eloquence did not matter; I was rapt by the music of his voice, the sinuous movements of his long, bony hands, the light which played about his pliant mouth and his pensive, sympathetic eyes. If only he could have stayed —if he, instead of the English General, had proposed to spend the night in the 'small private habitation'—I believe my troubles would have been at an end. Naturally he could not stay. But before he finally left me he made a journey to the kitchen and returned with a supper tray—I remember cakes

88

bursting with cream and jam, a mug of syrupy liquid tasting vaguely of raspberries, slices of thick, sweet ham lolling on wedges of salty bread. While I ate as much as I could of this exotic meal he continued to stand beside the bed, describing for our joint amusement the surroundings of his early, bare-foot days, the tumbledown buildings of his family's holding, the gang-law and the fighting at the Christian Brothers' school where he had learnt his letters; he would, I think, have watched over me till I fell asleep, but for the sudden appearance of a pulpous face between a gory picture of St Sebastian and a roll-top desk.

'Mr O'Kneale, will you not be coming back?' said its owner, a boy with a butcher's apron draping his enormous belly. 'There's a load of people waiting for their first course, and Mr Arvill's going tearing mad.'

Kevin pulled a face. 'Ah, tell him to be tranquil! If the customers knew what was in the soup they'd prefer to wait all night.'

None the less, he picked up the tray, preparing to depart. 'You'll say your own prayers, now?' he softly reminded me. 'Being Catholic myself, I can't assist you in that obliga-tion—I'm not acquainted with the Protestant manner of praying. But you have no doubt some comfortable prayers your mama would have supplied you? ... Is there anything you'll be wanting before I go?'

At this prompting, the thought of losing a guardian angel overcame my lingering shyness. I asked impulsively, 'Please, could you tell me—is salt very expensive?'

'Salt? Och, a few pence would buy you a cartload. But why, now?'

'Please,' I said, 'would it be a trouble to get me a bag of salt? Only a small bag. My father would pay, I know he would.'

'But Ryan, my dear, what would you be wanting salt for, when you've just put away your supper?'

'Oh, it's not for me,' I said quickly. 'It's to put on the leprechauns. My father says if they come at you hard it's the only thing to drive them away.'

My new friend nodded, slowly, with puckered eyes. 'Your dada told you that? Then he was dead right—ah, he knows a thing or two, your dada! But listen, now: a leprechaun would have never a chance in a great rowdy pub like this one. And tonight of all nights—when the Probities are having their dance and all—he'd be scared out of his wits to come a flea's jump inside the door.'

The glowing reassurance that statement brought me came not so much from the words themselves as from the waiter's valiant delivery: his eyes winked and shone, his wrists, elbows and shoulders worked together in the quick, dismissive gesture which a Frenchman executes when he utters the verdict, 'Je m'en fiche!' He might be imperfectly informed: a leprechaun or two, perhaps disguised, might yet slip in among the Probities (whatever they might be). But my friend would himself be a match for any dozen of them, and as long as he was within hailing distance I could reasonably count on coming through the night alive. I asked:

'You won't be far away?'

'Ah, no distance at all! Now you have a candle here—do you know how to strike a match? That's beautiful! Then I'll turn the gas a good way down, so it won't keep you wakeful, and you can light the candle if you chance to need it—but it won't be long before your dada comes, and if I was you I'd have my beauty-sleep in the meanwhile.'

With that he gave me one more dazzling smile, a brotherly squeeze of my shoulder, and was gone. For some time a rough image of his form and features remained with me, as the shape of a window frame will stay imprinted on one's closed eyelids when one has been gazing through it into the sunlight. In those five or ten minutes I had enjoyed my first experience of hero worship—one which no other admiration, no other love, would ever totally efface.

At that hour the sounds of the hotel—a constant traffic of

feet along the corridors, the muffled cadence of a hundred conversations—were almost as uniform as those of a liner's engines, and curiously soothing. Lying with my eyes—as I thought—wide open, resolved to stay awake till Howard came, I must have fallen asleep only a few seconds after the waiter had lowered the gas; and might have stayed so, but the first, ecstatic burst of music from the old shippon was enough to penetrate the slumber even of a tired child. On first waking I thought I was back in the train as it drew away from a station platform; for a line of frosted windows, hardly noticeable when the room was fully lit, had turned to panels of bluish light where a frieze of silhouetted heads, some sleek, some copiously maned, was moving past in a hubbub of bass waggery and piercing female laughter. When I remembered my true situation I cautiously explored the whole width of the bed with hands and feet, faintly hoping to find Howard beside me. In vain! I cried a little then. My father, who so often forgot my existence when in congenial company, might absent-mindedly have returned to Hendon without me. If so, how could I hope ever to find my own way home, ever to have another sight of Sonya's face or to hear her voice again?

On my recent excursion to Castlemagonagh I was at some pains to revive my memories of the Auction Room. It is that no more; it serves now as an extra dining-room, chiefly for the banquets which local societies are wont to organize on the flimsiest pretext. I found it hard to identify this chamber, its panelling painted cream and all the lumber gone, with the one which had been my bedroom, though the great stone fireplace had not been changed and the frosted windows giving on to an outer passage were much as I remembered them. One feature which had previously escaped my notice was of special interest: the roof, plainly of late Victorian construction, consisted of three skylights, cupolar in form, which in daytime gave most of the light it needed; that explained what had previously puzzled me—how, when I had occupied the great four-poster, the outlines of the room from end to end had still been visible when the gas was turned right down. It must have been a clear night, perhaps with a full moon. Though smaller details were hard to recognize (so that my clothes heaped on a music stool looked like a drowsing sheepdog), there was light enough to show the outlines of the crowding furniture; as I lay, wide awake now, my ears trammelled by the distant sawing of violins, my mind bent with longing for Howard to come, I could distinguish wheelback chairs and fire tools stacked on a grand piano, a rocking horse which lacked its head, a dog kennel perched on what looked like a pile of giant Swiss rolls.

Fear stands ready to invade a child's mind when he is idle and alone. Perhaps a small boy rigorously trained by an English father would have remembered just how his surroundings had looked in full gaslight and would not have given way to foolish fancies. For me, in the friendless state which the sounds of nearby revelry accentuated, every patch of darkness contained some mystery which grew more sinister as the minutes passed. In the couch and the deep armchairs there were bundles of different shapes and sizes; parcelled books, perhaps, or oddments of clothing; in the sepulchral light it was easy to imagine that those amorphous objects stirred and made faint noises, so that soon they turned to living creatures, menacing, biding their time, while the statue to which my waiter friend had pointed—a plaster cast, I suppose, of some undistinguished Hellenistic torso— became the chief focus of my fears: there, escaped from the rule of gravity, was a person who might well be my nurse Mavrusha, grown to twice her normal size and stripped for punitive action, waiting for the moment when my attention was relaxed to dive and crush me with her weight. Yes, I think now with some embarrassment of the craven infant who, ensconced in the comfort of a solid bed, submitted so feebly to absurd fantasies; but that sense of disgrace does not lie deep. Reviewing all the stages of my life I come on many spells of cowardice, physical or moral, of which I am bitterly ashamed, but I can view with some lenience the pusillanimity of a boy removed at short notice from familiar surroundings, one too near the start of life to have studied a rational attitude towards dark places, unaccountable sounds, or the sense of being callously abandoned.

The blurred invading pandemonium—an intermittent rage of music, a surging tournament of febrile voices—made it harder to disentangle the whispers and scratchings which came (or seemed to come) from within the room: it could have been mice I heard, or the creak of overloaded floorboards, or a flutter inside my own narrow chest. But by degrees a sound grew audible which differed wholly from the rest, a fluid rustle vaguely resembling that of the water pipes at Howes Croft and yet insisting in my fearful ears and mind that it had an animal source. For all his confidence, the waiter had not entirely banished my dread of leprechauns; now, supposing that the weird beasts described by the cabin-girls would be equally outlandish in their cries, I found it easy to connect this eerie noise with the ghoulish picture my mind had constructed. The rustle grew louder: now it might have come from a creature whose throat was being squeezed by another, now it was succeeded by a long, piteous wail. A few seconds elapsed and the hideous sequence started again. Unmistakably its source was at the far end of the room. For a while I lay as stiffly as if I had suffered a stroke, then terror itself so worked as to raise my head by fractions of an inch until I could see the little cycling tent which had been pitched between the rocking-horse and a kitchen dresser. It must have been imagination which made me think the canvas bellied and sank in time with the alternating whine and gurgle, but there could be no doubt that the tent was where the noises came from. They may have continued for only two or three minutes—it seemed far longer. I remember distinctly how the palpitating sound came almost to the loudness of explosion and then stopped abruptly; how the dreadful silence which followed was broken by a tiny, plaintive cry.

Though I cannot wholly detach myself, even today, from the small boy lying rigid in the vast bed, I marvel now at that instance of the power of fear to rule a child's senses and to stultify his reason. How, when the end flaps of the tent parted and two long pale shapes slid side by side into view, can I have seen them as the feelers of some exotic animal—how, even in that feeble light, can I have failed to recognize a pair of white stockings enclosing human feet or the pyjama legs which, like the shafts of a cart, slowly drew forth the obvious outline of a human posterior? The truth, I think, is that my mind (such as it was) had ceased to work at all. Consciously I made no plan to escape. As if my body were under remote control I found it slipping from the bed, feeling its way backward between the furniture, groping for the handle and stealthily opening the door. Panic must have sparked the vague idea of seeking Kevin's protection, and probably I should have run along the passage shouting his name if a fresh source of alarm had not come to change that purpose: I was just outside the door when from somewhere ahead a sound broke so suddenly that it seemed more terrible than any which had come from the tent—it was such a roar as I had often heard from the farmyard of the Express Dairy, but indoors so loudened and denatured that to my panic-stricken ears it might have come from a herd of buffalo. I stopped like a dog pulled up by the lead, and let out a scream.

Behind me a voice said, 'Trouble, old man?'

Simultaneously the light increased, and when I had recovered sufficent self-command to look behind me I saw a figure stretching to turn up the gas. It was human: a man in white pyjamas, white-haired, exceptionally small but otherwise distinguished from the common run only by his dried-up appearance, came near to gaze at me with sad, scholarly eyes.

'Stomach trouble?' he asked. 'There's a lot of dysentery about.'

I shook my head.

94

'I can't help at all? My name's Almore.'

As he seemed to expect some answer, I gave him the first that come to my head: 'I was going to look for Howard—he's my father.'

'Your father? Ah, then I mustn't detain you. I expect you'll find him in the ante-room. Give him my very kind regards.'

Those words were hardly uttered when the bellow which had frightened me a few seconds earlier came to my ears again. At that juncture it was easy to decide that of the two menaces which in turn had shaken me the one now clearly visible was very much the less malevolent. I said impulsively,

'I don't think I'll go now. There's a thing in the way.'

'A thing?'

'I think it might be a leprechaun.'

'Good God!' the old man said. 'I didn't know those things were still about. That's the trouble with Ireland, there's something round every corner—Molly Maguires, Ribbonmen —you don't get a moment's peace and quiet. Look, old man, I wouldn't go unarmed if I was you—not if there's any chance of an ambush. Wait, I'll lend you my Mauser, that's the ticket. You'll never have a better friend.'

This was not a development I cared for, but a child's wishes count for nothing: I could only exercise the rudimentary politeness which Mavrusha and Sonya had built into me. In deep embarrassment I waited patiently while my insistent benefactor crawled back into his tent and presently re-emerged in the same sequence as before, the white stockings and the minikin legs exuding like toothpaste from a tube, the exceptionally gibbous bottom following with the tremulous dignity of a sacred image borne over rutted roads. When the whole of his person was again in view he was holding what appeared to me a very large and fearsome gun.

He said, 'Here you are, old man. Five rounds in the mag. They may be a bit damp now—I bought 'em in

95

Jo'burg a long way back. They'll do for short-range work, though.'

With those words he put the rifle almost into my hands, and so earnest, so comradely was his expression that I was on the point of taking it; but in truth it looked too ponderous for me to carry, and, much as the boy David refused the loan of Saul's armour, I found just enough boldness to resist.

'Thank you,' I said earnestly, 'but I don't know how to use it.'

He was taken aback. 'What? You've never fired a Mauser? Well, it's much the same as the Lee-Metford—it's a better weapon, actually, though I oughtn't to say so. Same principles in handling. Wait, I'll show you.'

He spread himself expertly on the floor.

'Left elbow well under,' he said didactically, '—I can never insist on that too strongly. Butt well into the shoulder. Now then, we need a target. Ha, what about the lady— up there on the hatstand, improperly dressed! Bit unsporting? Never mind—ladies must learn! No discipline, wandering about the range with nothing on the top half. Distracting to the rank and file. You'll remember, old man, the correct trigger pressure is not so much a pull as a squeeze.'

This he must have demonstrated; all I became aware of was a flash, a report which seemed to split my ear-drums, then the patter of plaster as half the face of the statue fell to the floor.

'Bit too far left,' he remarked, in candid self-appraisal. 'May be a slight cross-wind. Steady now!' He fired again, and the statue became entirely faceless. 'Bit better—almost a bull. Like a go now?'

A boy of normal tastes would surely have had some pleasure from that *auto-da-fé*, and I am still unhappy in recalling that Almore's casual musketry left me ill at ease. In a sense I suffered, perhaps, from too conventional a rearing: Mavrusha had taught me that however ruthlessly Anastasia treated her toys I myself had no right to injure them, and from that indoctrination may have come my feeling that the old man was at fault—despite his kindly intentions—in performing so rough a surgery on things which evidently did not belong to him. More practically, I was afraid that the noise would attract my formidable great-aunt's notice, and that if she found me with a gun in my hand I was due for a lambasting which would make Mavrusha's punishments look like a prolonged caress. That fear was in fact groundless—in a place so full of noise and merrymaking the sound of sporadic rifle fire must generally escape attention—but it sufficed to stimulate my callow intelligence, and I said politely,

'I think I'd rather not, if you don't mind. I think I might spoil your gun—it's rather big for me.'

The General was by no means offended. 'I like your spirit!' he said fervently, laying the rifle on the bed and then gripping my shoulders. 'Respect for a comrade's firearm —that belongs to a great tradition. My name's Almore,' he said for the second time, and shook my hand. 'It's a privilege to meet you—not many fellows about these days who honour the old traditions. All the same, I want you to feel that rifle is yours whenever you may need it.'

'Oh, thank you, sir,' I said.

'Only one thing—you will remember the first and second pressures? And keeping the butt well into the shoulder? Wait—you'll see it better if I show you from here.'

This time he lay on the bed to take up a firing position, and it looked as if his next target would be a gilt-framed reproduction of *The Monarch of the Glen.*

It was then that I reversed my former conclusion, deciding that the old man was, after all, the less acceptable of the two hazards which were so impairing my peace of mind. This was ungrateful: no one could have shown himself more benevolent than he. But children like their elders to conform with patterns they know, and the mere fact that I had never before been approached on equal terms by a person so much my senior made this earnest shooting man seem uncanny and slightly sinister. He was lying with his feet towards me, his eyes fixed on Landseer's masterpiece, his tongue busy with the lore of marksmanship; here was my chance to slip away.

At that time the passage to the entrance hall was fortunately empty; when I had cautiously closed the door behind me I retained sufficient self-control to go quietly to the far end, and only then did I take the risk of calling, 'Mr O'Kneale! Mr O'Kneale!' Marvellously, he appeared from a door on the right in a matter of seconds, saw me, put down the loaded tray he was bearing and came, smiling, to my side.

'What is it, Ryan? A bad dream?'

'I want my father. I don't like the man in that room, he's got funny eyes and he keeps shooting things.'

'Ah, that's only the English General—he wouldn't show unkindness to a rattlesnake.'

Two deafening reports came from the Auction Room, each followed by the sound of falling glass and by exultant cries. Understandingly the waiter put his arm about my shoulders.

'Sometimes the General's not quite clear in his mind,' he explained. 'He lives in the past a good deal more than most of us. Well, now, we'll see if we can find where your dada's got to.'

He stooped and picked me up. Here was a friendship mysteriously different from General Almore's, a goodness which won my perfect trust. Held against Kevin O'Kneale's muscular body, calmed by his good sense, I realized almost at once that my recent qualms had been intemperate and shameful. Yet the shame hardly counted; for the second time that evening I was lost in adoring gratitude.

As he carried me through the swirling lobby I saw that the other source of my recent panic was equally innocuous: here was no flock of leprechauns, only a small black cow which a man and woman whose legs I had noticed earlier were dragging and coaxing up the main staircase. About that homely group the Sons and (I suppose) Daughters of Probity, crowding the stairs and the gallery above, presented such a scene—so rich a polychrome of trailing gowns, so dazzling a parade of laundered shirts and powdered bosoms—as would have captivated Veronese; to my childish eyes a cow looked out of place among those splendid gentlemen and ladies, but by now I had realized that the night life of hotels belonged to the vast desert of ignorance in which I had so far lived, and I had the sense to make no comment. There was an old woman in an apron whose view of the affair seemed roughly to correspond with mine; from the top of the stairs she was shouting into the dense cumulus of giggles and palaver, 'You've no cause to bring that creature into this hotel, Thomas Morrissey! Any time now she might forget her manners on the carpet, which Mrs Kearney paid nineteen pounds for.' But her rigorous attitude won no accord.

'That's a young cow of your grandfather's,' was Kevin's observation. 'They have their work cut out, those Morrisseys —she isn't used to stairs.'

I was glad that Howard, when we found him in a small bar at the end of a twisting corridor, seemed to have recovered from the worst of his misery. The cosy relation encountered in the train—Hanna someone—had somehow reappeared, and two or three other comforters, grave, serge-suited, whiskered men, were grouped about him. With an empty glass in his hand he sat in a corner of the settle, smiling at these friends with the look of sad and rather distant gratitude which is sometimes seen on the face of one recovering from the shock of a street accident.

'I've brought the wee boy along,' Kevin said, setting me down in front of him. 'He was rather lonesome in the great bed he has to sleep in.'

'Ah, it's a lonely world for all of us!' Howard said.

He glanced at me with tolerant eyes, but I could see that his susceptive mind was otherwise engaged. It was Hanna who drew me on to her knees, an indulgence which filled me with distaste. It is a misconception to suppose that infants will happily be mothered by any passing female; I found the salience of my cousin's massive chest inconvenient, the mechanism of her clothing painfully abrasive and her scent unwelcome. I should much have preferred to stay with Kevin.

Someone asked, 'Do you know, waiter, is Mr James still sleeping? Mr Howard here wishes to be up with him the first minute he's awake again.'

Kevin said he would make inquiries. He gave me another of his brilliant smiles and went away.

I have had to scan the fly leaves of a family Bible to fill some holes which time has worn in my memory of the talk that followed—talk displaying as much precision and purpose as recruits on their first parade. Hanna, like all her kind, was genealogically minded, and it was certainly she who said,

'You know who that young man is? He's Greta O'Kneale's child—Greta M'Taurey that used to be. Kevin, now, he would be her ninth, or maybe her twelfth—those Catholic families reach beyond accountancy.'

That must have been addressed to Howard, but I think it was one of the other men who answered: 'Greta O'Kneale—you mean Sawson O'Kneale's wife, the one that farmed a cantle of Mr Macartney's land over at Bowistown?'

'That's right, Mr Owens—if you call it farming, the pitiful day's work that man ever gave to his patch of rented soil. A wilful creature she always was, Greta M'Taurey—it was right against her parents' wish she married that lawless vagabond. Those O'Kneales of Gallinaulty, there was never a living man could master them, be he priest or proctor. A shame it was for Greta to go against her mother's will—in all Ireland you would not have found a greater saint than Cathleen M'Taurey, or yet a gentler woman.' Our kinswoman was once more directing her words to Howard, whose eyes were closed. 'It's your cousin we're speaking of, Howard—your cousin Greta. You remember, Cathleen M'Taurey was your father's eldest sister—Cathleen Hutchinson she was at the time her mother bore her.'

'Greta M'Taurey,' my father murmured sleepily, 'she married a wild rebellious man—one of the mad O'Kneales of Gallinaulty. The pair of them had never a penny.'

'And Kevin O'Kneale's her son,' Hanna reaffirmed.

'Greta was my aunt Cathleen's daughter,' Howard said dogmatically. 'Cathleen M'Taurey had never any son that I remember.'

There are those whose interest in others' consanguinity is easily exhausted: a man whose head resembled a goshawk's had been coughing a little restlessly, and now he spoke in a husky voice I recognized—it was he who, earlier that evening, had drawn attention to the capabilities of one Eamonn O'Callaghan. 'As I was telling you,' he said to Howard, 'if you want to be satisfied you've done the best thing, the right thing, then if I was you I'd go for the varnished oak every time.'

'Why not deal?' Mr Owens said.

'Because, Mr Owens, deal will never lend itself to the same workmanship. The craftsmen Mr O'Callaghan employs, there's a beauty in the work they do, Mr Hutchinson, that will make you the proudest mourner in all Castlemagonagh. And then again there's the durability.'

'This young Kevin,' Hanna resumed, 'they had him earmarked for the priesthood—no doubt they thought in their superstitious way to make him a sin-offering for their own misgoverned lives and laxities. It seemed the boy took to the notion well enough, he was a soft-spoken lad who never troubled the lasses any way and he had a queer inclination after piety of the popish kind. That ravening priest at Bowistown, he was not the sort to let a chance go by, he took young Kevin into his own teaching—Greek and Roman arguments and all the mystification—and set him in the line for St Finnian's College. Yes, and by what I heard at the time his mother was proud of him.'

'And is there any harm in honest pride!' the man like

a goshawk said. 'You have to think, Mr Hutchinson, of the Departed's reputation. Passers-by see a deal coffin, and what do they say? "Why, this must be some neglected pauper fellow, getting himself interred at bargain price, poor pollock."'

'She has a decent heart in her, Greta O'Kneale, when all is said,' Hanna continued. 'It fairly broke in pieces when she heard a year ago the College had turned her youngest into the street.'

'And why should the College do that?' Mr Owens asked.

Hanna shrugged her shoulders, and her face darkened. 'Who will ever know! Some kind of a royal rumpus he had with the Master of the Novices. They say to start with he had a laugh that troubled all of them, it was like a corncrake in a passion and he wouldn't stanch it even on Days of Obligation. But that was not the whole of it, to my understanding. If it came to a difference of opinion young Kevin there would have no law but his own—like all the mutinous O'Kneales that went before him.'

'So now he's turned over to hotel waiting?'

'Ah, that's only to keep him in shift and stockings till he finds a final occupation—his mother's hoping some bailiff will have the boldness to try him in a clerk's employment. A great kindness it was in my cousin Theresa—I mean your aunt Theresa, Howard—to fit him out with food and wages when he had no man or place to turn to. They say Theresa has the pride of an empress, but I vouch she hides a loving heart in the back of her high stomach.'

To a callow ear the insistent pulse of Hanna's speech brought a modest pleasure, like that which comes from dragging a stick along iron railings. As a rule such family talk is boring for the young, and what she said meant little to me at the time—I learnt the sense of it from Howard later on; my torpid intelligence was, however, wakened to the fact that my latest friend, my hero, had some blood connection with my father and hence (I supposed) with me. This was like finding one's own name on a coveted toy. I longed so much to blaze my joy and triumph that even Anastasia's presence would have been welcome then.

For all that, and in spite of the discomfort I was suffering from Hanna's stays, I must soon have fallen asleep; for I was not aware of anyone leaving the room, yet when I next opened my eyes there was no one present save Howard himself, Hanna, and the comatose colleen who appeared to be built in behind the bar. What woke me was the sound of a fresh arrival: the door was opening, and in a moment Kevin stood there, his head almost touching the lintel, his face solemn and dutiful.

'It's a message from Nurse Connolly,' he announced. 'She says the old gentleman's awake again—she thinks he might recognize you now.'

'Well, thank you, waiter,' Howard said, in the remote and cloudy voice he used when Sonya wished him to write a cheque or to get a nail out of her shoe. 'You will please present my compliments to Miss O'Connor, and say I hope to see her in the morning.'

There the business might have rested, but it was not in the nature of our cousin Hanna to conform with quietist procedures. In an instant she had put me down as if I were another woman's Pekingese; she said, rising, 'Tell the nurse Kevin, we'll be up in just a minute,' and in a matter of seconds she had my father on his feet as well. 'You will need a brave heart now, Howard,' she murmured, urging him towards the door as a motorized canal boat will coax its fellow into a lock. 'Your father will be looking to you for strength and fortitude.'

In such an emergency a child is naturally forgotten, and I might well have been left alone with the stagnant barmaid, had not Kevin taken pity on me once again. Lingering, he said,

'Will you not have Ryan with you, Cousin Howard? It might exhilarate the old man, to see the fine grandson he has now.'

My father evidently failed to understand that supposition,

103

but he did come to a halt and nod with a broad benevolence. 'Indeed,' he said a little vaguely, 'I'll deny no child his pleasures, be he Protestant or pagan.' That settled, with a cautious dignity he permitted Hanna to set him in motion again. Holding hands, Kevin and I took station behind them, and in that order we went upstairs to the Bridal Suite.

Sometimes one can trace a recurrent malaise to a particular experience in childhood. Twice, on visits to the Hague, I have had to hurry out of the Mauritshuis after finding myself face to face with Rembrandt's *Anatomy Lesson*. The disquiet I felt in the presence of that work is not, I believe, unconnected with the bewilderment and apprehension which attended the nocturnal meeting of my grandfather and me.

The cautious opening of a heavy door admitted Howard and his entourage to a room where the lamps must have been heavily screened: it was like entering a forest when summer foliage excludes all but slender shafts of pallid light. At first the only content which caught my eyes was the shapes to which that light was naturally attracted—the flamboyant structure of a nurse's headdress, patches like small white flags breaking the blackness of some man's clothes, pillow corners which might have been snow-clad crests projecting from a range of darkened hills. Young children instinctively recoil, I think, from pictures which achieve their grandeur through subtleties of darkness; here I was no mere spectator but a prisoner within the frame, and having suffered in the Auction Room the terrors—first—of solitude, I was caught now in fear of another kind. By the standards of my own home the room was enormous, and as my sight became adjusted I realized it was one of ineffable magnificence: above a vast fireplace the high elaborate mantel would have done for a reredos, along the farther wall the proudly tasselled curtains descended to the floor in a cataract of sumptuous brocade: simultaneously I saw that it was full of people, motionless, speaking only in low whispers, and because I knew little of illness, and nothing of death, I could only suppose they were engaged in some recondite worship—vaguely I imagined that from the space at their centre a spirit would presently arise, a creature made from wreathing smoke which might demand some dreadful sacrifice.

Was the reality much less alarming? A shift of the intervening bodies disclosed a huge extent of crimson counterpane, leading like a tract of ploughland to the foothills I had seen already. On that furrowed plain lay, as if discarded, two bony human hands; and when my eyes had travelled a little farther they descried in a shallow cavity something slightly darker and more angular than the humped pillows. Even in my tired confusion I was fascinated by so sinister a curio: the posture of the dim profiles clustered on either side showed it was the focus of the group's devotion, and when a woman's voice began a kind of whispered litany I could tell it was addressed to that magnetic shape—a frigid, shaggy object which strikingly resembled a human head.

'Your son is here now, Mr James. Howard. Howard is here. Your son Howard has come to see you.'

That patient annunciation had gone on for some time, and another movement of the figures at the foot of the bed had screened my view, when a male voice which seemed to come from underneath the bed brought a response:

'Howard? Howard's gone schoolmastering. He's away giving lessons to the English boys.'

'But he's back this evening,' the woman softly insisted. 'He's come back to see how you're getting on.'

'I'm tired,' was the answer. 'I don't want any sort of getting on.'

Now the whispering turned from solo to chorus—at least three women seemed to be in earnest consultation. In the old shippon not far away a polka was raging, and for some moments a tidal wave of music prevented me from hearing what they said. Then the voice of Hanna reached me with dreadful definition:

'We have the child here—Howard's little boy. It could be a treat for James to see his grandson.'

She waited for no one's agreement, least of all mine. Arriving at my side she put an arm about my shoulders, tore me away from Kevin and propelled me to the side of the bed, where with her stout arm hooked on my waist she practically held me captive. The head-like object among the bedclothes was now within inches of my face.

A human head it was, but one so different from any within my past experience that I could hardly recognize it as a thing of the same kind. It looked artificial, with a ragged nimbus sprawling on the pillow, grey tufts like pluckings of steel wool attached to the cheeks and chin; the immobility, the tightly fastened eyelids, the waxed appearance of the deeply folded flesh, all heightened the semblance of a manufactured thing. That immediate impression was defective. Tiny bubbles which formed and burst between the slightly parted lips, a small, incessant movement of the lock of hair protruding from one wide nostril, these conveyed even to an intelligence as raw as mine the truth that the owner of the head was breathing. From the corner of my eye I saw that one of the hands—now close to my own—had begun to make a feeble clutching movement. Soon there came from the effervescent mouth a sigh and murmur which finally convinced me that the image I watched was part of a living person.

I remember how, in the minutes that followed, I was oppressed not only by want of courage but by an anxious feeling of responsibility. Odious as she was, I could not doubt the rectitude of the woman commanding me, and if for some good reason she had made me the central figure in this drama it was incumbent on me to stay at my post. That sense of my own importance was enlarged by the signs of deepening sadness all about me. 'He was a good man,' one woman kept muttering, 'for all the hard things he ever said!'

while others, now, were sobbing without restraint. From some far corner I heard a tousled voice which I could just recognize as my father's, asking in pitiful confusion, 'Will someone have the goodness, please, to say what's happening?' but the last words of his appeal were stifled by the ardour of a quivering female voice: 'Ah, it will destroy the old campaigner's heart, to see the poor wee lad!' Only one person in the room seemed wholly to escape the contagion of grief —he who lay like one of Anastasia's abandoned dolls, deathly still, except for the hand which was creeping like a great white crab towards my own.

'Speak to him!' Hanna ordered from behind me.

Cowardice had made me dumb. I pretended not to understand.

'Say, "Good-evening, grandpapa! I hope you'll be better soon."'

Young though I was, I saw that form of words as incompatible with the immediate situation; and the disconnection between the invalid and me might have continued through the night, but for a fresh disturbance. The tissue of muffled sounds which emanates from corporate sorrow was invaded suddenly by one more urgent, a plaintive lowing which I easily identified; coming from the darkest area in the room, it told me for the first time that the cow I had seen on the staircase some while before had, like me, been brought to join this vigil. Her cry was promptly silenced by a gruff rebuke, but not before it had penetrated to that soundless desert which must have lain between my grandfather and the world he had known. The effect was startling. The great hand which had seemed to be stalking mine made its final assault, to fasten on my wrist; in the frozen mask before me the eyelids folded back, and while two small, light-blue eyes searched for my face a hoarse voice said sternly,

'Who made that rumpus? Was it you?'

With only Hanna to hold me I should have broken loose and fled; but the hand gripping my wrist exerted a surprising force.

'No, *barin*,' I said.

'You—are you Howard?' my captor demanded.

I answered, 'Howard's my father, *barin*,' in a voice which must have been too feeble for him to understand.

'Sure, don't I *know* I'm your father!' was my grandfather's indignant reply.

It was not an easy conversation for a small boy to take part in, and my confusion was aggravated by a tangle of sounds behind me. The cow had lowed again, and some of those present were protesting. 'She's no business,' a girl said, 'to make that noise in a sick man's room.' Others were less censorious. 'She's only asking to have her milk taken,' someone propounded, and his view started an anxious consultation. 'Why, it's hours before her time.' 'Ah, but the milk comes faster when they're feeling lonesome.' 'Would it be troubling you, Mr Waiter, to find a pail for milking?' Now the agitated voices gave place to Kevin's, forthright and serene: 'Why, the chamber here is empty, that will surely do.' His practicality was effectual in bringing the conference to an end, but this was not the end of my frustration. An aged invalid without his teeth must always be hard to understand, even when the listener is familiar with his speech; my grandfather's inflexions were quite unknown to me, and as I strained to catch his words the splash of jetting milk so embroiled my ears that the task seemed hopeless. A new sense of inadequacy made me ready to weep with shame.

I should be foolish, then, to pretend I can recover all his discursive talk—the larger portion must have passed me by. But I do remember vividly the awe which his worn old voice inspired in me—as if I had found myself in conversation with Moses or Elijah—and also, more strangely, the benignity which now and again broke the rigour of his declamations. I recall the warmth, the note of gentleness, which came into his grating voice when, imagining that I was Howard, he spoke of his own condition:

'Listen, dear boy: I'm old and sick, I won't be with you much longer now. There are things I'd like to say to

108

you before I go. You're not too proud, are you, to take a morsel of advice from a loving old father?'

Helpless and tearful, I could only murmur assent.

'You may go to Dublin if you wish,' he continued. 'The farm will have to get on without you—and indeed that will be no loss. But I won't have you getting entangled with those artists, do you understand! That's the thin end of the broad way that leadeth to destruction. Those painting men, they start with trees and cottages, and before you can turn round they're on to naked women.'

Here his tone had become so reproachful that I was moved to disclaim the identity he had fastened on me. 'Please, I'm not my father,' I said tremulously.

At once the sturdy voice of Kevin came to support my contention: 'It's young Ryan you have before you, Cousin James,' he said distinctly. 'It's the wee son of Cousin Howard.'

'Indeed, can I not see that for myself!' my grandfather replied. 'I could tell the boy from here to Malin Head—is he not the brawling image of my sister Theresa!'

'Ah, the master's a marvel for his observation, sick or sanitary!' an admiring voice cried.

'And a long ugly mug *she* has,' the old man continued huskily. 'Now listen, dear son: if nature's given you a cockle-kipper face like poor Theresa, I hope you'll one day have a heart as good as hers to go beside it. Little sense she ever showed, taking on that Michael Kearney who could never fasten his own boots without the instruction book, him and this mouldering barracoon some scoundrel sold him on a day the light was bad. But I tell you, lad, a loving heart outweighs a ton of foolishness. When I was old and sick and done for, and they threw me out in the street from that accursed pest-house in the god-forsaken town of Waterford, who was it but my poor young codling of a sister who'd kept a corner for me in her tender heart and in Kearney's balmy pub!'

Though I found it hard to follow his train of thought I was much affected by his mounting emotion. Was he, too, about to burst into tears? I was relieved, then, when the nurse who sat knitting at the other side of the bed provided an interruption:

'For pity's sake, Mr James, you'll wear yourself to the bone with all that blether! Will you lie quiet, now, and take a peg of the nice physic Dr Caheen has ordered you. It does you no good at all, the doctor says, standing gossiping all day like a Sligo fishwife in the very portal of Eternity.'

'Ah, to hell with the doctor—what does he know about me or anything else!' my grandfather replied. 'Harry Caheen has not opened his books for sixty years—he told me so himself. He has the letters after his name because the professor that examined him was drunk as a bombardier!'

None the less, the nurse's admonition seemed to have made some impression; he spoke more quietly, and presently fell into silence. I hoped then that I might withdraw my arm, but when I tried to do so his grip tightened, and though he had apparently returned to the comatose state in which I had first seen him he was soon talking again. From a spate of shapeless utterance a few words emerged which I could recognize:

'Janet Aruba. Where's she got to? Why don't I ever see her?'

The pathos in that appeal evoked a quick response; it came in a voice I knew—belonging to Thomas Morrissey, the man whose boots smelt of farmyard—and within its deferential tone there sounded a note of triumph: 'I have her here, maister!'

The sound of milking stopped. The noises which followed resembled those of a tap-room scuffle, embroidered with squeals of feminine alarm; something thrust against my buttocks, and a moment later what seemed to me a gigantic object installed itself beside my torso on the bed. It was the head of Janet Aruba. Town-bred, I had not realized that a cow's head was quite so large as this, and its presence might have aggravated the nervousness which had dogged me all that evening; but the eye which I found surveying my face was one of Franciscan gentleness, and the faintly asthmatic noise which came from the nostrils suggested an anxiety touchingly like my own. Again my chief discomfort derived from a callow conventionality of outlook: nourished in middle-class traditions, I was subconsciously disturbed at being neighbour to so humble a creature in a company as politely occupied as this.

Importantly, I was no longer friendless. I could not think of Hanna as an ally any more, and Howard was now noisily asleep, but in the undergrowth of whispered chatter I could always distinguish and draw comfort from Kevin's voice. It was Kevin who, when Janet Aruba started to low again, said, 'Mr Morrissey, will she not be more philosophical if you take the last drop from her?' and the soundness of his suggestion became clear as soon as it was adopted: when the splash of milk came to my ears once more, now from close behind me, she seemed to breathe more contentedly, and the minutes that followed were curiously peaceful; a regular movement of Janet's head caused one of her horns to scrape very gently across my shoulders, I found this massage soothing and I must have come near to falling asleep myself. Such tranquillity, however, could not last. I was picturing my return to Howes Croft, and the ravishing embrace I should have from Sonya, when the whine of hinges roused me; the door had opened, letting in a draught which attacked me like a cold sea wave, together with a burst of jubilation from the Sons of Probity, piercing squeals and hunting cries. In the wake of that uproar came a still, small, fussy, too familiar voice:

'Can I help at all? I heard there was some trouble with leprechauns.'

'Be easy, General!' Kevin answered at once. 'The last of them left an hour ago—they had their excursion tickets for Dingle Bay.'

But his report failed to satisfy the Englishman, whose small, pyjama'd figure I presently saw arriving, rifle slung, at the far side of the bed; he stared suspiciously at Janet

Aruba, and she at him. Myself deeply apprehensive, I was yet fascinated by the reaction of my black companion to this ominous encounter: the movement of her head stopped abruptly, and then, as if seeking reassurance from her old master, she stretched to lick his forehead. I heard the wife of Thomas Morrissey exclaim in a fervent whisper,

'Ah, she knows him, the witty creature, she knows him!'

But my grandfather was neither pleased nor flattered. 'That'll do, now!' he said impatiently, without opening his eyes. 'I don't fancy such foolishness, you know as well as I do.'

'Do you wish me to fire, sir?' the General asked, smartly unslinging the Mauser and bringing it to the standing-load position.

Much to my relief, the nurse intervened, saying with some severity, 'I will ask you, General Almore, not to excite my patient with unnecessary gunfire,' and thereafter I had the impression that nearly everyone was on her side; from all round me came murmurs hostile to the Englishman: 'Why can't he leave a poor sick man to die in peace!' 'Faith, it's no test of skill at all, shooting that size of cow at just three feet.' Whether Janet Aruba realized her danger I could not tell, but after pausing to survey the Mauser with the curiosity of her kind she renewed her attention to my grandfather's face, her tongue stroking his cheek with the delicacy a first-rate barber uses in his handling of a razor. For my part, I was impressed by her calm and tenderness; but my grandfather, still hardly awake, was not in a state to appreciate either, and the artless caress moved him suddenly to anger.

'*Woman,*' he cried, with astonishing violence, '*will you for God's sake keep your own side of the bed!*'

Almost at the same moment I heard the click of Almore's trigger. Fortunately for Janet—and perhaps for me—the Mauser failed to fire; perhaps the cartridge had lost its virtue in the years of idleness, perhaps the General in his keen rehearsal had exhausted the magazine. Glancing at his face,

I read there such overwhelming misery as I myself had suffered when some small naughtiness had disqualified me for a prospective treat.

For a child it is painfully distracting when even adults seem to fail in co-ordination. On the whole, then, I was thankful for the arrival soon after of my great-aunt Theresa; with her cultivated grandeur she was apt to spread a certain coldness about her, and here her presence immediately changed the atmosphere to one in which the product of a bourgeois nursery could more easily draw breath. Using her driest voice—but scarcely raising it—she quickly imposed on my grandfather's several comforters her own stringent sense of order:

'General Almore, you know as well as I do, if your wife was alive she'd never let you go shooting in that flimsy costume. Will you have the goodness, now, to go back at once to your own bed ... Thomas Morrissey, I do not buy superior chamber pots for the Bridal Suite just to have them used for dairy work ... If you, Cousin Hanna, will kindly wake my nephew Howard and put his face beneath a cold tap it will drown his sorrows better than anything he's tried so far.'

I feared that I might be next on her list for oblique reproof, but luckily her final proclamation was a general one:

'If it's not disturbing the party, I'd be glad to see this room with a smaller population. I don't doubt it's kind of you all to call on my ailing brother, but some of us prefer a little privacy to die in.'

I suppose the note of acerbity was needful, though it struck me at the time as somewhat ungenerous: certainly it had its effect—a shout of 'Fire!' could hardly have emptied the room at greater speed. I remember how, as Kevin carried me back to bed, I was oppressed by the kind of melancholy which always follows a large misunderstanding. Just in front of us the General walked with his head bent forward; he was holding his rifle by the muzzle, the butt trailing behind him, and his face was petrified with gloom. In the eye of

Janet Aruba, who was being dragged along beside me, I read an equal despondency; and I thought with a child's unreasoning desperation, 'Here are three beings subject to constant humiliation, simply because they are given parts to play which no one clearly defines.'

I learnt next morning that plans were being formed to get me out of the way. This seemed unjust. Already I had been brought to Castlemagonagh, suffering much homesickness and other inconvenience, so that I should be out of Sonya's way; now, apparently, I had to be moved again because I was in the way of everyone else.

One reason for the decision was, I imagine, that the Conor Maguire was showing corruptive signs of the good time had by the Sons of Probity throughout the previous evening: somehow the high chandeliers in the dining-room had been draped with petticoats and stockings, there was broken glass all over the place and a young woman ensconced among the half empty bottles on the billiard table had been found still totally insensible at breakfast time. More serious: as I learnt from Howard long afterwards, the youngish matron supposed to function as the girl's gooseberry had been surprised, in the company of one Commander Wolvenstone, in much the same condition; and though everyone was sympathetic about the hard lot of chaperones it was, in those days, considered a social solecism for one in her position to have quite so good a time as that. It is right to watch carefully over children at their most impressionable age. I see now that an infant freshly emerged from the sheltered life of a London suburb might well have suffered harm from the spectacle of moral anarchy presented by a pair of dancing slippers on the sideboard and the last remains of cream cornets strewn up and down the central stairs.

Another reason for getting me out of the building was that my grandfather had still not died. For Dr Caheen, who came after breakfast and was soon orating in the dining-room, in the kitchen and in the various bars, this was a matter for lavish self-congratulation. In others it engendered a certain tautness of the nerves. My father could respond to occasional demands for elevated emotion, but to maintain without a time limit a high solemnity of soul and countenance was a strain on his native resources. Most likely Theresa's sufferings were similar to his; and perhaps she could not quite forget that her brother, who all his life had treated her with the tenderness a schoolboy bestows on a favourite football, was now in occupation of quarters which could have been let at a fancy price to besotted honeymooners from Dublin or Belfast. To me only one thing was clear at the time: she and Howard were agreed that my grandfather's condition demanded absolute silence, and so long as a small boy was at large in the hotel this could never be guaranteed.

A solution came readily to hand. This was Saturday. My cousin Kevin had for some time been without a holiday, so it was thought desirable that he should go to his home for a long weekend, taking a generous supply of food, and me. The plan (settled, of course, without reference to my wishes) was not entirely unwelcome to me, since I vaguely hoped it might offer scope for some brave adventure. All along, the thought consoling me for my absence from home had been that of boasting to Anastasia about the various perils of the journey and my own heroism in meeting them. So far, unhappily, there had been no adventures; one could not brag even to a sympathetic person—let alone one's sister —about staring, under duress, at a very old man in bed.

3
Kevin at Home

All the same, I marvel that I set off so calmly under the wing of someone I had met for the first time only the day before; and if it is not uncommon for children recklessly to put their trust in those who have caught their admiration, I still find it remarkable that my cousin kept me contented through three days which afforded little comfort and no noteworthy excitements. Clearly he had special gifts for handling the young. His lanky frame, his easy acceptance of what to me was unfamiliar, the smile whereby he seemed to share with me his pleasure in being alive—those, I think, were the factors which continually heartened a nervous little boy through what might else have been just a cheerless extension of his exile.

Certainly it was Kevin's genial presence which kept me from tears on the six-mile drive, through incessant and blusterous rain, from the station at Ruckmore Gap. In a very small donkey-cart the three of us—Kevin, his brother Mairtin and I—were squashed together on a seat harder than iron; the tarpaulin draped over our heads did nothing to protect our legs, and the smoke from Mairtin's pipe reeked as vilely as anything which has since reached my nostrils in South American saloons. I felt slightly sick. The admirable motor road which runs to Ballygroyle had not been thought of then, and the lane we used, fenced here with broken walls, here with straggling hawthorn, was not unlike the dried bed of a stream; from so rude a surface a springless vehicle derives an irksome vibration, and to this discomfort a loose off-side wheel added a trying oddity in the cart's performance —it constantly veered to the right until the donkey, wise in the cart's ways and in the road's deformities, brought us back on to course by a sharp leftward twist of its robust small body. That kind of travel brings nausea to the inexperienced, and Kevin himself seemed to find it disturbing.

'Did Pearce not say he would have this wheel put right?' he asked his brother.

'Och, Pearce,' Mairtin answered, 'he's the one for talking!'

He himself—a squeezed, hump-shouldered, wrinkled man —seemed to be free from that failing; he had not said more than two sentences since leaving the station. Now, however, he extended his reply: 'He'll try again when he gets back, I wouldn't wonder.'

'Back? Where's he gone?'

'America.'

'So? He'll be back for harvest?'

'Not this year. Not if he has a job that takes his fancy.'

'What sort of a job was he after?'

'Pearce? He'll take a job of any sort, so long as it's not mixed up with any kind of labour.'

Kevin nodded. ''Twill be fine,' he said thoughtfully, 'if he can straighten the wheel a trifle when he gets back home.'

With the ice thus broken, the brothers went on to family affairs.

'How's the darlin' mother?' Kevin asked.

'She's much the same.'

'And the old grandad?'

'Much the same as he ever was.'

'How about Finnuala?'

'She's much the same.'

I had not the background knowledge for entering into this adult gossip and I could only occupy myself with what the frantically deviating landscape offered. The offering was meagre. A pair of massive gate-posts, standing alone, marked an entrance to a stretch of heath as bare as all the rest, a length of fencing made entirely from old bedsteads seemed to begin and finish for no reason. Sometimes, as the cart swerved and shuddered, a stack of peat or the carcase of a field-rake would show through the sweeping barrage of rain; once there were children staring listlessly from beside a decrepit cabin; once, in the entrance to a cottage still more ruinous, an aged wolf-hound barked as if he were paid at piece rates for that service. Tiring of this frugal scenery, my eyes turned to rest on a wreath of bedraggled narcissi which lay on Mairtin's knees. Kevin, his gaze following mine, asked,

'Where did you find the vegetation?'

'This? I took a walk to the Protestant graveyard while I waited for the train. They had a new grave there with a whole cargo of these trimmings, just sick to death for lack of occupation.'

'And this packet's for Finnuala?'

'Indeed, no—it's what Desmond has ordered for the Eoin Memorial. He's taking his grandad tomorrow—with a few more, most likely. They have to make the Annual Remembrance.'

'What—it's a year gone since last time?'

'As near as need be. They had it in mind to go last Sunday, but the weather was contrarious.'

'They think it'll clear tomorrow?'

'Ach, it's never yet been a dry day yet when they made their annual commotion round Eoin O'Kneale.'

Naïvely—in spite of what he had told me—I had pictured Kevin's home as similar to mine; I had supposed that the house, roughly in line with its neighbours, would at least stand facing an ordinary street. That was a faulty conception: in what turned out to be Bowistown there was (at that period) nothing to face, and every habitation was determined not to face it. The crumbling remnant of a castle which belonged to the days of Turlough O'Brien should have been the centre of the hamlet; in fact it stood on the rim of a shallow depression where the other buildings were strewn as Anastasia was wont to strew her toys on the nursery floor. A long barn with a roof of rusty iron stood back-to-back with the cottage it belonged to, an alehouse built of scarlet brick had its porch pointing towards the naked marshland, the Gothic windows of the one consequential house commanded nothing but the steep side of a hillock a few yards away; all that visibly connected these dwellings was a mazy pattern engraved by cartwheels in the grey mud, while the rest of the intervening space was largely filled with tall thistles and tangled hawthorn, or with banks of lusty nettles which served as a last resting place for broken furniture, tin baths, inverted pony traps and farming tools of every kind. I was never an accurate observer, but even my first sight of Bowistown drew my attention to the difference between that place and the London fringe.

In a phase of life so unpredictable I was not greatly surprised when, in one of his nicely calculated divagations, the donkey brought us obliquely through a broad gateway into the castle itself. This, it seemed, was where the O'Kneales were domiciled.

As I remember it, one large chamber in the keep, more or less intact, served them as parlour; for other accommodation they depended chiefly on what was left of a thin two-storied house which some resourceful squatter of the late eighteenth century had improvised in the bailey, overflowing into the range of penthouses and shielings which intermediate occupiers had added as the fancy took them with walls made from fallen masonry and roofs from corrugated iron. The whole was a residence of agreeable informality, but better suited to fair than to rainy days, and intimidating to so raw a visitor as I.

'So this is the English boy!'

I still hear the soft voice of Desmond O'Kneale as he greets me thus; I can see his aquiline face, shiny, black-a-vised, but imposing in its spare sculpture, as he critically regards me through his wire-rimmed spectacles. It was not the greeting I should have chosen, but I saw that he meant no unkindness; if a triple-headed toad had been brought for his inspection he would, I think, have examined it with just the same scientific curiosity, judiciously amused, perhaps faintly scandalized but ready to grant that no creature should be blamed for its congenital absurdities.

Kevin, of course, came gallantly to my defence: 'Ah, he lives in England, surely, but the biggest part of him is just as Irish as you or me.'

"Tis not a true Irish name, Hutchinson,' Desmond said. 'Did it not belong to one of our own great-grandsires!' Kevin protested. 'And with all honour to your learning, sib, I'd remind you there were Hutchinsons in Connacht in the days of Siol Aedha Slaine—except they were never certainly persuaded how to spell what people called them.'

I soon lost track of this argument, for which my presence had been no more than the point of departure, but I continued to look on my latest-discovered cousin with an interest not far short of fascination. Desmond wore a collar and tie —the high, starched double collar of those days with a tightly knotted ribbon of green silk—and although you might have seen a resemblance to his brothers he was distinctly a more urban personality. His handsome eyes were of the same minting as Kevin's, but more restless, more wary, readier to flash with moral excitement; when he fastened them on your face you could not look elsewhere. Sean O'Leighlin in his *Rebel's Odyssey* admits that Desmond O'Kneale often frightened him. Strangely, he did not frighten me; though (at an age when one is unresponsive to adult enthusiasm) I came to wish he had a little less to say.

Especially, at that first meeting, I regretted that the subject of my wretched surname had arisen to lock the brothers in debate. Soaked to the skin, I had assumed that on my arrival someone like Mavrusha would quickly take me to change my clothes and would give me something to eat; instead, I found myself sitting on an upturned beer crate just inside the open door of the parlour, no more regarded than the Gladstone bag beside me, while the eloquence of my cousin Desmond soared superbly, praising the wisdom of Greta M'Taurey in entering the Clan O'Kneale, and even my beloved Kevin turned his back on me as he doggedly insisted that some merit, even the patriotic sort of virtue, might yet be found in those M'Taureys who remained outside the Catholic fold. 'No more regarded': I have used those words without precision. A waterlogged spaniel which had followed us indoors stayed to sniff my knees fastidiously; some barefoot, fish-mouthed children came, one leading a goat on a piece of string, they were joined by a bearded and gaitered man whom I took to be another of the O'Kneale brothers, then by a blear-eyed woman with a man's jacket clutched about her shoulders and a crumpled cigarette stuck on a corner of her mouth. This unpretentious posse stood to inspect me in rigid silence. By now I was more or less resigned to my casting as a freak of nature, but I felt rather as in that dream—known, I suppose, to most of us—where a huge audience waits in sullen patience for the speech one has omitted to prepare.

Yes, in that queer interlude I was suspended, as it were, between two separate presentations; my eyes were tied to the arc of dumb observers, my ears to the engrossing ding and dong of the brothers' altercation. Though never loud or rough the voice of Desmond was falling as remorselessly as the strokes of a woodman's axe:

'Will you listen to me, young Kevin! Did they not teach you history at St Finnian's College! Did you never hear of the plantations—the Scots that James sent over in their thousands to settle on the stolen lands of Donegal?'

So may the major prophets have spoken. But Kevin's voice, unflagging in riposte, sounded no note of submission; it had a glint and swagger of its own:

'History? Indeed, we had it twice a week from Father Leonard, they kept him for no other purpose. But all the history Father Leonard knew gave out before the Scottish race was even started.'

'Then you never heard of Hugh Montgomery, the swindling laird of Braidstane? Or his partner Hamilton, the creeping spy, and the dirty deal they made with Con O'Neill of Clandeboye?'

'Ah, 'tis not the first time you've brought those gentlemen to my attention. Well now, will you and I dig them out from their unhallowed tombs and read a lecture to them? Will we tell them their behaviour was mortally indecent—will we earnestly request them to gather up the corpses of their vassals and transport them back to Ayrshire where they came from?'

'Why, for sure, Kevin boy, you can occupy yourself that way, if that's your fancy. Myself, I prefer to concentrate on their descendants, the ones that have their grip on us this day. When we're rid of the last of those vultures—'

'And that savage woman out there,' Kevin said, '—for all we know she's one of them as well!'

Directed by those words I saw, coming across the bailey, a wrinkled beldame in a black overall. Since then I have recognized her like all over Europe—you meet that grizzled, fibrous grandmother, with her black woollen stockings and her crudely doctored shoes, in the lowlier streets of every continental town—but I have rarely known an adult woman so small in stature: she looked like one of normal physique who has been shrunk by long exposure to an equatorial sun. Her shrivelled body was, however, far from feeble: her step was quick, the movements of her head were like a bird's, brisk and watchful; even at that first glimpse (some years before I had much interest in physiognomy) I believe I noticed the vivacity of her ardent, penetrating eyes. At the least, my earliest sight of the tiny creature left a deeply-etched impression on my memory, though that vision lasted only a fraction of a second; for Kevin, as he spoke, strode quickly past me, jumped clean over the goat which barred his way and with a cry of 'Mam-darlint!' ran out to meet her, for a few moments blocking my view.

Then once more my knowledge of life was widened. An adoration of one's mother was a sentiment I deeply understood already, and I had found the day before that a grown person—my father, to wit—could weep almost as heartily as Anastasia. But to see a man lift his mother off the ground, and clasp her tightly against his body while the two of them wept together, that was something new and marvellous to me.

They made up a bed for me in what was called the Farm Office, in one of the outhouses, where Kevin was to sleep in the loft above. "Twill be nice and quiet for him, away from the parlour,' Kevin's mother said. There was, indeed, no one working in the office on that Saturday evening (I find it hard to think of paper work being done at any time in a room without a desk or other clerical impedimenta) and its only other use, when I had settled for the night, was for a game of whist played by some of the brothers, my bed serving as table. One of them sat on a small ottoman, the rest on sacks or boxes; the light they used came from a single candle, and since I was very tired their talk and laughter did not greatly disturb me. I was only briefly awake when dogs were introduced to evict some rats which were found nesting on top of the dresser where I had put my clothes.

The question what was to be done with me while the others were at Mass was one of the subjects bandied at breakfast. Privately I saw no reason why I should not attend Mass as well; though baptized in the Anglican communion I had often accompanied my mother to the Russian church at Mill Hill, and at this date I had no grasp of liturgical distinctions. As usual, however, no one thought of consulting my own wishes, and I should have found it hard to express them in a setting so much more fluid than the meals over which Mavrusha presided.

'Can the lad not go with Finnuala when she feeds the Chinese sow?'

I think it was Francis, the bearded brother, who threw out that suggestion and almost at once left the kitchen (where the meal took place) munching a hunk of bread and cheese. Someone else, arriving at the same moment said,

'Better let Kevin do the feeding—he's professional.'

'Now there you have genius!' Desmond said, holding his plate for the porridge which Greta was ladling from a huge saucepan to anyone who came. 'A lad in full practice at waiting on the citizens of Castlemagonagh—who else would the Chinese sow desire to feed her!'

A burst of laughter came from three or four children sitting on a bench against the wall.

'Whist, now!' Greta said. 'You will please, Desmond, not to make sport of your young brother, who's occupied with as honest a trade as any other.'

'To say nothing of the genteel gratuities beneath the plates!' Desmond replied.

Kevin, who was fasting, stood near the stove, impassively regarding the desultory parade of breakfasters. He said,

'Ay, I'll feed the swine the next thing after Mass. 'Twill be a change from the Maguire Hotel, where the clients have no manners at all.'

'And speaking of manners,' Greta said, 'I do not greatly favour those of Captain Stevenage.'

'Stevenage? Who would that be?'

'He seems to be Mr Macartney's new collector. He came to the step yesterday, just when I had a piece of mutton roasting, and nobody but Finnuala to protect me from any wickedness he had in mind.'

'What—he came to pass the time of day?'

'That I couldn't tell—he spoke with an English accent it would take a conjuror to follow. But he gave me an impression the topic was financial.'

'So you set the dogs on him?' Mairtin said.

'Indeed, I did nothing so unsociable. I simply told him that as I understood the case the land hereabouts belongs to the Right Honourable the Earl of Lincoln, who would doubtless pay a visit to receive the rent according to his own convenience. But that was far beyond this person's education.'

'So then,' said Mairtin, 'he had the common decency to cease his persecution of a helpless woman?'

'He had not. He said this Mr Macartney he belongs to

has all this piece of country on a long lease from the Earl himself. I said I was greatly surprised to receive that information. I said my sons were great respecters of the law, they would require to see the legal documents to prove what he said was not some kind of joukery-pawkery to snatch the bread from the mouth of a decent English earl.'

'And did that put an end to the man's foolishness?'

'Sure, he moved himself away then, but he had the impudence to say he'd be back again today and pestering the menfolk of the family. I said I was astounded. I told him that before the Church had graciously received me to her bosom I was in the Protestant connection, I said it was a mournful state of things we'd come to if the English themselves would no longer show respect to the Sabbath Day.'

Naturally those exchanges meant nothing to me at the time. With my porringer on my knees I sat bemused, my eyes drifting from the gobbling cousins on my right and left to the statue of Our Lady above the door, now to the meat-hooks and the great cauldrons over Greta's head, now once more to the lank figure of Kevin sprawled against a French hall-clock and his withdrawn Gioconda smile. When he looked at his mother that smile took on the warmth of firelight, and I in turn could feel her magic. It belonged, I suppose, in great part to the sweetness of her tiny mouth joined with the astonishing brilliance of her restless eyes; but the spell she exercised on me came first from the music of her voice, where all the harshness of common experience, the quarrels and resentments, seemed to dissolve as in Daubigny's landscapes all the roughnesses of nature do.

Among her sons it was Desmond who—if my memory is accurate—most remarkably inherited the melody and rhythm of that voice. This I realized when, after breakfast, he took possession of me, quietly ignoring the several plans which the others had proposed for my amusement.

'So your father is some sort of Irishman?' he said, with a patronage which, considering his thirty-odd years of seniority, was perfectly inoffensive.

125

The question took me by surprise. I had heard Howard describe himself as 'a wretched artist conscripted to the teacher's trade', as 'a floundering expatriate' and 'a poor male thing that Providence has furnished to liberate your mother's maternal genius', but never in my hearing had he mentioned his nationality. I could only give a feeble answer: 'We live in Hendon, *barin*.'

He nodded kindly, as one not expecting brilliance from a hall-marked imbecile.

'Your father is not the only one,' he said, 'who ever made a pact with the devil to live in ease and luxury at the conqueror's postern gate.'

He had brought me to his own quarter, a shanty which leant against the largest building; it was furnished with books and rudimentary cobbler's tools as well as some aged bicycles and a double bed. Some of the children I had seen —they kept emerging in odd places, like spiders in an old bathroom—must have belonged to him, for there were boots of the smallest sizes on the unmade bed and the trestle-table; in a rather haphazard way he set about repairing these, remarking. 'On Sundays we turn the whole litter into lords and ladies.' But first, with notable good sense, he put a piece of leather on the floor and showed me how to help him by outlining soles and heels with a pencil. He was not, I think, a very able tradesman—he seemed to be for ever pricking his finger or sending nails flying across the room —but he never swore or showed impatience; his voice, as he worked, seemed to surround us with a dulcet harmony, like that of small, summer waves breaking on a sandy shore.

'So your papa will not have told you yet what the English came and did to this beautiful country? You have your letters, now? Then it's time, to my way of thinking, that a little history was brought to your attention.'

Mellifluously as they were spoken, those words made me somewhat uneasy; they were the first intimation to reach me that I was academically retarded. I said defensively, 'I know my tables up to seven twelves.'

He loftily ignored that rebuttal. 'So you've learnt nothing yet,' he said, 'about Niall of the Nine Hostages? Ah, let it be! But it might be convenient for you to know that in the time of the Thirty-two High Kings—all of Ui Neill stock, mind you—my fathers were the rightful owners of all these lands here. And no wonder, since they came of the royal stock themselves—the name we carry now is nothing but a bookless corruption.'

He was generously enlarging on this thesis when a raw-boned woman in carpet slippers came shuffling in to make the bed. Incensed by this intrusion, my cousin yet managed to rebuke her in charitable terms: 'Rosa, darlint, can you not find some other time to indulge yourself in those female amusements? This fine young Englishman and I, we're holding an important conference.' And when he had thus quelled the disturbance he quietly resumed his lecture:

'You will not have heard of Owen Roe O'Neill—he was among the noblest of my collaterals. But the name of the blackguard Cromwell, that will no doubt be familiar to you. Now I do not intend to sit in judgement on any countryman of yours, but when the commander of a great army overwhelms a small weak garrison, as your Cromwell did at Drogheda and again at Wexford, and when he slaughters every man, woman and child, not to mention every Catholic priest he finds there, then we shall not be far from the facts of history when we call that man a blaspheming anti-christ, a tool of Satan and a wholesale murderer. But hark you, now: let no one ever tell you this Cromwell was a foolish man. Ah, not at all! He had a problem he must deal with—there were the soldiers who'd fought the war to bring the Irish to their knees, and the "Adventurers" who paid for it, and the two establishments were crying out each louder than the other for some return. So what did this elegant administrator do but simply pass an "Act of Satisfaction", which means that the land of ten counties was taken from the rightful owners and given over to the greedy claimants. And what about the Irish folk that chanced to live there? Ah, that was easy: the whole brigade of them—with any poor beasts they had to live by—was bundled over into Connacht, to keep themselves alive by any means they might discover.'

He was faintly smiling, rather as a dilettante does when showing you a work of eccentric art which he himself has learnt to appreciate. Such smiles are commonly used for the persuasion of children, but I doubt if children often accept them as symptoms of geniality, and I remember how little—at that juncture—my discomfort was reduced by his appearance of bonhomie.

'You'll be saying,' he went on, 'that what I've told you was a long while back—you'll be telling me they were rough times your Master Cromwell lived in. Well, shall I tell you now what happened less than seventy years ago—in the memory of men who are living now? There was a blight that fell on the potatoes—it began in England but it quickly came to us across the water, like all the other plagues of nature. So here in Holy Ireland the crop was all destroyed —and that was the food the people lived on. In time the news got back to England that the Irish folk were dying right and left—it even got to the ears of a gentleman called Lord John Russell, who was head of the English government. Well, the English said the important thing was not to interfere with the Laws of Political Economy, which were made to be a comfort and a blessing to people who were dying of starvation. Lord Russell wrote it down himself, to make it all quite plain: "It must be understood we cannot feed these Irish people." There was a Law of Political Economy that public money must not be spent on relief work, because a part of it might find its way to the pocket of some private person. Another Law said that however poor the people were it was no excuse for letting them have food below the normal price, because that would have a bad effect on the traders' profits. Those laws accorded with the general notion of the English, which was that Ireland was a long way off, and a source of little profit, so the Irish must set to work and look after their own troubles, even if it killed the lot of them.'

The smile had gone, and he held me with his eyes so strictly that I felt as if I alone must answer for all the wickedness he seemed to be describing. Someone had entered the room by the door behind me. Anchored by guilt, I could not turn to see who it was, and even when I heard Kevin's voice I remained quite still, like a prisoner awaiting sentence.

'Des, will you leave off persecuting the poor wee lad!' Kevin said sociably. 'He will not have the time in this week-end to mend the wrongs that were done to Ireland in the last four hundred years.'

But his brother's moral temperature was now above the reach of flippancy. 'The lad's old enough,' Desmond said, 'to be acquainted with a few facts and figures.' His voice had grown dry, at last drained of its music. 'There's a place called Gonaghoe, just four miles along the road there—still in Macartney's land. Seven hundred and sixty-eight souls, that was the exact number in 1844—you'll find the names and holdings in Macartney's own office. In 1850 they took the number again, and how many would you think they found then? Two hundred and fifteen! And since you have the gift of figures, Master Ryan, that will tell you there were five hundred and fifty-three to be accounted for. Now then: Professor Thomas Guerin from Dublin took the trouble to make his own investigation, and when he reached the end of it there were ninety-one of the lost population he could never trace. But he found that two hundred and eighty-six were known to have died—some from typhus or relapsing fever, some from plain starvation. They died too fast for all of them to be buried, there were skeletons of babies and their mothers being found in the fields and woods for years after. Then there were nearly two hundred—of the ones who didn't die where they were—who'd been packed off in what they called "the coffin ships", old rotting hulks meant for transporting cattle. That lot were supposed to start a new life in America, but it's doubtful whether half the number even got there.'

The bitterness in those last words left a silence, like the smoke which hangs above the site of an explosion. It was broken by Kevin, who said simply,

'Ah, that was a cruel time, there's no denying.'

Then Mairtin came. He said, 'Would it not be time to start for the Memorial? They've caught both the donkeys. And the girls are putting grandpapa into his trousers now.'

'But certainly the lad can come—he shall be witness of a time-honoured Irish ceremonial.'

With those words Desmond stooped to lay a hand on my shoulder, smiling with the utmost benevolence. In a matter of minutes he seemed to have forgiven me for all the harm I had done to his land and nation.

'The man we go to honour,' he said, 'Eoin O'Kneale, was the brother of my great-grandfather. He was murdered by the English in the month of April, 1835. The place we're going to is Rory's Oak. That's the very tree—what's left of it— where Eoin was hiding with a few friends, patriots like himself, to interrupt the English soldiers who were on their way to lay hands on Michael Fortoul—he was an old peasant fellow, as innocent as you can well imagine, with a pair of sickly cows and a great litter of children. As luck would have it, the English corporal went to the top of a nearby hill, to have a general view of the countryside. That got him just one glimpse of Eoin; and without asking why or wherefore he shot him between the shoulder blades.'

Slightly mesmerized, I did my best to follow this compendium; my spirits were rising—I felt it was goodnatured of Desmond, and also flattering, to include me in what was clearly a grown-up and important expedition. True, I was also rather frightened: always slow in ratiocination, I failed to pull together the threads of his narrative; the word 'ceremonial' was new to me, and I vaguely supposed I was going to attend a display of musketry distinctly more lethal than General Almore's. But the risk of being shot in the stomach was not too high a price for a story which would make Anastasia's eyes pop out of her head.

Moreover the weather had the smell of pleasure in it. Those rotund clouds, black and violet, which so often gather over Ireland were today moving fast, hustled by a lively, brackish wind; they left, between their companies, wide intervals which the April sun filled with a silver light.

The waggon paraded for the party's use was not a large or obviously robust one: in the matter of vehicles the O'Kneales were never, I think, vainglorious. For the comfort of the passengers two forms such as you find in schoolrooms had been placed along the sides. Edward Carson, the donkey which had drawn me from the station, was between the shafts, and beside him a somewhat larger one named Queen Victoria; even to my inexpert eyes it seemed abnormal that the link which joined the harness of these beasts to the waggon consisted of nothing but knotted cords, some not much thicker than string, but I presumed my cousins knew their business. About this equipage the Memorial party assembled slowly; someone was always going back for something he or she had forgotten. I gathered from snatches of talk that Taoiseach Patrick O'Kneale—Kevin's grandfather —was to be the primus of the company and that his arrival would be the signal for starting. This was a happy circumstance: it meant that no one else need feel himself responsible for the prolonged delay.

I doubt if Patrick Cahir O'Kneale (whose title must have been a local honorific—it appears in no appropriate work of reference) was quite so patriarchal a figure as the one I see in the inflating light of childish memory; more exact records testify that his legs were pitifully short in relation to his immense breadth of shoulder. But Shane Lismore's portrait in the National Gallery at Dublin tells me that his great square head, with copious white locks falling about his neck, was not less magnificent than I remember it. When I saw him emerging from one of the larger outhouses that

131

majestic head was crowned (not, I think, to advantage) by a silk hat of the mid-Victorian shape, no longer quite large enough to encompass the cranium; an old frock coat gave a ceremonial air to the rest of his person, and in that rural setting it did not seem unorthodox that he should be without tie or collar, only a yellow singlet showing between the black lapels. His grandson Francis—the bearded one—was holding him on one side, a granddaughter on the other, but he hardly seemed to need their support; he moved very slowly yet with a dignified assurance, like a drum major matching his pace to that of a children's parade.

While this imposing personage was being shoved and hauled aboard the waggon by a team of his descendants, Desmond very amiably presented me:

'We have an English boy here, grandpa, who's aspiring to see the Remembrance. He wishes to expand his education on the side of history.'

Awkwardly suspended, with Francis tugging at his armpits and with one buttock propped on a granddaughter's shoulder, the Chieftain yet contrived to bend his head towards me with a touching courtesy.

'All are welcome, friend as well as foe,' he said, and the kindness of those words was enlarged by the radiance of his light blue eyes. 'On this historic day,' he continued, when he had been settled next to me on the off-side bench, 'we regard as members of our own fellowship all who salute the sublime courage of Patriot Eoin O'Kneale. As the nephew of that heroic fighter I am proud and happy to tell you, sir, that your nationality will make no difference to our feelings, no difference at all.'

At this stage Kevin was standing between the off-side wheels; almost as a matter of routine, now, he spoke up for me: 'You should know, grandpa, the lad has a good Irish father.'

'A good father?' As if those had been words of evil omen the old man's eyes clouded. 'Then let him keep the man away from Molly de Laney's Easter Ale,' he said. 'I once had a good Irish father myself—God rest his soul—and in his last forty years it was never safe to come within a dozen yards of him.'

On a day which felt so full of promise I was not much shaken by this warning. After descending the cobbled slope from the castle gateway our carriage went well enough, though without much speed or resilience; Finnuala and the other wives walked beside the donkeys (giving the turnout a curiously biblical complexion) and under their knowing management the animals pulled well together. The traces held. The face of my cousin Mairtin, seated opposite me and nursing the senescent wreath he had acquired at Ruckmore Gap, was steeped in gloom, but he, I think, was by nature saturnine; his brothers, in the main, looked cheerful enough. Between us the youngest infants in the party rolled, mewled and bickered among the many loaves and bottles strewn on the floorboards; older children gyrated erratically about their mothers, while a dozen dogs, conspicuously varied in design and stature, treated the cortège as base for raucous and neurotic forays into the passing countryside. In the way of ingenuous small boys I felt a joyous pride in belonging to this large, harmonious company, and I remember suffering a sharp distress when the expedition met with its first set-back.

The road bridge over the Sleane had not been built then; to cross from Bowistown to the main Gallinaulty road you had to use the Hard Post ferry. This was one of the simplest kind, a punt-shaped boat guided by a wire cable and propelled by an endless rope. When they were awake, and not too busy with their goats and vegetables, an aged couple inhabiting a cabin on the Gallinaulty side worked it; at other times the traveller did so himself, leaving—if he were finical—the fare of a penny a wheel on the mounting block nearby. The thing looked barely large enough to carry our equipage, and I recall some moments of alarm as we descended the cobbled slope by which it was approached on the Bowistown side; but in fact the women showed such skill in their control of the donkeys that the boarding operation was a quick success. At the other side (which we reached by our own efforts) we were not so fortunate. Here the ramp which had to be surmounted—upwards—was deep in mud. Again the drivers did their best, with Rosa mounted on Queen Victoria and Finnuala (I think it was) dragging Edward Carson by the head-harness. They had the waggon half-way up the slope when it stuck. In what must have been a reflex action the two women turned simultaneously, each to inflict a smart blow on her animal's quarter, but only Rosa's beast responded: she—Queen Victoria—plunged forward with such violence that the makeshift traces snapped. Fear, I suppose, will quicken the dullest child's observation: though the next few moments were tightly packed I clearly recollect some elements in the catastrophe—Rosa's manic laughter as her mount in the ecstasy of freedom bore her swiftly across a potato field, the fluid spectacle of dogs and children racing in hopeless pursuit, the trembling and the eerie bray of Edward Carson as he felt the waggon's weight dragging on him alone. An instant later I had reason to share his misgivings, for I realized suddenly that instead of Carson hauling us we were hauling him. Luckily (as I see it now) he made no sustained resistance: finding his driver limp with lunatic mirth, he put his four hooves together and glissaded smoothly backward through the mud. That was the last of the episode which I saw distinctly, for as our wheels ran back against the ferry's lip a jolt which toppled both the benches sent the lot of us sprawling on the waggon floor. Recovering, I realized by degrees that—a thing to marvel at—we were once more neatly waterborne. Carson's rear hooves had followed the waggon aboard, the front pair remaining ashore; his bray had grown louder and more petulant, as if he were making a speech on ferries, full of bigotry and passion.

'Now that's a lesson,' Mairtin said, when he had replaced his bench and settled in his old position, 'on the foolishness of having half a mountain at both ends of a river crossing.'

And Desmond added tartly, 'Well, what would you expect! The whole machinery's on Macartney's land—indeed, it's one of Macartney's special notions, to have a ferry that will aggravate the whole community.'

Francis asked at large, 'Will Rosa be back, would you imagine?'

He was sombrely answered by one of the women: 'It would not be like Rosa, with Queenie Vic in her lewd spirits and the day so fine. Rosa's a rare one for the riding—by now she'll not remember she had a waggon fixed to the Queen's arse when they began.'

We were all in our former places now, and the leisurely talk—of Rosa's interesting forgetfulness, of Mr Macartney's despicable failure to provide a decent crossing—went on for some time. My hopes for the grandeurs and excitements of Rory's Oak were dwindling. Oddly, it was the slow-brained Mairtin who at last conceived a means of escape from our predicament.

'Will we not do better,' he said, 'to go by water? The river underneath us has the same direction, except it goes another way altogether. It misses the Oak by half a mile—not more.'

'You mean, take the ferry boat along below the wain?' Francis asked.

His brother nodded. ''Twill save time and labour, in the last consideration.'

'Would it not be a kindness to put the proposition to Pat Coughlin and his old woman? They could be wondering if their old boat was away to join the fairies.'

'Ach, they wouldn't take it to their hearts at all. They have the turnip crop to occupy the little mind they have between them.'

'But there could be other folk will wish to make the crossing.' (That was Kevin's interpolation.)

'There's never more than a few small carts on a Sunday,' Mairtin replied. 'It might be to their advantage—who can tell!—to finish up on the same side of the burn where they began.'

Still another question was raised (I think by one of the women): 'Is it not Mr Macartney's property, the wee boat we're resting on?' And this point captured Patrick O'Kneale's attention. Since our tumble on the waggon floor the Chieftain had been silent, his thoughts doubtless wandering, as those of the very old do, in remote, recondite avenues. Now, raising his hat a little way, he turned upon the inquirer a gaze of refined benignity.

'Mr Macartney—' he said devoutly, '—my heart bleeds for him.'

It has been a convention among my other Irish relatives to speak of the O'Kneales as lacking in practicality. But no one—not cousin Hanna herself—would have laid that charge after seeing how ably the brothers diverted the ferry boat from her circumscribed routine to more ambitious voyaging. It was not an entirely simple task to loose the vessel from her guiding cable and to re-arrange her hawsers for free-style towing, nor was it easy to organize sufficient motive power: with her freight of waggon and passengers the boat lay low in the water, too ponderous a thing for Edward Carson by himself to get under way, so a protean team of children, some barefoot, a few stricken and rebellious in their Sunday boots and stockings, had to be assembled to reinforce him on the tow-line. If the exercise was performed without the polish of the Royal Marines it was yet completed with a reasonable dispatch and cheerfulness. Not long after noon (at a rough estimate) we were in fairly constant motion—Carson pulling manfully, the rest with intermittent zeal—along the frenzied writhings of the Sleane.

My own spirits rose again. I was not allowed to share in the towing—Desmond had fastened me beside him, and from an album labelled *British Injustice. Vol 5. 1896-1903* he was rather monotonously reading me newspaper reports of court cases and evictions. But the sun had emerged once more, and Kevin, busy handling a bargepole to keep our bows off the bank, could always find odd moments to hearten me with his dazzling smile.

The Memorial Celebration itself was so far outside my mental reach and so lacking in the drama I had hoped for that if left only a blurred memory. It consisted mainly of a speech by Desmond in Middle Irish—a language as unfamiliar (I imagine) to the main part of his audience as it was to me. To me his discourse seemed interminable, and I noticed that some of my cousins amused themselves with wagers on whether it would overrun the record of fifty-seven minutes which he had achieved three years before.

Not much was left of Rory's famous oak, and the rain of more than seventy winters had washed away the lettering which (so Kevin told me) had once declared its historic importance. I have retained a watery impression of the adjacent scenery—the meeting house of some austere sect (perhaps the Separated Campbellites) and a tavern of parallel simplicity, where at intervals the tap-room door would open with a longdrawn whine of hinges and a man or two would emerge to stand for a while, transfixed by reverent incomprehension, against the red-brick wall. The other listeners including me were seated on the convenient knoll from which the English corporal had fired the fatal shot at Eoin: there the women smoked and chewed their hunks of soda bread, pausing now and then to castigate their young for vexing the dogs, for a careless attitude to sanitation or for fighting with unnecessary noise.

There was music of a strange kind, delivered by a small shaggy man like a spider curled up in defence, ('He was a decent piper in his day', Kevin told me) and a daughter of twice his bulk who—if my memory is faithful—somewhat resembled Balzac as Rodin saw him; music for which Carson, to judge by his agonized vociferation, had as little taste as I. For the rest, I remember some disturbance when the Memorial Wreath, for a time lost, was found inside a small girl's jersey; and again when the Chieftain, charged to place it ceremonially on Eoin's stump, forgot his part and laid it with old-world chivalry on the piper's daughter's bust.

My kinsmen, none the less, seemed to be well satisfied with their Observance, and before we were back at the river the trifling deviation from rubric had plainly been forgotten. Rain had started, but no one seemed to be depressed by that annoyance. I heard a woman say,

"Twas the best Memoriam they ever circumcised. Ah, it was beautiful—I cried till I thought my eyes would float into my ear-holes.'

And another agreed; 'A proud speech it was—the best that Desmond ever farrowed. And a great comfort it must have been to Eoin himself, if St Michael and the Holy Angels gave him just the liberty to hear it.'

Only one in the company—a dark and lovely creature appropriately named Deirdre—spoke in a vein of sadness: 'It was mortifying, just the same, to have Carson palavering the way he did. Did he have to be bawling his agnostical opinions on such a day as this!'

'Boat-baling—now that takes feat hands and a load of patience. It's a trade for the womenfolk and bantlings.'

This proposition came from Mairtin. It was Francis who added, with his rudimentary kindness, 'Sure, if they're underneath the waggon it will keep them from the rain.'

He was, I think, too sanguine: against the sort of rain which is normal in those valleys the floorboards of a very old waggon will seldom make an acceptable shelter. But perhaps the question was academic. During the outward voyage our craft had shipped a good deal of water—the result, I suppose, of a kind of traction to which she was unaccustomed—and at the start of the return journey she was riding noticeably low. To the party of women and children who knelt in the bilge, scooping the water with mugs and bottles and often—through inadvertence or in a spirit of carnival—throwing it on to each other, the weather overhead cannot have been of much concern.

It was clear even to my raw intelligence that the crowded *Wasserfest* of the lower deck offered a more intense discomfort than any other mode of travel. Except for Desmond, who had spent himself too far for any more exertion, all the brothers were on the tow-line now; in a burst of colourable virtue I said that I must haul on the line as well.

On the whole our company's morale remained impressive: nothing, I suppose, so elevates the heart as a sense of having faithfully performed some duty, and while I myself had been no more than a confused spectator of the ceremony I was deeply infected by the cheerfulness of my friends. True, there was frequent wailing from the youngest children aboard, who may have suffered from hydrophobia of a special kind, but I was old enough even then to know that a strident hullabaloo is a natural concomitant of babyhood which wiser beings learn to ignore. On the upper deck (so to say) of our vessel there was sufficient dignity to neutralize the disarray below: with an old coat over his head Desmond had returned to his study of British Injustice while his grandfather, shielded by Kate O'Kneale with the remains of an umbrella, sat upright as before, gazing composedly at the watery screen ahead. With the rain increasing in force and volume the boat travelled as smoothly as the variable energies of donkey, men and boys allowed. Our retinue of sodden dogs was silent now, perhaps exhibiting contentment of a canine sort. Broadly, our progress made a damp but harmonious spectacle.

At a distance one can generally form objective judgements, and I see now that the people who disturbed our quiet passage were only following their own notions of civic or professional obligation. At the time, I shared the O'Kneales' resentment of their interference.

'Frank, we have visitors among us!'

'Ah, 'tis Pat Coughlin himself, come to take a pride in the old boat's performance.'

139

'And that would be his long-lost uncle he has beside him.'

'Indeed, it's the very one which got left over from the Battle of the Boyne.'

That colloquy between the brothers caused me to look across to the farther bank, where a pair of mounted figures was emerging rather operatically through the sliding portière of rain. Chance made their appearance a prodigy to me: I had lately been given Thackeray's version of *Don Quixote*, with C. K. Howe's illustrations, and in the turbid light of that moist late-afternoon the two riders abruptly revealed to an artless little boy could only be Quixote and his squire come to life. Granted, the taller of the two was beardless, but his face was exceptionally long and grave—showing a curious affinity to that of his high-backed, cadaverous Rozinante, which he rode as if with wooden thighs; while his fellow, though (like himself) in modern dress, had the stunted shape, the quickset moustache, the humility of aspect which for me were the whole stuff of Sancho Panza. So strong was this illusion that when the donkey he was riding called, in the manner of its kind, across the stream to ours, I was almost certain I heard the name Dapple embedded in Edward Carson's elaborate reply.

For all the modesty of his appearance, there was not much diffidence in the way 'Sancho Panza' opened his conversation with my cousins; some of the phrases which incised my memory were: 'Ye damned blackguards—ye thievin' bastard sons of Tipperary trollops—ye Satan-servin' buzzarfaced spalpeens!' And when he had reached the end of those civilities he continued, 'You take my word 'n' oath, I'll have the law on ye—this time next week the whole adulteratin' crew of ye will be in jail.'

'There—I told you it was Pat Coughlin!' Mairtin said. 'You could tell the cherub voice he has if you heard it coming from an old frog.'

'Is it something on your mind, Mr Coughlin?' Francis called.

'You know well enough what's on my mind,' Pat Coughlin shouted back. 'That's my ferry boat you've stolen.'

Francis nodded. 'Ah, that settles it—the daft gossoon we talked to along the river was right after all. He said the miserable raft we had was putting him in mind of the old Hard Post ferry. I said, "Then if it's Paddy Coughlin's boat we have—through some miscalculation—he shall have it back under him this very day, or sooner still."'

So pacific an answer left Coughlin with nothing to say. But now the man I had mistaken for Don Quixote spoke, with an English voice of a kind which—however familiar to me at home—sounded curiously artificial in this setting.

'You may like to know,' he said, 'that the boat you've stolen is Mr Macartney's property.'

At those words Desmond emerged from the shelter of his coat. 'Then it's an outrage and a scandal!' he said. 'A man who keeps a boat in this condition—who makes a charge for the public use of it—he's no more than a highway robber and a common criminal. There's a law of homicide even in this persecuted country, though you may not know it. Macartney may think he's safe and sound for ever through his foreign friends in Dublin city, but we'll have him jailed for manslaughter in the end.'

'Indeed?' the tall man said pedantically. 'But you will hardly blame my employer for one of your infants falling off his boat altogether.'

We had all been too much interested in the discussion to notice that occurrence; now, a few yards behind us, I saw a little, anxious face just protruding from the surface of the water. It belonged to a small boy who for most of the journey had been whimpering in a tiresome way, and with so many querulous creatures in the company I myself felt it no loss to be separated for a time from one of them; but women of the less sophisticated sort can never have too many children about their skirts, and one who was palpably the mother of the stray gave way to clamorous emotion.

'Tahm!' she screamed. 'Will you come out of the water

this minute! How do you suppose I can dry your clothes at a place like this! And you might have known it's a dirty river you're sporting in.'

This emphatic utterance had the effect of dislodging the Chieftain from his private meditations. While Tom, in heightened alarm, was scrambling on to our bank, his great-grandfather was turning slowly towards the other; his eyes coming to rest on "Don Quixote", he raised his hat and affably addressed the stranger.

'A beautiful morning,' he exclaimed, 'and a lovely country-side! You come from far, sir?'

For a moment the tall man was taken aback: the rain, indeed, had slackened, but he evidently lacked the inward poetry to see the landscape with the Chieftain's eyes.

'Taoiseach, it's Captain Stevenage you're speaking to,' Coughlin said. 'The Captain is Mr Macartney's new agent.'

'Then I count this a fortunate meeting,' the Chieftain said, 'for none of Macartney's servants rest long in their positions. I hope, sir, your sojourn among us, however short, may prove to be one of serenity and true refreshment.'

'I called at your house yesterday,' Stevenage said.

'Ah, that was an obliging courtesy.'

'And I left with Mrs O'Kneale an overdue account for eighty-seven pounds.'

'But what use would an account of any sort be to Mrs O'Kneale, God rest her, who for thirty-seven years come the Feast of Holy Innocents has not been under secular disposal?'

It was plain even to me that the two men had arrived at a point of mutual misunderstanding. Stevenage chose to ignore the obstacle.

'Mr Macartney tells me,' he said, 'that there's been trouble about the Bowistown rents for a long time past. I think you had better understand—'

'And Mr Macartney never said a truer word!' the Chieftain interrupted. 'It is not so far as three hundred years ago that all this Gallinaulty property was in the hands of my renowned progenitor, Cumann Liscasey O'Niall—indeed, according to law and eternal justice it belongs to him and his descendants now. It is on record that Cumann O'Niall was for ever at his wits' end to obtain a reasonable payment from those he allowed to use his land—Scottish vagabonds and other commonalty of the immigrating kind.'

Captain Stevenage seemed hardly to be listening. 'It's none of my business,' he said parenthetically, 'but another of your children has fallen off Mr Macartney's ferry.'

That was a belated observation: Kevin, wading in till the water reached his armpits, had already dredged the little girl in question and was even then replacing her in the boat. So the Captain was not allowed to evade the dialectic which had been ranged against him.

'What is needed now,' Desmond said sternly, 'is a scientific calculation of the total payment due to the O'Niall dynasty from the foreign tribesmen—the Campbells and McDougalls and Macartneys—who have milked our land for the last four centuries.'

'And when that is settled,' said Francis, 'there's the matter of the Jubilee barn Macartney claims to be his property, which he has left these twelve months past to crumble into rack and ruin.'

This brought a reproof from his grandfather: 'Francis, child, will you have the sense and goodness not to talk of business matters on the Sabbath Day. The Captain here will no doubt be of the Protestant persuasion, and I would not wish my family to lacerate his pious sentiments.' He turned to Stevenage again. 'That's a fine horse you have under you, Captain—I know him well. I broke him myself when I stood no higher than his hocks, and all the owners he's ever had speak well of him.'

'That is so?' the Captain said.

His tone betrayed a Laodicean attitude to horses. I suspect that Grandfather O'Knealc's statement came from a shaky memory, but the Captain's thin grey mount was patently past its colthood and its habits corresponded in some degree with those of the human elderly. The river bank was broken by numerous ditches, so narrow that a baby rabbit would have leaped them carelessly: Stevenage's horse had to ponder every one, and then, drawing its hooves as close as possible together, to teeter over like an old lady in a tight skirt. It had, moreover, a predilection for advancing sideways, leading alternately with the right and the left flank.

In fairness, then, it should be stressed that the Captain was negotiating under perceptible handicaps. When you are travelling on a zig-zag course, facing your respondent one moment and with your back to him the next, it must be easy to lose the thread of a discussion. Remember, too, that the conversation was in no sense tête-à-tête. To examine a difference of view with the aged and courtly person who was making a roughly parallel journey on the waterborne waggon would have been comparatively simple; even the younger, less amenable man with a collar and spectacles might not have proved an insuperable obstacle to final agreement; but while the towing party was engaged for much of the time in chanting the Ballad of the Lough Swilly Fisherman—rather breathily, like an underpaid chorus in provincial opera—its members would now and then turn aside to make tangential contributions of their own. Nor was Mr Macartney's agent greatly helped by the general acoustic environment. The boy who had given himself a ducking continued to celebrate his recent distress with a quavering, mindless lamentation. ('He couldn't be setting up more pother,' Mairtin complained, 'if he'd drowned himself altogether'.) And to the hubbub of the lower deck, interwoven with the susurrous of raindrops on the surface of the stream, the blatant camaraderie of Edward Carson and Coughlin's ass added a leit-motiv of exasperating monotony. I was a tender-hearted infant, and more than once I found myself feeling sorry for Captain Stevenage.

In that debate, however, the disadvantages were not all on the Captain's side. I will not say that the baling party was idle, but there was much to disturb its concentration on the work in hand—the need felt by women everywhere for social intercourse, the special interest aroused by the two riders on the left bank, the often irresponsible behaviour of the younger voyagers. The time came when only one woman was still baling (with what looked like a scallop-shell) while the others, noting how much of the water she poured on to her own lap, were content to spin a web of homely wit around her performance. By then it was perceptible that the boat was still lower in the water, and more stubborn in resistance to propulsion.

'We'd make better time,' Francis remarked, 'if the girls would work a little harder.'

'Ah, they've had no education in the craft,' Kevin said charitably. 'If this country was decently administered there'd be a College of Baling for the women. As it is, they're damping their stockings for very little purpose.'

It was then agreed that all the women and children should leave the flooded deck and spend the rest of the voyage up on the waggon, but as they had reached a state of hilarious excitement the change was not too easily effected: the boat rocked alarmingly as the whole party, like the Gadarene swine in reverse motion, swarmed up the waggon's starboard side, and the operation was only half completed when a fully grown woman fell overboard, rendering the others helpless with convivial laughter. I felt sorry for Desmond now. For the benefit of Stevenage he seemed to be repeating, *Anglice*, a generous portion of his Memorial speech, and once more he had to shout his sentences to pierce the mantle of ragged noise—a dismal wailing threaded with high squeals of merriment—which was enfolding him again.

'I will ask you, Corporal Stevenage,' he bellowed, 'to bring your mind to bear on the words of Lord John George Beresford, spoken in the English parliament during the debate on Emancipation in the month of April, 1829.'

'And what in the name of common sense,' the agent asked with a note of impatience, 'has Lord John Beresford to

145

do with the eighty-seven pounds you've been owing Mr Macartney for the last eighteen months?'

'And who's going to pay the repairs to my ferry?' Coughlin demanded with native inconsequence.

'There is no difference of opinion,' the Chieftain called back, 'which cannot be settled by peaceful conversation between honourable men.'

He, at least, seemed blind to any adjacent evidence of discomposure. To improve communication with the shore he was standing on the bench now, Kate hugging his legs as a measure of safety; and among the kaleidoscopic memories which that excursion left with me one of the sharpest (and most endearing) is of the aged man leaning far out like a tree about to fall, holding his hat in studied courtesy some inches from his head and smiling with a soft, seigniorial benevolence at the English Captain's unusual equitation. Not that Stevenage himself showed an inferior dignity in comportment. With his very long, straight body he sat his horse exactly as an old-fashioned clothes-peg would, and whether the animal was moving backwards or sideways, whether it stopped to graze or performed the act of spasmic levitation which it used to clear an obstacle, the Captain's long grey face maintained the serious expression of an upright, single-thoughted man.

'I must remind you,' he said, when one of his approaches to the bank coincided with a lull in the surrounding noise, 'that interest can legally be charged on rents which are overdue. So the liability increases month by month.'

'Would that be Macartney's announcement?' the Chieftain inquired.

'Mr Macartney has mentioned it.'

'And Macartney is in blatant health, I trust? I would ask you, Colonel, to present him at your next meeting with my distinguished sentiments. And as he's a Bible-loving man, he himself may like to be reminded of the person who was clothed in fine linen and fared sumptuously every day, while the beggar Lazarus was twisting his poor head this

146

way and that to catch the crumbs which tumbled off the rich man's overloaded table.'

'*And the Fisherman's heart was broke with toil, broke with toil,*' the towing party sang.

'Mr Macartney is a generous and patient landlord,' the Captain said, with his horse revolving as on a turn-table. 'Till now he has been anxious to forbear invoking the power of the law.'

'Indeed—and that was no doubt the kind of argument which Lazarus put to Abraham in the rich man's favour, though Holy Writ does not mention that particular. They're after saying, Colonel, that the Bible is a closed book to us poor uneducated Catholics. But a few crumbs of learning fall to us as well.'

'If you wish to argue from the Scriptures,' the Englishman said rather drily, 'we can start with the words of St Paul—"Owe no man anything."'

'Ah, but the prophet Moses went into the matter a long time before the blessed Paul did. And Moses said, "Thou shalt take no usury of a man that is poor and waxy."'

'Mr O'Kneale, I am perfectly convinced that Moses said nothing of the kind.'

It was shortly after the discussion had taken on this rabbinical flavour—which added strangely to its charm—that I myself made a remark of exceptional inanity: I said, 'I expect the boat will sink soon.' This is the sort of callow observation which narcissistic children make when they feel themselves starved of attention. Such ineptitude is always a burden to adults; and that utterance of mine must have been especially annoying, since—by chance—the contretemps I carelessly predicted immediately took place. In a sudden lurch the ferry's port-side gunwale went below the waterline; the river, like a trained assault force when a city wall is breached, rushed in to fill the little space its advance parties had not already occupied, and in another moment the boat, with a faint and slightly histrionic gurgle, had descended out of view. Sometimes mighty Nature seems bent on heightening the element of drama in the trivial accidents of human existence: it was just then that two of the great nomadic rain-clouds rolled apart and our troubled scene was abruptly bathed in brilliant sunlight.

A child's attention will always be caught by simple illusions. What remains most vivid in my memory of that spectacle is the quaint appearance of the sunken ferry's passengers, who now—as the waggon's floor was only just submerged—seemed to be standing on the surface of the stream. At this stage I was sorry not to be with them, for I felt that to walk on water must be a proud and stirring experience. But the change of situation had come too suddenly for the children actually involved—one could tell from a sharper note in their crying that the incident had only deepened their sense of grievance—and in the rising voices of their mothers I read a similar discontent. One who seemed to escape this wave of melancholia was the Chieftain; he, still standing on the bench with his legs clinched between Kate's arms and bosom, continued to expound to Stevenage his views on the landlord-tenant relationship—I caught the words, *'The poor useth entreaties, but the rich answereth roughly. Better is the poor that walketh in his integrity.'* I am not sure whether he noticed that his boots were some four feet nearer the water than when the discussion had begun.

'There, Master Coughlin—what did I tell you!' Those words of Mairtin's were delivered so trenchantly that they brought every other voice to silence; and the silence in turn was broken by a cry of reproach from Francis:

'To entice the public into a boat like that—I tell you, Patrick Coughlin, it's a shame and scandal, it's an act of hell-begotten wickedness that'll blacken Ireland's name for centuries to come.'

But Desmond, standing like his grandfather on the bench, spoke as it were from a rostrum, and his superb delivery made every other protest seem feeble by contrast. *'That settles it!'* he said, pointing at Stevenage with the inexorable hand and arm of a Prophet Nathan. 'Here we have attempted murder, naked and undisguised. You will have the goodness, Mr Captain, to tell the scoundrel who employs you that the patience of the O'Kneales has been tried beyond the final bearing. When it comes to floating a ruined hulk on one of Ireland's noblest rivers—when a man won't stop at drowning women and children by the cartload so he can batten on the profits of a stolen crossing—then that criminal has put himself outside the final tolerance of civilized man. You can tell him we will bring an action. We will hire the finest lawyers from the courts of Dublin. We will prosecute the murderer Macartney to the last gasp of his putrefying reputation—till he'll go to jail with gladness to escape the vengeance of the widows and the orphans, to hide his blood-stained features from the odium and the shame.'

'Selah!' the Chieftain added. 'Selah! Amen!'

At the opening of Desmond's address the Captain's horse had turned to face the grounded waggon, and it stayed perfectly motionless till the final chords had sounded. (Had I underrated that animal's intelligence?) Relieved of my responsibilities as towing-hand I was able to observe the Captain's face attentively. It showed little emotion. Retrospectively I see that he may have been heartened by the physical situation, which was now a good deal in his favour: while the side of the river where he stood was the one he lived on, the rival party were separated from their homes —and largely from their spouses—by dikes, too wide to jump, of muddy water. Clearly some time must elapse before the O'Kneales could open the legal campaign of which they had given him notice. In a few moments, however, the element of chance which has ruled the issue of so many historic battles came to reduce his tactical advantage.

It was Queen Victoria who restored to the encounter its lost mobility.

A noisy outburst from Edward Carson made me look upstream, where, on the farther side, I caught sight of Rosa's scarlet blouse above an extensive brake of whin, and almost simultaneously the sound of her laughter, like that of distant machine-gun fire, was lapping against our eardrums. The Queen, when she emerged from the scrub, was moving faster than I had thought possible for one of her species. She was clearly under her own control; what was in her mind one cannot tell, but it looked as if she had got wind (literally) of Carson's presence and was determined to rejoin him. That purpose was frustrated by the stream. Her next movements would be hard to explain, but neither her kind nor her sex has an unquestioned reputation for constructive reasoning. Seeming suddenly to realize the propinquity of Coughlin's ass she swung about, trotted to his side and nipped him in the withers: then, her rider still helpless with mirth, she tore away in the direction of Bowistown.

'That beast is the one for foolishness,' I heard Francis say. 'With just a pair of wings she'd be a dragonfly.'

Perhaps, girl-like, she had meant Coughlin's ass to follow her, and if so she had a notable success. That creature had so far behaved with a slightly priggish docility, often casting incredulous glances at his companion's graceless locomotion, as if he were a convent schoolgirl obliged to attend a corybantic orgy. His virtue was not, however, proof against Victoria's challenge: in a moment, without reference to his master's wishes, he was off in pursuit. It was now the horse's turn to seem censorious—to screw his head and watch these caricatures of his own species with an air of sublime detachment—but very shortly he too succumbed to the lawless contagion. Suffering, perhaps, from a crick in the neck, he suddenly swung about with an agility which greatly surprised me. It surprised his rider as well. The joint performance of horse and man was too swiftly over for me to follow it closely, but I should say there was a weakness in synchronization; all I distinctly remember is the sight of the horse cantering after the donkeys at a gait which, for all its stiffness, seemed insolently leisured, and that of the Captain, far from leisured, in ponderous pursuit. Again I felt sorry for the kithless Englishman. I hoped he would not imagine that the ribald cries which broke from all the marooned women had anything to do with him.

At supper I heard Kevin giving his mother a summary of the Memorial proceedings:

'A blithe and blessed day it's been for everyone. I tell you, mam-darlin', Desmond does better every year that comes, he has the whole of history put together like a fob-watch. A bit long, maybe, for some of the bantlings.'

'But Mairtin tells me,' Greta said, 'there was some small botheration with Pat Coughlin's ferry.'

'Och, indeed—Paddy Coughlin's past the age to keep a ferry-boat in any proper state for public employment. The girls might have got their skirts wet coming ashore, it was a lucky chance they were soaked from the rain already. But the day had no luck in it for Rosa. The Queen was in her mood of uncollaboration, they neither of them got to the Remembrance till after it was done.'

I often wish I had seen more of my cousin Greta—Greta M'Taurey, as my other relations never ceased to call her. I have a number of her letters to Kevin, written in the pretty, even hand which she doubtless acquired in the Presbyterian College for Girls at Enniskillen, but with a force and uberty of phrasing which can hardly, I think, be credited to that renowned gymnasium. Those letters alone would convince me that Sawson O'Kneale's widow was a person of more intricate mental structure than I, as a child, perceived in the tiny, bright-eyed woman who had entered the world some sixty years before I had and whose path so casually crossed my own; and this conviction is supported by every intimate of hers whom I have been able to question. Her tongue, often incisive, spun a web which screened the breadth and depth of her affections. She was servant rather than ruler of her numerous family, yet her influence was variously manifest in each of the children. On losing her heart to the scapegrace Sawson she had 'turned Catholic' with an outward indifference which might argue that these matters touched her lightly, if at all. Strangely, those who knew her best have said that the opposite was true: wayward as she sometimes seemed in her behaviour, her intrinsic life was steeped in her religion.

On that short visit to Bowistown I saw her mainly as a busy *mère de famille*, a figure of termless energy absorbed in producing at frequent intervals some kind of meal for her swarming descendants. But on the last night I had one memorable glimpse of her as a woman who could have lived richly on her inward resources.

Because we had to start at five next morning Kevin put me to bed early, and shortly afterwards retired himself to the loft where, as I have said, he slept above me. I had been asleep probably for an hour or so when an urgent voice came into my dreams:

'Kevin! Kevin, darlint, are you awake now? I have Father Killalee here to see you. Will I bring him up to where you are?'

That voice must have stirred me to wakefulness slowly; when my eyes opened I saw, by the light of a table-lamp which Greta was holding, that a marvellously fat man in soutane and cincture was already most of the way up the ladder which led to the loft. Above him, Kevin's face was dimly visible in the trap-door frame.

'Three more steps, Father,' Kevin was saying a little anxiously, 'and I'll have a grip on you myself. 'Twill be easy after that.'

'Now don't bustle me, Kevin,' the priest answered, panting between the words, 'I'm not so young as I was when I was a boy.'

I did not stir. My night-life under Mavrusha's management had taught me that from time to time much of interest may be witnessed by one who has the rudimentary sense to lie doggo when he is supposed to be asleep, and here, plainly, were the elements of drama—as when a huge vessel is being guided into a graving dock with inches to spare on either side. Nor was I disappointed. With no little effort, Father Killalee had ascended far enough for Kevin, stretching down, to start hauling him by the scruff of the cassock when the rung he stood on snapped. For a few moments, then, he hung on Kevin's hands, uttering little cries of exhaustion, merriment and fear, while Kevin, above, wheezed like a spent athlete and Greta, below, stood quivering with stifled laughter. 'I can't hold you, Father,' Kevin gasped, 'will you try for the next rung!' 'No use!' the priest panted back, 'I'll try for the last one!' and as Kevin let him go he did so. It was an unfair trial—the rung could not be expected to bear that weight with momentum added. Nor could the rung next below. A quick succession of small reports—each crack of breaking wood partnered by a little grunt of human disappointment—came to its climax in an awesome thud when the person of Father Killalee arrived like a roughly handled mailbag on the floor.

''Twas gravity that fought against me,' Father Killalee said.

As his laughter began to spirt like wine from a broken wineskin, Greta's was finally stanched. She whispered,

'If you'd keep as quiet as you can, Father! We have a wee boy from England in the bed here fast asleep.'

'Have no fear, Mrs O'Kneale!' the priest roared, struggling to his feet, shaking the room with his gargantuan mirth, emitting gobbets of a sound like coarse fabric being torn apart. 'I would not disturb the repose of a young child,' he bellowed, planting his massive behind within inches of my feet, 'whether he's from Salt Lake City, Kandahar or Sligo Bay.'

In truth I think the man had been a good deal frightened, and that shaken nerves were responsible for the effervescent state in which I first saw him; by the time that Kevin had descended what was left of the ladder and settled beside his mother on the ottoman he had recovered a measure of sobriety. Greta had placed the lamp on a sugar box; in its placid light I saw through my eyelashes a profile which a novice pastrycook might have fashioned out of dough, except that the eye was a work of such mastery as Holbein's, and the mouth so sparely cast that it seemed entirely foreign to the tumid flesh above and below. As his agitation subsided his voice grew quiet and musical, infused with an unmistakable affection:

'Kevin, dear son, it's a troublesome priest you have about you, spoiling your fine stairs and your beauty sleep.'

'Ah, the sleep's of no consequence, Father,' Kevin said, buttoning the coat he had added to his nightshirt. 'And the grand stairway you've bent a little out of shape, that's just a small piece of the Macartney property.'

The priest nodded sagaciously. 'It's the trouble with Mr Macartney,' he said, '—if the matter may be mentioned without departing from charity—that he will not maintain his belongings in substantial order. The Hard Post ferry, now— it's been in a sickly state for as far back as I remember.'

'Is that so, Father? That's bad news for all of us.'

'And now they're telling me Pat Coughlin has mislaid it altogether.'

'Indeed? He would feel the loss of it sadly. It was a shame to load an old man with that responsibility.'

I found myself observing Kevin's mother. I cannot have known so early in life the work of Josef Israels, but he is the master whose interiors I think of whenever I recall that vision of Greta in the lamplight—the doll-small head with its spume of wild, whitening hair; the face so long shrivelled to the colour and corrugation of fallen beech leaves that no further change seems possible, so motionless that the living, watchful eyes appear to belong to some other, hidden creature. Her stillness, I believe, was seldom that of repose; rather, it came from an immense vitality held exactly in restraint. Now, while I watched, her lips grew restless: it was plain that she could not indefinitely wait for the flow of masculine trivialities to peter out. At the first small

154

pause, then, she said intently,

'Kevin, love, Father Killalee has wonderful news. Will you just hold your dear foolish tongue and listen while he tells you.'

'Och, I wouldn't call it wonderful,' Killalee objected. 'I would rather say it puts an end—it *can* put an end—to a piece of trouble which ought never to have come about. I took the liberty—as indeed I had the right—to send a letter to the Prior of St Finnian's College—'

'And a finely written letter it was!' Greta said. 'He had the kind consideration to let me see the wording before he put the stamp on it.'

'Indeed, you might say, Kevin, your mother herself did the best part of the writing.'

'Ah, that's nonsense, Father—I did no more than suggest a word or two.'

'And beautiful words they were, Mrs O'Kneale.'

It was Kevin who sat silent now, his eyes moving gravely from the priest's face to his mother's, from hers to his; as if, like me, he was attending a play which was always some distance above his head.

'I put it to Canon Armiss,' the priest continued, 'that the difference which happened between yourself and Father Sestino was not so big a matter after all—a case, perhaps, of a bit of the devil we have in all of us, and each of the two not observing at the time the other's point of view. I said that in my opinion—and did I not know you from a baby-child better than most men—you had always felt in your heart and mind a true vocation to the priesthood. It would be tragedy, I told him, if a pin-size disagreement— a matter of conflicting temperament—was to rob the Church of a priest that would have the holy fire in him to serve Her faithfully. Well, today, now, I have the Canon's answer.'

'He'll take you back!' Kevin's mother burst out.

Fascinated by the tournament of words, I caught the blaze of joy in Greta's exclamation—the dullest child could not have missed it—and I thought that flame must set the faces of the men alight. There I was mistaken. Father Killalee's face remained intent and troubled, Kevin's expressionless.

'They'll take me back,' Kevin echoed woodenly. And then he said, 'With some conditions, I suppose?'

The priest hesitated. 'The Prior,' he said slowly, 'is hoping you will see the need for an apology of some kind to Father Sestino. It would need to be made before the other novices —that, you'll understand, is because the act of indiscipline was performed before them all. Now listen, dear son: it would be a sad thing, surely—a tragic thing—if you lost the prize of your high calling for just the fault of being stubborn.'

'Stubborn?' Kevin repeated, as if waking from a heavy sleep. 'You're saying I'm to ask the pardon of Father Sestino for the small hammering I gave him? And that's what the Prior is saying?'

'Ah now, Kevin, you must understand how it is with a man in Father Sestino's position. He has to think of his authority, else how can he do the work he's charged with?'

'Indeed? Then, Father, he shall care for his own situation, and I must be left to care for mine.'

At those words of Kevin's his mother may have caught her breath: I know that my eyes were drawn to her face before she spoke, and I remember being a little scared by the intensity of sadness in her eyes—that ancient grief which, as I recognize it now, must always torment the mothers of self-willed sons. She said, with a passion clothed in quietness,

'Kevin, that's pride! It's nought but sinful pride and arrogance to flaunt yourself against God's Holy Church.'

To the child stealthily watching the scene, held by the faces which the lamplight paled and magnified, it was astonishing that a grown-up man could be spoken to like that. I marvelled still more at the way Kevin flinched, as if his mother had struck him in the face. Just then it looked as if he might burst into tears—had I not discovered that my father, even older than he, was capable of weeping! But I was saved from so disconcerting a spectacle. A long silence fell; then, in a voice subdued but never wavering, the answer came:

'If it's pride, Mam, then it works so deep in me I'm past salvation. I've told you, surely, Will Dohben was my friend. There were boys with a bigger head-piece—he'd never involved himself in too much schooling—but you wouldn't find a better creature for his decency and kindness. Or a better Catholic either, to my observation. And that was the one Father Sestino has to pick on, to make the poor fellow's life a burden with his penalties and impositions and the dirty edge of his sly, sarcastic tongue. I tell you, Mam—I tell you, Father—I've seen that boy at nearly midnight still in the grammar-room by Father Sestino's orders, with a book open he could neither learn nor make the smallest sense of, and no food since the early morning, and crying as if they had the torture on him. It came to the time I could stand it no more, when Will was doing the best he could with his Greek translation and that great slimy blackguard was making him a joke to set the whole class sniggering. So I took the liberty to tell him—this great spittle-shooting Father Sestino—he was a muck-mouthed rattlesnake who'd no claim to call himself a teacher or a college-man or any kind of Catholic priest. And little good did that announcement do to poor Will Dohben. But now and then the telling of a simple truth is worth a sacking.'

He stopped. He had turned white and his jaw was quivering, as if his attack on the sardonic teacher had occurred only a minute earlier. But now, relaxing, he turned to clasp his mother's arm, and to bend until his forehead rested on her shoulder. I heard him say,

'*Mo mhurnin*, I'd give my eyes to go the way you're wanting. But not my tongue. Did Father Sestino ever say to Will that he was sorry! How should I grovel to a man that abused a helpless creature and would never ask his pardon! Sure, it would get me back into my own vocation. And with that hypocrisy behind me, how would I show my face again to God or man!'

My grandfather had still not died when Kevin and I got back to Castlemagonagh. Unjustly, I regarded this as a black mark against Howard, who had sent me off for a boring weekend at Bowistown on the pretext that his father needed a quiet spell to die in. The true fact, in my present belief, is simply that the old man had fought with success against the indignity of dying in his deceased brother-in-law's hotel.

He did, however, die in 1913, laughing heartily at one of his own stories, in the Second Class smoking room of the Finnish steamship *Hyrynsalmi*, a few miles off the coast of Ecuador.

4

Helma Examined

I have mentioned the talk on education and kindred topics which Anastasia and I had just before her first session with Helma. That conversazione was continued after the interruption. My sister said that of all the governesses she had ever endured 'this German person' was far the stupidest and most pig-headed. I felt obliged to answer, in effect, that it is always the unteachable who complain most noisily about their teachers. We had still failed to reach agreement when we were summoned to luncheon.

'*It is the shared meal,*' says the philosopher Duléry, '*which preserves and reinvigorates the unity of a human family.*' I have sometimes wondered whether there was in our family some subliminal flaw which interfered with the phenomenon he mentions, for during mealtimes at Howes Croft the signs of consanguineous harmony were never obvious to me. On this occasion Anastasia's face wore a look as friendly as Caligula's, and after staring hard at Helma for a few minutes she launched a sudden, gratuitous attack on Semyon:

'Semyon, what d'you think's gone wrong with the Russian soldiers? If they'd only fight properly—all those millions— we'd have beaten the filthy Germans long ago.'

'Anastasia, tais-toi!' Sonya said automatically, and that gave time for Semyon to mount his counter-offensive:

'You ask me why? Then, Miss Anastasia, I tell you why. It is because the Russian soldiers will not fight for a very few people to live in laziness and luxity so all the rest can starve themselves all day long. Who do you think it comes for, this war when after the soldiers are all killed they still have nothing to eat? It is for fat ladies like peacocks to march about

159

in their coaches and fill up their stomachs with caviare while a servant does her hair and is starving all the time.'

As he delivered this review of the eastern situation the obsolescent anarchist was pointing his fork with a whole potato attached to it at my sister, but his angry little eyes were fastened on Irina Nikolayevna. She, befogged by his unconventional phraseology, said rather nervously to Anastasia,

'Yes, Monsieur Semyon and I are agreed on this—for bravery in war there is nobody can match with the Russian soldier.'

'You're *not* agreed!' said Pavel, who had arrived with a second supply of potatoes, in an undertone designed to penetrate the hull of a battle cruiser.

'Be quiet, Pavel!' Sonya said. 'Nobody is praying for your opinion, and the potatoes are not cooked in the middle.'

Anastasia, as if giving a chairman's ruling, said, 'Well, I don't really care who beats these beastly Germans, as long as someone makes a good job of it, for always.'

Again Sonya pounced on her: 'Anastasia, if you cannot talk sensibly with your mouth full of meat and gravy you will altogether leave the dining saloon.'

While that conference was in progress I, racked with embarrassment, was covertly glancing at Helma. She, empty-eyed, attentive to all the practical courtesies (passing the bread to Irina, pouring water for me), might have been deaf to Anastasia's poisonous innuendoes, except that a slight quivering of her lips told me she heard them perfectly. I looked towards Sonya, who, in turn, was signalling to Howard at the other end of the table for his support. That was useless. My father, as always when a difficult lecture impended, had surrounded his plate with a rampart of text-books; he was shovelling cauliflower into his mouth with his left hand while making notes with his right, and all we heard from him was a spirt of small obscenities whenever the functions of the two hands were absently interchanged. I ached for this dreadful meal to end. In that period I was visited from time to time by the fear that if Anastasia were suddenly to die—and an immature theology suggested she might well be destroyed by lightning at any moment—I should find it hard to make a respectable show of brotherly sorrow. Today, however, I was troubled by no such cares: if my sister suddenly expired in fearful agonies I would chant the Toreador song as they lowered her coffin into the grave.

It was perhaps a weakness of Sonya's to rely too much on her intuitions, to cast her plans with insufficient ratiocination. Unquestionably she was right, that afternoon, to invent an errand for Helma, who was sent by bus and tube to Camden Town to deliver a copy of *Slovo o polku Igoreve* to a poor blind man who had once been postmaster at Lipetsk. But I think she was mistaken in supposing that Anastasia's mulligrubs would be relieved by a change of juvenile society.

Anastasia and I were not even warned: we were in the kitchen, helping Pavel to make a kind of vodka from some apples which had gone mouldy, when Mavrusha called from the hall that some children had come to see us. These, we found, were the two Dalbeatties, from a house near the top of Parson Street, and their invasion resulted from one of Sonya's parental brainstorms. Angela Dalbeattie was a year younger than I, with a broad, contented face and with fat white legs going up into a lather of lacy petticoats; her elder brother Osbert had spectacles and very good manners acquired at an expensive prep-school—he could not move a yard without apologizing for some fancied misdemeanour. After tea we told this insufferable pair that we had invented a new game called Cossak Companies and took them to the attic, where they had to keep as quiet as mice, we said, until we shouted up the first Clue for Action. To ensure their co-operation we took away and hid the ladder, then we went to continue our own conversation in the garden, where at that time of day one could generally hope for a little peace and quiet.

Though I knew that girls' brains functioned rather dottily

I was surprised to find that Anastasia had really worked herself into a state resembling high fever over Helma's appointment.

'It looks to me,' she said, throwing bits of stick on a smouldering bonfire which Loe the gardener had lit that morning, 'as if I'm the only person in this family who ever thinks about the war at all. I mean, what's the sense of fighting the beastly Germans if we let their dung-faced females sneak over here and butter them up and make them all comfy and let them propagate their Hunnish ideas to people who are young and impromptu, telling me that foul man Frederick the Great was a phosphate or something and all that buggle about the Hun poet Goitre who I happen to know did rude things with every woman he set his eyes on. I know I've got to be educated because obviously I can't get married, to get married you've got to be thin, with fuzzy hair like Susan Thornley and a loving sort of giggle, but I can't see why I can't have some say in who's going to educate me.'

It was really quite fascinating to hear this poor old bolster putting her case with so much passion. I felt a curious desire to lend a hand, but at the age of eleven one is indifferently equipped for introducing new ideas to a pitifully cloistered mind; I could only say, in a moderate tone,

'Well, I wouldn't call Helma dung-faced. Wouldn't you say it was more the colour of boiled potatoes just before the new potatoes start in June? And anyway, if she got married it shows that anyone can—it shows it doesn't really matter whether you look like the Queen of Sheba or a toadstool that's been trodden on.'

This fresh approach caught her attention. She asked, 'Do you think she really is married?'

'Well, of course—or was, rather. That's why her kid isn't indiscriminate. I told you all about it just before lunch, only you were spitting and sizzling too much to listen. I've found out she used to be married to Kevin, when he was alive.'

'But I said to you yesterday she might have been something to do with Kevin and you said she couldn't have.'

'Well, I've found out now she could.'

'But I thought when Kevin was here he was nice, and quite sensible. He must have been absolutely mad.'

She was beginning to sound calmer, and I felt I had shown some skill in irenic pleading. It was now desirable, I thought, to turn her mind to less emotive topics.

'It looks as if this bonfire's going out,' I said. 'It'll be hard on Loe if he finds he's got to get it going again tomorrow morning.'

That too was a successful move; we both began to work hard at reviving the fire, and in this activity Anastasia showed a surprising intelligence. The stuff on top was hopelessly damp, she said, so we got Loe's wheelbarrow out of the shed to serve as more palatable nourishment. The barrow was fairly old but it had new legs; those might be useful if ever I decided to make my glider a biplane, and we managed, with Anastasia lying across the barrow while I tugged, to get them off more or less intact. After that it was disappointing that the main part did not catch light directly we put it on top of the fire, but I persuaded Stasie to dance about on it to break it up. This started a smell of burnt rubber from her goloshes, which was a smell she liked; truly she seemed quite happy at last, and I was beginning to think the Helma worry was over, when I heard the 'Take Cover' sounding. That dismal ululation might have gone unnoticed—we heard it so often—had it not been followed by rebellious cries from Brigid and Polina inside the house: it was an *idée fixe* of Mavrusha's, probably derived from some atavistic super- stition, that all the babies must be taken down to the coal cellar whenever an air raid was in the offing, and they always resented this displacement. So undignified an uproar was bound to disturb our concentration on the work in hand, and it was not surprising that a noise with martial implications should recall to Anastasia her current grievance.

'Oh, it's too stupid!' she said. 'I get just one afternoon off from my ghastly education, I come out here to do some quiet work on a bonfire and in two ticks the whole place is buzzing with these idiotic Taubes. That's what comes of fawning on these Hun widows.'

Losing the thread of her logic, I could only say, 'There isn't one Taube that I can see, unless it's going round and round inside that cloud over there, in which case the poor Hun pilot must be getting pretty dizzy.' Then, 'Look,' I said, 'I don't think this stupid barrow's going to properly catch. We'll have to break it up smaller.'

Though she made no answer, Anastasia seemed to see the sense of what I said, and she got the barrow back on to terra firma by a rather clever hooking action with her left foot. For some time then we were busy tearing the thing apart; she was burning her fingers a good deal, but she seemed hardly to notice that—I fancy she had fallen into a daydream in which she was preparing a stake for Helma to be burnt at. I know the next thing she said was,

'Really, it would be too idiotic if we had a bomb dropped here to kill the whole lot of us while that O'Kneale woman is having tea and crumpets with Simeon Kozlov at Camden Town.'

'On the other hand,' I said to mollify her, 'it would be rather a rag, from your point of view, if they dropped a bomb on Camden Town which minced up Helma and Simeon together into tiny bits, which the poor could make into sandwiches with the crumpets, while nothing dropped on us at all.'

She would not be comforted, however. 'Now *is* that likely!' she said with her usual obstinacy. 'That woman must be getting messages all the time to say which bits of England they're going to bomb next. Obviously if it was Camden Town she'd be rushing off to somewhere like St Albans.'

This was an absorbing theme, and the afternoon was again becoming one of enjoyment. The bonfire was at last beginning to respond to the help we were giving it, and with this encouragement Anastasia worked harder than before, tearing the wood quite furiously into small pieces and using swear-words which I had not imagined were known to girls as she kept burning her hands in fresh places. With a good deal of patience I explained that I had scientifically investigated Helma's mode of life and was now satisfied that she was not in communication with the Enemy. This brought from Anastasia a long and eloquent but somewhat incoherent reply; every now and then she took in a chestful of smoke which made her cough and splutter, so that her rhetoric came to me in short, uneven lengths, as if from an early type of gramophone:

'... not going to propagate me, however hard she tries ... Sonya thinks I'm still just a kid, she thinks I can still just lap up whatever they tell me, all these squalorous widows and wurbling refugees ... Well, *I* think if our soldiers are getting killed and mucked about all day long and having pure hell in those filthy Flanders the least a person like me can do is to show a bit of patriotism, even if I'm the only living person left who does.'

I was greatly interested in this display of afflatus by a person who did not as a rule seem capable of mental activity. By now we were both more or less encircled by the thickening smoke, which a light breeze was wafting this way and that, and I was too much preoccupied to notice that a posse of grown-ups had approached us until Howard's voice came to assault my ears from a few feet away.

'That gardening fellow,' he was saying rather pettishly, 'he will always choose the least convenient day to start one of his bonfires. Look at all this dirty smoke now! On the last daylight raid we had a beautiful view from just where you're standing now. This time the smoke's going to spoil the whole picture.'

I moved back to see whom he was talking to and nearly collided with Mrs Dalbeattie, who had come to round up her young; she was the sort of parent who did that—I imagine that Hendon, in her flocculent mind, was carpeted with gangsters who were paid to kidnap smarmy-mannered boys and little odious girls with fat white thighs. My father was always soapily attentive to this lamentable woman, in the hope (I think) that her husband, who was something high up in the Board of Education, might put him in touch with people ready to pay large fees for fairly tedious lectures on Florentine Quattrocento painting.

'Ah, well,' he continued, 'if the German boys will steer their machines a bit lower today we may see something of them yet.' Then he deigned to notice me. 'Ah, Ryan, is that where you are! And Stasie too! What would you two be up to, now?'

Such brainless questions are scarcely worth an answer, and I gave him the first which came into my head. 'We're playing Joan of Arcs,' I told him.

'Good!' he said, with a vacant smile at Sonya, who was standing beside him, and he added fatuously, 'It's a grand way of learning history.' Then he turned to Mrs Dalbeattie again, giving her the warm, ingratiating smile which, I am bound to say, generally went down well with the junior sex. 'I think I hear the guns starting now,' he said hopefully.

'Oh, do you, Mr Hutchinson?' was her tepid reply.

She was a flimsy creature of the kind a fashion-artist dashes off to fill an empty corner in some advertisement; glancing at her Dutch-doll face, I myself could see that Howard's efforts to entertain her were falling on unfruitful ground, but it was left to Sonya—naturally a connoisseuse of maternal fidgets—to interpret her distrait expression.

'What have happened to Angèle and Osbaire?' Sonya asked me abruptly, after staring into the bonfire with what I took to be suspicious eyes.

Because our juvenile guests had not been at the forefront of my mind I was momentarily stumped for an answer. But Anastasia, with a flash of inspiration which took my breath away, promptly supplied one:

'I think they went to wash their hands,' she said.

She could not have done better. In those days that homely euphemism was generally as near as anyone would venture to a region recognized by English bourgeois society as one of moral quicksand: Mrs Dalbeattie was as likely to pursue so scatological a topic as to go dancing naked in Trafalgar Square. As if fortune were altogether on the side of Anastasia and me the sound of guns had become distinctly audible, and now the one at Summers Lane, not far away, began to bark like a close-chained dog, rattling the windows behind us. My father's enthusiasm mounted to a point where the proposal of other interests would have been a monstrous unkindness.

'Sure, they'll be coming this way after all,' he said, in a voice which recalled the father of the Prodigal Son. 'Will I hoist you on the shed, Mrs Dalbeattie, so you get the best chance of a view?'

His optimism was justified. In a stretch of clear sky between the chimneys we presently saw, far away, what might have been a small swarm of insects, travelling very slowly in our direction. It was an undramatic spectacle, relieved only by the tiny puffs of smoke which kept appearing fore and aft of the flight, but my father bent himself to showing it off as if it were a sumptuous pageant of his own devising.

'The ones on the outside, now, those are the English machines, Mrs Dalbeattie. The Gothas are all clustered in the middle there—that's so they can protect each other with their rifles.'

Here, it seemed to me, was a technical inaccuracy which should not be allowed to pass.

'Actually they're Taubes,' I said. 'Not Gothas.'

'Then we must be living backwards,' Howard answered somewhat discourteously, 'since the German High Command stopped using Taubes for this kind of work at least two years ago.'

'You can tell they're Taubes,' I said in firm though respectful tones, 'because they're biplanes. Gothas are monoplanes.'

'Do you know what the word "Taube" means?' he countered. 'It's the German for "dove". God forbid, Ryan, that I should presume to question your extensive knowledge of aeronautics—but have you ever seen a dove with two parallel sets of wings? I never have myself, but then I'm a mere painting fellow with no scientific learning at all.'

Though the subject was of interest I decided not to press my point, especially as I thought that Howard might unaccountably be right—possibly I had got the names the wrong way round. I felt moreover that our technological discussion might be boring for the ladies. Already it was apparent that Mrs Dalbeattie lacked the intelligence to follow either Howard's views or mine; she seemed to be straining her ears towards more distant sounds, as if hoping to pick out that of a favourite gun; while Sonya, in her feminine way, had now turned her attention to a purely social aspect of the occasion: Semyon had come out to see the raid in his hideous undervest and threadbare braces, and she, always sensitive about the comportment of her protégés, felt it necessary to expostulate:

'Semyon, I have told you before, in this house you need to wear your respectful clothes when you come to watch the aeroplanes.'

The noise all round was becoming an obstacle to conversation. Since daylight raids were few and far between it was natural that the gun crews should be extravagant in their rowdy labours—the appalling racket from the Summers Lane gun would alone have made it impossible to express one's views in an orderly, convincing way—and this martial pandemonium was reinforced by a constant hullabaloo from Brigid and Polina, still revolting against their unnatural confinement. Some element in what would now be called the 'unconscious' of that foolish pair must have made them allergic to coal cellars; regardless of Mavrusha's scolding they were hammering with their little fists on the cellar door, and their mutinous vociferation even provoked my brother Vladimir—by nature a genial infant—to howls of a tuneless and pessimistic kind. My father, still intent on parading himself as an expert in military affairs, had almost to shout to make himself heard.

'You see what they're doing wrong? The boys are firing
168

too far back—they ought to make allowance for the machines moving forward.'

He was at once corrected by Pavel, who had left his cooking pots to join us. 'It is the vind,' Pavel said. 'If the vind start from the east side, then you must shoot to the right—any Russian shooter will tell them that.'

But his thesis in turn was revised by Semyon, who said unequivocally, 'The English soldiers will aim right when they are given a proper wage. With a capitalist régime all the gun shooters are always underpaid.'

The raiders were now almost directly overhead. Flying very high, they were still a spectacle of no great interest, but the scientific talk—even when bedevilled by the tedious uproar from Summers Lane—made the occasion a pleasurable one for me: at that period I had few opportunities for listening to men in conference, and I remember feeling that though I was taking no active part in the discussion my sex gave me an honorary share in it, while the womenfolk, unable to grasp the finer points in aerial warfare, were no more than bemused spectators. For at least one of us, then, the afternoon was passing quite agreeably when a rapid sequence of mischances came to deform it. The first was the explosion of a bomb—perhaps intended, reasonably enough, to silence the Summers Lane gun. It fell, as we learnt afterwards, no nearer than the golf course (where it put the sixth green out of use for the rest of the war) but its blast shattered a number of local windows, including some of our own. I myself—owing perhaps to my encounter in infancy with General Almore—was over-sensitive to loud noises, and this one, combined with the feeling of being struck by an invisible bludgeon, would have shaken a child far less impressionable than I was then, but the brouhaha which followed was more alarming still: together with the sound of Osbert Dalbeattie crying 'Let us out!' in a voice pitched unnaturally high we heard a succession of piercing squeals from Angela—the eldritch cry of the suburban child at bay. That was the one sound which disturbed my father. Having started to resume his lecture on defensive artillery, he broke off to say irritably,

'Ryan, if your friends are stuck in the water closet you'd best go and haul them back to land.'

I should have hurried to oblige him—*mutatis mutandis*—but Mrs Dalbeattie was faster off the mark. The dynamic of maternal solicitude never ceases to astound me: before I had taken my hands out of my pockets that woman, with her fat feet squashed into finical court shoes, her legs shackled by one of the tightest skirts in Middlesex, was half-way to the french windows of the morning-room. Almost simultaneously Sonya was starting in pursuit: those cries of inflated discontent had alerted her as well, and however ignorant of English *mores* she had an acute sense of social obligation. She would have followed her restless visitor into the house, had not her movement been interrupted by a fresh arrival.

I can think of no one less theatrical in appearance or behaviour than Helma, yet often she seemed to have a gift for dramatic entrances. On this occasion I suppose she had simply fulfilled her mission at Camden Town as expeditiously as possible and returned by the next train; it was just by chance that, at the moment when Mrs Dalbeattie like a vexed rhinoceros *en grande tenue* was charging into the house, the figure of Helma, neat, sober, dutiful, should have issued from the tradesmen's door. Sighting my mother, Helma smiled devotedly, executed the small, respectful bob she had doubtless used for her professor at school, and advanced in a soldierly manner to address her; just then the nearer guns were silent, as if they had recognized the placing of the bomb as a decent admonition, and I caught almost every word of her virtuous little speech:

'The children in the upper loft ... much frightened. If you will tell me, please, where to find the ladder I shall quickly bring them down.'

Sonya's first reaction was to turn, in formidable anger, towards me, but I must have been wearing the look of utter bewilderment which—I have been told—often wrapped itself about my face on occasions such as this. Naturally, then, everyone stared at Anastasia.

Anastasia, standing almost on top of the bonfire, was worth staring at. Her work and mine had yielded fruit, the bits of Loe's barrow had really caught at last and the great plume of ochreous smoke was illumined by a core of lively flame. That by itself was a stirring sight, and the juxtaposition of Anastasia's person made it still more imposing. Normally, in those years, I thought of my sister's contribution to the world's aesthetic riches as a small one, but now her whole appearance—her skirt smouldering at the hem, the black and bleeding hands, the brick-red, sweaty face framed in a thicket of lawless hair—was so superbly matched with the fire itself that I was truly spellbound by the beauty of the total image. In that statuesque, defiant figure was the grandeur one associates with martyrs; and in the furious question which she flung at Helma I heard—clean contrary to my own will and sentiments—the triumphant voice of martyrdom:

'Frightened? What are they frightened about?'

The challenge had been better left unanswered, but a conscientious and scholarly young woman could never allow the threads of such an interchange to remain untied.

'I expect,' Helma said, her lips moving with the precision of a ballet dancer's legs, 'that the bombing can have frightened them.'

Anastasia stretched one arm as an orator does. She said, *'And whose fault is the bombing!'*

There are sequences in films which—today—force me to shut my eyes. Likewise I close my mind against the extreme moral discomfort of the moments which followed, when the two antagonists stared at each other with icy hatred, when my mother, for once losing her temper and her head together, screamed at Anastasia to withdraw her scurrilous insinuations and she, changing instantaneously from an image of heroic vengeance to that of a scolded schoolgirl, fell into such a convulsion of almost soundless tears that I seriously wondered if she would ever recover. Even Pavel, even Semyon, looked to be somewhat troubled, as if like me they felt themselves involved in the appalling scene which had come to us with the strangeness and violence of an accident to a smoothly running train. Only Howard was apparently unaffected: he had resumed his concentration on the pageant overhead, where three British planes were fiercely attacking an invader which had straggled from the rest, and as far as I could see he was unaware of any conflict on the ground. But there my observation must have been faulty; for when the rest of us were helpless, ourselves paralysed by Anastasia's frenzy, he, glancing at the stricken girl, called with seeming inconsequence,

'Stasie, darlin', there's a chore I have in the study that's got beyond me. If you're finished with burning the wee cart I'd be glad of a hand.'

With that he went lolloping towards the house—in his casual movements you could always see the farmer's son. At first it looked as if Anastasia had not heard him, but while he waited by the french windows she stirred and, as one walking in sleep, slowly crossed the lawn to join him. I have an oddly stereoscopic memory of his shaggily coated arm coming lazily round her shoulders as they entered the house side by side.

I think their tête-à-tête lasted about half an hour. What transpired I do not know: Anastasia volunteered no word of it afterwards, and I was sufficiently awed by the whole affair to ask no questions.

Her lessons with Helma went on next morning. I was not there: Sonya had thoughtfully arranged for Irina Nikolayevna and me to continue our literary collaboration in another room. But because of another setback in my own educational programme I was able, some days later, to see at close quarters how the movement to civilize my sister was progressing.

I was supposed to be starting at a school in Cricklewood

kept by two brothers with the scarcely credible names of Joshua and Eustace Dribble. Two days before term began, the senior Dribble wrote to Howard to say that 'owing to unexpected pressure on our accommodation' he was regretfully obliged to cancel the arrangement for my admission and was accordingly returning the fee paid in advance for one term's schooling. My father, greeted by this letter on his return from Scotland, was greatly surprised; holding that the education of young children was a matter entirely within the female province, he had always left such correspondence to Sonya and had never heard of Mr Dribble. Uncharacteristically my mother had kept Mr Dribble's earlier letter. She said that Howard must immediately put the matter in the hands of lawyers, 'who will send all the Dribbles into prison for their dishonesty', and he did get as far as consulting Mr Wilson, his Hendon solicitor; but Mr Wilson, who had been employed to disengage me from the aftermath of one or two negligible brushes with officious constables, advised that a legal campaign against the Dribbles was unlikely to succeed. Still slightly bemused, I think, by the sight of an unexpected cheque, my father thankfully let the matter drop.

It had long been evident from disheartening interviews between Sonya and the principals of local schools that they were all associated in a scheme of pooled intelligence. When Mr Stokes, the head of Hartside Lodge, was asked to add little Ryan Hutchinson to his galaxy of infant scholars he would send an urgent inquiry to some nerve centre of the local teaching trade and back would come exaggerated reports of my peccadilloes at other establishments—how at Miss Cubitt's Kindergarten I had 'grinned insultingly' at the First Form teacher's pronunciation of *Drogheda*, and at Manorhurst had bitten the Blackboard Monitor 'at least two inches' above her knee. This pedagogic conspiracy resulted in grievous problems for my poor mother, who was fiercely opposed to the English custom of sending young boys to boarding-schools. Very early she had tried me at the Brent Street Council School, but there I had formed an inharmonious relationship with a boy who addressed me as 'Rotten Russki', his parents had threatened legal action for 'malicious assault and battery' and the head teacher had earnestly recommended my removal to some proprietary school 'where they have time to teach manners to young hooligans'. Distressed and bewildered, Sonya had thought it best to follow his advice. Our neighbourhood—an expanding middle-class dormitory area—was fairly well equipped with private schools, but after a while the number of those where I had neither sojourned already nor been denied the opportunity to sojourn was shrinking ominously. There came a day when my mother in a mood of desperation wrote to Sir George Cave, the Home Secretary, asking if he knew of any 'good class' reformatory in the North London area which I might attend as a day-boy. She was further disheartened by a prosaic and unimaginative reply.

These scholastic difficulties stemmed chiefly from a minor element in my youthful nature—a taste for individual contests combined with a certain sensitivity about my non-English provenance. Had my childhood taken place a few years later this syndrome would have been observed and deftly classified, parents and teachers alike would have recognized in me an invalid requiring a sympathetic approach and expert therapy. But in the reign of George V the axioms of mental philosophy were not widely known, and so far from being regarded as a sufferer I was treated—especially by the educational world—as a person deliberately hostile to society. Nothing is so adhesive as a sullied reputation, and often sheer mischance deepened the disfavour in which my elders held me. If, for example, the brothers Dewson had insulted me within the curtilage of the school we were attending (Manorhurst, if I remember rightly) I should have taken appropriate action in the playground and that would have closed the matter. But it was in The Burroughs, on a fine Saturday afternoon, that 'Pig' Dewson chose to shout at me from one pavement to the other the vapid couplet, to which young Dickie Dewson added as *codetta* his girlish giggle; of necessity the next phase in that transaction took place in the centre of the carriage-way, where 'Pig' was kneeling on my neck (but Dickie with his head among the horse-droppings was under both of us) when a motor-car with a Councillor's wife in it had to swerve abruptly to by-pass our small reunion, and that intrinsically private affair must needs be witnessed by an ultracrepidarian reporter from the *North London Express and Star*. Again, it was a singular misfortune that the only boy who ever lost three teeth while wrestling with me—one Reggie Pyke, a foxy ten-year-old who thought it witty to call me 'The Russian Steam Howler'—turned out to be the sole and treasured offspring of a Police Inspector at Mill Hill. Still less—as I review the facts—was I to blame in the disastrous matter of Miss Lottie Budge, teacher of the Transition at Windsor Grange. When Miss Budge stigmatized me before the whole class as 'a rude rapscallion from the Irish bog' mere self-respect demanded that I should make a categorical protest; perhaps I acted imprudently in throwing that mannerless woman's goloshes out of the street-side window, but it was simply a harsh coincidence that one of them should have struck the forehead of an emotional neighbour whom Sonya had justifiably insulted at a meeting of the Soldiers' Dependants' Friendly and Philanthropic Society only a week before. With a little patience, some attempt at understanding, on the part of my preceptors all such troubles as these might have been avoided. In the light of today's concepts I was really a gentle-natured child, who fought with other children only to alleviate a certain loneliness, and for the pleasure of healthy exercise.

Howard, unhappily, was the last person to appreciate my psychic situation.

'Ah, it's just a sinful extravagance,' he said, 'paying decent money to these bow-bellied gurus to teach a boy whose only aim in life is to bloody the nose of every other boy he sees.'

With that obscurantist dictum, addressed to my mother at the other end of the breakfast table, he rang down the curtain on the *affaire* Dribble, and as my own patience with the educational process was long exhausted I allowed the slander to go unchallenged: I meant to discuss my future with Sonya at a more convenient time. But now my incalculable father came out with a proposal which made me miss a heart-beat:

'If Mrs O'Kneale will have the goodness to take him on,' he said light-heartedly, 'there's no reason at all why Ryan should not be schooled alongside Anastasia. Of course he'll need to follow a simpler brand of study, but if he'll use the wee portion of mother-wit God gave him he could finish up not far behind. What do you think, Mrs O'Kneale?'

'It will be a pleasure for me,' Helma said (looking and speaking, as she sometimes did, like the cheaper sort of marionette), 'to have a second pupil also.'

'But Howard,' I said, when I had got my breath back, 'you must be being funny. I'm a boy,' I reminded him. 'A boy can't be educated by a governess, at home.'

'Why not?' he asked.

To answer so naïve a question I had to borrow from a man of larger worldly experience than mine; using the words which Lieutenant 'Dare-all' Lusty had addressed to his stay-at-home cousin in *A Hero's Choice*, I said, 'Sir, it would sap my manhood.'

'Manhood!' Anastasia said in her childish way. 'A fat lot of that there is to sap!'

I had not used the last shot in my locker: from an old *Spectator* which had been lying about in the lower lavatory a sentence sprang to my support:

'It would be tantamount,' I said, 'to spiritual emasculation.'

'Ryan,' Sonya said, 'you are not to use such street-boy words. Wipe your mouth and pass the salt to Irina Nikolayevna.'

The idiot Semyon started laughing. I was nearly in tears—no one in this petit-bourgeois circle had the mental refinement to understand me.

Howard said, 'You may as well start today, while the iron is hot. Keep a note of how much your spirit is emasculated every day and report the aggregate figure once a month to me.'

By then the dining-room had proved an inconvenient site for Anastasia's mental development: Pavel was always arriving with a tray of utensils, and even when sober he would generally stay to read the papers and to fire his political opinions at anyone he found there. In view of its peace and cosiness Howard's study was chosen (by Sonya) as the alternative venue; as a rule it was free in the daytime, and it could readily be warmed by a primitive gas-fire whose angry crepitation one ceased after a while to notice. In the period when Howard had taken a fitful interest in photography one end of the room had been partitioned off with the necessary plumbing for service as a darkroom; that portion was now much used by Semyon as a laboratory—he was understood to be working on a formula for 'a humane explosive'—and his research was apt to be attended by splutterings and hissings which, with many puzzling smells, came through the partition; otherwise the study was a quiet room except for the palaver of a cuckoo-clock, some years out of adjustment and habitually eccentric in performance.

The time for lessons had been changed to nine-fifteen. I went to the study at twenty-to-ten. At the long desk-table Helma was seated in Howard's office chair, apparently lost in a one-volume Shakespeare. She glanced up when I came in and pointed perfunctorily to a chair on her right, saying,

'You will sit here, please, Ryan.'

'I always like this chair,' I replied, taking one at the far end of the table.

She continued: 'On this paper you will find some English history questions. I want you to answer those as well as you can. Your answers will tell me where we have to commence our historical study.'

To that I nodded broadmindedly, answering, 'I'll have a look at them later on.'

I had no wish to be harsh towards this woman, who was, after all, mother of the adorable Cathleen and with whom I had taken some trouble to cultivate satisfactory relations; but I felt it important at that stage to make my position clear. My father had desired me to attend these occasions. I was ready to humour his caprice. I was not, however, prepared to enter a feminine milieu *in statu pupillari*. Turning away from the table, I occupied myself for a while in studying a half-finished portrait of Pavel on Howard's main easel; it was the usual mess of unnatural greens and screaming purples—*Verlaine on Guy Fawkes Night* might well have been the title. Helma, meanwhile, was obviously impressed by my independence. All she said—as if talking to herself—was:

'Ah, Ryan is not yet ready for his studies.'

From where I sat I also had a fair view of Anastasia, who, dumped on Helma's left, was laboriously writing; she had scarcely raised her eyes when I arrived, and I concluded she was struggling with some sort of imposition. Just then it was not easy to read her face, which had congealed in a leaden caricature of itself; it would have passed for an abortive work by Madame Tussaud; but the way her body was hunched over the table—behind far back, front far down—seemed to tell me the whole story: Howard, I inferred, had broken her spirit with a full 62-gun pi-jaw, and she had now to stay in scholastic bondage until, at about nineteen, she would be allowed to put her hair up and some myopic mortal might be roped in to marry her. I was somewhat moved by this spectacle. Of course she had behaved disgracefully, and was in need of discipline; but when you see a dog miserably chained to its kennel no amount of reasoning will withstand the wave of pity which washes over you.

That was the general shape of my meditations when they were disarranged by a sudden grunt—a strange, Teutonic, pectoral sound—from my sister's gaoler. It was followed by '*Ach, du lieber Gott!*' and then, 'This English tongue, it is

178

mad, it is a jungle without a pathway!'

The vehemence in that observation was so foreign to the Helma I knew that I stared at her in some disquiet. She did not look up; as if pursuing a form of devotion, she read out, '*"We'll put you, like one who means his proper harm, in manacles"*,' and added, 'Hopeless, hopeless! This English, no one in a hundred years will learn such a tongue—every sentence in a different form, words that mean never the same thing a second time.'

It looked as if Anastasia had grown accustomed to exclamations of that sort: I thought I saw something like a smile pass across her face, but she went on steadily with her writing, only murmuring, 'English? It's the easiest language there is.'

Helma must have heard that, and I expected her to be resentful. But all she said, with a weary patience, was: ' "Manacles"—what could it mean, that word?'

'Handcuffs,' Anastasia said.

'Hand cuffs? *Ach, ja,* from the *lateinisch "manus"*. Thank you, Anastasia. But this "proper harm"—I have not understood how harm can be "proper".'

Clearly Shakespeare had put the poor woman into dreadful confusion, and I saw it was time for me to come to her rescue.

' "Proper" means "respectable",' I explained. 'You can have respectable harm, or unrespectable. In this country we don't talk much about doing the unrespectable sort of harm—Sonya will tell you about that if you really want the details. As a rule it's degurgitated from the best English families.'

My exegesis was totally ignored—I might as usefully have addressed the stern of a grazing cow. And now, with an air of assurance which greatly surprised me, Anastasia chipped in again.

'It means "his own harm",' she said. 'It's the same as *"propre"* in French.'

That made Helma sit up, much as my younger sisters did if they heard someone unwrapping a toffee.

'You are sure of this?'

'It's like *"amour propre"*,' Anastasia said laconically. 'At least, that's what Mademoiselle Letellier told me. I did *Coriolanus* with her.'

Smiling gratefully, Helma made a marginal note. She said, 'Ah—thank you—that is most useful.' And in a curiously helpless way she added, 'For me the nature of this General, this Marcius Coriolanus, is difficult to understand. It demands perhaps an English understanding.'

Anastasia nodded—I could see that in a simple, rather pathetic way the old dunce was getting quite pleased with herself. She launched out once more.

'That's more or less what Mademoiselle Letellier said. She said "Ziss Coriolanus can only be an English man. He iss a vair prood bougaire who fight on bote sides of zee var".'

'Ah, that I must keep in mind,' Helma said. 'But please, Anastasia, if you will leave your composition for one minute I shall be thankful for some more direction—there are more things I have still to understand about what you have called "this prood bougaire". Can it be he ever loved his own country? You see here—this talk he has with his mother, it's hard for me to know what all of it means. *"Then let the pebbles on the hungry beach fillip the stars."* This word "fillip" is not known to me.'

A literary question of that sort could have had no possible interest for my cowboy sister, but a girlish curiosity made her move an inch or two to look at the open book which Helma was nudging towards her. She said,

'I don't know either. "Fillip" is a thing you do with little rolled-up bits of blotting paper.'

'But of course,' I put in, 'you can do it with pebbles too.'

Neither of the two females seemed even to hear my contribution—at least, they lacked the courtesy to acknowledge it. They were sitting elbow to elbow now, their eyes stuck to the open Shakespeare, like a pair of schoolgirls sharing a copy of *The Rainbow*.

Their behaviour was not entirely a surprise to me. I had learnt a good deal about women from a friend, Gus Wipple,

180

of my Windsor Grange days; Gus, at nearly fifteen, had only been sent to the Grange because he was backward, having one loose eyeball (it wobbled in quite a remarkable way when one wrestled with him) and a Dutch mother, but he knew more about life than most of us, and he explained to me that women liked to get into tight clumps and then pretend they didn't notice any men who happened to be about—it was a dodge, he said, for making themselves feel less subjunctive to the opposing sex. But even when I remembered Gus's illumination I found it slightly provoking to be treated as no more than a piece of stage scenery. By degrees a singular desire to weep came over me, and I might even have committed that absurdity, but for the timely arrival of the person I was really aching to see.

For two or three days I had scarcely set eyes on Cathleen: more and more the heartless Mavrusha was holding her captive in the nursery, to serve—I supposed—as playmate for my dreary sisters while Mavrusha herself was valeting my brother. So, when the door was boldly opened and the neat, black-stockinged creature marched with total self-possession into the room, I felt afresh all the wonder and exhilaration of our first meeting; the world, I thought, might be overfull of unsociable women, coalescing to tease themselves with books they had no hope of understanding, but there were still others of the sex whose mere appearance transmuted everything about them, whose fragility and grace brought you the sense of a swallow's flight, of sunlight on rippled water, the flute notes in a Mozart concerto, the tang of earliest spring. One hardship supervened: facing me as she entered, the enchantress did not notice me at all. She was clutching in her pinafore some variously coloured balls of wool, attached to a sort of birdcage shaped like an hour-glass; going straight to her mother, she planted this conglomeration of wool and wire in her lap, uttering the one word, '*Mücke!*'

That sounded to me a correct appreciation.

The moment has remained in my memory as the sight of an exquisite miniature will do: it taught me for the first time that Helma O'Kneale might on occasions be beautiful. Not that the word 'beauty' would have occurred to me then; but only a cretin would have failed to see how her Teutonic face, generally taut with conscientiousness, was changed by the child's sudden presence to a soft and glowing thing, the incarnation of warmth and tender affection. My resentment of her authority was not relaxed; yet strangely, I believe that glimpse of her in an access of radiant maternity brought to an end the period in which she had figured merely as an established visitor: here was a person whom one accepted as—like Sonya—an enduring part of one's own existence.

Her mood of extreme gentleness was, however, evanescent; her smile had hardly come alight before she said quietly, deliberately, 'Cathleen, I am busy. Yes, busy. Anastasia and I have things to talk about.'

Cathleen, as far as I could see, made nothing of that. (Probably her mother, when they were alone, spoke to her mostly in German.) I thought there would be tears; and upon a mindless impulse I said, 'Here, I'll see to it!'

Without hesitation Helma accepted this solution. 'Ryan is not so busy,' she said. 'He will put it right for you.' Those words Cathleen seemed perfectly to understand, and she came at once to my side.

Here was a kind of ecstasy one knows, as a rule, only in dreams. After laying the frame and the tangled wool on my knees, the adorable small person stood close to my chair, regarding me with admiration linked to a grave expectancy; simply to watch her face—the miniature perfection of its sculpture, a faint smile which lit the tiny mouth, the trustfulness of the large dark eyes—was a pleasure I would gladly have protracted through the morning. Only, the patience of the most complaisant child might not have lasted. The privilege of keeping this divine creature at my side depended on my own practicality, on putting right the sorry mess into which her handiwork—surely through no fault of hers —had obviously fallen.

The apparatus she was using, called *Kiddiknit* or some such nauseous name, had directions in five-point type on the underside of its wooden base. These—as far as memory will reach—recommended the infant user to *'cast on in the normal manner'*, to *'repeat, now threading over and under in alternate apertures'*, and to perform other feats of mental and manual agility appropriate to a seamstress of outstanding skill and experience; they advised him or her at all costs to *'avoid overlooping two or more colours in successive circulations'*. It appeared that Cathleen had overlooked that warning. Examining the remarkable budget of knots and tangles into which she had guided her red, blue and yellow skeins, I saw that what I needed was a large open space, together with an hour of peace and solitude. Some space I did acquire by moving the whole Augean hotch-potch to the middle of the carpet where, kneeling, I could attack it from different points of the compass; but the presence of Cathleen herself, following me from point to point like a humble student of witchcraft, was equal in moral effect to that of a numerous, critical audience, and for silence the pet shop in The Burroughs would have served me just as well. The cuckoo clock was in its most loquacious mood, and some trouble which Semyon was having with his work in the darkroom produced a continuous rustle of Slavic imprecations; yet those sounds were a trivial annoyance compared with the plodding duologue between governess and pupil above and behind me:

'These workmen who drive Coriolanus out of their city, I find it hard to know what opinion Shakespeare has of them. But the tribunes he admired, I think so. Is that how it appears to you?'

'I suppose he does.'

'And this Coriolanus whom your early teacher calls "a prood bougaire", how does he think of him? That also I find it hard to know.'

'Well, sometimes I think he admires him too. For being so brave and so on. I think he thinks it makes up for all his ghastly swanking.'

'Perhaps. Yes, I think so too. But when he makes him say,

183

"My birth-place hate I, and my love's upon this enemy town," you think he is still admiring him then?'

'Well, I really don't know. What do you think?'

'Me? I cannot truly examine Shakespeare from the inside, as you can—because you are born with the same tongue as he uses. To me it is strange, it is—?—a great enigma, when the enemy lord is made in the end to speak of him, *"the most noble corse that ever herald did follow to his urn"*. I cannot know how your Shakespeare is thinking then.'

Such futile chatter was so distracting that I had to make some conversation with Cathleen as a kind of protective screen.

'What I'm trying to do,' I told her, 'is first of all to clear the blue wool out of the general mucko. Then we'll begin to see where we are.'

'Allo, Bub!' she replied; reminding me that her obvious intelligence was still some way ahead of her powers of speech.

'I want you to hang on to the yellow wool,' I said, 'then the main part of it won't get mixed up again.'

She nodded happily, seizing the red wool.

'No—the yellow!' I said composedly.

She tugged hard at the wool in her hand, tightening the knot which I had started to unravel. 'Allo, Bub!' she said again.

Certainly the linguistic barrier limited her usefulness as an assistant; in practice I had to labour single-handed, scarcely avoiding harsh thoughts about the fool who had given this contraption to my loveling. (Such mischievous inventions are always in the toyshops, a lure for aunts and uncles whose brains fall short of their benevolence. I myself have never bought them except for children with adequately leisured mothers.) The yellow wool was the most recalcitrant; when a length was loosed from the wire cage it adhered to the blue and simultaneously formed little tangles of its own. Then, while I was freeing enough of it for one end to be fastened to the door handle, the red wool in turn sprang loose from the chair I had tied it to, caught itself on one of Cathleen's

184

shoes and again became tightly involved with the yellow. Of course it was a pleasure to help my youthful friend, but the conviction grew that work of such an ephemeral kind was unworthy of a male person's time and powers, and this sense of squandered endowments was aggravated by the obtuse behaviour of the distaff side. From cussedness, as far as I could see, Anastasia was playing now—however awkwardly—the part of dedicated disciple; while Helma, pretending that Cathleen's activities were no longer any concern of hers, went bubbling on as if she really hoped to overcome my sister's intellectual narcosis by a process of attrition:

'I shall admit to you, Anastasia, that this Volumnia is a lady I do not greatly admire. Shakespeare has made for her some noble speeches, yes. But she, also, appears to me a prood bougaire.'

'I think "bougaire" is masculine,' Anastasia mildly objected. 'And actually if you're prood and female as well it means you're a person who thinks that chorus girls ought to wear more clothes than they very often do. But Volumnia is nothing but an old swank-bag, that I do agree.'

'Thank you,' Helma said, making another note. 'All this is most valuable to me.'

Soon I was beset by the miserable feeling that all the world was determined to spoil my concentration on Cathleen's handicraft. That morning the smells which seeped from the darkroom were peculiarly noisome, the tide of guttural oaths was always rising and at a moment when I was trying to handle all three skeins together Semyon must needs emerge in person. His appearance then reminded me a little of Anastasia's on the bonfire, his cheeks were poppy-coloured and his eyes running, he had singed his hair with the bunsen burner and his expression of bleak despair was pitiful to see.

'All through Golders Green,' he said, 'I seek high and low for a thing so commonplace as nitric acid. I ask for one thing only, for purity. There is no purity, high or low, in Golders Green.' He held up a test-tube as concrete evidence. 'This is what Boot the Chemical have sell me.'

Helma said, 'Oh, I am sorry, Mr Semyon.'

In its irritating way the cuckoo-clock was giving tongue again. Touchingly, Cathleen went up to the poor old man and presented him with the end of a length of yellow wool which had straggled from the main body, saying sympathetically, 'Allo, Bub!'

'Cuckoo! Cuckoo!' the clock said.

'And you tell me,' Semyon declaimed, with a withering look which embraced us all, 'that you have here the capitalist régime for his efficiency!'

'Cuckoo!' the senile clock repeated.

Still holding the strand of wool, and so towing behind him the whole complex on which I was working, the weary nihilist went back into the darkroom and slammed the partition door.

All this was distressing to me, for even in youth one has periods of tenderness, and in man-to-man conversation Semyon had told me much about his life of successive disappointments. Somehow the friends of his stirring Hampstead Garden Suburb days had all deserted him. 'As for Vladimir Ilyitch,' he had once confided, almost anaesthetising me with clouds of rum and garlic, 'that man who calls himself now Lenin, I tell him to his face in the Lyon teahouse at Kilburn Road he have miscomprehended all the bottom philosophy of Engels. For that he is mad with jealousy, he thinks I will chase him from the party-leadership, he rouses all our old comrades to have me in contempt.' By now it was plain even to my callow observation that his chance of final recognition as the chief philosopher of the Movement was always declining, and today something of his desperation seemed to infect my own spirit. With tireless perseverance I had extricated many feet of wool in all three colours, with scientific care I had secured the liberated lengths to limbs of the room's furniture which should prevent their creeping back into the old entanglements, but the clotted maze which clung to the wires of the *Kiddiknit* appeared to have grown no less substantial. My delicious Cathleen still enchanted me: she had started addressing me by a new name, Dummkopf, and though my lack of German left that appellation meaningless her smile and her dulcet voice turned it to music. At the same time, her discipleship added something to my burdens. In a room which has become an enormous spider's-web of coloured wools the presence of a little girl will never be wholly remunerative: her movements, eager and imprecise, will often complicate the existing pattern, her legs will become entangled, she will fall, roll over, drag a dozen strands from their moorings and form a kind of pupa-case about her own small person, laughing and crying 'Dummkopf' all the time. To remain entirely philosophic in the face of that complication one needs to be without an audience; and if women have to crowd the horizon they should manifest some sympathy with the person obliged to play the part of Laocoon before them. Anastasia, at least, ought to have noticed my predicament and even to have offered me some help. It is depressing to record that throughout that wretched morning she was too much absorbed in her own shallow pursuits even to take a look at mine. Of course she was under duress, but no longer—it appeared—altogether regretfully: in that dreadfully familiar face I detected a peculiar conceit—that of one who, to win a dare, sits quietly in the corner of a tiger's cage.

Here I am not suggesting that there was in Helma anything of the tigress; she was, however, a person whose stature quietly increased. I cannot acquit her of insensibility, on that occasion, in regard to her child. A wholly conscientious mother would surely have realized that an immature girl and a *Kiddiknit* were together too much for one individual to organize. Helma, like Anastasia, behaved as if what was happening five feet away did not concern her—to all appearance she might have left her daughter at a reliable boarding school, to be called for at the end of term.

The rigour of my own situation was perfectly exposed shortly after the female party turned from toying with Shakespeare to an attempt at European history. While I was moving to release the yellow strand which Semyon had carelessly trapped in the partition door my left foot was caught by a small network which I had fixed for the time being between the *Kiddiknit* and a table leg; in consequence I fell full length, grazing one hand and bruising a knee. As I was trying to get up, a blue thread which went to my father's easel attached itself to the top button of my jacket, so that the easel was dragged some way towards me, interfering with other strands as it came. My counteraction was to lie down again and, while I was thinking out some way of escape from the Daedalian network which had formed about me, to manipulate another portion of the blue wool which, with one end temporarily attached to a plaster Apollo Belvedere on the chimney shelf, had re-ravelled itself with a vagrant tussock of the red. These developments had been watched by Cathleen with candid admiration; now, in the innocent way of the young, she thought to walk rather slowly across my abdomen and, having found the going good, to return by the same route. When she had twice repeated this ramble I made a hesitant appeal:

'Cathleen, if you don't mind—that hurts.'

She laughed understandingly. 'Dummkopf!' she said, and knelt on my chest.

It was gratifying to be approached so trustfully, but also inconvenient. 'Look, Cathleen,' I said, 'if you want me to go on helping you, you must find something else to kneel on.'

That point of view was too complicated for a person of such small experience to grasp; all she could do was to murmur 'Dummkopf' intermittently while she trod my ribs with her lively little knees and went on laughing. At that point I should have expected even the least perceptive woman to appreciate my problem and offer some small assistance. Instead, Helma was busily speechifying, emitting so continuous and fervid a current of sound that Anastasia, when I caught sight of her face, appeared to be mildly stupefied.

'This Catherine of Russia,' Helma was saying, 'this second Catherine, they call her Catherine the Great, but I do not see her as a great woman at all. She has an education, yes—

unlike that poor ignorant creature the first Catherine. She has studied some of the encyclopedia Philosophers—Diderot and Montesquieu, Voltaire also. But what has she *done* with all this atheist philosophy? At the start of her reign she thinks she will be kind to the poor people. Then more and more she finds it is less trouble to please the rich military people who have given her the throne, and after Pugachov has frightened her with his rebellion she does *not one thing more* for the poor people at all. And she is after all a woman. Can we expect nothing better—nothing more sensible, more kind, more *good*—from a woman in such high position!'

I should have liked to turn that question back on to Helma herself, but her daughter, smiling benignly as she gripped and twisted my ears, was inhibiting my powers of disputation; it was Anastasia who, in a voice of unexpected mildness, put in a challenge:

'Perhaps you're not awfully keen on Russians anyhow?'

The answer came like a warm breeze: 'There are Russians of whom I am most fond—your kind mother is one example. But it happens that this Catherine the Great is not a Russian at all, she is a German girl, her father is the prince of a small place, Anhalt-Zerbst, and she is brought up at Stettin. I must tell you as well that I have no hatred against Catherine herself—instead, I feel sorry for her. Her foolish mother Johanna carried her away to wed with that disgusting man the grand-duke Peter. Then when she bore a child the Empress Elizabeth seized him away. It is hard to think of more unhappiness for any young woman.'

Those words seemed to offer me an opening. I said, raising my head as far as Cathleen would allow, 'Mrs O'Kneale, if you want me to return your child now I will.'

'Oh, shut up, Rin-bin!' Anastasia said. 'Helma, why do you call the grand-duke Peter disgusting? What was wrong with him?'

'Wrong? It cannot be often,' Helma said with a startling venom, 'that the grandson of two great men is a man so contemptible! In his looks he was a monster, he was pleased

189

with himself for no reason, the way he lived we can only pardon if we accept he had some damage to the brain. He had one idea only in his ugly head, it was to admire the militaristic notions of Frederick the Great and copy them as well as he could.'

Anastasia pounced on that: 'But you told me the other day you admired Frederick the Great yourself!'

'You have not understood me,' Helma said deliberately. 'I am sorry for Frederick as a boy who was cruelly managed by a brutish father. I admire in him his respect for learning, and we have to think of the many reforms he made inside his country. But I do not think with admiration of the wars he made, or his love of fighting. In that he had a mind of the Prussian sort, which I do not admire at all.'

By carefully shifting Cathleen as far as my legs I had succeeded in sitting up, and I was interested to see the look of wondering incredulity on Anastasia's face. I suppose it had not occurred to her before that it was possible to esteem a person in one way and despise him in another; indeed, even to me it was a new idea that one might look at people who had been dead for more than a hundred years with such discrimination as well as such intensity of feeling. I was about to give that thought expression when we were all physically shaken by a thunderous detonation in the darkroom. Such barbarous noises—as I have said already—always upset me; this was the most vigorous explosion Semyon had yet engendered, for an instant it silenced Cathleen's merriment, and when a quantity of plaster fell from the ceiling even Anastasia's face turned a lighter shade than its normal colour of Camembert. Helma, however, was too much engrossed by her own train of thought to notice the disturbance.

'We have to accept,' she continued, looking into Anastasia's eyes as earnestly as a lover would, 'that men consider wars as something needed for their manhood—they dream of the glory of great victories, forcing more land and more people under their power. They will not consider what is known to women (unless such women as that wicked Volumnia), that war is a cause to destroy their husbands and their sons, to burn the fields and make a ruin of their houses, taking cold and starvation and every kind of misery to all the innocent people which wish no part in it at all. I tell you, *liebe* Anastasia, this war that men and emperors consider such a noble thing, I say it is a godless thing. I hate and despise it with everything I have inside my heart and brain.'

I cannot think how Anastasia would have answered that affirmation. She was relieved from doing so by the obtrusion of Semyon's hoarse, despairing voice:

'All my reasoning is correct. All my calculations prove themselves right. *And still* this democratic artifice I plan to send itself on one course only, still it spreads itself on every course together.'

He was standing just on our side of the partition, holding the calcined remnant of a cocoa tin in which, I suppose, the explosive had been concocted. His whole appearance had worsened since his earlier entrance: his face had now the look of a poorly grilled cutlet, his eyebrows and a good deal more of his hair had gone; some of his clothing had been so badly mauled that a portion of his chest was exposed and there a little rivulet of gore was coursing through a dense thicket of grey and chestnut-coloured hair. Although his legs were fouling important strands of my wool-work the pathos of that spectacle made me almost forget my own trouble; nor could it fail to draw some pity from Helma, who reproved him only with a gentle courtesy:

'Mr Semyon, we are busy with our studies, really I must beg you not to keep interrupting. This evening I shall be free to admire your new combustions if you wish.'

But the old man would not be soothed. 'You, Madame Professeur,' he said, 'how do you hope to understand my technic work, you who have never searched the social-dialectic which lies below it!'

'You must tell me about that this evening,' Helma said equably, while Cathleen, who had parted from me to take a closer look at Semyon's ravaged torso, was murmuring,

'Hurty-Bub!' in a tone of neighbourly compassion. 'Cuckoo! Cuckoo!' the fatuous clock said once again.

When he finally returned to the darkroom, Semyon left behind him a peculiar sense of indetermination. What was lacking in our little company, it seemed to me, was any unity of purpose: even my sweet Cathleen—prone like others of her age to *accidie*—was evidently losing interest in my work on the *Kiddiknit*, and as that empty morning crept towards midday I had the melancholy feeling that all my life was running to waste. How thankful, therefore, I was when Helma, winding up a rigmarole about the virtues of some female Austrian potentate, said decisively to Anastasia,

'That is sufficient study for today. If you can find the time to finish your composition I shall have the pleasure to read it when we assemble tomorrow.' After which, turning to me, she asked in a reasonable tone, 'You will like to make an exchange now, Ryan? I will continue the arrangement of Cathleen's handwork, and you I expect will like to consider the questions I have written out for you.'

I was disinclined to waste more time in detailed negotiation with a woman of her obsessive rectitude—especially when she must be weary from combating my sister's ineradicable torpor. Moreover it seemed to me now that my friendship with Cathleen might flower more luxuriantly in a setting different from this. By degrees I freed myself from the woollen labyrinth which had evolved by a kind of parthenogenesis from the *Kiddiknit* and settled in grateful comfort at the table. The questions which Helma had devised for me showed a considerable intelligence; there were even one or two which proved to be beyond my own intellectual reach.

I think my faint but persistent prejudice against co-education may derive from that period. In the field of learning Anastasia and I were perhaps not innately fitted to labour in double harness, and the saddest aspect of our scholastic partnership was a weakening of those bonds of close and affectionate undertanding by which a brother and sister are naturally united. True, in the earliest days of that semester we discussed our impressions with the freedom one expects in colleagues. I can still hear Anastasia's corncrake voice as she bellows across the harness room:

'That old Frau you said was going to put the stingo into my education, she had *you* through the mincer all right this morning—in the geog lesson. Ha ha.'

'Ha your silly self ha,' was my reply. 'It was all arranged between Helma and me just as a way to make you remember that Labrador isn't a part of Nova Scotia.'

'Hoo!' she bawled. 'You are a drippy liar—you can't even think of lies that *sound* right.'

To that gratuitous abuse I responded with perfect simplicity, throwing a piece of saddle soap to rivet her attention, 'Really it's not much good my explaining the Labrador business to someone who simply doesn't know a thing about educational methods.'

'Well, thank you, Rin-bin, all the same,' she said. 'I like hearing all about educational methods from a little snotnosed guinea-pig who thinks that Labrador's a small Canadian valley stuffed with great black dogs.'

That exchange of views, though it brought us to no positive conclusion, illustrates the frank and open way in which we could discuss our tutor and her procedures in the initial stages of our corporate schooling. Later on, when I tried to find out if Anastasia had modified her censorious view of Helma, she was generally evasive and often noticeably hostile.

'It's no good talking to you,' she would say. 'All you ever think of is showing off the two things you happen to know—the thing about doing square roots and the one about which of Henry the Eighth's nine wives got their heads chopped off—in the hope of the Frau being knocked so flat by your ommonitessence she'll shout, "Ah, bravo, *hoch-hoch-mein-Gott*, what a clever little boy our Ryan is!" And then you're always sucking up to her by pretending to be a sort of grinning auntie to her ghastly kid.'

But only a little later, when I happened to remark that Helma had been in rather a wax that morning, she came back at me as tartly as if I had criticized her own deportment.

'Who wouldn't be!' she barked. 'At least half an hour she spent on Thursday telling us what this French person Victor Hugo did to get himself famous, and then today she asks you who he was and you say you *think* he was "a rather Protestant sort of boxer from Glamorgan". If I'd been her I'd have sent you straight off to work in the darkroom with Semyon.'

'My dear old fathead,' I answered patiently, 'until this morning I didn't have a moment to check over what she'd said about that Hugo person. A good scholar never accepts what the first person who comes says about anything. So I tried her out with an alternating hypotheosis.'

'What—you mean to say you think you can dig up righter answers than hers out of books?'

'Well, of course I can! After all, *her* answers come out of books, and she—poor old cow—has to do the best she can without a masculine intelligence.'

'Huh!' Anastasia said, pretending to laugh (which she was never much good at). 'If you'd got just a hundredth of her brains we'd be getting somewhere in these classes instead of going back and back all the time to try and cut things up small enough to squeeze into your tiny little noddle.'

That hysterical remark showed me that my sister had reached an interesting but hazardous stage in her educational pilgrimage. My answer was:

'If you wish, my dear, to make a complaint about your fellow-pupil you would do best to lodge it with our parents. Good afternoon!'

Though I recognized that such outbursts were part of Anastasia's growing pains it grieved me to find that she and I were drifting apart. She was spending more and more out-of-school time with an undersized girl called Lorna Cheevey whose acquaintance she had first made by more or less treading her into the ground at a dancing class. Lorna was really only sixteen but her father was in the Foreign Office and she seemed to be quite grown-up. Before the War she had been to Rouen, so she knew about Paris fashions and things of that kind, such as lipstick and French mistresses, which she explained to Anastasia were used in France for teaching grown-up men as well as children. I did not much care for this new and intimate association: the Cheevey girl was altogether too far advanced in her ideas for a healthy friendship with one of my sister's simple mind and careful upbringing; also I found it intolerable to have to listen from afar to the chirruping and giggling which went on in the stable loft through half the evening.

Concurrently I was in some anxiety over Helma's mental condition. Often she looked weary, and one day when she and I were alone she said impulsively,

'If you, Ryan, would only work at your lessons in the way Anastasia does, instead of seeking to display a cleverness which is so easy and so shallow, you could be making such progress as would please your wise father and your most kind mother.'

For some time I was so astounded by that quaint remark that I failed to place it in its true perspective as the utterance of a tired woman who still used the English language with greater confidence than comprehension.

No doubt her duties kept her at full stretch, for she had now four people in her charge. Cathleen, to my delight, was nearly always with us, as a rule quite happily employed with an affair of wooden pegs which I had got her with eight-and-sixpence borrowed from Pavel (it appealed to me because it involved only a single ball of wool) but now and then needing some attention from her mother. Then, too, Semyon had accepted an invitation to join us as a student of German, since he ardently desired to read *Das Kapital* in the original text; by this means we were freed from a daily diet of chemical smells and desultory explosions, but that immunity was paid for by heavy demands on our teacher's patience and time. As I look back across the years at Helma's classes it strikes me that they make, pictorially, an unusual contribution to the history of English schooling. There is Anastasia sprawling over the table, her lavish top-half couched on Abbott's *Elements of Logic,* her fishlike mouth agape, her eyes boring into Helma's face—for by then she had fallen into the habit of imbibing everything Helma uttered, regardless of whether it was meant for her and whether she understood a single word. On the other side sits Semyon, still in a state of some dilapidation, his cheeks brindled with dangling shreds of blistered skin, his sparsely tufted skull resembling a Scottish moor ravaged by summer fires; he too gazes at the teacher in rapt discipleship, his hands are spread towards her as if begging for alms and he smiles with unwonted humility as he plies her with nervous, staccato questions: 'If you please, I wish to know who appoints the committee which makes this *Bühnenaussprache....* Please, what does this writer intend when he refers about "secondary stress"?' While Cathleen—whose unmethodical behaviour is at once her weakness and her fascination—laboriously twists her wool about the different portions of Semyon's chaotic braces, coaxes it through one hole in his vest and withdraws it through another, then winds it tightly round an ear-piece of his spectacles. It cannot have been easy for one teacher to manage and to mould a group so heterogeneous: often Helma showed signs of wear and tear, and fatigue sometimes led her to a wild injustice; as when she shouted,

'All would be easy for me, Ryan, if you would keep to your own studies, in place of staring at the others with the proud grin of an imbecile.'

But in spite of such aberrations one was bound to respect the woman for her perseverance, her professorial agility, and for my part I could never dislike her for more than a few minutes at a time. That she was mother of so rare a creature as Cathleen would alone have sustained my secret admiration. Now, occasionally—and more often as the days passed —the duteous German features would permit the visitation of a smile: a sad smile indeed, but one to awake—in a person still, perhaps, a little short of maturity—something hard to distinguish from affection.

Because I had not yet learnt to put separate segments of experience side by side I seldom thought of the connection between Helma and Kevin O'Kneale. There were, however, questions about Kevin himself which for a long time had vaguely puzzled me, and it may have been Helma's incursion into my life which reanimated that curiosity.

One day Howard was taking me on the step of his bicycle to a small munition factory where, according to local rumour, there was labour trouble which might soon end in rioting. It occurred to me as we went along that this was a good opportunity for putting my questions to him.

'Howard,' I said, 'what happened in the end to Kevin O'Kneale—after the last time we saw him?'

'Kevin?' he said. 'Ah, he's dead now, poor fellow.'

'I know. But what did he die of? Did he get killed at the Front?'

'At the Front? Well, now, in a war you get all sorts of ways of dying.'

As if to illustrate that proposition he suddenly pedalled hard and swerved in front of a bus which was about to pull out from the kerb, shouting—in response to the driver's observations—'Have they not told you, brother, that steam gives way to sail!' Then, with a geniality which even I found irresistible, he returned his full attention to me.

'Listen, old son,' he said, sweating hard against the gradient of Child's Hill, 'I don't want you to be upset if we find there's no rioting at all. As often as not some busybody from the Government comes tearing out and humbugs the men into work again before anything of interest can happen.'

I saw then that Kevin's death was a subject on which my father did not wish to be questioned. Recognizing that streaks of curious decency were to be found within this man, I did not raise it again.

5

Kevin Translated

One's memories of early years are seldom chronologically ordered and I am hazy about the date of Kevin's arrival at Howes Croft. It occurred, of course, at a time when he (and we) were unaware of Helma's existence: but it cannot have been so very long before the War.

Naturally there were rumours of that war (the '14-18 War, I mean) among grown-ups some time before it started; Commander Macdonald, whenever he looked in to pass the time of day with Howard, spoke of nothing else. I remember taking a somewhat fictitious message from Macdonald to Mr Pimmle, cubmaster of the 9th Hendon Wolf Cub Pack, asking him to investigate a report that an Austrian submarine had found its way up the river Brent and was hiding in the watercress beds just above the Waverley Grove bridge. It had not occurred to me that anyone could believe so silly a story, but Pimmle had the whole pack, with some senior scouts to reinforce it, hunting for the intruder throughout one Saturday afternoon—some boys prodding with their poles, some rather optimistically trying to hook the thing with ordinary fishing-lines. A few from this industrious band fell into the water, and that started an inexorable chain-reaction: fusspot mothers went after Cubmaster Pimmle, Pimmle pursued the affair with Macdonald, Macdonald informed my father that 'what that boy of yours needs is a damn good hiding'. Luckily, Howard was at that time bored beyond endurance with the verbose Commander; he replied with flaming Irish indignation that he would not thrash me till Macdonald had himself produced 'indubitable scientific proof' that the watercress beds were entirely free of Austrian submarines.

None the less I was punished for my indiscriminate message-bearing, by loss of privilege: instead of eating in the dining-room I was made to return to nursery meals under Mavrusha's supervision, with strident and malodorous younger sisters as my only social resource. That must have been how I came to hear nothing of the plans my parents were making for Kevin to be employed in London and housed with us.

It was a wretched period for me. Talk at my parents' table might fall short of Attic brilliance, but I had found it notably less gruelling than Mavrusha's reminiscences of children far more virtuous than I whom she had nursed at Tsarskoye Selo in 1877. Moreover the floating population of Howes Croft included at that time people in whom I was interested— among them my Swiss-domiciled great-uncle Nikolai Stepanitch Rachinsky—and I felt the indignity of banishment more keenly because my disgrace must be known to them. It seemed to me that I was suffering chiefly for the shortcomings of other people: Pimmle had surely been guilty of some laxity in committing his pack to the Brent operation before making a personal reconnaissance, and I thought it ridiculous that any trained wolf-cub should be incapable of spending one afternoon searching a watercress bed for submarines without making a slovenly attempt at suicide.

With Sonya's friends and relations infesting every corner of the house I had to sleep in Pavel's storeroom on a folding bed—it afforded the sort of comfort one would expect from a chain harrow. Lying awake one night, with this abomination chirping to itself as it sawed my thighs, I brooded on the world's unkindness, and especially the injustice done to me by my parents, until I could endure the misery no more. Getting up, I walked for a while about the passages, but no peace was to be had there: it was long past midnight but my Russian relatives were largely noctambulant, in the sepulchral light from the low-turned gas-jets my meditations were frequently disturbed by pattering footsteps, the glint and flutter of brocaded dressing gowns, little squawks of

199

embarrassment or alarm. I made my way at last to Howard's study, in the hope of perquisites: Howard was inclined to keep under lock and key such things as we both took pleasure in, but once or twice I had found in an ashtray a cigar stub of decent length, good for at least ten minutes smoking. That night I was surprised when I entered to find the light still on; here, I thought, was a piece of carelessness which I might put to use next time my father scolded me for being wasteful; then, on the sofa where his models were occasionally allowed to rest, I noticed in succession a sheet of the *Irish Independent* spread like a mainsail, the hem of a buff nightshirt and a pair of inordinately long, naked legs. I was still staring, silent and doubtless open-mouthed, when the paper was lowered and a well-remembered voice said sociably,

'Ah, 'tis Ryan himself! And how is the great wee man nowadays?'

Sleepy and confused, I answered, 'Thank you, sir, I find myself very well,' and added vacuously, 'Are you waiting for my father to paint you?'

'I wouldn't put so good a man to that much trouble,' Kevin replied. 'No—Cousin Howard has kindly allowed me to sleep for the present in this private parlour he has. I had the opportunity your gracious mother gave me to share a room with a Mr Simeon, but your thoughtful father had a notion that that gentleman's manner of snoring might disorganize my dreams. Now tell me, Ryan, is there any small service I might do for you? Were you hunting perhaps for a story-book? Or just making a small patrol to be sure that all is well?'

Those questions, lazily delivered, still came too fast for a sleepy little boy; but the man's charm was already working again, so that I felt in his presence a heartening security.

'I just came to look round,' I told him simply. 'Sometimes Howard leaves a bit of a cigar in his ashtray.'

He nodded pensively. 'And he would naturally wish you to tidy it away?'

He was sitting up now, and he peered towards the ashtray which was lying on Howard's table.

'But this time no luck at all?'

'No.'

At that he pulled a sympathetic face. 'It's a poor make-shift,' he said, 'is all I have to offer, but I beg you to accept it as a favour to myself, in honour of our long acquaintance.' From the jacket he had slung on the back of a chair he extracted two crumpled cigarettes, put one between my lips, one between his, and lit them both. 'You've grown,' he said, 'since we were last together. Almost a man now. Are the days sweet and joyful that you spend in this big and beautiful mansion?'

'No,' I said.

'No?'

'It isn't big *enough*,' I told him, 'now that Sonya's started having babies two at a go and all her relations come swarming in to goo-goo at them. I don't think it's beautiful either. Most of the time it reminds me of hell.'

'So?' He fingered his chin distressfully. 'And that is always a mortifying memory. But the worst part of hell—to go by my own experience—is knowing you wouldn't be there at all unless you had yourself to blame. That's only speaking for myself, mind you.'

His voice conveyed no sort of innuendo, but something prompted me to self-defence. Impetuously I began to relate the facts of my situation just as they occurred to me rather than in strictly logical sequence:

'It wouldn't be so bad if Mavrusha was stone-dead, only she's past the age when people ever die, she's been going about a hundred years already. It isn't Sonya's fault. Sonya quite likes me really, at any rate she thinks I'm more civilized than Stasie, she'd have me back for meals any time, only she's under Howard's influence like always when he's in a stew and he's just trying to show that bilgy old captain he's not afraid to tan me if he wasn't too busy with lectures and things. And I only said about the submarine because of his being such a

201

slop—Pimmle, I mean. You should see him after he's had cocoa, with skin dangling from his moustache. Anyone who saw him then would have done the same as me.'

That abstract of my case closed in tears: I must have been preternaturally lachrymose in infancy—a weakness which gravely embarrassed me. On this occasion it might well have embarrassed Kevin too, but he betrayed no irritation or contempt; his splendid eyes seemed to burn with compassion as he said,

'Ah, I know just how you feel! It's a pitiful thing when a man can't keep his moustache clear of his cocoa-skin.'

Having shown he was on my side, he waited courteously for the visible tide of my distress to recede. I snivelled for a while, trying but failing to complete my apologia, for perhaps two or three minutes I alternately pulled at my cigarette and blubbered noisily, while he, standing in just his shirt by the empty fireplace, blew uniform smoke-rings towards the ceiling as if fulfilling a firm order for that decoration. When I had quietened he said slowly, sitting on the edge of the sofa and frowning at his rugged knees,

'I was thinking just now, there's one sort of trouble you only have to go through once—that's being young. And thankful I am to have that affliction well behind me. When you're young, as I can still remember, you have the whole world making rules according to their own convenience and you're the one who has to obey them. Ah, that's a dis-heartening situation, to be the one small captive in a prison yard filled with enormous gaolers. And well do I remember the joy I had when I came to man's estate—I was in the neighbourhood of twelve years old when my next brother's man-size breeches came down to me, proving I was far enough grown-up to make my own rules for behaviour. But I'll tell you a queer thing, now: the very moment you're big enough to be free from the old rules, that's the time you find you've grown in some crazy way to be fond of them. You get an upside-down sort of joyity from not doing the things you think of first of all—from not getting into bed to say your prayers, or telling bigger lies than you can comfortably manage, or even making a fool of some poor wight when nature has beautifully done the job already.'

I cannot have followed his homespun philosophy at all closely (I was only eight or nine then) but his gentle conviction impressed me. Now, inconsequently, his face surrendered to a prodigious smile as parchment yields to flame, and I felt as if that burst of sunlight gave me a passport to the country my peerless cousin lived in: soon—not in some remote and cloudy future—I might turn into such a man as he, high as the picturerail, with a head like the Sennen cliffs and a laugh which broke and echoed as thunder did among the Irish hills; one who could turn out smoke-rings as uniformly and as lazily as Pavel did piroghi; a person far too large and too engaging for anyone to order or condemn to the gall and wormwood of Mavrusha's table. I had loved the man at our earlier meeting; now I saw him as one of almost messianic endowment, a bridge between my dark exile and the halcyon world of which I had formerly been citizen. So long as he remained with us I should never be totally unhappy.

'Are you staying here long?' That was my first question when I was calm enough to speak like a rational being.

'As long as your generous parents can bear the encumbrance,' he answered, 'or until I make my fortune in the town of London, whichever period will be done the sooner. Now tell me, Ryan, where in this gigantic habitation would you have your own bedroom?'

I explained (with a martyr's licence) that at present I shared a shallow cupboard with a lot of tinned food and Pavel's burnt-out saucepans.

'Ah, that's the brave life of the pioneers,' he said approvingly. 'And I observe you scorn the use of an outside coat for your early exercise. Are you never plagued at all with pneumonia? All the same, I'd like to see you back to your own pallet now—a pinch of sleep will fortify us both for the griefs and glories of tomorrow.'

He was raking the contents of a carpet-bag; now, triumphantly, he unearthed another cigarette to equip me with. So subsidized, I took the hand he offered and we made our way to the store-room walking side by side.

When my mind goes back to that anodyne reunion it discovers no thought of how things looked to Kevin. But then, how often do young children suspect that adults have feelings comparable with their own?

Had I known the details of Kevin's journey as he described them to his wife a year or two later—a boisterous crossing in the crowded steerage of the *Duchess of Ormond*, the fruit and soda-bread in a paper bag which served as his only nourishment between Bowistown and Howes Croft—I might have been slightly less self-absorbed in my ruminations. I doubt it, though—my egotism was absolute then. Today I have no trouble in picturing his arrival in the huge turmoil of Paddington: I see a Norfolk jacket, bought secondhand at the Gallinaulty People's Rights bazaar, hanging loosely on a man whose chest has not expanded to match his upward growth; creaseless hop-sack trousers, so short they leave an inch of ankle bare above the socks, with less than ten shillings (at a guess) in both the pockets; above that scarecrow outfit my cousin's gaunt, amused, indomitable face. I see him accosting—probably—the most important-looking man in sight and asking, gentleman-to-gentleman, the way to Hendon ('No, not Heaven—*Hendon* ... Ah, no, I wouldn't be troubling the underground railway—what did God give me feet for!') then setting off, tired as he is, to cover the six or seven miles, mostly of pavement, with his elastic rural stride. Yes, that vision haunts me now, but at the time of our nocturnal meeting in the study I was disturbed by no such excogitation: here, simply, was a hero-friend, discovered in my babyhood, tonight restored to me by an erratic but sometimes genial providence in the very week when ruthless parents had consigned me to the stringent mercies of a Ciscaucasian shrew.

In truth, Kevin's migration had not been casually arranged: the project must have been in his mother's mind for a long time before it came to fruition.

> 'The future of my little Kevin is a great perplexity to me, now that the wickedness of Father Sestino has turned him away from his true Vocation.'

That sentence, placed with feminine guile as a postscript, occurs in the first of a sheaf of letters, now in my possession, which Greta O'Kneale sent to Howard at intervals of a fortnight or so over a period of several months. My father was not wholly obtuse in the field of family machination, and I can hear now the note of outrage in his voice as he cries wearily, 'Another six-page billet-doux from Greta M'Taurey!' (The Hutchinsons would never accord her another surname.) 'She'll have to wait this time—I'll compose her a counterblast on Sunday.' Yet I doubt if his replies ever fell short of forbearance—there was no meanness in the man when you came to know him. Those letters of Greta's are all in a surprisingly neat, artistic hand; they cover many topics, for her mind travelled mercurially and it took to sentences as the feet of little girls take to dancing, but a keen exegetist would judge, I think, that every one of them enfolds the same purpose—to call attention to the abilities and the occupational needs of 'my little Kevin' (who must have been some eighteen inches taller than she). She writes:

> 'Our aunt Theresa Kearney has nothing but praise for my little Kevin. He is a hard worker, she says, and as honest as all the Holy Apostles put together (except for Judas Iscariot, as you will understand). All the same she is not persuaded any more than I am myself that the boy is cut out for the trade of waiting at table. He cannot always contain himself from laughing at the English travellers who are apt to foregather in her establishment, and that is a distress to them, since they have come into

this world with little appreciation of their own foolishness.'

In the next letter she is writing:

'Kevin has always been as gumptious a bairn as any in my brood, Father Killalee will tell you any time you ask him he has no less philosophy packed in his forrid than his brother Desmond, and the Christian Brothers at Ballyfaheel did a royal work with his schooling.... I had a mind to put him in the business of land agency, I thought he might start in Mr Macartney's office—they have had since some while back a new manager there, Captain Stevenage, he's an Englishman with very little brain to him but as fine a pair of legs within his stockings as ever man or woman saw. I have been to see this person and I gave him a small hint of my admiration for his figure, supposing it would gratify a military man, and I told him my Kevin was the very gossoon he needed to take all his worries from him, seeing he could add up figures like a racing man and even turn them into algebra. But the Captain has a foolish pregidice upon the O'Kneales, all because a ruin of a boat Pat Coughlin was keeping for Macartney must choose to sink itself below the river the very day my poor boys had the loan of it.'

One watches, fascinated, the development of Greta's tactics in the letters which follow. Her friend Dr Eugene McEvoy, she writes, has mentioned to her that for men of education England offers opportunities for employment in many ways superior to those available even in Dublin or Belfast. Cousin Howard would doubtless confirm that opinion? Soon she is advancing on a narrower front. From the letter next-but-two one gathers that the city of London (according to intelligence received by Greta from the well-informed Dr McEvoy) is hungry for young men of first-class schooling—such young men as, for example, her own Kevin. Would Cousin Howard, 'being a close acquaintance with London's leading professors and other gentlemen of the same complexion', have heard, perhaps, of one among them who would realize the particular advantage of taking into his employ a youth recommended by all who knew him for honesty, sobriety and exceptional mental attainments? Their aunt Theresa had been so kind as to say that, having regard to the great value she had received from Kevin's services, she would be happy to contribute some portion of the fare to London should such an opportunity be offered him.

Howard must have been sorely tried by his cousin's remorseless circumvallation. At that time Kevin was known to him in person only as a rankly grown young man in a monkey-jacket very far from clean who bustled energetically about the Conor Maguire dining-room but who never shrank from taking a lion's share in the customers' gossip and arguments. That was hardly a picture of the office clerk whom prospective employers dream of, and the young man's family might seem to them an insufficient recommendation. Many of Howard's closer friends in London were themselves Irishmen, and though a few of them might never have heard of the O'Kneales of Gallinaulty there could hardly be one to whom the name of Sawson O'Kneale was quite unknown. It has been said of that rugged individualist that 'there was no real vice in him' and I have myself ascertained that some of the stories about him are apocryphal: for example, it is simply not true that the cell he occupied in Carlow gaol had his name engraved in a metal plate on the door and was always kept vacant, as a matter of courtesy, in the intervals when he was not in residence. But a man who acquires so much livestock by other means than purchase, and so many descendants through other procedures than the matrimonial one, will never be highly regarded by the employing class of persons, and that prejudice will often add to the difficulty of finding a post for any of his children.

I suspect, moreover, that for Howard the project of bringing Kevin to England meant some difficult negotiation with his wife as well as with influential friends. The penniless youth would have to be lodged, for a time at least, at Howes Croft. Howes Croft belonged to Sonya (or, strictly, Nikolai Rachinsky) and she was accustomed to filling it with necessitous relatives and friends of her own. Celtic in-laws were another proposition.

'There's a crew of rapscallions called O'Kneale,' Howard had told her in the early days of their marriage. 'They're no connection of mine, except my cousin Greta M'Taurey had the misfortune to wed with one of them on a day when her mind was out of its best condition. It's a tribe that's said to have the most accomplished horse-thieves in all Ireland. But that's just tavern talk—they have no more skill in stealing horses than any other family of the same class and inclinations.'

My father needed now to modulate that thesis; he had to win from his wife a welcome for one of those dimly collateral O'Kneales with the argument that the young man's mother spoke of him in terms of warm approval. Simultaneously he had to persuade some well-placed friend that this young man was deserving of respectable employment, having spent five terms at a famous seminary, blacked the eyes of one of his tutors there and subsequently occupied himself in roasting Saxon tourists while engaged as a servant in his great-aunt's hotel.

'I will tell you, Howard, I say this cousin in *Irlande* who must send you one great letter after the next about her little boy is nothing but a scheming woman.'

In those words Sonya, as she told me herself in later years, expressed her early opinion of Greta M'Taurey. That wholesale view of Greta's character is very far from mine; but if for simplicity one accepts it, the appendix is that Greta's plotting was crowned with total success. Among the latest in the batch of letters about Kevin is one she addressed to Sonya herself, where maternal anxieties and gratitude seem to march so close together that one has the faint impression of watching a well-matched pair in a three-legged race.

'It is impossible that I can ever thank you and your estimated Husband enough for the kindness you are holding out to my Kevin, but God will bless you both, notwithstanding my cousin Howard remains in the Protestant connection, and you may rest in certainty that Kevin himself will repay your goodness by every contrivance he knows of, he has always been a useful boy and your Husband's aunt Theresa who is my own aunt besides has schooled him thoroughly to wait at table and the rest of such politeness. He can reform his own clothes better than a girl. He was trained when he was quite small to change his stockings for early Mass on Sundays but in London where the stone footpaths are cruel to the feet as I am told by Dr McEvoy I expect he will need to change on another day as well, perhaps Wednesday would be the best day. I am sure he will be diligent at the work which the kindness of your Husband has found for him and as he studies the work he will become most useful to his employer and earn money to pay for his own lodging. You will find, dear Cousin Mrs Hutchinson, that Kevin's heart is full of goodness in spite of what happened to him at St Finnian's College because of Father Sestino. I shall put in his travel case enough soap to do for about 3 weeks and a new flannel, and if he makes any mistake in the service he does for yourself because of not knowing the English ways you can be sure he will put it right at once if you will have the goodness to explain. I know I am nothing but a foolish old Irish woman, but o my dear if you can do anything to care for my Kevin when he is so far away from his own mother then I know that God and his Holy Angels will always care for you . . .'

It would be pleasant to record that my mother surrendered without hesitation to this inter-maternal wooing, that she accepted with a perfect grace the cuckoo so gently inserted in her nest. That would be too large a claim. I will not allow that the natives of St Petersburg were tainted—as some say— by a peculiar antipathy to strangers; but the lively air of that place, like the air of Edinburgh, does breed the kind of person who thinks twice before entering a sixpenny raffle for the crown jewels. There is evidence that my parents argued rather stiffly about where Kevin should sleep: Sonya simply could not see why a portion of the noisome tenement in- habited by Semyon would not do well enough for a stray limb of the Irish peasantry, and when Howard tactically suggested his own study she objected—through sheer feminine perversity—that you could not put a homesick boy where 'a screeching clock' might execute its entire repertoire three times in a single hour. My father replied that to a man who had spent his formative years among the sucking pigs, the cockerels and other fauna of Bowistown the vagaries of one cuckoo-clock should not result in permanent mental damage.

That cleavage helped to solidify my mother's resentment of Kevin's invasion. On his arrival she greeted him—by Anastasia's account—with no more than prescriptive civility. It took him almost twenty-four hours to convince her that he was the most agreeable guest she had ever entertained.

The first employer to profit from Kevin's scholastic and other attainments was a Dorset man, Dobey Barnes, a rather moody character with a frayed ginger moustache and a caustic tongue whom many retired City men still remember; he was London agent for a Lancashire insurance firm and had an office close to Holborn tube station. For some years Howard had been visiting that office to split hairs over the insurance of Sonya's knick-knacks; he had come to relish Barnes's sardonic observa- tions and must have perceived a fundamental goodness in the old man as well—else he would not have put Greta M'Taurey's son under his command. I imagine that Barnes took on Kevin mainly out of friendship for my father; he used him chiefly for press-copying letters, and for enhancing the tortuosities of a chaotic filing system.

The association of Dobey Barnes and Kevin outlasted four whole days. On the fifth morning one of Dobey's regular customers came to make a tiresome fuss about a racehorse called Patricia's Pet which Dobey had covered against accident and theft and which had died of old age a few hours after running in the Rhayader Coronation Handicap; this man soon exhausted the meagre patience of Dobey, who, as soon as he was gone, kicked the wastepaper basket into a corner and shouted to Kevin,

'That bastard's Irish like yourself, and a Catholic into the bargain. Half the trouble in this world comes from Catholics, with their childish superstitions and their damned superiority.'

One minute later Kevin had resigned his appointment. He explained his action to Howard some time afterwards:

'Father Killalee gave me my orders when I left the parish —I was not to fall into a passion over true religion or to knock the top off any man in the cause of charity. Mr Barnes has doubtless an estimable nature of the English kind, but to save myself from the impropriety of ruining his face I needed once and for all to get it out of my sight.'

Remarkably soon he found himself a new job with Curtice Powell, the travel agents in Cheapside. The *mise en scène* of his engagement, as he himself afterwards described it, has always impressed me as a strange one. Mr Hull, the assistant manager of the establishment, found facing him across the counter one morning a man like a fractured hop-pole who, smiling with a Santa Claus benevolence, made without a single pause a carefully fabricated and mellifluous speech:

'My name is O'Kneale, sir, and I should be glad to purchase one of your useful tickets except that I lack the necessary funds, being presently in need of employment. I have lately been diverted from the Catholic priesthood, and also from hotel service. I have the Greek language up to a fair standard and my Latin is not beneath contempt. The writing of Mr

Chaucer has given me some insight into English travel customs. I could address your envelopes in a fair hand, sir, and I have enough arithmetic to manage the smaller parts of your accountancy.'

In normal circumstances Hull—as he later confessed—would have saved his own time by sending for the police, but an epidemic had left him short of staff. So he said in his chisel-edged cockney voice,

'If it's work you're after, how'd you like to clean the ink-pots and wash the office floor?'

'Sir,' said Kevin, 'those are labours which would give me the highest satisfaction. And for such tasks—if I may presume to advise you, sir—you can do no better than employ a retired hotel waiter.'

He was hired for one week and the engagement was extended; he was promoted from cleaner to office boy, from office boy to counter clerk, first on the rail-ticket and then on the European tours counter. All the time he lived with us he was still working there.

In deference to the City's aesthetic sensibilities Howard had taken him to the Polish tailor he patronized at Willesden Green (one who had been expelled from Bolivia in 1902, I cannot remember why) and garbed him in the uniform of the salaried class—black jacket and striped trousers; Hopes in Ludgate Hill had completed the glory of this attire with white shirt, high, starched, independent collars and long, starched, independent cuffs. But no one could supply him at short notice with a less lank body or a more metropolitan face, and in consequence even I, seeing him in his working clothes, was conscious of some incongruity; I felt the faint embarrassment which arises when, in dreams, one meets one's Airedale dressed in a gay bodice and crinoline. Even so, it did not occur to me that Kevin himself might suffer from being so respectably equipped. Often, I suppose, a massive egotism exempts young children from vicarious distress. From the window of my bedroom when it was restored to me I used to watch my idol going off to work in the mornings, shoving the anomalous bowler to the back of his head and thrashing the suburban air with his umbrella (Sonya's gift) as if he wielded a shillelagh. I never imagined he was anything but happy.

My mother's immense affection for Kevin began, I think, with her discovery of his abilities as a kind of equerry: there was no domestic or other service he would not perform for her, in a manner neither obsequious nor condescending—quaintly but without affectation he always addressed her as 'Sonya-ma'am' and where occasion offered he would greet her with a bow which Richard Nash would not have been ashamed of. Staying the other day with Henry and Anastasia I dipped into the old family albums, and in that deadly expanse of artless snapshots I came on one of curious vitality: Kevin stands loaded with a great pile of carriage rugs to which Sonya, facing him, is about to add another; they are both laughing (how uncannily the picture recalls to me my mother's arpeggios of effervescent laughter) and it is clear from their congruent posture, the way their eyes are joined, that they perfectly understand each other. In retrospect I discover some attitudes they had in common. Both—as I see them—were realists; expatriate, they accepted sturdily the facts surrounding them—the proliferating squalor of the English scene, the pathological aloofness of the English, the cultural vacuum contained in lunatic formalities; at the same time both were always ready to outflank reality when it passed the limits of their toleration.

It occurs to me that the photograph I noticed may have been taken on the day of the Totteridge excursion, an event where the parallelism of my mother's and my cousin's outlook is sufficiently exemplified—though a gala so foreign to accepted patterns could have had its source in the incognizable operations of my mother's mind alone.

*　　*　　*

213

I can think of nothing common to Sonya's mind and that of Rubens except a certain extravagance in invention. Yet whenever I stand in speechless admiration before *The Rape of the Sabines* my thoughts erratically return to that small park at Totteridge where my childish conceptions of adult behaviour were fearfully and dramatically enlarged.

'For us it is a happiness that Nikolai and Héloïse must stay for eight days more because this foolish Bank of England will not make up his mind. But for them it becomes a tragedy.'

When Sonya delivered that thoughtful speech I had just been re-admitted to the grandeurs of dining-room life, following a grotesque complaint from Mavrusha that Brigid's and Polina's table manners were being debauched by mine; so my senses were unusually alert, and I have retained a lively visual impression of my mother's performance. Only the three of us are present—Kevin has gone off to work and the others are not yet down. Sonya is standing (as she often did to pour the coffee—her 'English' manners owed not a little, I think, to Shaftesbury Avenue); she is wearing a full-skirted dress of crimson cloque—too showy, in my present view, for breakfast time—and about her shoulders is a Bokhara shawl; this she cannot have needed for warmth, but she liked it as a histrionic property, a thing she could gracefully let droop behind her and with equal grace restore to its former emplacement. The gas mantle above the fireplace illuminates the high cheek bones, the apparently translucent skin, of a face made lovely by the marriage of preternatural youth with mature intelligence. And I know—for children are not devoid of intuition—that her mind is gravid with unscrupulous plots and stratagems.

She played, as so often, to an audience of one: my father's eyes were engaged with the *Burlington Magazine*, his jaws with toast and marmalade. But when his mouth was clear enough for speech he did acknowledge her signal.

'When I contemplate the cruel sufferings inflicted on rich bankers,' he said agreeably, turning over a page, 'it just breaks my heart in two.'

With the ease of incessant practice my mother leap-frogged over that avowal. She said, 'But Howard, *mon ange*, I think you have not understood: on *samedi* it is for Nikolai and Héloïse their marriage day.'

'What? I thought they were married years ago.'

'On *samedi*, twenty-five years! And it is long-time arranged that all the people of Lausanne arrive at their estate to make a fête for them, there is a big *orchestre* and twenty-five small virgins shall dance on the *pelouse*. And now because the Bank of England will not make up his mind there will be no Nikolai at the château for the fête, and no Héloïse, and no *orchestre.*'

'Nothing but twenty-five undersized virgins dancing in the void?'

'*Non-non,*' Sonya said with some impatience, 'they would have been covered altogether with their dancing suits. But listen, *chéri*—this morning when I waked myself I chewed some cuds, and I have thought it will not be so anguishing for Nikolai and Héloïse to lose their fête if we shall make a very small wedding party to jubilate them in this house. I suppose we shall gather some professors of your college, and a very few bank-keepers which Nikolai meets at London—it will all be in a very modest style.'

Howard put down the *Burlington Magazine*. 'Now Sonya listen!' he said.

My mother changed at once to an image of wifely submission; her face became reverent, her head tilted meekly to one side. Watching her in total fascination I could almost see one sentence of my father's pouring out of her left ear as the next one entered her right.

'What I can never make you understand,' he pronounced, 'is that we live here far beyond our means and far above my own station in life through nothing but the lovingkindness and generosity of your good uncle Nikolai. (Ryan, will you stop sitting there gaping like the village imbecile! This has nothing to do with you—just get on with your barbarous mastication!) And if Nikolai gets a front-rank view of us using

215

his money to organize great banquets for all and sundry with wine, women and the Silver Prize Band of the Salvation Army what is he to think of our sense of obligation! Well, if I was him I'd send a telegram this very minute to the head clerk in my high-class money-shop underneath Mont Blanc or wherever it is, I'd say, "Stop all payments to my niece Sonya Hutchinson without the smallest delay."'

Sonya said, 'Yes, Howard.' Her head was still bent over, a silence of two or three seconds ensued. Then she continued: 'Last week I have a nice talk with Yelena Mintslova, she is living now in the Kensington Street with Albert Hall. She has told me it is best of all to go to the Harrod shop for caviare.'

'Who's talking about caviare?' Howard said.

'I think Sonya is,' I said courteously.

'Ryan, will you shut your muddle-headed mouth!' Howard said, without any courtesy at all.

In a story Sonya had read me long before, a boy called Theodoric de Beauvoir had monotonously rescued his parents from connubial strife by resourceful diversions: here was my chance, enlarged by a wide educational background, to emulate that filial paragon. I addressed the estranged pair in a quiet, reasonable voice, but with a note of firmness:

'I'm sure we shall find some solution. Burton II at school says the most exciting thing about weddings is when the man and the lady jump together—*boomp!*—into the same bed.'

Sonya said, '*Tais-toi, Ryan, je t'en prie!*'

'I was only thinking,' I said, 'it would be quite a cheap sort of wedding-birthday party if we got the bed from the big spare-room down to the drawing-room—'

'Ryan, for God's sake—!' Howard interrupted.

'—and then had Nikolai and Héloïse in their night things and just one or two people like Mrs Dalbeattie and Commander Macdonald to watch. With perhaps just tea and cakes.'

'Yes,' Howard said, in a voice frozen with grown-up superiority, 'it's not unlikely the gallant Macdonald would consider it quite a cheap kind of entertainment.'

To be fair, he may have been worried because our little circle had been enlarged during that conversation: I had felt at the back of my neck a high-powered beam of brainless cordiality, and there when I turned was Héloïse Rachinskaya herself, all five-feet-two of her. I myself sometimes felt shy with this pyknic Vaudoise who gave the impression of being out on parole from an exhibition of primitive sculpture, and I fancy that her prodigious virtue, equally revealed by her cow-catcher bottines and the merciless binding of her khaki hair, was to Howard something of what the slain albatross had been to the Ancient Mariner. He had hardly finished his ungrateful speech to me when he jumped to his feet, stuffing his napkin into an outside pocket and wiping his mouth with the magazine.

'You will please excuse me, Mme Rachinsky?' he said with makeshift urbanity. 'In just forty minutes I have an engage-ment with a number of juvenile yahoos who seek to elude the drudgery of labour by calling themselves art students. I am committed to establishing some kind of bridge between the infinite profundity of El Greco's mind and the chronic super-ficiality of theirs.'

Familiar with that exit speech, Sonya arranged her features in her most commodious smile—it said to Howard, 'The thoughts of your adoring wife will follow you through all the hours of your absence,' and to Héloïse, 'This foolish man will soon be out of our way.' The remains of that smile lasted, like those of snow on high ground, until my father's departure was confirmed by the slamming of the hall door; then, dropping comfortably into French, my mother turned upon our visitor all the radiant warmth of her benignity:

'Héloïse, darling, Howard and I have made up our minds to give you and Nikolai a beautiful party for your anniver-sary, so you'll forget the sadness of being away from home. Howard has spoken of hiring a military band, but I think such noise would be too exhausting. All the same, everything will be most festive, and in quite good style so far as the

English manners allow. You must tell me who are your best friends in London, and this morning Ryan will quickly write out the invitations.'

At that point I felt bound to remind the dear reckless woman that I had a prior engagement to spend the morning with (if I remember rightly) the Misses Bristowe at their school in Horley Drive.

'Ah!' she said. 'Then I must write you a little letter to give to these Bristowes tomorrow. I will say that today you have a small disease of the stomach, with quite a tall temperature, but tomorrow you are once more healthy for your lessons.'

'Or could you say,' I suggested, 'that I was knocked down by a motorbus when I ran out into Church Road to rescue a poor little kitten which had strayed from its mother and father? You could mention I was suffering from grazings and confusions but I'm being wonderfully brave and the doctor thinks I may be fit for school again in about a week's time.'

By now my mother was so deeply absorbed in her social fantasia that she phrased my excuse-note very nearly in the terms I advised.

I was myself admitted to the grand luncheon because even Sonya lacked the pluck to ask Mavrusha if I might spend a few hours more under her jurisdiction. An attractive element in the affair was the absence of Anastasia—I think she was spending the day with a girl called Audrey Thaynes who wanted to get into a ballet school but never could because of her gnarled knees and kept a natterjack as a pet. Despite this advantage I did not look for much enjoyment at the party itself: I thought of it rather as the price to be paid for for the week's exeat which Sonya was generously procuring for me.

Everyone has heard how boys at expensive schools suffer when their parents attend some particularist occasion— 'Founder's Glebe' or 'Lords Connivance': Father is sure to carry his umbrella by the point-of-balance instead of the handle; Mother will wear a dated hat or casually accost someone in the First Eleven to ask the time. But I believe that children in less eximious strata can suffer equally from a conviction—perhaps universal—that the two adults who have brought them into the world are largely ignorant of its social niceties. From my earliest days I saw that many people admired and loved my mother hardly less than I, that there were men such as Mr Gill and Mr Fry who mysteriously found pleasure in my father's company; yet I was always certain that when faced with ordinary people—people they did not know—my parents would sooner or later commit some solecism which, unrecognized by them, would deeply humiliate me. This disquiet was progressively reinforced by a callow snobbery about our domestic framework: I came to feel that Mrs Deekes, the milkman's wife who on special occasions waited at our table, should wear some sort of uniform instead of her patchwork apron, and that Pavel, who in his softer moods would leave the kitchen to help her, ought to smell less saliently of Old Tom and to sound less brusque when he joined in our guests' conversation. Those infantile conceits and fears were in strenuous operation on the late spring day of the Rachinskys' Silver Wedding. The emergence at mid-morning of the sun, after a week of densely clouded skies, was not enough to dissolve my private gloom, and Sonya's face, preoccupied, secreting a dark, irrational delight, only augmented it.

'When the *déjeuner* is quite finished,' I heard her say to Nikolai, 'I shall have a grand surprise for everyone.'

I was very young, but I had known Sonya all my life, and that blithe utterance seemed to me heavy with foreboding.

The actual opening of the meal only intensified my gloom. Rather as one is punished for over-eating by hideous dreams, I suffered for my slight equivocation in regard to absence from school by feeling as if I had been thrust into a dungeon

crammed with maundering buffalo: all around me there
seemed to be persons of monstrous bulk and antiquity, uttering sentences as gay and gossipy as those of the Commination
in the Book of Common Prayer. I had hoped that at least
Kevin would be there to give me moral support, but throughout the first two courses the place laid for him was empty.
Alternatively I should have been content to sit by Nikolai
Rachinsky, for despite his birth in Paris and half a lifetime
spent in Switzerland my great-uncle remained intrinsically a
leisured Muscovite whose urbane intelligence enabled him
to ignore the awkward gap between his years and mine; he
was, moreover, with his noble brow and the silver beard
which fell like an icicle to the top button of his brocaded
waistcoat, as beautiful an old man as I had ever seen. If,
again, I had been allowed my choice of companion from the
female element I should have gone for the youngest, with
her dimples, her big plum-purple mouth, her conical pro-
trusions and her Gainsborough hat, since at that time my
taste in women was largely execrable and for me the miasma
of patchouli in which this houri moved and had her being
was an added attraction. All those consolations were denied
me. I was inserted between one Mademoiselle Lerévérand,
who I think had some post in the Swiss Embassy, and a
skirted monolith called Lady Thelma Vowell. The fluorescent
smile I received from Lady Thelma told me that a person of
my age was *persona non saepe grata* with her.

Looking back at that sepulchral feast I remember how my
sense of isolation, combined with an immature theology, drew
me into pessimism of a desperate kind: suppose, I thought,
advancing years should make me virtuous and I should finally
arrive in Paradise, might not Paradise itself turn out to be a
place where adults in serried rows sat mournfully ingesting
course after course of promiscuous grown-up food? This dire
commemoration was at any rate what lay in wait for a couple
who had sustained their marriage for twenty-five years,
and I looked with some apprehension so see how Grand' tante
Héloïse, seated opposite me, was taking her punishment. Her

primitive wooden face showed me a far from negligible courage; she was straining every muscle, as a young girl would, to simulate polite attention while her partner, a bull-necked magnate called Mr Caudlemaster, raked her fore and aft with a cannonade of political indoctrination. As if his voice had been mechanically recorded I hear it now, abnormally high, polite but insistent, that of a schoolma'am whose duty and pleasure are to share her wisdom with others less happily endowed:

'We must all agree,' he pronounced, 'that the idea of Social Insurance is a charming one to contemplate. On a small scale it might even operate with some success—in the village of Llanystumdwy, for example, which Mr Lloyd George himself honoured with his early years. Unhappily a mind which really belongs to a small Welsh village, as Mr Lloyd George's does, can only court disaster when it applies itself to the financial affairs of a great nation.'

'Ah—so?' Héloïse responds devoutly.

The woman whose dimples have won my boyish admiration interrupts: 'But Reggie, dear, if Mr Lloyd George is so absolutely unbrainy as you always say—'

'Quiet, Pansy!' Mr Caudlemaster says connubially.

So the famous scented lady must be the wife of this lugubrious bison! Already I loathed Mr Caudlemaster—his knowing eyes, his sneering over-lip, the perfect tailoring of his funereal clothes. Why on earth had 'Pansy' married him? Perhaps he had drawn her in one of those outsize charity raffles where you saw things like Norwegian skates and even three-speed bicycles on the list of prizes. And now another Englishman—a grown-up version of the hamster-faced boy at Horley Drive whom one had to be decent to because he had lately been de-tonsilled—was starting to give tongue:

'What you say,' he called to Caudlemaster across the bosoms of two women, 'has some relation to what I myself said in the House on Tuesday. I was speaking—'

'My dear,' said Lady Thelma, as if to a favourite dog caught scratching for bones among a friend's delphiniums, 'I think everyone knows by now what you said in the House on Tuesday.' She turned her head a few degrees to direct her long-range fire at Nikolai. 'Don't you agree, Prince Nikolai, we British would get on better if we left all business matters to business men? You can't learn about finance from books by long-haired professors. My father used to say that what they call Political Economy is just a parlour-game for innocent romantics who'd be bankrupt in a week if they tried to run a sweet-shop.'

'But my dear,' said the hamster-faced man, who was evidently Mr Vowell, 'we do after all need politicians to channel and co-ordinate the efforts of business men. I myself—'

'Yes, dear, we know about that!' Lady Thelma said briskly.

Spontaneously, Mrs Caudlemaster opened her luscious mouth to say, 'It would be rather interesting to get a lot of people who keep sweet-shops and make them into economical professors. Then we could see—'

'Hush, Pansy!' Mr Caudlemaster said.

Nikolai was cryptically smiling, like the sandstone Buddha of Manura. I confess that I myself have a high regard towards professors,' he said suavely. 'There is my marriage-nephew, for one example.' He made a graceful gesture towards Howard. 'From him I learn more of painting in one hour than ten painters will teach me in a year.'

'No one can teach anything about painting,' Howard said morosely. 'Art lectures are just one almighty shenanigan.'

From the other end of the table my mother shot at him a glance of affectionate patronage. She said at large, 'My husband loves to wind himself in a coat of humbleness so thin we see through it a naked man of shameful vanity.'

And while her other guests were trying with lowered eyes to unravel that announcement, Caudlemaster came freshly into action:

'We can forecast the final outcome of Mr Lloyd George's Insurance Act without going very deeply into the basic axioms of public accountancy. Let us first examine its effect on the profit-earning potentiality of those who, quite shortly, will be faced with the enormous bill.'

In a kind of corporate palsy we set ourselves to examine this special result of Mr Lloyd George's thoughtless legislation.

For myself, I began to wish I were back at school, where at least one had Harcourt-Byrd to help exploit the awfulness of Miss Ruby Bristowe reading aloud *My Strength is as the Strength of Ten because my Heart is Pure*. For till now I had scarcely imagined the sadness of adult amusements. I shall not pretend to recall more than a fraction of Caudlemaster's dissertation, which pursued its course like a radio set left on in an empty flat. Vowell must have been listening, since now and then he offered a nascent footnote—'Or to put it another way...' 'To be strictly accurate...' 'If I may illustrate that point...'—as one who plays a soda-syphon on a forest fire; and Nikolai, his eyes vitreous with courtesy, may have been listening too, while Howard smothered yawn after yawn with forkloads of *pommes Duchesse*. Otherwise, I observed no active listeners.

Indulging what has proved a life-long curiosity I scanned the women's faces, marvelling at their fortitude. My mountainous neighbour Lady Thelma was accepting the financier's eloquence with laudable composure, perhaps in expectation of taking the floor herself as soon as he had done with it. In the crouching posture of Mlle Lerévérand I thought I saw a hint of indiscipline: she was a creature of compact design— stripped, she would have done for an army instructor in physical training—and I fancy her intelligence was fundamentally not less athletic than her person: certainly the eyes which examined Mr Caudlemaster through thick-lensed pince-nez betrayed no ardent admiration. I doubt if Miss Brenda Seccombe, a brawny pupil of Howard's who also sat on my side of the table, worshipped him either, but as a painter of cubist inclination she may have seen the rhomboidal doyen of British Discount Banking as a possible subject for exotic portraiture. Acoustically the most vulnerable of his

223

audience was my distant cousin Yelena Alexandrovna, who sat immediately on his right, but she must have been armoured by her long experience as a lady-in-waiting and by an almost total ignorance of the English tongue; taller and finer-boned than the average of Russian women, expertly marcelled and corsetted, tightly fastened in a grey moiré dress which conceded nothing to the styles of the new century, she contemplated the crusading financier with eyes in which a stable charity hid every trace of boredom and incomprehension. The resilience of these ladies still failed to reassure the small boy intently watching them: thinking what shame this dreadful party must have brought to Sonya, I found it hard to look at her so long as Caudlemaster was in spate. When I dared to do so, however, I was much relieved: as if we were undergoing a recitation from a simpering child my mother wore the most multifarious of all her smiles—simultaneously it seemed to offer to the speaker an expression of profound esteem, to the listeners her sidelong sympathy and her gratitude for their patience. Adoring this woman as I did, I was yet faintly scandalized by her duplicity. If she wished, I thought, she could turn herself into a poltergeist; and would do so in a trice for any social advantage.

I kept wondering if Kevin would turn up in the end. Only his presence, I felt, could provide a window for the cell of loneliness in which I was held captive. To be fair, Mlle Lerévérand made conscientious efforts to entertain me, describing a boy called André Saint-Arnoult who apparently did nothing except help his widowed mother drive a flock of sheep round a smallish mountain at the back of their farm; it was, in fact, while I was listening to the life story of this tedious child, and rewarding Mlle Lerévérand with comments like *'Vraiment? Ah, c'est extraordinaire, Madame, cette histoire!'* that I heard Sonya say genially,

'Voici notre beau cousin qui vient d'Irlande!'

And there he was, bowing to her and quizzically smiling, just inside the door.

*　　　*　　　*

I must record, to my indelible shame, that I felt at first more than my usual discomfort about his appearance: straight from the office, he wore his business clothes—they were, I suppose, the only 'respectable' ones he had—and even I, looking from him to the immaculate Englishmen, could see that those garments were equally unsuited to the man and the occasion. No one could have cavilled, though, at his party manners. Responding to Sonya's casual introduction he briefly spread his smile to embrace the company and then slipped without a word into the empty place on the right of Yelena Alexandrovna; unobtrusively he stretched to move a cruet nearer to Miss Seccombe, gave a friendly wink to me and placed a butter dish in front of the lovely Mrs Caudle-master. There had scarcely been a pause in the conversation, and as if no more than a piece of furniture had been added to the scene it effectively absorbed him.

By then Caudlemaster's lecture on the absurdity of social insurance had finished prematurely, Lady Thelma's patience being exhausted. Lady Thelma's own theme was the good-ness of her father; her unpretentious intellect must have been faster in action than Caudlemaster's, for whenever he tried to launch some new objection to Lloyd George's fiscal policies she blocked his path with a fresh example of the gratitude shown by those who had benefited from her father's prodigal philanthropy—it was like watching one of those films where a swordsman of extreme dexterity holds another against the banquet-chamber wall. She thus performed a useful service, setting her fellow guests at liberty to converse with each other. For a time my own attention was occupied by Sonya, who was playing all her charm on Mr Vowell as she explained to him the subtle differences between the British Parliament and the Duma.

'We have had a *ministre*,' I heard her say, 'called Pyotr Arkadievitch Stolypin who was well known by my mother. He was quite a sensible man, he made the Duma pass some good laws about the land, and when they would not pass some more laws he passed them himself by what we call "Emergency

Method". In London you have not, I think, the "Emergency Method"?'

On my own side of the table Miss Seccombe was ruthlessly describing to Nikolai the new Shikubu school of modelling, while Semyon and Loe the Poor Gardener (as Howard inevitably called him) were engaged in a somewhat irregular discussion; through one of Sonya's least prudent *tours de force* Loe, who like many domestics at that time was an ardent Conservative, had been brought in to help the professional waiters supplied by Collitts of Hampstead, and Semyon was seizing every chance to bait him in a caustic undertone. I found this hubbub less burdensome than Caudlemaster's monologue, but it still seemed to me depressing that adults could not foregather to enjoy a baron of beef without emitting a foam of chatter on topics roughly as vivacious as the bye-laws of Stoke-on-Trent; mesmerized by such boredom as only children suffer, I heard the flying sentences as one hears the continuing shouts and curses when lying concussed on a football field:

'Now I shall tell you of another little boy who also helps his mother with the sheep. His name is Armand, and he has gay blue eyes.'

'So, Mr Loe Tovarish, you find it a grand honour—you who are a worker on the soil—you find it is your social complement to carry plates of food to these idle *bourzhui* and their fat mares who do no work at all?'

'Well, what I always say is—'

'That'll do, Pansy!'

'Marvellous, really, these scraps of Japs, the punch they've got. They grab whole handfuls of this muck they use—like plasticine, only twice as tough—and simply bung it all to-gether, then they whack it and thump it about with all the spunk they've got till they get Significance. Marvellous, when you come to think of it.'

'So at last they shoot this busy man in the theatre—like Mr Lincoln in America. In your English parliament they do not shoot the *ministres* for passing laws they do not like—

that is what my husband says. He says such men are carried away and shut up in the top house instead.'

'There were tears in the poor woman's eyes. She said to my father, "I shall never forget your goodness, my lord. The first thing I shall do when my husband is in work again is to send you a postal order." '

At least the group which Sonya had so wantonly brought together seemed content with this travesty of conversation, which went on with the jolting rhythm of a slow suburban train. To that extent I was relieved. But presently the rhythm was broken. Caudlemaster had got his second wind, and he turned once more to address Yelena Alexandrovna, pronouncing every word with extreme care, as one who teaches tricks to a dog of minimal intelligence.

'In my belief what is needed is a return to political integrity. I say boldly that the world looks to this country as the great exemplar of Integrity and Justice.'

'So interesting!' Yelena said graciously.

Howard for some time had made no contribution—he might have been posing for a sculpture entitled *Boredom through the Ages*. Now, with his head on one side, seraphically smiling, he said, 'If you're running short of English justice, Mr Caudlemaster, we could send you back a decent helping from the part of Ireland where I come from. Over there we've had a little more—these last few hundred years— than we quite know what to do with.'

The clap of silence brought by those words was followed instantly by Sonya's voice, sweetly allegro, from the other end of the table: 'It is the custom of my husband's family, Mr Caudlemaster, to revolt against the English. So Howard must always be revolting also. In my country we have a place called Sakhalin where we send such dangerous people.'

Mr Vowell, seated beside her, laughed politely—his laugh made you think of someone trying to start a motor boat on a wintry morning. Mr Caudlemaster refrained from laughing: to me, anxiously watching the great banker's face, it appeared that he was not much mollified by my mother's intervention.

A new silence spread over us like a snow-cloud, till salvation came, preternaturally, in the high, virginal, Brook Street voice of Mr Caudlemaster's 'Pansy':

'Mr O'Kneale, I believe you've made it up—all that about The Day of the Singing Waters!'

To which Kevin answered gravely, 'I assure you, ma'am, I have no powers of invention.'

'"The Day of the Singing Waters",' Mlle Lerévérand echoed dreamily. ' "*Le jour des eaux qui chantent*"!'

Miss Seccombe put down her knife and fork. Squaring herself, as one about to bully-off at hockey, she said, 'Well, can't we *all* have this, Mr O'Kneale? "Singing Waters"—sounds like a cartload of tripe to me!'

Kevin for the first time appeared to be overcome by shyness.

'Ah, 'tis nothing at all,' he said evasively. 'It's just an old custom we have where I come from—on the nineteenth day of April in every year they carry the girls over some small piece of water. They say it brings good luck to the girls themselves and the men who carry them.' He turned to me. 'You may remember, Ryan, there's a wee twisting river called the Sleane where we had a piece of trouble with Pat Coughlin's ferry-boat. As often as not that's where the Gallinaulty people do the carrying.'

He was using almost the same quiet voice in which he had conversed with Mrs Caudlemaster, but now, mysteriously, he had captured everyone's attention. Nikolai asked,

'But how has it commenced, this custom?'

Kevin shrugged his shoulders, as if he had forgotten. Then he said hesitantly, 'Well now, the story they tell is about St Dirwyn, when he was naught but a poor ploughboy. He had his home then in the Isle of Inishbofin, but the call came to go preaching in the country between Cahirciveen and Ballinskelligs Bay, so he set out on foot, having neither horse nor other beast to ride on. He was a tender-footed man, and after three days of travel and starvation—being too poor to buy fresh viands—he sank down beside the river Kilcrow in a state of terrible exhaustion. He slept for a while, and when he woke a woman stood beside him, old and ill-favoured, asking would he carry her across the stream. That was indeed a challenge to the poor fellow when he felt he had not an ounce of strength remaining in his body. But her pleading was so pitiful he said he would oblige her if he was able, and with all the force he had left he raised her off the ground to the height of his two nipples and strode with the whole weight of her on his arms to the middle of the torrent, which at that time was fleeter than a hunted hare. He sang as he went forward; and the strange thing—so the story goes—is that when he reached the deepest and most dangerous part the water itself began to sing. "The Day of the Singing Waters"—that's how the name began.'

'Interesting,' Mr Vowell said sagely, 'those old tales!'

'But that is all the history?' Héloïse asked.

'Ah, the rest of it, ma'am, would sound the least bit fanciful in the ears of practical folk.'

Mrs Caudlemaster said ecstatically, 'Oh, but Mr O'Kneale, you *must* tell them!'

Her fervour evoked no response in Kevin, as far as I could see: he was staring at the wall above Miss Seccombe's head as if, viewing there a private world, he had no wish to share it with his present company. When some moments had passed, however, with no one else speaking, his soft, rather dreamy voice began again:

'It will sound unnatural to folk who've never known that country—the magic there is in its dark woods and curling streams.' He paused, seeming to smile at some grateful re-collection of his own, and then continued pensively: 'The brave Dirwyn struggled to the farther bank, and when he set the old woman down she went off along a woodland path, telling him to follow. He did as she bade him, with his legs still weak below him, and he came soon to a small cabin where he found a meal set out—cakes of barley bread, and steaming broth, and every kind of fruit you can imagine. The old woman herself was there, commanding him to take his fill—but she would not eat with him. So he ate and mightily refreshed himself, till all his strength returned, and when he had done he rose and placed a modest kiss upon the old woman's forehead. At that very instant she was changed altogether to a woman of surpassing beauty, and he saw she was none other than the Queen of all the woodland fairies. A moment afterward the lovely creature had vanished away, and the wee cabin with her. But he knew from the strength in his body and the fresh fire in his spirit that the strange happening had been no dream.'

As music does, the low, singing voice left a hush behind it. Glancing left and right, I saw the face of Miss Seccombe absorbed, that of Héloïse enraptured. Then Vowell said,

'Extraordinary, really, these old fables. One wonders how they started.'

'You're not telling me,' Caudlemaster said, 'that in Ireland they still take them as true, stories of that kind?'

'I can only assure you, sir,' Kevin answered slowly, 'that on the nineteenth day of April no true Irishman finding maid or matron on one side of a running stream will fail to lift her over it—you would learn that for yourself, sir, if you took a stroll this day along any river bank from Malin Head to the Harbour of Glandore. Indeed, you'll find our people following that practice in places round the globe, be they beside the Potomac or the Murrumbidgee, for so I have it on the best authority. As for the good luck which follows, you may call it just coincidence if you prefer.'

'But *does* it follow?' Miss Seccombe asked.

'I personally have no use for such childish superstitions,' Mr Caudlemaster said with finality.

'Indeed, sir, I greatly respect your wisdom,' Kevin said.

There the discussion ought to have ended—even I could see that our English guests should not be subjected to an overdose of Irish folklore. But my mother, for all the refinement of her intuition, had never quite attuned herself to

English sensibilities. It was she who said, with a girlish impatience,

'But still, Ke-veen, you need to tell us what you keep in your own mind. What sort of "good luck" will come to such people who bring the women across the water—or the goblins or what they may be?'

'Good luck of every kind, Sonya-ma'am,' he answered soberly. 'In my own village there was Brian McKevitt who carried Maureen Parbell—a daffy girl and no featherweight either—and in less than a week he had a hundred pounds from a great-uncle in America that he'd never yet set eyes on, one who'd put him in his last will and testament and taken the trouble to die of Hodgkins Fever that very day. Then there was Biddie Sewell, she was lifted over quite a small wee burn, but by her own account it sang like a choir of angels. And not a month had gone when her husband—a great ugly brute with as foul a temper as you could wish to imagine— fell off his waggon seat when he was in the drink and broke his neck as clean as a sugar-stick, leaving her free to wed with a very decent cattle auctioneer that was after her for years. Well, chance that may have been. But I find it hard to explain, myself, the luck that came to my friend the doctor, Stephen Delayne. Three times—three years running—when he himself was in a mortal hurry to reach the poor sick folk awaiting his contrivance, he found himself obliged to dismount and lift the same winsome lass called Julie Wabe across the stream at Dragman's Bend. And those same three years running he drew the *winning* horse in the Catholic sweepstake on the Kilnacullen Open Challenge Plate.'

'Remarkable, certainly!' Mr Vowell said.

'Howard, do you know of this?' my mother asked.

'Doc Delayne? Ah, he's famous in those parts,' my father said somewhat absently. 'Ay, if his wife was not a demanding woman he'd leave the doctoring alone, he'd just be lifting girls across the river all day long.'

'Quite frankly,' Mr Caudlemaster said, 'all this strikes me as the greatest balderdash I ever heard.'

231

Here my mother seemed once more to remember that it is the duty of a hostess—as of a boxing referee—to keep her men out of clinches. 'After the *café* and the gentlemen's *contes gras*,' she announced with a radiant dignity, 'there will be a beautiful surprise.'

In later life one comes to view one's parents more sympathetically, and I think I understand now the mental mechanism which resulted in Sonya's singular arrangements for the celebration of the Rachinskys' silver wedding. As a young woman she had often stayed on her grandfather's estate at Krasnoborsk, where her fellow guests, mostly cousins, exhibited a quasi-morbid aversion from anything which savoured of routine; in the very middle of a dinner party her cousin Evgeni Arishkin would suddenly cry out, 'Oh what a bore this house is—for God's sake let's *do* something!' and without a moment's hesitation the whole party would wrap themselves in their furs, pile into sleighs and drive off into the forest, shouting and singing, to start a wolf hunt by torchlight; they would return at perhaps three or four in the morning, all the servants would be roused and a dance would begin. Howes Croft was dismally lacking in apparatus for diversions of that kind. I see now how my mother must sometimes have been driven almost frantic by the dreadful sameness, day after day, of English life, and with that much sympathy I am ready to forgive her for the embarrassments she inflicted now and then upon her family. I think she was truly determined, that sunny April day, that as far as happiness was possible in a place so remote from Krasnoborsk as North London we should all of us be happy.

With allowance for the ground mist in a old man's memory, I can present a sufficiently faithful record of the graceful speech in which, standing near the drawing-room window, she explained the 'beautiful surprise' to her guests:

'Nikolai—dear Héloïse—all my friends! This morning when I have seen the sun strip himself from the clouds (like my dear husband when he takes the bath) I have said to myself, "This is an English sun which burns for my dear Oncle Nikolai and his Héloïse on their wedding birthday. So, the *fête* we make for them must be in the English style, and what the English love most of all on such a day is the *fête champêtre* —the *pique-nique*," I am right, Mr Vowell? So, I have commanded Mr Pope at Finchley to send two coaches, and if you will so kindly take three persons more in your nice motor, Mr Caudlemaster, we shall all go away to the *campagne* in a grand carnival. See!'

She turned theatrically, and everyone moved to look out of the window. In the short half-moon drive, behind Caudlemaster's Windsor limousine, two victorias had been drawn up in échelon; in the rear of that file stood our own governess-cart with the veteran skewbald Vyacheslav between the shafts, while the three drivers were bunched with Caudlemaster's chauffeur among the laurels, smoking like a bacon factory. Measured against our usual scale of living that conflux made an impressive promenade.

Was there a burst of congratulation—did excitement and pleasure suffuse the face of every guest? I still wish to believe so, but in that matter I am no use as a witness, since something had drawn my whole attention to the face of my father.

His expression disturbed me: he had the slightly haunted look of one who, asked to say a few words before he is publicly hanged, can only remember the speech he has always made in proposing the health of the bride and bridegroom at weddings. In retrospect I seem to understand his disquiet. Though bred on an Irish farm he had somewhere learnt, I suppose, that the English make a distinction between a luncheon party and other forms of hospitality. The sun still shone, but the behaviour of a monkey-puzzle on the other side of the road showed that a frolic wind was blowing, and I doubt if any of the ladies was dressed for outdoor amusements; that was perhaps immaterial—in those days, as far as I remember, that class of women did not often dress for other activities than being looked at—but it was patent even to me that the men would have clad themselves differently had they expected to be dragooned into close contact with nature. I give Howard some credit, therefore, for the apparent calm with which—when he had recovered speech—he asked,

'How far, my love, have we to drive?'

'Ah, a very small way—five, six versts. We go to Totaire-Reege, where Mr Green has his lands—you remember, last year we are there for a great *réception*. I think it will be nice to have our *pique-nique* in the park against his house.'

'And Mr Green,' Howard asked, as if with rheumatism in his vocal chords, 'does he think that will be nice?'

'Oh, today he spends with Mr Asquith, so he does not need to think at all. But this morning I advise his maître d'hôtel with the telephone that we all arrive this afternoon.'

'He was pleased—the maître d'hôtel?'

'One cannot know—he seems to be a fairly stupid man. But when I ask him to boil the water for the tea he says he will do what I wish.'

'Sonya Mihailovna has all things sumptuously arranged,' Héloïse said with shining loyalty.

Her tactful intervention should have saved my poor mother from further questioning, but now the wretched Vowell had to take a hand, asking, 'You don't mean Sir Rushden Green? *His* place is at Totteridge—Brocken Chase.'

Hearing that name, Sonya nodded gratefully. 'Brocken Chase—that is right!' she said.

'But Sir Rushden is Deputy Attorney General.'

Sonya shrugged her shoulders; in her *exaltés* moments she was apt to be impatient of masculine pedantries. 'He is a little ugly fat man like a monkey,' she said. 'Perhaps he is a turning General also.'

Nikolai had long been silent, his face glazed with inveterate urbanity. Now, including us all in a regard of demure benevolence, he said in his graceful English, 'It is fortunate this ugly man keeps a park for the picnics of his friends. Let us journey to Totaire-Reege as quickly as we can.'

* * *

And how absurd, I thought as our modish procession ascended Bittacy Hill, that anyone—let alone my bucolic father—should have demurred at Sonya's imaginative plan! In those days there was open country all about Mill Hill, and in that green playground a child could forget he had only just escaped from the sullen bricks and mortar of London's fringe; above the quaint hill-top barracks great white clouds today were drifting high and harmlessly, already the devouring boredom of the dining-room seemed far behind. As the road bent to left and right I had glimpses of Sonya in the pony trap handling the reins with flagrant *joie de vivre*, of Vowell's face resembling those of captives in a Roman triumph, of Caudlemaster's hideous motor panting and belching smoke as the chauffeur strove to curb its natural élan: the size and diversity of our parade persuaded me that I was sharing in an event of some importance, and in that exhilaration I was freshly proud to possess a mother so enlightened, so lavish in her hospitality, so abundant in resource.

Once more I had Kevin to thank for a great part of my contentment. Directed to the occasional seat in the second victoria, he had spontaneously invited me to share it.

'What do you say, Ryan? I need another fellow to keep me in countenance, and the wee seat will prop one half the backsides of you and me together.'

As bounty, I had Pansy Caudlemaster facing me: although she became in transit almost as giggly as one of Anastasia's friends I still found it thrilling to be so close to a woman who smelt like the whole scent department at Whiteleys. Mlle Lerévérand was with us too, but as she seemed to have run out of stories about dutiful small boys I did not so much mind her presence, and between those two young women space had just been found for the elegant person of Yelena Alexandrovna. She, I fancy, had no idea where she was being taken or for what imaginable purpose; she sat as queens do—erect, tranquil, delicately smiling—whether on their way to enthronement or to the guillotine.

In truth Yelena was by no means an empty-minded woman,

235

as history has since proved, and as that short ride to Totter-idge would have taught me but for the poverty of my own intelligence. She scarcely looked at me—herself childless, she was, I suspect, invariably bored by children—but she was manifestly interested in the vigorous sculpture of Kevin's face, and we had not travelled far before she was putting questions to him, using Mlle Lerévérand as interpreter.

'Sonya Mihailovna tells me you are a student of theology?'

'I was, ma'am,' he answered, 'in a piece of my life that's gone altogether behind me. Indeed, I was intended for the priesthood, but it came to light I had not the disposition such a calling demands.'

'So? That is sad for you,' Yelena said. 'My mother was partly Polish, so I have many Catholic friends and I know a little of what priesthood means to them. I also have a philosopher friend of my own communion, Nicholas Berd-yaev, who talks to me of these things.' She smiled pensively while Mlle Lerévérand translated, and then she asked, 'But perhaps that part of your life is not really over? Perhaps the call will come again?'

The effect of that question—gently asked and sympathetic-ally translated—was startling. The Kevin I knew was always a fount of cheerfulness, but now he looked as a man does when suddenly reminded of a friend who has died. He said miser-ably, looking out at the passing fields,

'Indeed, ma'am, that would be a thankful day for me. But first there are things inside myself I have to get the reach of. A queer figure I should make, celebrating the Holy Mysteries and betweentimes blacking the eyes of any passing citizen whose manners failed to please me.'

His words must have set the Swiss woman a stiff task in translation, and before she was through with it his bout of despondency seemed to have passed. To escape, I suppose, from a painful subject he turned to me, asking lightly, 'And you, Ryan, do you yet know what sort of work you mean to do when your education is finally disposed of?'

'I shan't go in for work,' I answered easily—for I had given

236

some thought to this matter. 'I'm going to write books instead.'

'And you don't think there's any work attached to that?'

'Oh no,' I said.

'I went drinking once with an author fellow from Dublin,' he said reminiscently, 'and he told me writing was such hard work it almost killed him.'

I answered, 'Yes, I believe it's hard for some people.'

'But it won't be for you? And you think you could earn your living that way?'

'Oh, easily. Mr Kipling goes in for writing books and he told Howard he gets paid half a crown a word.'

'Then it's a fine thing,' Kevin said with his grave kindness, 'that you have one of life's most pestilential problems fairly beat already.'

Refusing to concern themselves with my economic prospects, the two young women facing us had started chattering about the iniquitous price of summer coats. But now Pansy Caudlemaster—never, I should say, one to treat a male presence wastefully—leaned forward to gaze into Kevin's face with the timid, trustful look which nature had put at her service for occasions such as this.

'Do tell me, Mr O'Kneale,' she said, '—if one of those Irish girls wants good luck from the Day of the Singing Waters, can it be just any man she gets to carry her? I mean, could it be just her husband or someone like that?'

'According to the old saying, Mrs Caudlemaster,' he answered promptly, 'It needs to be "a true and loving man".'

'And that's the only rule?'

'It is indeed. Except they have both of them to sing St Dirwyn's magic anthem as they go over.'

'St Dirwyn's anthem? What's that?'

Kevin put a hand across his eyes. 'Ah, how does it go? ... Wait now, I think I have it! It's the girl who starts the singing.' To a tune remarkably resembling that of *Hark, the Herald Angels* he sang in a dulcet baritone a couplet which went (as nearly as I can remember):

> *Hausted high a-brode the water,*
> *Ah-day, brach-day, rankin-ho.*

'And then,' he said, 'the man sings,

> *Dorsal-wyde I will support her,*
> *Mistog, mastoch, leasing-low.*

After that they both sing together,

> *Let not vischil gnobes alarm us,*
> *Fish nor fowl hath power to harm us!*
> *Lush not, pish not, onwarde stryde,*
> *Bear the brund, whate'er betyde.*
> *Dirwyn lodist maiden bore,*
> *Dumpen on ye fairther shore.'*

On a child's inexpert ear this simple prothalamium fell with a singular charm, and it was plain that our ladies were not less delighted.

'This is without doubt a song of the Irish Middle Age,' Mlle Lerévérand said ardently.

'Och, it's much older than that,' Kevin assured her.

Pansy said, 'It's rather mixy-uppy, but awfully sweet, really. Do sing the first bit again, Mr O'Kneale—the girl's bit.'

He did so, and she sang it after him in a voice which, though high for my taste, probably did credit to some Kensington music teacher. Then I found myself joining Kevin as he sang again,

> *'Dorsal-wyde I will support her,*
> *Mistog, mastoch, leasing-low.'*

Now, under pressure from the younger women, he taught us the concluding couplets, one at a time, with such winning patience that even Yelena Alexandrovna was drawn into our corporate performance; and although she cannot have followed the song's meaning closely her face expressed a benign thoughtfulness as she bravely strove to render the unfamiliar vowels.

> *'Loosh note, peesh note, onvairde strite,'*

she sang in a dignified contralto,

> *'Bar dee-brahnt voteer be tight.'*

I remember vividly my glad amazement at finding that

even grown-ups could sometimes enjoy themselves with manifest intelligence, and how proudly, exultantly, I merged my
reedy voice in the sonic commotion as my elders and betters
attacked the final lines, singing in a multiplicity of keys and
accents but with uniform civility and zest:

    'Dirwyn lodist maiden bore
    Dumpen on ye fairther shore.'

Those were almost the best moments in my day. Vaguely
I felt I had penetrated to what the magazines in barbers'
shops called 'good society', and now through Kevin's peculiar
agency the splendour of my situation was no longer private:
children, women and even men were staring into our equipage
as we passed them, and if faces here and there were incredulous or disrespectful I realized that in the remoter tracts of
Middlesex it was vain to look for manners of metropolitan
refinement. I was thus in the highest spirits when our proud
procession drew near to the confines of Brocken Chase.

That estate has for long been a sub-depot of the Royal
Army Pay Corps. When I last saw it a year or two ago the
entrance looked much the same: only a nameboard and a
lick of whitewash had imposed a tang of Aldershot upon its
wistful romanticism—the twin castellated lodges, the slightly
bashful gryphons standing sentinel above a gateway wide
enough to admit two coaches abreast. The demesne, however,
has been much changed by wholesale felling, so that the
sub-Palladian mansion is now starkly visible from the road.
At the time of the Rachinskys' Silver Wedding you began
your approach to the house through an avenue of trees; escaping from their protection, the drive swung rightward and
ran for a little way beside a stream called Dollis Brook, which
it presently crossed by a rather picturesque Venetian bridge;
at that point the house was screened by a larch coppice which
the great McGoyle had characteristically planted to em-
bellish the view from its ballroom windows, and you hardly
saw the full extent of the atrocious pile before you arrived at
the carriage sweep. Let me record, for honesty's sake, that
on that spring afternoon I did not think it ugly, or alarming.

I was simply impressed by its magnificence.

No, the faint, fresh disquiet which began to chafe me came from some kind of presentiment—a subtle foreboding which attached itself to the sight of the tranquil stream. For all my adoration of Kevin, a poorly focussed memory of earlier days made me feel that O'Kneales were better kept away from any kind of watercourse. Here the clouds, coalescing, had drawn as it were a blind across the sun: I saw Yelena Alexandrovna discreetly shivering. When I noticed Pansy staring at the brook, with eyes which made me think of a cat's outside a fish shop, I experienced a curious dread of some new, refined humiliation—a cowardly desire to be back at home, playing with Anastasia or anyone else whose feelings did not count.

Yes, reviewed from an elderly man's coign of vantage that picnic does appear to be—as my mother had promised—a distinctly English occasion; an event in the extravagantly open air, close to the soil; one of needless discomfort high-heartedly endured. I find it moving to reflect that it was mounted by a woman whose only claim to be English rested on her adventitious marriage to a Tipperary farmer's migrant son.

Children, of course, reason in the simplest terms, and on that increasingly wintry day it seemed to me pure lunacy that we should be eating out of doors when a building possessing half a hundred rooms with wind-proof walls stood only a few yards away. I ought to have recognized that Sonya knew to a hair's breadth the limits of the licence canonically extended to attractive women. On the telephone she had evidently persuaded the Italian butler Girolamo that she was among his employer's most intimate friends; the man's assiduity in taking and returning her teapots was beautiful to witness, and had she asked for the loan of the library or drawing-room he would probably have obliged her, but she prudently refrained from asking: I think a special power of divination told her that English Deputy Attorney Generals are as a rule less

powerfully swayed by aesthetic impulse than Latin manser-
vants. Moreover she had, after all, proclaimed a picnic. Here
were the cakes and sandwiches she had brought in two large
hampers, here were the carriage rugs to sit on; here, again,
was Sir Rushden's faultless croquet lawn, ideal for the spread-
ing of rugs, and here an adequate sample of the English
race, known the world over for its attachment to alfresco
alimentation.

As I recall the scene I would not say that one ethnic group
responded more admirably than another to the spirit of
Sonya's hospitality. The English naturally did well: even the
face of Mr Vowell, basically designed to symbolize the triumph of reason over hopefulness, displayed from time to time
the indomitable smile which press photographers demand of
persons rescued from the sea, while his wife, who may well
have been in agonies of cramp as well as cold, uttered no
word of complaint as she crouched on a folded blanket like a
brave toad at bay. Yet I do not think that our Slavonic
kinsmen failed to match the home team—so to say—in
staunch composure. The behaviour of Great-uncle Nikolai
was perhaps less stoic than the others', but also, I think, more
sensible; instead of pretending he could squat on mother
earth as serenely as a native of Sibsagar, he kept on the
move with a cover-plan of helpfulness, acting as Girolamo's
satellite, circulating canapés, discreetly extracting from the
house an ancient sociable on which his wife and at last Sonya
herself gratefully subsided. Yelena Alexandrovna, on the
other hand, would not be persuaded to sit at all, or to stir
from the place where she had elected to stand, leaning
familiarly against a terracotta Venus. Closely watching them
—as a small boy could without offence—I saw with childish
wonder how those two very different faces which chance
had brought together in a setting alien to them both wore
exactly the same expression, one of inexhaustible forbearance.

What the party lacked, I think, was a sense of intimate
cohesion. My father, for example, seemed to be for ever
marching keenly away, bearing food to the drivers who

were huddled in the shelter of a greenhouse, while Semyon, still embittered by Sonya's command to wear a collar and tie, stood some way off from the rest, smoking a small cheroot and staring scornfully at Girolamo, who fluttered anxiously between the guests like a moth in a lighted fairground. No one knew exactly which way to face, and one noticed a lack of ordered conversation. My mother's beatific smiles never declined in radiance; but these were not quite enough to weld a group of people mostly unacclimatized to English picnicking, or to dissipate the gossamer of sadness which attends a late afternoon of grey, accumulating cloud and recurrent gusts of freshening wind.

For myself, I suffered little hardship, since the mind of the immature will often triumph over physical distress. I amused myself by supposing I was about to start on a one-man expedition over the Great Ice Barrier, entailing some seventeen weeks without food or water. '*My advice to you, Hutchinson,*' I imagined King George V remarking as I took leave of him at Balmoral, '*is to fortify your frame with a bellyful of sustaining viands before you embark on your hazardous enterprise.*' Accepting this wise counsel, I stuffed myself with all the cream cakes which the others were leaving—and most adult women eat marvellously little at tea-time. I must have put away nearly a pound of bedizened pastry before Kevin, whose attention had been in fairly brisk demand by the ladies, came to rescue me once more from spiritual isolation.

'Ryan, my friend,' he said tactfully, 'will it not modify the enjoyments of your supper if you eat a second sugar-cake now? Will you and I not take a constitutional and explore the wee wood over there?'

Most willing was I to exchange a merely sensuous pleasure for a moral one—that of walking beside so popular a man, exhibiting myself as his chosen companion. As we went to join the path leading downward through the coppice I had my hands in my breeches pockets and I took such enormous strides that they almost matched my friend's curtailed ones.

'It's a shameful thing,' Kevin said, 'that the weather has not the Christian decency to support your lady mother in her fine philanthropy. 'Tis the only piece of apparatus that will not yield to her thoughtful appointments.'

I expressed agreement with that thesis.

'You're among the luckiest of mortals,' he continued, 'to have such parents—large in their cogitations, with hearts great enough for the mastery of their intelligence.'

This was a new idea to me—that Sonya and Howard could be spoken of in the same terms. To me Howard represented as a rule no more than the rougher side of nature's remarkable provisions—an instrument for rationing the comfort derived from one's mother's benevolence. Lacking the scholarship to put that view into words, I simply said,

'They're not enjoying it much, these people, are they!'

'Ah, different folk delight in things in different ways,' he answered scrupulously. 'No doubt it's a new sort of experience for some of your mother's visitors—taking their tea in a sharp wind on a gentleman's croquet field, and that will give them something to clack about at many a dull party, as far as their friends will abide the information. Then there's the poor wretch from the Parliament, Mr Vowell; he's a body made for misery—his own brave conduct in the face of suffering is all he has to take a pleasure in. I make no doubt that this is a mighty day for him.'

Somewhat out of my depth, I said, 'I wouldn't like to have the wife Mr Vowell's got. She's *awful*.'

'Awful?' he echoed.

'Well, she's so pig-ugly.'

He considered that assertion, frowning pensively. 'It's all a matter of opinion,' he said. 'There may be other women you or I would prefer to look at—indeed, the most of simple men like you and me might own to the same sort of prejudice. But there's nothing in your opinion or mine that the poor ladyship's to blame for. You know, Ryan, it's the hardest thing can happen to a woman, to be landed with a face that

243

other folk are apt not to fancy. With a man it's another story. Give a man a face like a piece of dough the cook's sat on, he can still pass for a fine fellow if he's useful in a hurling game or some other destructive occupation. With women, on the other hand, it's a sonsy face or nothing.'

Later in life I was often to recall that primal dictum on aesthetic tolerance, but I cannot pretend that it made a profound impression when I heard it. For me the virtue of that hour lay in having Kevin to myself, in the soft modulation of his voice, his comradely demeanour. I longed to sustain the enchantment, but like all blissful experience this one was harshly curtailed. Having reached the brook, we were standing with our backs against the huge trunk of a beech tree which slightly blunted the teeth of the wind when a troubled cry of *'Mr O'Kneale! Are you there? Mr O'Kneale!'* told us that Mrs Caudlemaster was drawing near us in remorseless pursuit.

When she appeared, coming along the path which we ourselves had taken, she betrayed an understandable confusion. 'I thought it might be warmer down here,' she said apologetically—and indeed the poor thing looked frozen. 'I just had to take a walk—up there by that ghastly house it's simply arctic now.'

'I agree, ma'am,' Kevin answered. 'The weather side of the afternoon has given none of us entire satisfaction.'

'Oh, and I was going to ask you,' she pursued, '—did you tell us it's the man who gets good luck when he carries someone over the water, or is it the girl?'

'They say it brings good luck to both of them.'

'Does it really!' Pansy gave a glance at me which suggested (in the way of adult glances) that she would like me to go for a long walk by myself. 'I was only wondering,' she said to Kevin, 'if you yourself are in need of luck at all just at present. I mean, we've got the river here and everything—we could have just a try.'

'Indeed, Mrs Caudlemaster,' Kevin said earnestly, stooping to take off his shoes and socks, 'it would be socially indecent to disregard so providential an opportunity'.

I am ashamed to say that as I watched my hero rolling up his trouser legs I suffered pangs of jealousy. Unabated by the freezing wind, the fragrance of Mr Whiteley's scent department still hung about Pansy's clothes, and in a puzzling way I felt that this poor lady who had been lured into marriage with the hideous Caudlemaster was in dire need of my protection. How readily would I have taken Kevin's place! But a rudimentary appreciation of problems in dynamics told me I should hardly raise the lovely creature off the ground. I could only look on in deep dejection while my beloved Kevin robbed me of romance, and the woman I would have succoured stole my friend.

'Are you ready, Mrs Caudlemaster, ma'am?'

She giggled: perhaps she was, after all, rather a silly lady, however nice to look at and to smell. And I could not escape a fresh admiration for Kevin as he bent to his task, placing one hand in the small of Pansy's back, the other below that part of her toilette which I think of as a vestigial bustle. '*Up!*' he cried, and raised her high and marched nonchalantly into the brook. They had reached the middle of the stream, where the water came up to Kevin's knees, when she cried out,

'Stop! I've forgotten what I have to sing.'

Obediently he halted, and standing there rehearsed her afresh in the opening couplet of St Dirwyn's anthem. This time she seemed slow to learn.

By then the pair had plainly forgotten my existence, and in a new access of loneliness I was glad to hear the sound of chatter in the wood behind me. A man and woman were talking in French, and it was Nikolai whose voice I first recognized, saying,

'Yes, my dear niece has attuned herself remarkably to English ways.

'And this I imagine is the English custom also,' his companion said, as they emerged from the wood.

It was Mlle Lerévérand. Standing at the water's edge, she and my great-uncle surveyed the river-scene with the quiet intelligence of travellers who take a scholarly interest in foreign folklore. Unaware of their presence, Kevin, still supporting his pupil in midstream, sang the opening couplet once again, and Mrs Caudlemaster with her head deliriously thrown back sang it after him in her tremulous soprano:

'Hausted high a-brode the water
Ah-day, brach-day, rankin ho!'

'For a young woman it can only be agreeable,' Mlle Lerévérand said indulgently, 'this ceremonial of ancient times.'

Nikolai slightly raised his luxuriant grey eyebrows.

'For *any* young woman?'

'Why, certainly! At least, I should imagine so.'

With his tongue between his lips, Nikolai nodded soberly. 'Then I count myself most happy,' he said, 'to be faced with so delectable a duty.'

For a second or two that announcement was as puzzling, I think, to Mlle Lerévérand as it was to me. But when he bent to untie a shoelace she gave a little squeal.

'Oh no, you mustn't! Princess Héloïse might not like it.'

Nikolai smiled, as if in opiate meditation. 'Like myself,' he said, pulling off his shoes and detaching his socks from their neat suspenders, 'my dear wife is an earnest student of primitive mythology. As soon as possible,' he added, delicately furling his trouser legs, 'one must find amphibious transport for her as well.'

Disgruntled as I was with this development—since no one was paying the slightest attention to me—I could not but admire the old man's versatility and courage. The normal duties of a Swiss bank's president must differ notably from those of a male ballet dancer, and my great-uncle's slender body was not visibly muscular, yet he met the challenge to his chivalry with apparent unconcern: standing barefoot, wearing the civilized smile which devoted amateurs show to the paintings of Mantegna, he studied for a moment or two the person of Mlle Lerévérand, then seized her by the waist and placed her gracefully across his shoulder. He asked,

'You are ready, Mademoiselle?'

246

'Ready? Well, I suppose so.' Then, with a burst of irresponsible laughter, she cried, *'En avant, cavalier!'* and he carried her robustly to where the other pair still occupied the centre of the stream.

My sense of desertion was increasing. To be noticed is a psychological necessity with children, who moreover look to adults for a certain constancy in deportment and action. Here was a recondite traffic in which I seemed to have no place. Freezing as the water looked, I should gladly have bared my feet and entered it with any reasonable excuse—but where should I find a female of appropriate weight? More members of our party, lured perhaps by the sound of singing, were descending through the wood, and I prayed that by some fantastic chance a girl of about my size would be found attached to them. My prayer was unheard. My malaise only deepened when Héloïse came into view, shivering from the cold, with Howard looking bored and cross beside her.

For a few moments they both observed the riverine spectacle in silence. When my father spoke I was painfully conscious of the Munster inflexion which thickened in his voice whenever he found the discommodity of life beyond all bearing.

'Kevin,' he called irately. 'there's no sense at all in what you're up to—you can't behave that way in a damned highfalutin' country like the one we're landed in. That's Caudlemaster's lady-wife you're rafting now—there'll be hell to pay if you drop her in the water.'

This utterance struck me as unduly censorious; I was not surprised that Kevin seemed hardly to understand it. He glanced at Nikolai, who was smiling like a little boy possessed of another's teddy bear. 'This gentleman wishes me to assist him with the Anthem,' Kevin called back. ''Twill not take more than a small minute or even less.' Together, then, raggedly but with scrupulous discipline, the two womenbearers began to sing:

> *'Dorsal-wyde I will support her,*
> *Mistog, mastoch, leasing-low.'*

247

At this juncture I myself was slightly disturbed by the pendulous face of Mlle Lerévérand, which showed an unmistakable disquiet. Her position on Nikolai's shoulder may have afforded something less than physical luxury, and I supposed that her unaccountable fear of upsetting Héloïse might still be weighing on her mind. Héloïse, indeed, appeared to have lost a little of her normal equanimity, and before the couplet was finished she was calling to her husband with a note of impatience:

'*Nikolai!* It's foolish for a weak old man to go paddling in the arctic torrent! Put that lady down and put on your stockings at once, before a visitation of pneumonia conducts you to an early tomb!'

My sympathy was now transferred to Héloïse, whose distress was palpable. I had always considered my great-aunt-by-marriage a tiresome character, with a gift for demanding from my mother time and attention she might else have given to me, but now I was touched by observing in this stolid female a fondness for Nikolai at least equal to my own. Here, it seemed, was the chance I had longed for to show myself *sans peur et sans reproche*. Though stocky in build, Héloïse was not much over five feet tall—a dwarf beside the other women. In a moment I had whipped off my shoes and stockings.

'Madame Grand'tante,' I said with a decorous bow, 'I believe I have strength to bear you at least a little way towards the man you love.'

Her response was far from what I had hoped. Like a sausage fried too fast her wooden face was split transversely by a monstrous smile. '*Ah, qu'il est ravissant,*' she exclaimed, '*ce petit bonhomme!*'

I cannot think how I should have dealt with that nauseous utterance if Howard had not been there. He, perhaps, was scarcely less revolted than I; at any rate he must have read the horror in my face, and this, unexpectedly, brought out his better side.

'Och, listen now, Ryan,' he said with a gallantry I had

248

hardly known in him before, 'that's a bigger job than you can handle at the stage you've come to. This is a two-man load, make no mistake about it.' He was removing shoes and socks as he spoke, and reassuring Héloïse with the seraphic smile he always wore when putting money on impossible horses. 'You look after the tootsy end,' he said to me, 'and I'll manage the rest from the crupper up.'

It looked as if my great-aunt was taken aback by this eruption of chivalry, but she made no comment: her command of English was inadequate, I think, for expressing to Howard any views of her own, and in any case she may have been a little overwhelmed at receiving so much male attention. For my part, I often felt a certain respect for my father when he had a purely practical problem to deal with, and this affair he conducted very capably, coming behind Héloïse and lifting her with his hands in her armpits, while I found it best to turn my back to her and tuck one of her ankles under each of my small arms. In that way we bore her very easily to the middle of the brook, which the others had vacated now—under Kevin's leadership they were struggling through the rest of the anthem as they clambered on to the farther bank.

That was a stage where I was able to prove my worth. Héloïse was either too shy or too dim-witted to sing St Dirwyn's opening couplet—the only duty required of her. I therefore sang it on her behalf; and to cope with Howard's habitual laziness I sang his couplet too.

By now the rest of the party had assembled on the bank we had left. They had in general a solemn, even a depressed appearance. This was where one saw most clearly that Sonya had planned her 'beautiful surprise' with too little time, too slight an understanding of meteorology, at her disposal: a flurry of snowflakes seemed to emphasize the fact that none of her guests had dressed with rural pleasures in view. She herself, however, did not appear disconsolate. She called to Howard, without perceptible anxiety,

'What is happening, chéri?'

'Part of the host,' he answered rather phlegmatically, 'have crossed the flood, and part are crossing now.'

This can have meant little to my mother, who cried with a note of irritation, 'It is not right for Ryan to stand in the water without his stockings. There is quite a cool wind beside the river, and all the ointment I bought for his chilblains is finished now.'

'I can't hear you with all this damned caterwauling,' Howard shouted back. (But I doubt if he was trying—he never took much trouble with interspousal communication.) 'Just hold your patience for half a minute—as soon as I'm done with this load I'll be back to lift you over.'

That last assurance provoked my mother to a burst of wicked laughter. 'Do you think,' she called, 'I wish to override the river on a stuffed old husband! I shall give my permit only for a beautiful heroic man to cart me.'

With those words she turned to bestow a melting smile on Vowell, who imprudently was standing close beside her. An infantile percipience told me, as I looked across the water at the lean politician's frozen cheeks and meagre chin, that his private ambitions did not include the attendance on my mother in the role of St Christopher: his answering smile lacked fervour, and he seemed ridiculously slow in taking off his shoes. Kevin, however, was a good deal more alert. With a rapid grasp of the situation—and adoring my mother as he did—he went splashing back to the embarkation side, bowed to Sonya as an old-fashioned footman would, picked her up and had her at midstream, joyfully laughing, before Vowell had succeeded in baring his feet.

Almost simultaneously my father went back to the embarkation side as well, wearing his calmly-efficient look—in moments of confusion that least methodical of men was subject as I see it now to a Born Organizer fantasy. It was he who lifted Miss Seccombe. I am not sure that she wanted anyone to lift her—she had been standing, feet apart, reviewing the carriage of the other women with an artist's slightly supercilious detachment—but Howard in his more rhapsodic moods would never neglect to help a lame dog over a stile and if there was no stile in sight he would scour the country-side to find one. I confess I felt some filial pride in the man as I watched him and Kevin advancing side by side towards the disembarkation point, each bearing his load so sturdily, while the four of them joined in the central lines of St Dirwyn's chorus with a spiritual ardour which counter-balanced any weakness in musical finesse.

'*Lush not, pish not, onwarde stryde,*'
they sang fortissimo,
'*Bear the brund, whate'er betyde!*'

Hardly, I thought, could queens have been more bravely borne.

We on the arrival bank were now compassed about with a cloud of witnesses—mostly infants from the lodges with a few estate workers who, bicycling home, had stopped to gaze at the transfluvial operations with the manic curiosity which any departure from normal occurrence provokes in simple persons. The children were joining in the anthem—the speed at which they had learnt an approximation to the unfamiliar words did no small credit to their primary educa-tion. Unhappily their presence induced in Sonya one of her bouts of maternal solicitude; she again remarked my lack of stockings and ordered me to the other bank to put them on.

I crossed over the more reluctantly because the small party still stationed on that side seemed shamefully to illustrate the less desirable results of my mother's erratic hospitality. Bound by ties of sex and suffering, Yelena Alexandrovna and Lady Thelma stood close together. They did not speak. Their frozen faces were still tolerant, composed, but I recognized their kind of valour as one belonging to my own tin soldiers, who wore it alike in victory and defeat, whether marching, stricken or dead. Near them stood Girolamo, who, finding Sonya's handbag on the croquet lawn, had very decently come to restore it; on his face was the strangely mystified expression one so often notices when foreigners meet with some fresh example of English usage. On the whole I preferred his bearing to that of Semyon, who as always stood well apart, arms folded, coat collar turned up, bestowing on the total situation a kindergarten teacher's caustic patronage.

A little way upstream the two Englishmen, one barefoot, their heads close together, were marching back and forth with long, slow strides as serious males do when their brains are working at maximum power. I naturally attached myself to this masculine pair, taking—as far as my dimensions allowed—long, slow strides immediately behind them. From them I learnt, that afternoon, yet another lesson: that the English, even if they fail to scintillate in social life, are matchless in vigour and resource when faced with a concrete challenge.

'I'm glad, really,' Vowell was saying in a carefully lowered voice, 'that my wife has that Russian woman with her—can't quite get her name. I mean, a woman feels it rather if she's left entirely alone, if you see what I mean.'

Caudlemaster pondered that formulation. 'I know what you mean,' he said judiciously, keeping his voice to the level of Vowell's. 'Pansy—my wife—takes quite a lot of trouble not to be left out of things. I suppose—if the opportunity came—your wife wouldn't like to join in with this lifting business? I mean, I'm not suggesting there's anything in the good luck part of it—all tommy-rot in my opinion. Only I've noticed women as a rule do like to do the same sort of things as other women, if you see what I mean.'

'Yes, I do see what you mean,' Vowell said. 'Actually I did think of putting the idea to Thelma, only there's rather a practical difficulty. You see, she's what's called a fairly well-built woman—she played middle-centre in the Second Netball Seven at St Winifred's, Llanfairfechan. That introduces what you might call a technical question.'

'I do see that,' Caudlemaster said, nodding rather anxiously. 'Yes, I can see your wife isn't one of those skinny creatures who are all the rage nowadays—starve themselves till they're nothing but skin and bone, foolish things. Lady Thelma might be—perhaps—a trifle over seven stone.'

'Well, actually, a bit more like seventeen.'

Both men thought for a while, pausing in their promenade, lighting fresh cigarettes, trying (I suppose) to take a Berkeleian view of seventeen stone. Then Caudlemaster began again:

'I remember in the corps at Wellington they showed us a way of getting guns over an obstacle. A sort of block-and-tackle thing. You fixed it on the branch of a tree.'

'Yes,' Vowell said, 'they showed us something of that sort at Lancing. One of those Sapper fellows rigged it up. Can't remember just how it worked, but it was damned ingenious.'

'I was wondering—'

'Yes, old chap, I see what you mean. Only the thing about a gun is you can take it to bits, and then as far as I remember the barrel's quite an easy shape to handle, comparatively speaking. I mean, it hasn't got clothes and things.'

'No, I suppose it hasn't. I don't remember an awful lot about that demonstration.'

'I mean, supposing you were told by your housemaster or someone to get the barrel of a gun over a river, using this block-and-tackle thing, and you found a hell of a great flouncy skirt tied round its middle, and then a lot of whalebone and all that sort of thing—'

'Yes, that would be tricky.'

'Damned tricky, I should say. If you had to do it in front of a mixed audience, I mean.'

'There must be some other dodge,' Caudlemaster said ruminatively. 'Wait! I've thought of something—a thing I saw beside the path as we came down.'

To a boy as yet ungrounded in military engineering the technical flavour of their talk was becoming wearisome, and when they went off into the wood I did not trouble to follow them. Instead, I returned towards the ladies, a little apprehensively, fearing they might have guessed the subject of the men's discreet exchanges. Here I found a dramatic change in the situation. It appeared that Semyon had at last become bored with his own aloof behaviour: with the Homeric dignity which every muzhik can call on when it suits his mood, this scourge of aristocracy stood before Yelena Alexandrovna and addressed her in Russian, much as if they were old acquaintances meeting at the Winter Palace.

'You want to be carried across, Comrade Old-lady?'

She made a gesture of indecision, asking, 'Is that necessary, do you think? May one not go round by the bridge?'

He in turn shrugged his shoulders; then he said with rare goodhumour, 'We Russians, we can't be beaten by these English softies.'

Yelena delicately smiled. 'That is a point of view,' she said.

Now, with a soldierly decision, Semyon turned to Girolamo. 'You, *Camerta-cameriere*,' he said with the confidence which is part of the Marxist's stock-in-trade, 'do you know how to make the Prophet's Chair—*Sedia di Profeta*? Come, I'll show you.'

Girolamo, always obliging, was quick to learn; in a matter of seconds the two men had linked their hands and wrists to form the seat which Boy Scouts are supposed to provide for their wounded friends.

'All ready, Comrade Auntie! Please to mount!' Semyon cried.

It was a charming thing to see, the benign complaisance, the perfect grace, with which the tall old lady took her place in the makeshift palanquin, hooking her arms in the accepted manner about the men's shoulders.

'Do we have to sing?' she modestly inquired.

'Sing? We can beat the weasel-throated English at that!' Semyon said robustly. 'Do you know the Mosalski Trooper's song?'

'Why, I learnt it in childhood.'

'Then please to sing it for our pleasure—we accept it as your fare for the voyage.'

In her slightly quavering voice Yelena sang the opening

254

line of Zagoskin's famous ballad, and Semyon quickly joined her in his ponderous baritone. It seemed the song was unknown to Girolamo, but he was evidently keen to show a cordial unanimity; without direct incitement he discharged the opening bars of *La donna e mobile* in a tenor of such explosive power that the voices of his Russian partners were almost wholly submerged. In that crescendo of synergic sound the close-knit trio advanced with measured steps to the water's edge. There I thought it would surely pause for the pedestrian part to denude feet and legs, but no such pusillanimity was shown. Without either haste or hesitation the dedicated bearers and their stately passenger went into the stream, heedless of saturate trouser legs, flooding the wintry air with hybrid song.

I might have gone with them—forgetting Sonya's orders I was still barelegged—but the stirring of a rudimental conscience held me back. With Yelena's removal Lady Thelma was left entirely alone, and though there were no tears on her virile cheeks it was manifest that a less courageous person would have shed them then. In the least developed of the human young there is, I suppose, a tiny germ of feeling for other creatures of his own species. I had very little regard for this woman, who I felt had treated me with scant courtesy at luncheon; but she was, after all, the guest of my wayward mother, and even a notoriously obtuse small boy could faintly imagine how it would feel for a member of the more receptive sex to find herself, at a ceremonious Lifting of the Women, the only one neglected. With an embryonic sense of duty, then, I presented myself as comforter to that massive image of feminine distress.

'Rather disagreeable weather,' I said in a friendly tone, 'for the time of year.'

She stared at my face in a nebulous way, as if I had addressed her in Cassubian dialect. I continued steadfastly, however, adopting a gambit I had heard my father use with shy people:

'I hear the going was terrible at Lincoln. But then I never

put my money on two-year-olds—it's too like gambling.'

There was still no answer, and I began to suspect that this old person's mind had been slightly unhinged by her humiliation. The contrapuntal uproar from midstream would in any case have been a hindrance to social intercourse, and I was much relieved when the two Englishmen emerged from the wood again.

They were carrying between them a dilapidated rustic seat, which they delicately set down as near as possible to Lady Thelma's stern.

'Look, dear, Mr Caudlemaster saw this bench thing,' Vowell said modestly. 'He thought you might like to rest for a bit.'

'Oh, but how very kind!' she said, bowing gratefully to Caudlemaster and sitting down.

'Not at all—a pleasure!' Caudlemaster said.

I saw a swift glance pass between the two men. Unobtrusively, standing behind the seat, Caudlemaster was taking off his shoes.

'We were just wondering,' Vowell said cautiously, 'if you'd care for a lift to the other side. The rest of the party seem rather to be collecting over there.'

'There's no need,' Caudlemaster put in, 'to pay the slightest attention to all that superstitious Irish nonsense. That's all the most absolute rubbish—I've tried these good-luck things again and again, they get you simply nowhere. But what I mean is, we don't want to hurt the feelings of these poor muddle-headed foreigners.'

'Indeed, no!' Lady Thelma agreed. 'My father had a great saying which I've never forgotten; he used to say, "Do in Rome as Rome does."'

'Well, that strikes me as absolutely sound,' Caudlemaster said. 'Though actually I haven't travelled in Italy much,' he added honestly.

'It's a quotation, actually,' Vowell explained.

'I mean,' Caudlemaster continued, 'I doubt if we could get hold of one of those gondola things, or anything like that.'

By then he, like Vowell, was barefooted, with his trouser

256

legs rolled to the knees. I wondered if two men of such disparate physique—Mr Vowell's figure so stooped and lean, Mr Caudlemaster's as short and ellipsoidal as Humpty-Dumpty's—could jointly handle a burden as awkward as the grossly overloaded seat, but my fears should have been extinguished by the quiet confidence of their faces. There was a brief traffic in politeness: 'Are you quite ready, Lady Thelma?' 'You're sure it's not too much trouble, Mr Caudlemaster?' Then the intrepid pair solicitously raised the bench, adjusted their grips to correct the sway, made—with a sliding sidewise movement of their vulnerable feet—the first short advance. They rested, breathing heavily, but not for long; the second effort brought them to the water's edge, with the next they were ankle-deep. For the rider on the bench it cannot have been a carefree journey—any small clumsiness on the men's part might have tipped her in the stream—but she showed a composure equal to theirs. None of my recollections of that impressive afternoon has remained more vivid than the expression of those three faces, made uniform, like those of soldiers in a death-or-victory assault, by a common valour and a common purpose. On the farther bank the attention of all was occupied by the Russo-Italian trio, who had just made their landfall, so the arduous and skilful work of the Englishmen went unregarded. I marvel still when I think of the quiet dignity, the unassuming confidence, with which those untrained bearers pursued their formidable task without a single voice to cheer them on.

At midstream they took, deservedly, an extended rest. There were inconveniences in this: the swiftly flowing water here invaded the tucked trouser legs, Lady Thelma herself had to draw her Brobdingnagian feet on to the bench to keep them safely dry. But half the journey was done, and the spirits of all three were at the highest point.

'Do you think we ought to do a bit of this singing thing?' Vowell asked rather bashfully.

Caudlemaster, while he recovered breath, considered this

motion. 'Well, just as you like!' he said at length. 'What do you think, Lady Thelma?'

She in turn pondered the proposal. 'My father,' she answered thoughtfully, 'had a saying I've never forgotten: "Do not spoil a ship," he used to say, "for the sake of saving a half-penny-worth of tar." '

Looking at Caudlemaster's earnest face I could see that, trained in rapid appreciation, he at once grasped the sense of Lady Thelma's father's apophthegm and saw how it should be applied. 'That's a clever way of putting it,' he said. Then he called, 'Mr O'Kneale! D'you mind telling us what this thing is we're supposed to sing?'

But Kevin's ears were under shorter-range bombardment. Once more the way was open for me to show that I was no mere parasite at this ritual observance.

'I know the whole thing,' I cried, splashing my way towards them.

'All right, young feller-m'lad, let's have it!' Caudlemaster said.

Distasteful as I found that appellation, I decided to let it pass, and entered at once upon my new engagement. Lady Thelma mastered the opening couplet quickly enough, and sang it very much as a shrewd landrail would after a few terms at the R.A.M. The men were more difficult to teach. 'I never get the hang of these Saxon things,' Caudlemaster confessed. 'They used to give us Chaucer for impots at Wellington, but I never quite saw what the chap was driving at.' The two of them worked conscientiously, however, and in time I had them singing more or less together, if in slightly discordant keys:

'Dorsal-wyde we will support her,
Mistog, mastoch, leasing-low.'

Intent on my tutorial work, I paid little attention to the large motorcar which had halted on the drive, close to where the rest of the party was standing: with a faulty sense of direction I vaguely supposed it was Caudlemaster's machine, brought round to fetch him. Only when the door of the car opened, and a short, wide, bountifully whiskered man stepped down from it, did I look hard enough to realize that a new interest was being added to a varied and unusual afternoon.

At Oxford some years later I was passing Elliston and Cavell's windows early one Sunday morning when I noticed, among the delicate and neatly ordered drapery, a large recumbent undergraduate of the football-playing kind in evening dress. (I learnt afterwards that he had been ingeniously placed there the night before, while in a vinous coma, by other Brasenose men.) Now, amid the random furniture which litters an old man's memory, I always find two portraits standing side by side: the beardless face of that young man just waking to a startling view of Magdalen Street in a frame of rayon underwear, and the hirsute face of Rushden Green as he surveys from the footboard of his Daimler the latest result of my mother's gregarious ebullience. As if their owners, setting out for Tunbridge Wells, had arrived without warning at Bir el Ksalb, those two faces reveal a striking identity of emotion: a total incredulity, illogically tinged with an acute distress.

With a child's vacant curiosity I went ashore to examine the stranger more closely, leaving my choral pupils to continue their practice independently. Joining the little group which had turned towards him, I had an excellent view of Sir Rushden's face when the look of stunned incomprehension gave place to one of palpable annoyance.

As I review the incident with the tolerance one learns with the passing of years I find a measure of excuse for Sir Rushden's unfriendly attitude. He had spent some hours with Herbert Asquith (not always the easiest of premiers for a junior minister to deal with), and a man who, after an exacting day, finds a number of strangers making free use of his private estate is apt to be ruffled by anything unconventional in their deportment; nor will he be reassured by seeing among them, drenched up to the thighs, his own principal domestic.

259

Green's first biographer, Mr Harwin Spode, tells us that he was largely unresponsive to music, and this deficiency may have aggravated the lawyer's sense of alienation; for although Girolamo had stopped singing, Semyon—with the constancy one sometimes regrets in the Russian temper—was still proclaiming the complex nostalgia of the Mosalski Trooper in a voice designed (one had supposed) to carry to the purlieus of Potters Bar. All in all, I think Sir Rushden may be forgiven for the touch of acerbity with which, when the ballad at last petered out, he delivered a general question:

'Will someone tell me just what is happening here?'

His tone had a strangely stifling effect on everyone except Kevin, who may have been comparatively insensitive to the symptoms of English displeasure. It was he who asked, perhaps with excessive geniality,

'Would you be forgetting, sir, 'tis the Nineteenth Day of April? Or do they not know in these parts about St Dirwyn and his beautiful behaviour?'

'I do not know anything about St Dirwyn,' the Deputy Attorney General said succinctly. 'I do know that this is my private property.'

'And an elegant property it is,' Kevin replied, 'with the wee burn and all! It could have been just made for the Lifting of the Women.'

Looking at Sir Rushden's face, I could tell that the Lifting of the Women was another subject on which he lacked information.

'What I want,' Sir Rushden said, 'before I send for the police, is a complete explanation of this act of trespass.'

'You mean, sir, you would like the whole story of St Dirwyn from the time he left his home in Inishbofin?'

Apparently this was not what Sir Rushden was in need of. In any case the talk between the two men was roughly broken by a shout from midstream; it was Caudlemaster, calling with despotic impatience,

'Mr O'Kneale, d'you mind coming here a moment! We don't know how this damned song goes on.'

'If you'll excuse me, sir, for the short end of a half-minute,' Kevin said to Sir Rushden, retiring gracefully into the brook.

By now my mother had recovered from the effect of Sir Rushden's incivility. Pictorially she was not at her best, for her party dress, already crumpled from the Lifting, was being turned by successive squalls of sleet and rain to an amorphous bundle of sodden taffeta, but her morale was unimpaired. Stepping into Kevin's place, she addressed the Deputy Attorney General with a radiance which would have thawed the snows of Greenland.

'Sir Rushden, it is so philanderous of you,' she said, 'to lend me your little park for the marriage fête of my uncle.'

His response lacked warmth, however: 'May I ask, Madam, who you are?'

'You don't remember me? But of course, when we meet in the past year I am wearing a yellow gown.'

'Indeed? From time to time,' Sir Rushden said pedagogically, 'I meet a number of ladies in yellow gowns.'

'And it have shown,' Sonya continued, struggling to keep her patience with this brainless man, 'a little more of my *poitrine*.'

Between these two there seemed to be little hope of any advance in understanding, and I was thankful when Howard, in his incalculable way, decided it was time for him to cut the Gordian knot. He came to stand in front of Sir Rushden, much as Horatius stood before Lars Porsena in a similar conflict of intentions.

'Will you listen, now, while I explain,' he said in a straightforward and manly way which I could not help admiring. 'My wife's uncle here has been wed to the same woman for twenty-five years—that's this one here, a trifle damp from the English climate and all but none the worse for that—and the policy was to celebrate the grand occasion with a whole menagerie of dancing virgins in the central pastures of Lausanne. Then the godforsaken Bank of England must needs put its foolish oar in.'

His rationale was interrupted by a burst of song from behind him:

'Let not vischil gnobes alarm us,
Fish nor fowl hath power to harm us!'

And as soon as speech was again possible Nikolai, with his usual generosity, came to develop the theme which my father had propounded.

'I also have to explain,' he said with his exquisite courtesy, raising his right and left legs in turn to dry them with a silk handkerchief. 'For a long time my charming niece has made me understand that among the beauties of Grande-Bretagne the estate of Sir Rushden Green has the most grandeur of them all. So, when our Irish friends wish to handle the ladies above the water, it is natural that your handsome torrent, Monseigneur Green, is selected for this traditional campaign.'

'In my country,' his wife added helpfully, 'we have greater waters, but the ladies are not so transacted. We find the steamboats a better convenience for the to-ings and from-ings of the female portion.'

'At the same time,' Mlle Lerévérand said fair-mindedly, 'such a traffic of the women is not so picturesque.'

And now, in a way which greatly touched me, Yelena Alexandrovna made a little contribution of her own to the seminar. Groping for the English words, she delivered them with fastidious care: 'Always it remains,' she said, smiling with regal complaisance, 'that the carriage of women procures for the workless a useful employment.'

Sir Rushden made no attempt to surrejoin that argument, which seemed scarcely to engage his attention. Like some other lawyers he was, I think, a man of narrow interests; moreover he had just caught sight, with evident relief, of one face which he knew. Rather unceremoniously he broke through the circle of people who were labouring to enlighten him and went to stand at the water's edge, where—in a small boy's eyes—he closely resembled Napoleon as Orchardson has pictured him aboard the *Bellerophon*.

'Mr Vowell,' he called, 'perhaps *you* can tell me what is happening here?'

To a rank-and-file M.P. a Deputy Attorney General is doubtless a person of some significance. Mr Vowell was manifestly alarmed by Sir Rushden's challenge, and it looked as if he would hurry ashore like a schoolboy summoned to the form master's desk. But Mr Caudlemaster foresaw that move and was quick to prevent it.

'We must get this job done first, old man,' he said decisively.

And indeed the face of Lady Thelma had started to betray a certain despondency. Physically her contorted position must have been one of minimum comfort, and however masculine in fortitude she was, I suspect, sufficiently a woman to deplore the ruination of her costly furbelows by the combined assault of rain and hail. But now—a thing to wonder at—her intrinsic virtue blazed again. Her features suddenly relaxed in the look of moist benevolence which served her in the place of a smile; with undiminished dignity but with almost girlish eagerness she cried, 'How do you do, Sir Rushden! I think we met at Mr Lowther's Reception last July.'

I doubt if Sir Rushden remembered Lady Thelma's face (now quaintly waterlogged) any better than he remembered my mother's, but the Speaker's name was one he could not disregard. Moreover he was not a man devoid of social grace.

'How do you do,' he said.

That promising reunion was disturbed by an appeal from Kevin, who had taken up a central position at the back of the bench. 'We could do with another hand here,' he called. 'This accursed thing has got its feet stuck in the mucky bottom.' My father and Nikolai at once responded, wading out and taking station on his right and left. With the five men heaving together the legs were freed and the bench lifted clear.

'Now the next piece!' Kevin ordered.

Standing straight and firm, as they would have for the National Anthem, the five sang with a manly fervour, and in tolerable concordance:

    Lush not, pish not, onwarde stryde,

Bear the brund, whate'er betyde.'

The east wind had become more ruthless, the fall of sleet was thickening. But for my part, I was almost tearfully happy now. A day of much moral discomfort, of many infantile alarms, seemed to be reaching a beatific dénouement. In the short silence which followed the singing, Lady Thelma sought to advance her emollient mission.

'I believe your brother used to know my cousin, Admiral Colgaught,' she called to Sir Rushden.

But some inward derangement—caused perhaps by political anxieties, perhaps by some intimate emotion—seemed to hinder the fluent operation of Sir Rushden's mind. 'I used to have two brothers,' he called back, with a note of rather pitiful confusion. 'There was Hammerstall and there was Trudd. I don't think either was a sailing man.'

This conundrum Lady Thelma might have disentangled, but now, with her seat borne by five men of varying stature and temperament, she needed to concentrate once more on her own equilibrium. This stage was critical. Slowly but sturdily the five moved forward, breaking once more into song. It is something I can never forget: the dauntless faces of the bearers advancing through a barrage of hail, and the invincible calm of their distinguished burden; a piquant blending of Irish and Russian voices with unschooled but resolute English ones, the swelling note of triumph with which, as they pressed towards the farther bank, the singers thundered forth the final chorus:

'Dirwyn lodist maiden bore,
Dumpen on ye fairther shore.'

As the bench was carefully lowered on terra firma I moved to get a better view of Sonya's face. It was rapturous. She in turn glanced towards Kevin, and I think their eyes met. It may be only in retrospective fancy that I see, connecting those two faces, a ghostly filament of perfect sympathy, of uniform delight.

*   *   *

It is something to be thankful for that a child sees only a little way into adult feelings. Many of the letters which Kevin sent to his mother at that time came later into Helma's possession. Through her indulgence I have before me the one he wrote on the day after the Totteridge fiesta.

'... The English are a better crew than I was given to imagine, they do their best to show themselves friendly, but oh their dullness would turn Heaven itself into a place of lamentation.... I gave them to relieve their mournful vapours the most I could call to mind of the old story of St Dirwyn you used to tell me. But oh, Mother mavourneen, it only set my own heart aching for all I've left behind, for you, for the great paps rising from the blue hills of Gallinaulty, for the calling that I fell in love with and was not within my reach...'

6

Kevin and Helma

I suppose that before the second decade of this century the Arranged Marriage had become—at any rate in most of Western Europe—the exception rather than the rule. So when I say that the union of Helma and Kevin depended on coincidence I am practically stating a truism. But to me, at least, the detailed operation of such coincidence is often of no small interest.

The providential instrument which brought Helma and Kevin together was a telegram dated from Hohenwald, in Bavaria, which arrived on the desk of Mr Hull, Assistant Manager of Curtice Powell Ltd, travel agents, in Cheapside, London, at nine o'clock on a Friday morning. The wording was:

> *'Completely stuck here. Many complaints from party. Food short and toilet situation far from satisfactory. Please wire further instructions. Wrimple.'*

From several conversations with Helma, in years when she and I had come to know each other better, I was able to piece together the circumstances of that agonized communication.

For all his imperturbability, it was fortunate for Herr Wilhelm Rinderspacher, Bürgermeister of Obervelden, that his daughter was home from the University of Regensburg (where she had recently added a Diploma in Education to her degree in Political Science) to help him with final preparations for the forthcoming Banquet at the Herrenhaus. His office staff was small and somewhat rustic in mental process. Long widowed, Herr Rinderspacher greatly loved his daughter, and his faith in her good sense was unlimited: if he made her responsible for the Banquet the whole affair would go through like a carriage on well-greased axles.

'It's rather a nuisance,' he told her at a preliminary conference, 'the army wanting exclusive use of the railway-line for their summer manoeuvres at this of all times.'

'The army is always a miserable nuisance,' Helma said.

'Hush, my dear—you mustn't even breathe such unnatural sentiments. The army is our only bulwark and our greatest pride. All the same, I wish they could have postponed their summer manoeuvres till sometime in the winter. I ventured to send a long letter to the Corps Commander. I told him that Hans Krommer's sow Elisabet Kirschenzweig—truly a marvellous animal, of lovely proportions, tenderly devoted to her twelve offspring—had won the first prize in competition with all the other sows in the great tournament at Vurgensburg. I mentioned that she is named after the fourth wife of the great philosopher Kirschenzweig, reminding him that Kirschenzweig was born and bred in this town—whatever ridiculous claims may be made by the arrogant village of Untervelden. I made the modest request that a special permit be granted for the transport of Krommer's sow and her progeny by rail from Vurgensburg to this place, of which she is—one may say—an honoured citizen.'

'And what did the Corps Commander reply?'

'To put it in a nutshell, he sent no reply at all. A busy man, I suppose. Never mind, we've got over that. Hans Krommer is sending his finest waggon, newly painted, with a team of four percherons, to meet the prize-winner at Viechengarten. From there the homeward journey will take less than three hours—the waggon should arrive at the Abbey gateway shortly before five-thirty. The procession will form up there with the band leading, and the waggon will enter the courtyard of the Herrenhaus at six o'clock. The Banquet will commence at precisely six-thirty, as you and I have already

267

agreed. In fact, I can't think of anything more we have to worry about.'

'I can,' his daughter said.

There can be no question that Helma Rinderspacher was fond of her father. Say, if you will, that some contact with a larger world had made her critical of the small one she had previously belonged to: it remains that she was a young woman of serious mind and affections who felt it important to guard her father from any kind of indignity or distress.

'Papa,' she said, 'do you really think it's essential for Elisabet and her brood to remain on view while the Banquet's going on?'

'But my dear, Elisabet and her offspring are what the Banquet is *for*—it's to celebrate her triumph over all the other sows who competed at Vurgensburg. The glory really belongs to Hans Krommer, who bred her with such incomparable skill. Hans would be utterly mortified—he wouldn't enjoy a single course—if his masterpiece wasn't there to be admired throughout the feast.'

'Hans Krommer,' Helma said unemotionally, 'is in my view the most absurdly conceited farmer in the whole neighbourhood. When his jack-ass Karl Mittermaier won a bronze medal three years ago *that* animal had to be in the Herrenhaus courtyard too. And he got loose—surely you remember—and gobbled up all the salad before the guests arrived.'

'That was quite a different matter, my dear. Karl Mittermaier was highly temperamental—he was excited over his medal and rushed about and ate the salad through an attack of nerves. Elisabet Kirschenzweig is the gentlest creature imaginable—as philosophic in her own way as the great man whose name she proudly bears.'

'That is something,' Helma said, with small conviction.

'I confess,' her father continued rather wearily, 'that I've been bothered with a lot of quite unnecessary disturbance. That abominable machine, the telephone, keeps interrupting my work with all sorts of stupid messages, including my Aunt Hanna's—she thinks I can find her a new maidservant. And

268

then there's that pack of philosophic tourists at Hohenwald, making a fearful commotion because the commandeering of the railway seems to have upset their plans.'

'Tourists?'

'Yes, a whole crowd of professors and such people who want to make a song-and-dance about the second centenary of Kirschenzweig's birth. They seem to have accepted the preposterous theory that Kirschenzweig was born at Untervelden, and they're grumbling because the railway people won't take them to that wretched hamlet. Well, as I said to the stationmaster, that sort of foolishness is no concern of mine.'

Helma was scarcely attending. 'I can't see why anyone in the world should fuss over Kirschenzweig and his fantastic notions,' she said. 'What worries me is dealing with General Nichtberger.'

'But why, my love?'

'Do you think the General will be pleased to find himself dining within a few metres of Elisabet and all her little ones?'

'Is that likely?'

'More than likely. All the sleeping accommodation in the Herrenhaus has been reserved for four nights for the General and his Staff. The order's driving Herr Lindenstadt half out of his mind, he has to search the town for other accommodation for all the earlier bookings.'

'Very well—if the military people want their meals in the hotel George Lindenstadt can offer to serve them in a special room, not in the terrace restaurant. Then in all probability they wouldn't even know that the *Feiermahl* was taking place. Sometimes, Helma my sweet, I think you go a little out of your way to manufacture difficulties.'

'Papa, darling,' Helma said gently, 'if we are to talk of manufacturing difficulties, I would remind you it wasn't I who invited Graf Otto von Lunichshofen to attend the *Feiermahl*.'

'But my dear,' said her father, 'Graf Otto would have been deeply hurt if he had not been invited—in a way, he still thinks of the Herrenhaus as his own hereditary property.

Besides, I don't regard the poor old man as a difficulty at all. A little wandery, perhaps, but perfectly innocuous. It is some time since I had the honour of meeting him myself, but everyone tells me he is not nearly so mad as his father. The grandfather, Graf Rudolf, was of course totally insane—he imagined he was a reincarnation of the Decemvir Appius Claudius, he used to travel to München especially in order to make lascivious gestures at the sculpture in the Glyptothek. Graf Otto has never been known to do anything of that sort.'

'I am glad of that, Papa,' Helma said.

A part of Helma Rinderspacher's mind was deeply engaged with a problem of her own. She had been offered the post of Assistant-Principal in a renowned school at Passau. Never before had such an appointment been offered to one so young. She had not yet told her father. Was it her duty, now, simply to refuse it? If she chose to stay at home, as only-daughters of widowed fathers were expected to do, she might accomplish other things besides managing the domestic side of her father's life; she might bring some order, a degree of efficiency, into the public side. The approaching banquet was only one example of the extravagance with which the affairs of Obervelden were being conducted. By degrees she could change all that: she could reorganize the little town's touristic possibilities, the development would bring in money which was badly needed to deal with disgraceful conditions in the old Malzhaus quarter...

For the moment, however, the important thing was to get the Elisabet Kirschenzweig *Feiermahl* mounted, smoothly served—and done with.

'Completely stuck,' Mr Hull read aloud from the telegram on his desk.

'*Completely stuck!*' he repeated, in a voice where incredulity competed with mounting indignation.

'*Wire further instructions,*' Mr Hull shouted in a tone of savage burlesque which broke into the uproar of Cheapside, alarming passengers on the upper deck of a passing bus.

'This Wrimple,' Mr Hull said to Mr Taylor, his personal clerk, 'is what they call a highly educated man. He has "B.A. Cantab" stuck on the end of his name. This is what happens when bloody fools of rich parents, not content with passing a boy through a normal schooling, which don't do any harm worth mentioning to most of us, have to go and buy a whole lot more of what they call education and have it piled on to the after end of the little twot.

'Here,' Mr Hull continued, 'we have this Mr B.A. Wrimple, some cousin or something of the owners of this godforsaken house of business, being told to use his precious education to cart no more than thirty other learned imbeciles to some twopenny-halfpenny German town which any normal person would get to as easy as the Rose and Crown at Tooting Bec, and before you can say "Jim Jugglebottom" this prize educated cuckoo has lost the thirty other learned nanny-goats in some public bog as far as I can make any head or tail of what he says and doesn't know where in hell he's got to or how to get anywhere else either, and what does he think of doing but come bleating to me for "further instructions"! Just when Mr Mountcaswell's up at Glasgow—that *would* happen! Well, we'll have to send someone to dig the silly bastard out of wherever it is. Where's Hoggett? On his summer holiday? He *would* be! No one in this damned ticket-shop does anything except go on holidays. Where's Petticorn? No, that's no use, he'd only go and get himself lost in the public bog with all the rest of them. Where's what's-his-name—that wily Irish bastard, O'Brien, O'Connor, O'Some-dam-thing-or-other —O'Kneale? Get O'Kneale, somebody! At the *double*!

'Now the first thing,' Mr Hull barked at Kevin, 'is to get an atlas—you'll find an atlas in Hoggett's desk somewhere— and look up where this place Hohenwald is, if there is such a place at all, which I wouldn't count on. Then sell yourself a ticket to it, wherever it is, whether it's there or not. Then go and hunt the public bog at this place till you find this madman Wrimple, B.A., and as many as you can of the other

271

dunderheads traipsing round after him—foreigners mostly, as far as I remember, and it doesn't so much matter about these damned Dutchmen and dagoes, but if the English lot don't get back sooner or later there'll be questions asked in Parliament and hell to pay with the Boss. You'd better get some travelling kit and put it on the expense sheet, I fancy you need a thing called an alpenstock, ask Hoggett—only you can't, 'cause he's on his blasted holiday. And most likely you'll want a Tyrolean hat, or a sola topee, that sort of gew-gaw. Only whatever happens don't go sending footling telegrams back to me...'

At Hohenwald, where my kinsman Kevin O'Kneale arrived in the late afternoon on an ancient bicycle he had bought for seventeen Marks at Kunzeldorf, 26 km away, there was much to disturb a man of orderly mind and to distress a tender-hearted one. The china-clay seams, which with their ancillary workings have permanently disfigured the Hohenwald valley, had been disused since 1905; deserted, the sprawl of shanties which had served the workmen and their families were now in ruins, the Wolke Gasthaus had practically ceased to be anything but a bar for the owner's friends, the one remaining shop opened for the sale of paraffin and crumbling biscuits only when the Widow Schunemann was finding boredom less endurable than her arthritis. In this lugubrious canyon a railway coach containing the devotees of Kirschenzweig had already stood in a siding for more than forty-eight hours. The pilgrims were hungry, and those teetotallers among them who believed that to drink unbottled water on the mainland of Europe was the surest recipe for typhoid were thirsty as well. This (as Kevin later reported in a letter to my father) was a harrowing situation. My cousin was by no means stony-hearted: he cannot have been unmoved by the spectacle of famished and bewildered intellectuals who, after paying more than they could easily afford for a bout of cultural advance-ment, now found themselves marooned in one of the least exhilarating valleys known to exist between Tarifa and Hammerfest. He had learnt, however, from the stringent milieu of his youth that the commonest provisions of life are untidiness and hunger. Piles of rubble and rusted iron, a ragged carpet of hawkbit and sowthistle which threatened to obliterate the siding rails, these did not strike him as symptoms of disaster on a cataclysmic scale; the grey, despondent faces at the carriage windows stirred him to pity but not to ultimate despair.

'Will we not dig out some daft old railway pensioner,' he said to Mr Wrimple, 'and slip him a handful of the local coinage to hitch an engine on this misbegotten truck and drag the damned thing to wherever these poor loonies want to get to?'

'But you don't understand,' Mr Wrimple said with almost tearful indignation. 'It's the stationmaster you've got to deal with. *He* gets his orders from the military. And I can tell you this, old man, they take the military damned seriously in these awful continental places.'

Walter Wrimple, at forty-three, had a thin, bluish, melancholy face, a scalp which had already lost most of its flaxen hair and the basic plan of a moustache which had never come to much. He wore rimless spectacles. Nature and a widowed mother had designed him as a teacher of languages and history to lewd adolescents of the baser sort at a progressive school in Worcestershire. He was right about the Stationmaster.

'I have told you twenty times already,' the Stationmaster said to Wrimple, 'I have direct orders from Military Headquarters. All lines to be kept clear for troop movements. For a country like ours, surrounded by jealous rivals, movements of military personnel are of the highest imaginable importance.'

Not that his tone was harsh or his mien unfriendly. The Stationmaster was a round family man with a moustache many times more copious than Walter Wrimple's; he was devoted to the pleasures obtainable from the music of Wagner

273

and from Westfälischen Schinken. The discussion, starting in the station office, was continued in the Gasthaus, where Herr Wolke, the Stationmaster's brother-in-law, had unexpectedly discovered in a drawer beneath his winter vests an encouraging supply of Weihenstephan.

'For heaven's sake tell this numbskull,' Kevin said to Wrimple, 'that I represent an important company working in close connection with the British Parliament. Talk to the old moke about international complications and suchlike— tell him there'll be hell to pay if he doesn't get our truck moving. Ask him who runs his beautiful army—which we all admire and love like our own sweethearts—and tell him to get the silly fellow on the telephone.'

Obediently, but with diplomatic reservations, Wrimple rendered these representations into German. Tankard in hand, the Stationmaster received them with a grave attention.

'Much of yesterday,' he said, 'I spent in trying to make some special arrangement by means of telephonic communication. The telephone, you understand, gentlemen, is a delicate contrivance. At one point I thought I had the ear of the Director of Military Transport at Straubing, but the call was interrupted and I found myself listening to a lady—a member of the distinguished Rinderspacher family—who was in conversation with her nephew, the Bürgermeister of Obervelden. She was hoping he might find her a servant girl to replace one she had been obliged to dismiss for barefaced dishonesty.'

Again Kevin prompted his colleague: 'Can't you remind the old gas-bag that what our crew has come all this way for is to pay their respects to what's-his-name—one of his own great philosophers. Kirshen-something, they told me at the office.'

Wrimple, faintly shuddering, wiped his forhead. 'Kirschenzweig,' he said; and added, 'but I've said that over and over again. I've told him as well that I've got a speech of my own to deliver at Untervelden—that's the central part of my assignment. Three thousand words. Most of it pinched I must admit from Böhme-Böhland—I had to review that book of his for *Philosophy Today*. My mother has most kindly typed it out for me.'

'Well, try him once more on Kirshen-whatever-it-is,' Kevin said stubbornly.

Wrimple did so.

'Kirschenzweig—indeed, yes, one of our most famous thinkers,' the Stationmaster said. For the third time he emptied his tankard and refilled it. 'In my own household we have troubles of the same kind,' he continued reflectively. 'It becomes harder every year to find girls for domestic service —the sort of wages they ask for, you'd think they were Duchesses.'

It was the Stationmaster's wife who, in the way of woman-kind, arrived to curtail the tripartite conference.

'In the Railway Regulations,' she announced, in the plausible tones of Jael the wife of Heber the Kenite, 'it says that the Stationmaster may be absent from his office, if circumstances permit, for thirty minutes during the hours of duty for purposes of physical necessity or other forms of recreation. It is now more than an hour since you left the office. The Assistant Clerk is threatening to resign his appointment. A soldier has come—a very handsome officer with epaulettes and all the rest of it. He gives you the choice of returning to the office within one minute or being shot on Platform 1 with a revolving pistol.'

The short walk back to the Stationmaster's office was—as Kevin later described it—the bleakest episode in that weari-some day. He himself had found the Weihenstephan a cum-ulative depressant. The lowering sun had left the air both clammy and stifling. In the dismal siding the abandoned rail-way coach still stood as the stark evidence of failure, a lamentable reproach to Europe's cultural pretensions; within it the more nervous pilgrims had remained, staring vacantly

275

through the fly-infested windows, while the bolder stood in little groups among the slag-heaps and the mouldering bothies, forlornly hoping that Frau Schunemann would once more raise her shutters to sell them another kilogram of time-worn oatmeal biscuits, and agreeing in their several tongues that the English travel bureaux existed solely to practise monstrous frauds on unsuspecting strangers. Only in one aspect had the scene changed dramatically: where the main railway line was ruled between the station building and the signal box a train of seven coaches had been placed, as if by expert scene-shifters from the Bayreuth Festspielhaus, against the scarred hillside.

That phenomenon caused the Stationmaster to stop, blinking.

'Great God in Heaven above!' he said to his wife. 'I never heard any train coming.'

'If you happen to be drinking Weihenstephan in Albrecht's bedroom when the Last Trump sounds you won't hear that either,' she briefly replied.

Wrimple was polishing his spectacles with a piece of chamois-leather supplied by his mother for that purpose, with the words *For polishing Spectacles* embroidered in her own hand. Falling back a little way, he took Kevin by the arm.

'This is something you and I had better keep out of,' he whispered. 'I've not been a schoolmaster all my life without learning a thing or two. When fellows start actually tearing each other to bits, the only thing is to pretend you've got to rush off into the town and order stationery or something.'

Kevin did not share this view. 'Why,' he said, 'is this not a perfect chance we have to get our pop-eyed customers moved over into that train!'

'We can't!' was Wrimple's sensible answer. 'To start with, it's bound to be a military train—there aren't any others allowed. And even if we could, how do we know it would take us to Untervelden?'

'Does that really matter?'

'Of course it matters! Untervelden's where Kirschenzweig was born.'

'Does *he* matter?'

'Kirschenzweig? My dear chap, according to Böhme-Böhland he was one of the World's Greatest Thinkers.'

'But don't the World's Greatest Thinkers crop up all over this damned country like nettles in an old chicken-run? Would there not be one of them born and bred and did his wee piece of world's-greatest-thinking in any one-horse town this train might have a mind to go to?'

'But I tell you,' Wrimple protested, again almost in tears, 'it's Untervelden where I'm booked to do my speech. I've got it here—I've had all the German vetted by a chap who knows it better than I do, and my mother's been kind enough to type the whole thing out, though she suffers frightfully from rheumatism in the finger-joints.'

In the Stationmaster's office they found that two officers were standing side by side. It was the younger, taller and more handsome who was addressing the Stationmaster as a schoolteacher addresses a pupil caught reading shockers under his desk.

'The Brigade Major demands to know why a train conveying military personnel on a movement of the first importance has been held up at this piffling station.'

Standing against the wall, swaying a little and visibly trembling, the Stationmaster knew with dreadful precision the true answer to this inquiry. He himself, confused by the hubbub on the telephone, had told the afternoon-duty man in the signal box (who was his nephew by marriage) that no train of any sort could arrive earlier than 7.30 that evening; on receipt of that intelligence, his nephew would have taken his normal action—he would have set all signals in the *Halt* position and bicycled off to spend a couple of delicious hours with his little friend Martha Tomschin in her cottage two kilometres away. These homely arrangements would not have been easy to explain to a young man bursting with martial grandeur and impatience. The best the Stationmaster could say was:

'The matter will be rectified immediately, Herr Hauptmann. You'—he turned to address the Assistant Clerk—'will proceed at once to the Signals Compartment and see that all up-line signals are altered to the *Proceed* position. Meanwhile,' he continued, now facing the short, fat, more elaborately bedizened officer, and making intelligent use of the smoke-screen which chanced to be at hand, 'I respectfully ask leave to present to you these two English gentlemen, Herr Doktor Rimpel and Herr Direktor Niel, who have made the long journey from London to honour one of our great philo-sophers.'

Mr. Wrimple bowed to the officers. The Brigade Major briefly acknowledged that courtesy.

'Tell this worthy popinjay,' Kevin said to Wrimple, 'that I greatly admire the elegance of his uniform.'

Somewhat nervously Wrimple did so.

'And say that the efficiency of the German army is known to the entire world.'

'That fact we proudly understand,' the Brigade Major admitted.

'And for that reason,' Kevin pursued, 'we have no doubt at all that he can arrange for the coach containing our dis-tinguished party to be attached to his train, so they can continue their journey.'

Still more nervously, Wrimple translated. The dour, machine-made face of the Brigade Major began slowly to show that it contained the apparatus of human cerebration.

'I also,' he announced to Kevin, 'I am a scholar of the English. *"Henry Eight is a mighty monarch, he keep in his bed six wives for the constant sleeping. When they do not please him he cut off their heads, one after the next, chop-chop-chop."* I have it correct, *ja?*'

'Your English, Colonel, is quite remarkable,' Kevin assured him. 'You and I, we understand each other perfectly. You understand me when I say, "Please give a quick order for my

278

tourist coach to be fixed to your train." '

'I understand quite good,' the Brigade Major agreed. He turned to the Captain. 'Duncker, can you arrange for this Englishman's coach to be attached to our train?'

Captain Duncker flinched, as if he had been ordered to embrace the Corps Commander's wife in the centre of a parade ground. Recovering his poise, he said smartly,

'Sir, it is laid down in *General Orders for Army Transport*, Paragraph 83 (c) (ii), that no coach without military markings is permitted as an element in a railway-train designated for the conveyance of military personnel. I understand the coach these foreigners are fussing about is full of philosophic tourists. I can't see, with all respect, Sir, how people of that sort could be described as "Auxiliary Civilian Personnel".'

The Brigade Major nodded sagely. 'My transport officer,' he said to Kevin, 'tells me that the Regulations put your request outside of the possibilities. If your tourists were all beautiful young women we could speak of them as "Auxiliary Military Personnel"—you understand? I think so, ha-ha-ha! But those I have observed are not I think quite young or very beautiful.'

'They could be called "Interpreters",' Kevin said.

'But for what intention have we the need for interpreters?'

Kevin shrugged his shoulders. He said, 'All my life they were telling me that German Officers were the best you'd find in all the world—clever gentlemen who'd be as brave as lions. Now I find to my pity and amazement they're frightened for their lives because of some small piece of clerking which says they aren't allowed to risk their soldiers' lives by putting a few old women on the end of their train. It's a sad chapter, Colonel, that you've added to my education.'

Mr Wrimple, listening to that speech, stared aghast at his colleague. It seemed inevitable that the two officers would produce their pistols and shoot the madman dead, unless they decided to strangle him slowly with their bare hands. Would he, Wrimple, be strangled for good measure as well?

Indeed, the Brigade Major's face was that of the Emperor Nero being casually insulted by an Ethiopian slave. Yet after some fifteen terrifying seconds it was visited by that crumpling of features which nature had devised for him as the rough sketch of a smile. Another few moments passed, then he said abruptly,

'This is all a ridiculous waste of time. Duncker, you will immediately instruct all the foreigners to return to their coach. You will then personally seal the doors. You will then have Brigade markings with the words *"Reserved for Interpreters"* pasted on every window. After that you, Mr Stationmaster, will quickly have the coach shunted on to the rear of my train, which will then haul it without any more damned nonsense as far as Obervelden.'

The name Obervelden brought Wrimple out of his mental and physical paralysis. 'Herr Brigade-Major,' he said with palpitating humility, 'while we are profoundly grateful for your most generous action, I would beg leave to mention that our proper destination is the birthplace of your immortal Kirschenzweig—*Unter*velden.'

'Enough!' said the Major curtly. 'You will execute my orders, Captain, without a moment's delay.'

At 3 pm on the day of the Banquet the conscientious manager of the Herrenhaus at Obervelden was still calling at private houses, seeking accommodation for travellers who had made earlier bookings. In the covered courtyard the platform on which the band was to play had been decorated with expensive flowers, and a small strawed pen where the victorious Elisabet was to exhibit herself and her offspring was being rigged with coloured lights and bunting. On the terrace flanking the court the main banqueting table was in an advanced state of preparation, while other long tables were being rather somnolently clothed and set by shirt-sleeved youths who would presently be transmogrified into waiters.

In his own cubby-hole near the entrance from the square

Herr Schmidt, the Head Porter, after a late and generous luncheon, was lying half-asleep on his bunk. Near his head was a small embrasured window through which, himself hardly visible, he might observe any occurrence in the court-yard demanding his personal attendance.

At that hour dream and reality are sometimes hard to distinguish. With his eyes just closed, Hermann Schmidt seemed to hear an august voice informing him that he was to receive an Imperial Decoration in reward for his many years of diligent service at the Herrenhaus, and now he saw the Decoration being actually brought towards him on a velvet cushion; the cushion was borne by two ladies, both young, both of exceptional beauty, who in the course of their journey from the Capital had had the misfortune to lose every stitch of their clothing. He was about to suggest a way in which that catastrophe could be turned to advantage when, his eyelids vexatiously rising, he caught sight of two other ladies, neither young nor handsome, who so far from being *in puris naturalibus* appeared to him as creeping monticules of travelling coats, hats, veils and every other sort of feminine superfluities.

Hermann got up as quickly as his hundred kilograms' body-weight allowed and put on his black jacket. In the courtyard he found that the two ladies had been joined by several others, while more were straggling through the great archway. There were gentlemen as well, most of them old and rather lame, laden with ear-flap caps, binoculars, photo-graphic apparatus and other touristic impedimenta, as well as with Gladstone bags and travelling rugs and canvas holdalls. In common they had a look of weariness and wild-eyed hunger and thirst. The man who first approached him was a good deal younger than the rest; a miserable creature he looked to Hermann Schmidt, with his chestless body, his rudimentary moustache, a chin which appeared to be no more than a slight protuberance on his scraggy neck.

'Good afternoon,' this man said meekly, speaking German rather as one with artificial arms and legs rides a dromedary.

281

'Have you, please, accommodation for my small party of distinguished scholars?'

'I regret, sir,' the Porter said majestically, 'that the Herrenhaus is closed absolutely. The entire hotel has been requisitioned by the Military.'

Mr Wrimple appeared to be stunned. 'But this is extremely awkward,' he said. 'My party consists of persons of European reputation. We are on our way to attend the Kirschenzweig Bicentenary Celebrations at Untervelden, our coach has been unaccountably detached from the rest of the train. At the very least you will, I hope, provide us with a substantial meal.'

'A meal? Quite impossible!' the Porter said. 'Our catering facilities are fully engaged with an important banquet.'

The word *Feiermahl* seemed to have a powerful effect on the woman standing nearest to Wrimple, whose name was Karlotte Zschokke. She was short and robust, with the elephantine ankles and sturdily sandalled feet which are not unknown in the Swiss countryside—she belonged, in fact, to a suburb of Schaffhausen.

'This is the greatest nonsense I ever heard,' Frau Zschokke said, in the manner of a six-inch field gun firing its sighting round. 'We are here to honour the memory of a great German philosopher. This is a public hotel—it is listed as such in the Gohrmann Guide. And you have the monumental impertinence to say you can give us nothing to eat.'

Kevin, meanwhile, was conferring with Wrimple. 'The thing is,' he said, 'to tell this illustrious bumpkin we *are* the Army—we are all official interpreters appointed for the seasonal manoeuvres. Find out how many rooms he has, and we'll help ourselves to about half of them.'

'I can only repeat, madam,' the Porter was replying to Frau Zschokke, 'that my orders are to exclude the general public from this hotel, categorically and absolutely.'

'How many rooms have you?' Wrimple dared to ask.

'That, sir, is quite immaterial. All nineteen of them have been commandeered by the Military. I could show you the

Army Order from Straubing—it is in the Manager's office.'

'Indeed, if you are telling the truth I should very much like to see it!' Frau Zschokke said.

Though the movements of Hermann Schmidt—at the age of 62—were somewhat ponderous, it did not take him long to reach the Manager's office at the end of the east corridor, and in less than five minutes the Order (tucked with other such papers into the copy of *Des Knaben Wunderhorn* which Herr Lindenstadt had won at school as a prize for Good Conduct) was in his hands. Five minutes, however, are time enough for some activity on the part of people galvanized by physical hunger and spiritual exasperation. No sooner was the Porter out of sight than Kevin picked up the largest valise from the pile around him and mounted the terrace on which the tables were being set. From there he beckoned to his party. The tourists may or may not have supposed that a fresh decision had been made in their favour: obediently, picking up their baggage, they formed a ragged procession which wound its tired way across the restaurant terrace, through the lobby, up to the first floor. When the Porter returned, triumphantly bearing the Requisition Order and now determined to have no more nonsense from the mob in the courtyard, he found that the mob was physically on a higher level than he.

The foot of the staircase was blocked by a Danish couple, resting with their baggage beside a half-blind Reader in Experimental Eudaemonism from the Institute of Advanced Technology at Rochdale and a large asthmatic matron from Zagreb. Hermann Schmidt therefore stood quite still in the centre of the lobby, his face set in such an expression as Moses may have worn at his first sight of the crowd around Aaron's golden calf.

'This,' he proclaimed, 'is a matter for the Police.'

Upstairs, Kevin was busy. Having found that No. 5 Bedroom was exceptionally commodious, he was considering whether with some delicate contrivance it could be made to serve as dormitory for two married couples (one Swedish, one Bulgarian) and a pair of female philosophers from the Duchy of Luxemburg. From these cares he was diverted by a young woman's voice which asked, in a tone of patrician authority,

'*Welcher ist der Führer dieser Gruppe?*'

Turning, he saw in the open doorway a figure as different from the lady tourists as it was possible for a woman to be: she was young, compact, bare-headed, neatly dressed in a white overall with grey collar and cuffs; in no ordinary sense a beauty, but with eyes of such deep intelligence, cheeks sculptured with so spare a dignity, a small mouth so resolute, that he felt the sharp pleasure which an evening breeze brings at the end of a sultry day.

'Good afternoon, ma'am!' Kevin said. 'Delighted I am to make your charming acquaintance.'

The young woman repeated her question in confident English: 'Who is in charge of this party?'

'Well, roughly speaking, you might say that I am.'

'Then you will roughly remove it from this building in two minutes, or else I shall have you arrested by the Police.'

'Indeed? Have I the honour, then, of speaking to the owner of this hotel?'

'You have not.'

'Then who are you, may I ask?'

'That is no concern to you at all. But I happen to be the daughter of the Bürgermeister—the Mayor of this town.'

'Ah! My compliments to your honourable father—I trust he is in the best of health. He will need to be, when I tell him what I think of this godforsaken place you say he's in control of.'

'Mr Englishman, I have told you already—'

'My name is Kevin O'Kneale. If I was an Englishman I would cut myself into wee small slabs and sell them in the nearest dog-food market. But I am indeed the representative of an important London business-house, and at this moment I'm sick and tired of putting up with one piece after another of ball-eyed German inefficiency and pig-headed German

284

obstruction. I have come out here—'

'Mr Neal, I have already warned you—'

'Miss Daughter-of-the-almighty-Mayor, will you have the goodness to hold your tongue while I inform you of the situation! I have here a party of learned people, men and women of the highest reputation, who've come from all over Europe to pay respect and honour to the memory of your great philosopher Kitchenwig, if I have his name correctly. At every point—'

'Then I shall tell you, to begin with, that Heinrich Kirschenzweig was an uncommonly foolish person from a small village called Untervelden who wrote many books of extravagant rubbish, and only simpletons pay the least attention to his so-called scholarship. If your friends wish to waste their money—'

'What you say is no surprise to me at all. At the Catholic college I myself attended the general opinion was that German philosophy included a large proportion of the purest spittle-and-bunkum. Nor would it astonish me to find that all these people I'm steering round this accursed country are just as daft as they appear to my own naked eyes. But that is no excuse for locking them and me in a moth-eaten railway coach for something like nineteen hours without food or drink at the back end of a so-called military train being dragged along at one mile an hour by a steam-engine which if it came to my country would be taken to the nearest knacker's yard and humanely put to sleep with a pole-axe. What I'm telling you—'

'What I am about to tell *you*, Mr Neal—'

'Be quiet, woman! What I'm telling you is that these poor loonies with an average age of about ninety-five have gone for more than two whole days without anything like a meal. From which it follows on that your *first* business, as daughter of the head-man of this prehistoric hamlet, is to stir up the paralytic bodies who are meant to run this tenth-rate so-called hotel *and get my party something to eat*. When you've done that—'

285

'Mr Neal, the Staff of this famous and very efficient hotel is not lazy or stupid in any small degree. They—'

'Indeed, no, they are lazy and stupid in a very *large* degree. When I—'

'Be quiet! Hold your teeth! Every person in the Staff of this hotel is extremely occupied in preparation for a great feast of celebration which has long before been constituted for this evening. This preparation—'

'Feast? Celebration? And may I please ask what you have to celebrate? *Another* half-cooked philosophic author, would it be? Or the end of the Thirty Years' War, which no doubt you've just had the news of?'

'What we celebrate is nothing to do for you! Even if you think this a very small and unpraised town, I believe we have the right to honour a special victory by one of our very skilful farmers. To us agriculture is of the highest importance, it is not a small thing that one of our hardworking farmers has cultivated the best pig in the whole of this region. If you—'

'The best *pig*? What—you mean to tell me that all the great men of this mighty town have to gather themselves tonight to make a feast of the best pig?'

'Not *of* the best pig. *For* the best pig.'

'You mean the best pig is to feast on all the great men of this town?'

'Mr Neal, you are being extremely foolish.'

'Fräulein Whatever-your-name-might-be, I am not being foolish at all. You have just told me in plain English—on which I take the liberty to offer my congratulations—that here, tonight, in this highfalutin hotel, there's to be a great feast in honour of a philosophic pig. That means—'

'I did not say "a philosophic pig"—'

'I'm not arguing whether the pig is philosophical or plain foolish. Here is this preposterous doss-house, stacked up with food to the honour and glory—may all the Saints in Heaven preserve us!—of some blessed holy *pig*. And here am I with around thirty poor feeble-witted souls without a meal inside them for God alone knows how long, through the damned interference of your swaggering empty-headed army and the general godforsaken inefficiency of this antiquated country, and you have the stark effrontery to tell me you don't care a twopenny toss in Hades if the whole lot perish from starvation, so long as the guzzling burghers of this pagan parish have their evening's pig-worship with no one from the outside world to observe their wretched and revolting greed. You think I'll stand for that, because of the sweet womanly way you have in putting it. Well, let me tell you, you're wrong, Miss Bürgermeister's-daughter. There are some sorts of damned nonsense I will do my best to put up with, and some sorts I will not.'

The practical uses of music are manifold: one is to halt and extinguish intemperate oratory. The renowned Municipal Band of Obervelden (augmented by several instrumentalists from the far-famed Municipal Band of Pfarrkirhausen) had been assembling in the Market Square, preparatory to marching to the rendezvous with Elisabet Kirschenzweig and her entourage at the Abbey Gateway. It was not a band which wasted time in silent marching. At the moment when my cousin was reaching a dangerous state of verbal auto-intoxication his voice was abruptly drowned by the opening bars of *The March of the Meistersinger*, delivered with astounding violence almost directly below the window of the room where he was standing. For nearly a minute, then, further parley was out of the question. This should have given Helma the time she needed to compose an appropriate retort —a speech at once so rational and so imperious that the foreigner's impudence would be finally overwhelmed. Such a counterblast she did in fact make ready. But, so intricate is the mental process in women, she never delivered it. When the dwindling uproar opened the way once more to vocal intercourse she said, with a taut simplicity,

'I make no promise. But I shall ask whether the hotel can arrange for giving your people some food at one of the side tables.'

At this my cousin gravely nodded. He took a short step forward. Placing his long, bony hands upon the Bürgermeister's daughter's shoulders, he said with a sage deliberation,

'When I see in a woman's eyes the beauty that I'm seeing now, then I know there's a heart of gold inside her that's beyond her own control.'

Deriving from one of the older families of Braunschweig-Wolfenbuttel, Generalmajor Nichtberger was a man of native good humour. As other soldiers do, he liked to have his own way: this he had just achieved in overriding the foolish inclination of Generalleutnant Hartwig to allot the area north of Lorschdoft to his Division while he, Nichtberger, knew from every experience that the country to the east of Obervelden was superior both as camping ground and as a basis for the forthcoming manoeuvres. Obervelden, moreover, was a town he was personally fond of; he liked its old-fashioned flavour, he enjoyed visiting one Gustav von Triebsch, a friend from his cadet days who had retired to live in the neighbourhood. When, therefore, a little after six-thirty, he arrived in his flagged motor-car at the Herrenhaus, where a Colonel on his Staff came forward with a face tortured by anxiety and guilt (while an N.C.O. and two Police Corporals stood at the full-salute), Generalmajor Nichtberger was ready to approach the trials and tragedies of a soldier's life in a spirit of courageous equanimity.

'A most unpardonable blunder has been committed,' the Staff Colonel said, 'by the management of this hotel. They've allowed a small horde of tourists to invade the sleeping accommodation.'

'Have they indeed!' said the General. 'You mean that I shall have to share a bedroom with some stray civilian? Of which sex is my partner to be?'

'To share—? You, Sir? Oh, emphatically not, Sir,'

'Ah, a military career is full of disappointments,' the General said.

The face of Oberstleutnant Berghauer was one which Nichtberger had long grown tired of. Turning, he saw in the archway a civilian whom he vaguely recognized, waiting to greet him.

'Rinderspacher!' the civilian announced, taking a smart pace forward. 'My very humble respects, Herr General.'

'Good evening, Herr Bürgermeister!' Nichtberger replied, noting at a glance the insignia of Herr Rinderspacher's office.

'A private dining-room has been arranged for you and your officers,' the Bürgermeister said smoothly, 'but the citizens of Obervelden have been wondering whether you would care to delight and honour us by sharing in a modest *Feiermahl* arranged to celebrate an agricultural victory. We have taken the liberty of reserving special places for you, and for your distinguished Colonel, should you be graciously willing to join us.'

To Generalmajor Nichtberger (as he tells us in his memoirs, *Meine Militärische Laufbahn*) the nature of Bürgermeister Rinderspacher's invitation was not entirely clear. He had, however, an oblique view of a long table adorned with candelabra, smothered with bottles and demi-litre glasses, while mentally he envisaged a more austere dinner-table surrounded by the reverential faces of his Staff, officers whose conversation, almost exclusively on military topics, bored him almost more painfully than the puritanical face and utterance of Colonel Berghauer.

'Delighted, Herr Bürgermeister, delighted!' he said.

The augmented Municipal Band of Obervelden in its gold and plum-purple uniforms was rendering *Ho Bruder, nimm das Gläschen* with frenetic zeal. Deafened and slightly dazed, the General responded with his usual assurance but without much understanding to a series of introductions: '...the greatest citizen of all our neighbourhood, Graf Otto von Lunichshofen ... And please allow me, Herr General, to present to you also my daughter, Fräulein Helma Rinderspacher...' Seated, he bent a courteous ear towards the shrivelled octogenarian on his right, whose tiny, glinting eyes he found faintly disquieting.

'Welcome to my hearth, Herr Feldmarschall!' Graf Otto screamed against the uproar from the band. 'Our families have, of course, long been acquainted. When I first knew your grandmother her head, I remember, came exactly in line with my navel.'

'Graf Otto is famed for his phenomenal memory,' the Bürgermeister explained. 'I trust the goose is to your liking, Herr General?'

'Indeed, it is delicious.'

'An admirable orchestra!' Graf Otto observed, when the music at last died away. 'That tune, you may like to know, was composed by my aunt, Elisabet Olrich. The verses she wrote it for were of course by Heine. You would like to hear it again, I expect?'

'Well, a little later on, perhaps.'

'So! I take it you are here, sir,' Graf Otto continued, with his upper denture somewhat tangled in sauerkraut, 'in connection with this war the newspapers tell me is to start almost immediately. May I inform you how I myself—a lifelong student of military history—should lay the basis of our initial strategy?'

Nichtberger assumed the infinitely patient expression which he kept for use with civilian strategists. He said, 'If I may express a personal opinion, sir, it is that the newspapers talk a great deal about an imminent war in order to increase their circulations.'

Fortified by an enormous glass of Forster Jesuitengarten, the General contrived to preserve a countenance of respectful attention to his neighbour's eloquence while he scanned the company with eyes trained in methodical observation. The Bürgermeister's daughter, seated opposite himself, had nothing in her looks to compete with his own pretty daughters', but what intelligence he saw in her splendid eyes! How gracefully was she veiling her deathly boredom while Oberst-

290

leutnant Berghauer, beside her, made dutiful conversation, no doubt explaining with excruciating dullness the problems of providing rations and appropriate bedding for Other Ranks in the Field. To left and right extended a line of senior citizens, Councillors, no doubt, transferring immense forkloads of food from their plates to their stolid faces, while their fat-cheeked wives heroically preserved their party smiles. But who were the foreign-looking diners at the farther table, the heterogeneous collection of male and female oddities which seemed to be dressed rather for a ramble in the Schwarzwald than for Municipal banqueting?

'Old as I am,' Graf Otto pursued, 'I still have strength to carry a rifle, or to man a howitzer, if that is what you would recommend, in the cause of our threatened Fatherland. I have also some detailed plans, in coloured crayon, for a sweep through Constantinople aimed at the final encirclement of Quetta and Lahore.'

'I venture, sir, to applaud your patriotic sentiments,' Nichtberger said.

And now his discreetly exploring eyes, as they travelled a little to the left of the second flautist in the band, came on a fresh and singular spectacle: a fenced arena where—at his first glance—a trio of hamsters appeared to be rushing round and over an ellipsoidal sand-dune with every symptom of terror and dismay. The wine! he thought: it was foolish to have accepted an outsize glass of the local beverage in a stomach fastidiously upholstered an hour before with von Triebsch's admirable Spätlese. He looked again. The sand-dune stirred—it was alive. A young beige elephant? Now he recognized it as a sow, very much the largest that he, town-bred, had ever seen. She lay on her side, her eyes very slightly open, her mouth—he could have sworn—blissfully smiling. Nichtberger was strangely stirred; not so much by the discordance between this vision and the adjoining scenery as by a striking resemblance between the sow's face and that of Frau General Hartwig. That likeness would alone have been unnerving. But this stupendous animal was wearing on a collar of goffered silk a huge crimson rosette, and to every one of her mammae, more numerous than he would have thought to be physiologically feasible, was attached a tiny miniature of herself, each embellished with a blue or a vermilion ruff and a rosette hardly smaller than its mother's own. The band was again in full eruption with *Die Wacht am Rhein*, but the Generalmajor was hardly conscious of the din. The family of Elisabet Kirschenzweig held him in a peculiar fascination. Those three piglings who still tore about the small arena, tumbling and squealing, were they anti-pathetic to music, or devoid of patriotic feeling, or victims of some congenital neurosis? Could it be that, of all those innumerable mammae, none was at present vacant for any of them?

'And now, ladies and gentlemen,' the Bürgermeister announced when the most illustrious of the guests had been toasted with musical embellishment, 'it is my great pleasure to refer to a number of our distinguished visitors who, how-ever unexpected, are none the less most heartily welcome at our table.'

The attention of Generalmajor Nichtberger began to wan-der again, as a new small drama started to unfold for his entertainment. The place beside the Bürgermeister's daughter's had for a while been empty—Oberstleutnant Berghauer was out of sight: somewhere behind the scenes that insufferable but admirably conscientious officer was no doubt wrangling again about his own and his colleagues' sleeping arrangements. But now the vacated chair was again occupied—not by Berghauer, but by one of the foreigners, an elongated, carrot-haired young man who had quietly moved in from the farthest table. A curious specimen, Nichtberger thought, with his long-nosed, brown-skinned, bony face—perhaps the result of some casual alliance between a Nor-wegian sailor and a Spanish nursemaid—a shockingly attrac-tive vagabond whose roving eye and pliant lips suggested, at

292

the best, a genial disrespect for the distinguished company in which he found himself. Was Fräulein Rinderspacher displeased by this intrusion? The face of that perfectly mannered young woman betrayed no special feeling.

'It is a happy chance,' the Bürgermeister was declaiming, 'which has brought this galaxy of eminent scholars here for their bicentennial solemnities, since, whatever claims the boastful village of Untervelden may fabricate, it is now established to the satisfaction of all reasonable historians that the great philosopher our friends have come to honour, Heinrich Kirschenzweig, was in fact most appropriately born in the very house where we are assembled this evening.'

Kirschenzweig? Nichtberger knew that name, but philosophy was not his province: a deviser of eccentric theories, he fancied, perhaps something of a mountebank. His interest was still centred on the intruding foreigner, who was eating heartily, from time to time smiling at Fräulein Rinderspacher, manifestly at ease. And now Berghauer had reappeared. What would happen? For a few moments the Oberstleutnant stood, puzzled, dignified, just behind the interloper, then he touched the fellow's shoulder. He said stiffly,

'*Bedaure, Sie sitzen auf meinem Platz.*'

Clearly the foreign rascal was baffled by that simple statement. Fräulein Rinderspacher translated:

'The Colonel is reminding you, Mr Neal, you have taken his seat.'

'Well now, I thought he must have finished with it,' the foreigner said cheerfully. 'No matter—there's an empty chair at the table over there. He'll find himself beside a charming Swedish lady—a grandmother and all. They'll have a rousing time together.'

With discreet circumlocution Fräulein Rinderspacher transmitted this suggestion to the Oberstleutnant. He, incredulous, his facial muscles already twitching with a kind of ague, showed signs of imminent apoplexy: it was unlikely that he saw much to choose, as table companion, between a

293

young female intellectual and a Swedish grandmother, but for a man in his position to be coolly displaced by a rough-necked foreigner was the climax to a series of intolerable blunders and indignities. This situation General Nichtberger, much enjoying his Limburger and the emollient rumble of the Bürgermeister's elocution, observed and fully understood. Nichtberger was not without experience in diplomacy: a few words from him would have brought the affair he witnessed to a decorous conclusion. Unhappily the potent wine of Obervelden had slightly blunted his sense of propriety. He called softly across the table,

'Herr Oberstleutnant!'

The Colonel came to attention.

'Sir?'

'There seems to be some disorder among the animals over there. I've noticed there are three small pigs who've had nothing to drink at all.'

'Indeed, Sir?'

'The trouble seems to be that the natural sources of supply are all engaged. The only remedy I can think of is to detach three of the other junior pigs and compel them to fast for a while.'

'I follow your reasoning, Sir.'

'And it occurs to me that you, with your immense experience of commissariat problems, are the very man to organize that adjustment.'

'Me, Sir?'

'As a personal favour to me,' the General explained, smiling benignly.

'Commissariat problems?' Graf Otto said. 'There again, Herr Feldmarschall, I have a scheme to put before you which I think may be of some value.'

'Ah, but my highly efficient Staff Colonel always attends to such matters,' the General replied. And a little later he added suavely, 'Oberstleutnant Berghauer is a man I always rely on to handle our most troublesome quandaries. Yes, he is the

294

officer you see down there—the one with the rather worried expression who's climbing into the pig-pen beside the band.'

'We are especially honoured,' the Bürgermeister said in conclusion, 'that Herr Professor Walther Rumpel, from the Academy of Cambridge in London, has made this long journey to pay tribute to the greatest of Obervelden's sons. I now have pleasure in calling on Professor Rumpel to deliver his oration.'

Frau Zschokke, seated next to Wrimple, poked him smartly with her elbow. As if wakened from an engrossing dream, Wrimple stood up, steadied himself with one hand on a huge salt-cellar, felt in his inside pocket with the other. The speech, thank heaven, was there. He carefully unfolded it, brought the slightly erratic typing into focus and hectically cleared his throat.

'Herr Bürgermeister, ladies and gentlemen,' he began, in a high, quavering German which even to himself sounded a little strange, 'every one of us visitors is conscious, tonight, of a great privilege—the honour of being present in this famed and beautiful town of Untervelden, now universally acknowledged to be the birthplace of one who ranks, in the eyes of all the intelligentsia of Europe and America, with Immanuel Kant and Hegel: the immortal Heinrich Kirschenzweig. How happy must you, Worshipful Mayor and Citizens of Untervelden, feel in the knowledge that you can claim as your own a philosopher whose transcendent genius has revolutionized the thinking of the whole civilized world.'

'Tedious it may be,' Kevin whispered in Helma's ear, 'but I find the voice of my learned colleague a more bearable abomination than that barbarous band.'

'So?'

'Indeed, this is an evening which gets better every moment it goes on.'

'How pleasing for you!' she frigidly replied.

'But not for you?'

'If you had taken so much trouble as I have, Mr Neal, to arrange a feast of dignity, one for doing credit to my father; if all your plans had been overturned by a herd of stupid tourists who insert themselves at the final hour—'

'But everyone looks perfectly contented.'

That was approximately true. The citizens had reached the state of congenial satiety which speeches do not gravely interfere with. Among the foreigners a few, cupping their ears or hopefully traversing their aural trumpets, appeared to follow the speaker with some perplexity; but the Danish couple were nodding with quiet approval, the Latin tourists seemed to be well satisfied, an aged Doctor of Metaphysics from Szeged was blissfully asleep.

'So, in surveying the apocalyptic aspect of Kirschenzweig's teaching,' Wrimple declared (somewhat inconsequently, as two sheets of his manuscript had slipped and drifted under the table), 'I feel that I can do no better than quote to you a passage from a paper delivered at Obervelden some years ago by Dr Pencho Slaveykov of Trnovo ...'

'It is intolerable to have to listen to such baby-talk,' Helma murmured.

'For you it is indeed,' Kevin answered softly. 'For besides being a beautiful woman you are also one of intellectual distinction—even a creature of my own simple schooling can see that, as plain as the Four Courts in Dublin City. But for me, when I have beside me a girl of your sort, it makes no difference if some poor noodle of an Englishman is spouting balderdash on his own weskit like water dribbling from a leaky drain. I tell you, Miss Helma—if that's what I heard your father call you—for me it would take a lot more than that addlepated gabbler over there to contaminate the pleasure of an evening such as this. And if it had no other pleasantness at all, I would still be happy to sit here for the rest of my mortal days so long as you were sitting here as well.'

'Mr Neal,' Helma said, 'I think you have been drinking something more than you should.'

'Miss Helma,' he answered truthfully, 'this evening I have been without the time or the inclination to drink any liquor at all.'

With the kindly help of a savant from Coimbra, Wrimple had recovered the missing sheets of his dissertation; with the vigorous assistance of Frau Zschokke he had got one of them the right way round.

'Can we wonder,' Wrimple read dramatically, 'that a man of Kirschenzweig's spiritual profundity, surrounded by all the beauties of your beloved Untervelden, enjoyed a home life of tranquillity and supreme contentment! He—I beg your pardon, there's a word here I can't quite read—ah yes, he was the fortunate possessor of four modest and devoted wives. I hardly need to remind you of the virtues—the simplicity, the amiability—of the last of these, the lovely Elisabet Kirschenzweig.'

The most fervent admirers of Wrimple's eloquence would not have claimed that the citizens of Obervelden had been following his speech with breathless concentration: it was the more remarkable that those last words brought every one of those citizens to his feet.

The bandmaster was not slow to take his cue; the band was already at the alert, the shouting had hardly reached its height when the thrilling strains of *Heil Dir im Siegerkranz* burst out to join, to shape and finally to overwhelm it. When that blaze of harmony was in turn exhausted a man whose face bore a striking resemblance to the Emperor Servius Galba's was seen to be standing on his chair. Another shout went up:

'*Heil Hans Krommer!*'

'Ladies and gentlemen,' Hans Krommer boomed, 'I thank you from the bottom of my heart. You will, I know, wish me to give you some account of how my Elisabet was bred and brought to her present glory.'

There were cries of assent.

Wrimple was still on his feet. Though slightly confused by the combined assault of wine and commotion, he had not lost sight of his objective: these warm-hearted folk deserved the best he had to give, and since this dreary Kirschenzweig was their hero—as their bawling plainly showed—they should have his speech (which Mumsie had taken such pains to type) to the very last full-stop.

'It is charming to reflect,' he read, raising his voice, 'on the thoughts of Elisabet when as a young girl she first gazed, as if from afar, on the mighty figure with whom she was one day to be united.'

As if in Wagnerian duet, Herr Krommer continued his exposition. 'From the time she was weaned,' he said, his voice a little glutinous from the Forster Jesuitengarten but his eyes adhering resolutely to the sheaf of notes his broad-based wife had placed before him, 'I knew instinctively, from my long experience, that Elisabet was destined to higher achievements than what we may call the Life of the Trough. I remember well the first occasion when I felt her hind quarters with my sensitive hands. I—'

Graf Otto, happy and excited, was also standing up. 'I should like,' he said, 'to say a few words in support of our friend Herr Kinderheimer's hind quarters—or rather, if I may speak of something which deeply touches me, the inward, spiritual qualities of the lady to whom he has referred, and to whom our foreign visitor whose name for the moment escapes me has paid such eloquent tribute. Elisabet, dear Elisabet Olrich, as I chanced to mention to my military friend only a few minutes ago, was an aunt of my own.'

His revelation drew respectful applause.

Herr Krommer bowed appreciatively and pursued his thesis: ' "There," I said to myself, "we have a future champion—one whose capital need will be for a mate of her own calibre." Soon I was weighing up several possibilities, and meanwhile it had occurred to my good wife that she should be named after Elisabet Kirsch-whatever-her-name-was, the favourite wife of the great citizen of this town who they say was one of the most important professors in the days of old in our beloved Fatherland. Even in her days of maidenhood the growth of Elisabet's belly—I speak from matchless experience—was phenomenal. The moment came when I knew without a doubt that an appropriate partnership was due. I had been measuring the rival merits of two splendid hogs of my own breeding. My practised choice fell upon the elder of the two.'

'And how moving to reflect,' Wrimple read, 'that this mighty figure, looking forward to an old age of melancholy loneliness, should have found at his side, in the closest of all companionships, one whose tender heart, whose simplicity and grace, were able to supply his soul's deepest needs.'

Certainly Graf Otto was moved. He too had now climbed on to his chair, and there were tears on his shrivelled cheeks as his fluttering voice invaded a moment of silence left by the other orators: 'I can only emphasize what that Dutch gentleman has said. I too, how well I remember the new, sweet, wondering expression in my dear aunt's face, the new gentleness of her voice, in the days which immediately followed the happy culmination of that long courtship. Ah, that melodious voice, I seem to hear it now.'

'Hrrugh!' the prizewinning Elisabet said.

The face of Hans Krommer's prodigy was changed indeed: the contentment, the tranquillity, had given place to signals now of impatience, now of mounting ill-temper. As Kevin afterwards related (in a long letter, based on some experience in husbandry, to our cousin Michael M'Taurey) her asperity was not unjustified. At the end of a wearisome journey she had been subject to such public exhibition as the least modest of female creatures might well have resented, as well as to ruthless bombardments of flamboyant music, and now a sour-faced man in uniform was desperately clutching three members of her family who screamed as if he were roasting them alive. Provoked beyond endurance, Elisabet heaved her tremendous body on to her short but sturdy legs, letting her other offspring cling or fall as their strength allowed, like commuters in a suburban train. With her formidable snout she went for Oberstleutnant Berghauer's knees. The Oberstleutnant executed a shrewd lateral movement of tactical withdrawal. Elisabet, swinging her vast bulk at surprising speed, advanced upon Berghauer again.

'It is most kind of your officer,' Herr Rinderspacher said tactfully to General Nichtberger, 'to amuse our prizewinner in this way.'

'On the contrary,' the General gracefully replied, 'it is all to Oberstleutnant Berghauer's advantage. Like every good soldier he neglects no opportunity for physical exercise, especially in field-sport.'

Wrimple, too, continued to do bravely, but he had lost his way; the sheets of his script had got out of order, and with a vague sense of disquiet he was reading, as well as his tired eyes allowed, the first of them again:

'Every one of us is conscious tonight of this famed and beautiful town of Untervelden, now universally acknowledged as the breeding-place of Immanuel and Hegel Kant, whose penetrating genius has revolutioned the thinking of the civilized world.'

'The time of her pregnancy,' Hans Krommer declared, 'was an anxious one for me. Day after day I got up early to examine her expanding underside.'

Slightly harassed, Wrimple turned his top sheet over. 'No,' he said, 'I don't think there's anything on the underside.'

'And a great happiness it was to my aunt,' Graf Otto said, 'to know that her condition was in the experienced hands of the medical gentleman who has been so eloquently addressing us.'

The Bürgermeister rose again. 'Just so!' he said. 'We are all of us most grateful to Graf Otto for his condescending and most illuminating address. And now—'

'I think I have spoken already,' Wrimple said, recovering confidence, 'of Dr Slaveykov's discovery that the meteorite which fell in 1863, closely connected with the book of Ezekiel, was large enough to be compared with the Trilithon temple at Baalbek.'

'I myself,' Hans Krommer insisted, putting down his notes

300

and glaring at the irrepressible foreigner, 'can assure you that by the fourth week Elisabet was already *twice* the size of the animal at Buhelbach that gentleman has mentioned. When I took my wife's measuring-tape—'

'We are all agreed,' the Bürgermeister pacifically interposed, 'that the measurements of Herr Krommer's wife—I beg your pardon, I meant to say, the measurements of the splendid creature to whom Herr Krommer has so long given all his wonderful devotion, are something in which every one of us may feel a glowing civic pride.'

'And I will confess to you,' Hans Krommer added, 'that when, at Vurgensburg, I saw my loved one crowned, triumphing over no less than seventeen other competing sows and their litters, my sense of achievement, my overwhelming joy, brought tears to my eyes.'

Those tears now returned, wonderfully softening the Roman outlines of Herr Krommer's corneous face. In sympathy, Graf Otto wept; and among the assembled citizens of Obervelden there were not a few whose manly emotion found in tears an overdue relief. The Bürgermeister stayed calm; and once more it was he who did the right, the perfectly sagacious thing. He flashed a signal to the bandmaster: in an instant the band was playing *Heil Dir im Siegerkranz* all over again.

Often it is hard to establish with precision some detail of events which have happened many years before they are systematically recorded. At Obervelden they will tell you it was one of the piccolo artists borrowed from Pfarrkirhausen who played a faulty note. That assertion may rest on local prejudice. There seems to be no doubt, however, that a wrong note was played. One does not think of the sow Elisabet as a fastidious connoisseur of harmonics; but since her victory at Vurgensburg she must have listened to *Heil Dir im Siegerkranz* a number of times, and among husbandmen of the more thoughtful kind I have found considerable support for the view that to her a clumsy rendering of the familiar air was an annoyance sharp enough to heighten her already alarming rage. Within the small area at her disposal she drew back a little way, gathered her forces and charged Oberstleutnant Berghauer once more. The Oberstleutnant lacked nothing in valour: his *raison d'être*, so to say, was to die for his Country. But neither is patriotism fulfilled nor dignity advanced by the act of falling down and being trampled by a ferocious female pig. Besides courage, Berghauer possessed the other qualities of his profession—a sharply observant eye, the gift of lightning appreciation. He had long since located the well-built gate by which Elisabet had been admitted to her place of honour, he had even seen that it was held, top and bottom, by bolts on the outer side. His action, now, was first to put down the three small pigs he had taken into his charge; in the course of a fresh tactical movement he spared a quarter-second to lean over and release the upper bolt, in his next evasive circuit he paused again, leaned further, and slid the lower one. By every account—and the incident is still described at length by aged Oberveldenians—it was Elisabet who now behaved most prudently, or else with a touching forbearance. The seat of Oberstleutnant Berghauer was a target such as every exasperated sow must dream of. She refrained. She waited till the tiresome intruder had nimbly slipped outside; but before he had time to bolt the gate again she swiftly followed him, with her whole brood at her heels. Those diners who had descended to the courtyard to stretch their legs scattered to left and right. In a matter of seconds Elisabet, with a cadenza of grunts which some say were contemptuous, some grateful, had led her progency out to the Market Square. The band, entranced by the intricacies of its own performance, continued fervently to play.

Graf Otto had resumed his seat. 'Do your soldiers always bring their pets to affairs of this kind,' he asked courteously, his mouth pressed against General Nichtberger's earhole.

But the General would still not be enticed into discussing with any civilian the details of army organization. 'To officers above a certain rank,' was all he replied, 'we allow in such matters a sufficiently broad discretion.'

'Another thing I like about this place,' Kevin was saying

302

to Helma, '—it makes me feel as if I was still at home.'

She was alone next evening in her own kitchen; in the absence of the servants Fritz and Anna, enjoying their weekly night-out, she was busy preparing Bratwurst in a sauce with olives and garlic—the way her father liked it best.

Well, that dreadful *Feiermahl* was past and done with: in time, she hoped, it would be forgotten. This morning she had visited Herr Lindenstadt, Manager of the Herrenhaus, to apologize profusely for the stupid feebleness on her own part which had allowed the invasion of those wretched excursionists; that mob, she was told, had now departed—Lindenstadt himself had arranged for their transport by road to Untervelden, where their cretinous orator might even now be reading his speech all over again. From Papa, dear Papa, she had received no word of complaint about her responsibility for everything which had marred the dignity of the evening. How much she owed to him ... Was it merely tiredness which accounted, now, for her deep depression, her sense of waking from an ugly dream to a landscape where every congenial feature had been flattened out?

The casserole was ready for the oven, she was readjusting the damper when a sound behind her made her jump. A man had quietly entered by the tradesmen's door, he had placed himself only two metres from her shoulder, to gaze at her with the concentration of a devoted amateur before a Rembrandt. Her fright lasted only for a moment, giving place to an almost congenial surprise: the intruder—for all the trouble he had occasioned yesterday—was a man whose eyes, now, declared him to be a harmless, even a rather amiable creature, the one she knew as 'Mr Neal'. The amiability came partly from his look of sadness; a little, perhaps, from her realization—in this more intimate setting—that in his exotic way the man was not ill-favoured.

He stood with his hands clasped before him, his head and shoulders bent to reduce the great superiority of his physical height to hers. He said, 'I meant to come before. This was the first moment I could find.'

To that announcement she saw no obvious reply. 'I do not understand,' she said. 'Why are you come to this house?'

'Miss Helma,' he answered, 'I wish to ask your pardon. It's not often I've been so rough with a woman as I was when I saw you first of all—I had that circus of old dodderers on my hands, I was bothered out of my proper mind and the devil himself got a hold on my tongue.'

Helma was still unable to deal with this. 'I thought you were gone,' she said confusedly. 'They have told me at the hotel, all the tourists are gone away.'

'They have—good luck to the poor souls!' he said nonchalantly. 'And my own business orders are to be back in London the fastest way I can. But a man at times must act according to his own mind, you understand. I was not intending to leave this place before I had your pardon for the shameful things I said. So I took a cleaner's job the boss of that classy pub had the decency to provide me—it will keep my soul and body fixed together for a week or more. Do you think in that amount of time you could find the kindness to forgive me?'

He had taken off his coat, this curious man. As if it were she who had engaged him, he passed behind her to where a pile of utensils stood on a table behind the sink, he took a used saucepan and began to wash it out with the easy efficiency of one experienced in such business.

'I'm not saying,' he resumed, 'that I have any right to ask it. Only, seeing the cross you had about your neck last night I supposed you'd be Catholic like myself. I thought it might make a difference, if you follow my meaning.'

He had given her the time she needed to bring her thoughts to some kind of order, one which could overcome the hindrances of foreign speech.

'I myself often speak with rudeness,' she said simply. 'That is when I have some hardship of the mind, as you have had, with the voyagers who had no food. All of us at some time suffer such hardships.'

Kevin put down the saucepan and turned to face her. 'But now,' he said, 'you're talking as kindly as could be, while I see your mind is full of troubles just the same.'

'Troubles?' she repeated.

'Is it not right, what I'm fancying?'

Taken by surprise, she answered, '*Ja!* You have right.'

'What sort of troubles?... Or is that an impudence for a foreign fellow to be asking?'

It looked as if she would go no further. But when some moments had passed she said haltingly, as if in Confession, 'I am a person who cannot know how to do with her life. I have a little learning, there is a quite good teaching post prepared for me if I wish it. But my father also needs me, for the management of his house.'

Nodding gravely, Kevin considered this.

'There's yet another occupation,' he said, 'which appears to be in favour with many women—I mean, the wish of getting married. Have you never thought of that as another possibility?'

She faintly smiled, with ancient wisdom. 'I am a person with some intelligence,' she said quietly. 'I have in my own room a good looking-glass. It tells me I am not a woman such as men wish to marry.'

'Is that so!'

He had started work on another saucepan, and it was some time before he spoke again.

'I too,' he said at length, slowly, so that she might easily follow, 'I have what you call "a little learning". A *very* little —almost nothing at all. But it teaches me about myself, just a little at a time. Yes, I was studying for the priesthood, but that was not for me, with the quick temper that I have— that was one thing I had to learn about myself, the hardest thing of all.... Would you have some sand handy, or a pot-brush? I need one or the other for this skillet.'

305

'There's soda in that jar,' she said abstractedly. 'That perhaps will do the service.'

'Why, that will do it to perfection.... Now, I'll tell you a queer thing. Being set for the priest's vocation, I put away the thoughts which other fellows have as to marrying. And after I was turned away from the priest's calling that part of the training stayed in me like a kind of habit—the way some men will not go under ladders all their lives because of what their mothers said when they were children. Och, I liked the girls well enough, but I had no need to go to bed with any one of them. And that has been a great convenience, seeing I've never yet had a wage for two to live on.'

Helma said, 'I think it is not very useful, such talk of girls and other things.'

'Will you please give me your patience,' he pleaded, 'till I finish what I have to say! We have a word in the queer English tongue, "To fall in love"—would you know that one? Well, as I was telling you, that was a thing that didn't happen to me—I was sure as could be it would never happen. And then there came a day when my thoughts were on something different altogether, and by chance I had a lovely girl beside me at a foolish party, and it came to me like a flash of lightning that my own life was no use to me any more unless that girl would have the pity and the goodness in her heart to share it with me. You can call that what you like—I call it a message from God Himself.' He crossed himself. 'I'm simply telling you what happened to me, all in a moment of time.'

Helma put down the wooden spoon she was holding. She stood perfectly still. She asked,

'But you have spoken to this girl? You have told her of your strange emotion?'

When she dared to turn and look he had dropped on his knees, shaking all over like one in the second stage of fever. As a child might, he flung his arms about her legs, letting his forehead fall against her apron. He said almost voicelessly,

306

'My dear, my mavourneen, my darling, that's what I'm trying to tell you now.'

Wilhelm Rinderspacher's supper reached him—sadly over-cooked—nearly thirty minutes late. Because his daughter's face was very pale he uttered no word of discontent: she was worn out, he surmised, from her work and worries over the *Feiermahl* the day before.

'Papa,' Helma said, when they had eaten for a time in silence, 'a very upsetting thing has happened.'

Her father put down his knife and fork.

'An upsetting thing? Then leave it to me—the main busi-ness of a Bürgermeister is to deal with upsetting things. What is it has upset you?'

'It's the Englishman who was at the *Feiermahl*. Not the idiotic one who read out all that nonsense about Heinrich Kirschenzweig. The tall, thin one who came and sat beside me.'

'But what has he done?'

Resting her forehead on her wrists, Helma stared at the table. She said, as if in pain, 'It's terribly hard to tell you. He has turned out to be slightly mad.'

'My dear,' said her father, 'all Englishmen are as mad as March hares. Don't worry! With people who go mad there's a regular procedure. They're required to be examined by a suitable doctor. If they refuse, it becomes in the first instance a police matter. What form has it taken, the madness of this man?'

'He wants to marry me.'

'To marry you? When?'

'He says, "immediately".'

'And you say he's entirely a lunatic, this man?'

'Well, I suppose so. Only, the trouble is, I seem to have become a little bit mad myself. I mean, his madness seems to me—in some strange way—attractive. It's hard to explain it—something so new to me.'

307

' "Attractive"?'

'Well, yes. I mean—it sounds so foolish—to me he is more adorable than any man I've known.'

She seemed about to weep, a feminine weakness which since childhood she had always avoided. All her father could do was to pretend he did not notice. He resumed his supper. Emphatically the cooking of the Bratwurst was not up to Helma's usual standard—for one thing she had slightly over-done the garlic—but thirty years of married life had taught him that women are never at their best as cooks when suffering from some disorder in their emotions. The sausage itself was by no means inedible. When he had thoroughly cleaned his plate with a slice of pumpernickel he addressed himself once more to the subject his daughter had introduced:

'It is quite ridiculous, this man imagining he can get himself married "immediately". What they do in less civilized countries I've no idea, but in Germany we have decent rules for the regulation of a thing so important as matrimony. Proper notice has to be given by both parties, preferably in person. The notice has to be posted at the Town Hall, and fourteen days have to elapse before the ceremony can pro-ceed. All those requirements you must explain to this wild young man—I myself have so far forgotten the English they taught me at school that I should have no hope of making him understand the legal technicalities.'

He stretched to rest his capacious hand on his daughter's slender one.

'And then,' he said, 'since you tell me the man is adorable and since I have explicit faith in your judgment, you must order him to report at my office at nine o'clock tomorrow morning, in order that we may commence the necessary formalities as quickly as his understandable impatience seems to demand.'

It amuses me to think that Kevin's marriage with Helma took place—in the Church of Heiliger Jakob (which, strangely,

308

had once belonged to the Irish Benedictines) at Lorschdoft —exactly eighteen days after their first meeting. It is not so amusing that the date of the wedding, in the Year of Grace 1914, was the Twenty-ninth of May.

7

Message from Kevin

It must have been seven or eight weeks, perhaps a little more, that my pupillage under Helma lasted. Characteristically it was Howard—the very person who had conceived that singular plan for the advancement of my learning—who suddenly decided that I was not a suitable subject for co-education. Far less characteristically, he set himself to do something about it.

From a colleague—a Reader in Zoology—he learnt that the well known school at Rugby was the one best fitted to impart a sterling character to a boy notably lacking in such moral refinement; he therefore wrote to the principal of that establishment to say that I should presently be joining it. Some kind of secretary person replied in a courteous but unexpansive letter that I should not. My father next consulted Sean Cloghearn, who was an old friend of his and who happened just then to be at liberty, after his six months' sentence for a woefully amateurish attempt to set light to the cavalry barracks at Hounslow. Cloghearn was always a mine of information on every subject and he at once supplied the name of the ideal academy: one not far from Northampton, called Duke's Devise.

This was a school for what the commercial world knows, I think, as 'seconds'—articles which fall a little below a firm's regular standards in manufacture. It was run by an Old Cliftonian, Colonel 'Crasher' Finglestone, formerly the popular Governor of a penitentiary in Saskatschewan. If the Colonel had failings a narrow outlook was not among them. He accepted as pupils those in whom Borstal institutions had been unable to cultivate any *esprit de corps* or equivalent virtue; he took on boys of fourteen who had driven and wrecked their fathers' limousines, boys of twelve who had made unsuitable advances to women of twenty-five. From all over the country headmasters who had come to despair of some of their charges transferred them with the minimum of fuss to Finglestone. I hope I shall not be thought immodest if I mention that among my fellow-students at Duke's Devise were some who had been removed from the most famous schools in the land.

My memories of 'Crasher' are on the whole agreeable. 'Any more humbuggery from you, Hutchinson,' was his favourite war-cry, 'and I'll flog you till the flesh hangs in ribbons from your dirty neck to your verminous feet,' but in practice he was too short of wind to pursue that mode of improvement. When he and I finally parted, after a difference of opinion too paltry to be worth relating, the argument had cost me a greenstick fracture of the left clavicle and him a new pair of bifocals, but the incident left, I think, no permanent animosity between us. He was quite a good teacher, who had retained from his own Fourth Form days a respectable smattering of the classics: I learnt more from him than from any other of my preceptors about the manners and customs of ancient deities. He claimed, indeed, to be 'fundamentally a religious man'. In his sweeter moods, and when partially sober, he would read aloud to us from Balzac's *Contes drôlatiques* on wet Sunday afternoons.

Inevitably my removal to Duke's Devise accelerated the weakening of my fraternal ties with Anastasia. I saw her now only in the holidays, and little enough then, since she came more and more to prefer Lorna Cheevey's company to mine.

The results of that unfortunate association were increasingly apparent. My sister started doing things to her hair, persuading Sonya to buy her clothes which were far too fashionable for a young girl, and generally behaving as if she belonged to the great world while I remained a mere school-boy. These absurd affectations increased my brotherly anxiety about her future. Earlier, I had preserved the intermittent hope that she might finally settle down to the harmless life of a stable-girl, which seemed her obvious *métier*. Now I suspected that she had visions of trapping some half-witted male into marriage—and my own broadening knowledge of the implausible facts of life told me that in this unscrupulous design she might one day be successful. (Had not some of nature's most egregious lapses—Lady Thelma, for example —acquired something in the approximate shape of a husband!) My reflections upon the possible victim were comfortless indeed. How would he feel when he found himself joined for life to a girl whose gastronomic sensibility was limited to a boundless appetite for apple charlotte and who could not occupy a room for five minutes without making it look like the Stamford Bridge football ground after a Cup Final? Some years later I recalled those early anxieties of mine in a private conversation with Henry St Auberlin. He replied in his slow, soft, rather whimsical voice that owing to the formidable industry of his ancestors he could afford to employ a highly competent domestic staff.

'But Henry, a staff, however efficient, has to be supervised,' I suggested.

My brother-in-law agreed. 'That is one reason,' he said, '—though a very minor one—why I persuaded a woman with nothing short of genius in the art of management to become my wife.'

Once, in the Duke's Devise epoch, I ventured to ask my hyperborean sister how she was getting on with her schooling. She told me, in the superior tone she had caught from Lorna, to mind my own business. I persisted, however:

'I mean, do you still think Helma's a rotten governess? You did to start with.'

A thoughtless pendant—naturally she had no wish to be reminded of her atrocious behaviour at the time of Helma's arrival. So I should have been ready for her evasive answer:

'You, Ryan,' (she had ceased, disquietingly, to call me 'Rin-Bin') 'don't care twopence about Helma either way. So why badger me! It's just that you've worked yourself into an idiotic calf-love for that pocket-size child of hers, so you think you've got to fuss over Helma like a little Sir Galahad over what's-his-name.'

Calf-love: I was then unfamiliar with that phrase, which she had doubtless acquired from the Cheevey excrescence, but the manifest vulgarity of such an inane remark greatly vexed me. My response was a dignified silence.

That short exchange taught me that between the new-model Anastasia and myself the subject of Helma was off the conversational menu. By chance, however, I learnt something of her developed feelings about her governess through our joint encounter with a third party.

Dear Sonya, in her reckless way, had been showing a maternal attitude towards a fair-haired local youth whom I shall call for convenience Reginald Bates. He was about nineteen, lately commissioned, and lacked a mother of his own. He arrived one afternoon, in the grandeur of a new second-lieutenant's uniform, when Sonya was out. Pavel, who answered the bell, mechanically showed him into the drawing-room, where Stasie was sprawling on the sofa with some magazine of female fripperies while I was at work on designs for a new anti-submarine weapon, the patent of which I meant to offer the Admiralty for a very reasonable fee. Though annoyed by this interruption I moved a chair towards the fellow; he took it without saying 'Thank you' and sat staring at Anastasia in the way that men of his age will goggle at anything within the girl division of humankind. She, of course, was flattered and at once put on her best Lorna Cheevey manner.

'I'm *so* sorry my mother isn't in,' she said in a voice which sickened me. 'She should be back before very long.'

'Oh, not at all!' Bates said; meaning, I supposed, that he could happily make do with Stasie herself for the time being —the cock-eyed clod.

313

'If you'd like to wait a few minutes—?' she said.

'Well, if you're sure I'm not in your way—?'

He was very much in mine; one cannot concentrate on problems of secondary recoil while a pair of vacuous persons are talking, a few feet away, as if they had learnt their lines from a Victorian manual of bourgeois etiquette. I bore with this nuisance, however, because I could not face the trouble of moving the drawing-board and all my coloured inks elsewhere.

Presently the door opened and I thought, 'Ah, here is Sonya at last, she will take this goof to another room to make a fuss of him and I shall get a little peace.' But it wasn't she, it was Helma, murmuring, 'Oh, I am sorry, I thought your mother was here.' In her bashful manner—for she was still shy at any first encounter with our visitors—she slipped away.

'Was that a relative?' Bates asked politely.

'No,' Stasie said. 'Actually she's my German tutor.' Her mincing voice conveyed the fact that in her view it was absurd for a fashionable young woman to be still in the process of education.

Bates put on a sort of smirk. 'How odd,' he said, 'to have a German in the house!'

That was the wrong thing to say. Looking up, I saw a change in Stasie's face.

'Is it?' she said.

Evidently Bates did not observe the altered climate; the supercilious grin stayed on his face. Now he said, with a note of patronage, 'Oh, I remember now, your mother told me about her. She was married to that fellow O'Kneale—the Irishman.'

'Which in fact makes her non-German,' Stasie said tersely.

'How do you mean?' Bates asked.

'Well,' Stasie said—and now her voice made me think of a wound-up watch spring—'you can hardly go on calling anyone a German when she's been married to someone who fought on our side.'

Obtuse as he was, Bates must have seen at that point that he had provoked in his hostess a certain hostility. A sensible man would have said, 'Oh, of course, I agree!' and changed the subject. Bates, I suppose, was not old enough for such discretion.

I particularly want to be fair to the man, because he himself was mortally wounded at Passchendaele only a few weeks later—in those days Platoon Commanders were highly expendable. (That is why I have withheld his real name.) From the present distance I see that boy with different eyes from the childish ones I was using then; I realize now something of what the youngsters who came to maturity—theoretically —in the First War years, who were turned overnight from schoolboys into fighting men, must have felt in their lonelier hours; I see that their swaggering and laughter, their glancing, feline sneers at 'conchies' and everyone who appeared to be escaping their own martyrdom, were all a *cordon sanitaire* woven around the deadly fears which they must never show. Yes, I have long forgiven Bates—if forgiveness was needed—for the broad insensibility of his answer to my sister's sponsorship of our Helma:

'But I rather gathered,' he said bleakly, 'from what I read in the papers that O'Kneale wasn't really on our side at all. Well, naturally, I suppose, with a German wife and all that.'

Anastasia did not at once reply; she looked, for a few moments, like one concussed by a nasty fall. Then she said, in a voice with hardly any sound in it, 'I'm not interested in what people read in papers. Or what they say about my friends.'

Bates let out a little, wobbly laugh. He said, 'You're not by any chance pro-German yourself, are you?'

'Mr Bates,' Anastasia said, 'I don't like people inventing things about my friends' husbands. Mrs O'Kneale is a person I admire and—and a person I love very much. And—and her dead husband is a person I admire and love as well.'

I was glad those white-hot, terrifying words were not aimed at me.

'Oh,' Bates said—and I thought it was all he could possibly say. Yet he added, 'I'm sorry. But there is a war on, you know.'

Anastasia said—now quite evenly—'Mr Bates, I want you to get out of this house, and never come near it again.'

He got.

It was a long time, and we were both grown-up, before Anastasia and I talked of that encounter. But I know now that it haunted her as it haunted me, provoking among her secret thoughts the same devouring curiosities, the same shapeless fears, which it stirred in mine.

Naturally we never mentioned Bates's innuendo to Helma herself, and neither Stasie nor I had the confidence to question our parents: in the cloudy intercourse between children and adults there are nearly always, I believe, areas which the children are frightened to invade. At that time neither of us had formed the habit of reading newspapers, and we were unaware of places where old ones could be studied—I myself imagined that, once read, they were invariably used for lighting fires. Later on, when I was old enough to know a little about the use of libraries, I did dig out some of the articles—they were enigmatically allusive—to which Bates must have been referring. By then my friendship with Helma had advanced to a stage where she could tell me a good deal about the weeks which immediately followed her marriage; later still, when old letters came into my hands and when my circle of friends widened, I came to learn something of what happened to Kevin after he became a soldier. But years elapsed before I had fitted the fragments fairly well together.

Only once did Kevin bring his bride to Howes Croft. Anastasia and I were both away from home at the time; she (if I remember rightly) in Wiltshire helping our cousin

Ludmilla Fyodorovna with one of Sonya's more imaginative projects—a stud for cross-breeding bloodhounds with salukis —I at one of those seaside camps designed to furnish defective boys with a healthy outlook, 'grit', and other British attributes. The young couple's visit lasted for only one afternoon. My generous mother would have housed the pair indefinitely, even if it meant consigning me, as usual, to Pavel's storeroom. I think it was Kevin's pride which forbade him to take further advantage of her philanthropy: he did not wish to advertise his precarious situation.

He had lost his job with Curtice Powell. Unlike 'Crasher' Finglestone, Mr Hull of that firm was capable of puritanical attitudes. He had ordered 'that damned Irish specimen' to return to Cheapside as soon as his mission was accomplished; a postcard crudely depicting a castle near Obervelden, with a scrawled announcement that O'Kneale had decided to prolong his absence for the frivolous purpose of getting married, fell short of Mr Hull's notions of correct behaviour for junior counter-clerks. Arriving in London three weeks later, with a wife and with Wilhelm Rinderspacher's wedding present of a thousand Marks as almost their only resource, Kevin found himself among the unemployed.

Answering an *Evening News* advertisement, he took the first post that offered, that of 'Man for general duties' at an institution in Deptford called—in full—*Mr Gorboyle's Charity for the Relief and Sustentation of Eleven Aged and Indigent Seamen*. The wage was minimal but an attic room, equipped with a small gas cooker and a bed just large enough for two sympathetic persons to sleep in, went with the job. Helma, presently, was able to supplement her husband's earnings by part-time teaching at the Haberdashers' School nearby.

'In those weeks,' she told me in later years, 'I knew for the first time what it meant to be happy.'

And Kevin, did he share that contentment? Was he never exasperated by the menial and sisyphean nature of the work, the ruthless tyranny of his overseer's wife, the bareness and

317

constriction of the room which was all that he and Helma had to call their home? Was he never troubled about the future, which the earliest signs of Helma's pregnancy must surely have made more intimidating? Did he never read the papers—did the thickening war clouds never alarm him?

I surmise that he was perfectly aware of all the trouble which might lie ahead—he was not an empty-minded man. But love can be a potent medicine. He was further armoured, I think, by an optimism which may have come first from the incorrigible rogue who begot him; and then, perhaps, by something which one or other of his teachers at the Christian Brothers' school, or such a man as Father Killalee, may mysteriously have transmitted—what I can only describe as a transcendent, indestructible belief in an ultimate goodness lying beyond the harshness of human experience.

Howard took the trouble to visit him at Gorboyle's Charity, and the afternoon he spent there made so lively an impression on his ominivorous mind that he was able long afterwards to give me a minute account of the experience.

'*Gumboil's Charity!*' my father said, with that luxuriant sarcasm which is achieved only by persons born and bred in the province of Munster. 'There were absent from that ex-cremental plague-pit faith, hope, charity, these three, and the least observable of these was charity.'

The Master, Captain Eli Munro, had long withdrawn (wisely, my father said) into a second childhood, spent mostly in the private bar of the nearby Admiral Blake; his desiccated wife, a native of Queensland 'with a face God put together under the influence of Hieronymus Bosch', was the real ruler of the place. No doubt that product of a Brisbane orphanage had deep-seated troubles of her own, and aged men fall seldom easily into a neat domestic framework. The wear and tear of life had serrated a voice which can never have been musical; Mrs Munro used it copiously to discipline her protégés, and especially she used it to preserve her latest serving-man from the sin of idleness.

'Ocknel, where've you got to now? Ocknel, you never took

out the dustbins like I told you ... You haven't done the window in the Trustees' Room.... *Ocknel!* Simpson's been in the bottom toilet for half an hour, go and holler him out through the window!'

Those cries from the half-open door of the kitchen, married with nauseous gusts of chutney and steaming linen, seemed to ravage the building at intervals of two or three minutes, discomforting my inflammable father as he sat on the narrow deal bench provided for visitors just inside the street door. From different parts of the house he caught the sound of Kevin's tolerant replies:

'Coming, Mrs Munro, ma'am ... In one minute, Mrs Munro ... Ah, poor Mr Simpson, he has the diarrhoea a good deal on his mind today. I'm just attending to the needs of Mr Greeney, he has his two thumbs stuck in a drawer that'll neither shut nor open.'

That was what made the work a burden: the fact that each of the residents had always a private problem, that the services they called for seldom dovetailed with Mrs Munro's conception of an orderly household. Huw Llwyd the Cardiff man expected a letter from his mother (who had died in 1903) and was sure that Mrs Munro had hidden it out of spite. Stibbald from Yarmouth was devoting his retirement to a favourite occupation of sailors, the construction of a model schooner in a bottle, but had failed to grasp the artful stratagem on which that ploy depends; in months of patient workmanship he had made a recognizable four-master and he had lately filched a bottle of appropriate size, but the bottle's neck still stubbornly refused to give the schooner passage. These decent, worried men supposed that 'Mr Ocknel' could always turn aside to help them. One wanted pills to cure the bunions on his feet, another with chronic laryngitis desired that Mr Ocknel would constantly divert the Master's wife's attention while he spat on the messroom floor. To oblige *pari-passu* Kevin's customers and his real employer was a task, my father said, which would have daunted the Angel Gabriel in partnership with Gunga Din.

319

It was the Master himself who arrived, that awkward afternoon, to end the long half-hour when Howard sat alone 'with that infernal bench ploughing a mighty furrow in my bum'. Captain Munro stood before my father, hazily smiling, trying to focus his vagrant eyes on the visitor's face, as tired travellers seek to identify some landmark on a distant horizon.

'Why, Tickles,' he said at length, 'it's a rare treat to see you again! Great times we had at Tsingtao, all those years ago.'

My father stood up and steered his hand into Munro's wandering one. 'Delighted, sir,' he answered non-committally, 'that you find an old friend in a person of so little consequence as myself.'

Again the kitchen door had come ajar; a barbed, familiar voice ripped out to interrupt the chimerical reunion: *'Eli!* There's a bloke in the passage, come after Ocknel. I've told him it's not a visiting day.'

'It's nobody but Jim Tickles, lovey-sweet,' the Captain called back. And to Howard he said obligingly, 'I'm not sure if he's still here, Hocknell—Hocknell who was Dibben's mate, you're speaking of? We buried one of the hands last week, out at Plumstead. Hocknell, it could have been.'

Kevin himself appeared just then at the top of the stairs.

'Cousin Howard,' he cried, 'it's tearing kind of you to come and see me all this way! I'll take you up in half a minute to the wee compartment Helma and I have for ourselves at the top of the house ... Is there some small trouble, Master, you have gnawing on your mind?'

'Captain Tickles here has come to look for Hocknell,' Munro said despondently. 'Was it Hocknell we buried last week at Plumstead?'

'No, Master, that was Matt Talbot ... Now, Mr Baldwin, I've told you already twice today, Mrs Munro doesn't care to see those details on the bottom floor.'

From one of the lower rooms a tall man of incalculable age had issued, bearing a chamber-pot with hieratic absorption, as one who means to offer a libation in a temple of peculiar sanctity.

'Put it round the corner, man, under the bootstand,' Kevin directed. 'I'll care for it myself, the moment Mr Simpson has done with the bog.'

Mr Simpson, as it happened, was at that moment returning to public life.

'There now!' Kevin said to Mr Baldwin. 'Mr Simpson has kindly cleared the way for your small operation.'

'Now listen!' Simpson said to no one in particular. 'I will not have that woman bawling at me in the times of my private engagements. To every man his own bowels, as the Frenchies say. I could do you a picture of mine, Mr Ocknel, as would make your hair stand up on end and holler out for pity.'

'Ah, now that's an entertainment we might leave till Sunday,' Kevin suggested kindly. '...No, Mr Baldwin, *not* the kitchen, the other place ... And what is it that's trampling on your mind now, Captain?'

'It's Tickles here,' Munro said mournfully. 'He was reminding me of Hochnitz, the Dutch fellow we used to have a noggin with at Tsingtao. It doesn't seem right to have old Hochnitz under the ground at Plumstead—that one-horse town with not a thing to see but squealing kids and fudge-faced nursery maids.'

'All you men ever do is gossip all day long!' his wife screeched from the kitchen. '*Take that dirty thing away, Baldwin!* Ocknel, will you stop your jawing and get on with your job! Five times I've told you now to take out the dustbins.'

'Be easy, ma'am!' Kevin called back. 'I have them at the tip of my mind, the bins you're fretting on.... Yes, what is it now, Mr. Stibbald? Ah, that's too bad, it's a foolish kind of bottle they make these days, with the necks too small for a tidy ship to go in. Wait now, I'll hunt you out a bigger one, the first moment I have to call my own. We might take the smallest quarter of an inch off the masts of the fine ship you've made, then it would likely fit a jam-jar as snug as a babe in the womb.'

'Will you tell me, Skipper,' Simpson was asking earnestly, 'has your wife no bowels of her own? Do they never squeak and bubble like an old frog in a pond?'

But the Master was deep in professional conversation with his visitor:

'You know, Tickles, it's a leaky old tub I have here, but we've a fine spirit aboard. Discipline, that's the main thing. And a first-class female cook I found a long time back in Sydney—never quite get her name—Biscuit, something of that kind. Got her spliced on me at the Passion to Seamen. Apple-sauce she does a masterpiece—makes all the difference to the men.'

A new *cri de coeur* took Kevin upstairs again: the one-legged bosun Edwards was complaining that 'the Captain's bitch' had stolen his singlet to use for a dish-clout. He said when he returned,

'I'll not keep you waiting long, Cousin Howard. The wee wife'll be back from her school directly, she'll make you a fine cup of tea, bless the darling.'

'It's a hell of a job you've landed in,' Howard said *sotto voce*. 'It's a mortal pity, really, you never quite hit it off with Dobey Barnes.'

'Och, the job will serve me well enough when I have the hang of it,' Kevin said blithely. 'Would you lend me a kind hand, Captain, for shifting the bloody bins that have themselves stuck in your good lady's mind.'

'Here, I'll give you a hand myself,' Howard volunteered.

To reach the back yard they crept, all three, through the kitchen, as quiet as thieves, except that the Master stumbled and groaned from a spasm of lumbago: less cautiously, two or three of the clients followed, in the way that trustful children do. Still bearing his utensil with a sexton's dignity, Mr Baldwin drew up the rear of the procession.

For once the mistress of the house was almost voiceless in her rage.

'Let him bring it once again, that dirty man,' she managed to pronounce, 'and I'll drown his face like I would a bed-bug.'

With dexterous courtesy Kevin sought to change the subject, murmuring as he passed her, 'We're shifting the rubbish bins this very minute, Mrs Munro, ma'am. Your kind husband's helping me.'

The master's wife was unappeased. 'Next time I try my luck at marriage,' she said, perhaps with pardonable venom, 'I'll pick on twenty demons out of hell. That'll make a better life for me.'

Plainly Bequette Munro did not relish having within her province another woman not directly under her command. That, I am told, is an attitude not without other examples in the feminine world. Here the climate of resentment was aggravated by the older woman's oddly expressed conviction that 'on top of everything, this lazy bloke Ocknel has to bung up my house with a pig-faced *foreign* bitch!' For with dim memories of a Belgian mother, and more vivid recollections of a sad Australian girlhood, she had adopted sentiments which were vehemently British. In practice there was little occasion for contact between the two ladies; but if they passed on the stairs the Master's wife steered a course which made it plain that the right of way belonged to her, and when—through one of life's routine mischances—a camisole of Mrs O'Kneale's strayed into Mrs Munro's washing basket the displeasure of Mrs Munro did not stay sheathed in silence.

'*Twelve* dirty men I've got to wash for,' she rasped, 'and now I'm expected to work my guts to the bone for the foreign bitch belonging to the servant-man!'

In moments of unprejudiced reflection I can feel for Eli's consort, whom the fates had treated without much generosity. It was, moreover, natural that the historic events of August should define and intensify her emotions. 'It's not right, it isn't safe,' she pronounced, 'to have a German female sleep-

323

ing here among the British navy-men.' Her fears were perhaps extravagant, but her outlook is understandable. When Liége fell it was reported in the English papers that the German commander Emmich had driven Belgian women in the front of his storming columns. On one whose blood was partly Belgian the effect of such reports could not be trivial.... With painful industry Mrs Munro composed a letter to Rear-Admiral Dubberley, Chairman of the Gorboyle Trustees, and required her husband to sign it: it earnestly requested a special meeting of the Trustees to review the alarming situation caused by 'the German female person who that workman O'Kneel you have engaged have smoggled into the Charity.'

In the event, there was no need for such a meeting. On Thursday, August 27th, Kevin remembered to carry out the dustbins. Less happily, the time he found for that operation was when Mrs Munro was bending over her cooker stirring the midday stew, and in the narrow space available he allowed one of the bins to graze her salient rump. This is the kind of mishap, small in itself, which ignites the gases formed by a long period of mental ulceration. It is likely that Bequette had been brooding as she worked on the horrors and humiliation of Liége, on her own hardships and helplessness. She turned now, blazing with righteous wrath.

'So, Ocknel, you go out of your way to insult me! You treat me like a Chatham tart, you think you can rape me any time you've a moment to spare! You start by getting at me from behind, like a savage beast!'

That volley of diverse indictments took Kevin by surprise. Reacting according to his nature, he let out a small bubble of laughter.

'Ah, Mrs Munro, ma'am,' he said, 'you know it was naught but a piece of clumsiness I let the bin come against the elegant skirt you're wearing! I'm sorry, and that's the truth of it. I'll take more pains the next time.'

With that ephemeral apology he would have gone his way, but Mrs Munro, her legs no less agile than her tongue under the stress of fury, had by then slipped past him to stand with her back against the door. Her face was deathly now, her body stiff and vibrating as if from electrocution.

'Now you're lying!' she fulminated. 'You, you dirty idle bastard, you're no bloody use to me or anyone, d'you hear me! You're nothing but a lazy tyke what's hiding in my house to keep out of the War which all the decent men have gone to fight in. If I was the Government I'd have you whipped and stuck in jail.'

Kevin waited in silence for the storm to blow itself out: this was not his first acquaintance with the verbal eruptions which may serve as therapy for an overwrought woman. When the chance came he said pacifically,

'Now be easy, ma'am—let yourself be calm, now! I know it's a hard place you have here, and you need a first-rate man to take a part of the labour off your shoulders. But I'm learning all the time. Give me time, now, and you'll have a serving-fellow that'll make the place less of a burden to you.'

She wasn't listening. A woman raised in a gentler school might have found relief in tears, but crying had been discouraged at the Brisbane 'Home' where Bequette Aggs had been deposited at the age of five. She could only return to the attack:

'And now,' she blurted, 'you keep that German female in my house. Those bloody beasts—those German swine—look what they're doing now—sticking their bayonets in Belgian babies, mucking the women and killing the men! And you think it's nice for me to keep a German woman in my house, and wash her mucky clothes, while she grins at me down the passage. I tell you, Ocknel, I keep this house for British sailor men. I put up with the bugs they bring, I wash their mucky drawers, I put up with the rats and mice and filthy stink what come with British sailor fellows. I will put up as well with a bloody good-for-nothing idle serving man, but when he use my house to keep a dirty German whore, *then I'm done with him!*'

Those words sufficed. The Master's wife had, in fact, no

authority to dismiss without consultation one who was formally an employee of the Trustees, but that argument is academic. With the minimum of necessary force Kevin removed the frenzied woman from the door and gained the passage. Followed only by her imprecations he went up to his own quarter. When Helma returned from her work that afternoon she found him on the pavement guarding their worldly goods, which he had packed in their two valises and a wooden sugar-box.

'We're getting out of this,' he told her unemotionally. 'I can stand a woman in her tantrums like the next man—did I not learn that exercise with my great-aunt Theresa Kearney, the one that first employed me! But when that hell-cat of Munro's sets her filthy tongue against my wife, then it's over for good and all between her and me.'

They were put up for a few nights by Terence Rosscairn, an amiable journalist from Antrim whom Kevin had kept in touch with since his schooldays. Thereafter they luckily secured a first-floor room in Mountfield Lane, Norwood, a narrow street embanked on either side by bay-fronted villas, spawned in 1906 or thereabouts in the style of laboured hideosity which might be classified as Outer London Pride. The rent was low. The room was furnished for their comfort with a superannuated sofa and a mountainous Victorian side-board. A bathroom on the third floor, when not in use by any of three other families, was available for theirs.

That house still stands, now numbered 105. There, some six months after their instalment, their only child was delivered by an able midwife, one Pieta Galleti, belonging to the Society of St Vincent de Paul.

'I'll nobble another job soon enough,' Kevin assured his wife, on the night when they had shaken from their feet the dust of Gorboyle's Charity. 'With all the men going for soldiers there'll be places needing to be filled all over the town.'

That was true: he found fresh employment almost at once, as invoice clerk in the London office of a West Riding firm busy with government contracts. The work was dull but undemanding, the pay comparatively liberal. Why, then— long before compulsory military service was introduced— did he enlist?

The question is not insoluble. The moral climate in the autumn of 1914 was one of crusade. The Celtic peoples (as one loosely calls them) turn readily to soldiering. It is easy to argue that Kevin's paramount duty was to stay with his wife —among all the difficulties a foreigner would meet with in war-time London—at least until she was safely past her confinement. But obligations which look plain to the vantaged historian have often been less obvious to those who had to make decisions at the time he is reviewing.

Helma was never unperceptive. In the man who flung his arms about her when he returned from work each evening, who watched over her health and comfort as a professional nurse would, who found unfailingly some cheerful topic to keep the War out of their conversation, she could still detect a current of restlessness, of self-dissatisfaction. In late September (I think it was), on an evening when Kevin had fallen into abnormal silence, she stretched her courage to put the question:

'Tell me, *mein Liebling*, sometimes you would wish to be in uniform, like the young men we see everywhere about the streets.'

Taken unawares, he looked away, and then at her face, profoundly troubled.

'Och,' he said, 'I'd look a peepshow in the uniform, a fellow shaped like I am!' But presently he continued: 'If it was Dancing Dervishes they were at war with, or the Mongol tribes or some such specimens, I could likely try my hand in the business. But there's other things I have to think of— there's your father's goodness to begin with, him letting a roving Irish fellow go off with his daughter, the only one he has, and never a word or a hard look to complain of what it cost him. That's not the sort of folk I'd wish to be fighting.'

Such a speech is not easy for a wife of high intelligence —and tempered virtue—to answer in a language not her own. Helma allowed the subject to submerge in a fresh silence. Only when another day had passed did she raise it again:

'Kevin *liebling*, are there men in your work-place to mock at you because you do not go to the War? I think there could be older men who say that one who is young should be a soldier now—now that this Prussian Ludendorff has done such wicked things. That would be hard for you, if other men should call you a coward—if they should say you are afraid to fight.'

Again he seemed to be surprised. 'Och, what should I care!' he said. 'There are Tom-fools everywhere who think they know the other fellow's business better than he does himself —the sort that feel themselves that much the bigger when they're laughing at some other man. I tell you, darlin', the stupid jokes fall off me like the rain off a duck's feathers. I've a girl to be caring for, and a babe in the offing besides. That's the proper work for a freshly married man. The boys can call me a shirker till they wear their tongues out—I know my own state of mind better than them!'

Helma nodded pensively, and went to the shared kitchen to put a kettle on. Returning, she spoke with a slow deliberation—she had spent some hours setting in order what she meant to say:

'I myself, I know there is no-body less a coward than you can be, Kevin. But I do not like that he should be laughed at, the good and brave man who is become my husband. You will understand, I do not want to have you away from me, not even for a little time. I hate this war, I hate all the wars that have ever been. But I want that everyone shall know how little he can be called a "Shirker", that tender and brave and—and *herrlich* man who has married me.'

328

So in truth the decision was Helma's. I find it moving, that decision.

My fragmentary knowledge of Kevin's military career came first of all from one or two members of my young brother Vladimir's club to whom he introduced me between the Wars; in particular from one Clevedon Pasquell, a Sandhurst product, who at an early stage had been Kevin's company commander.

Those who poke fun at professional soldiers (a sport I scrupulously refrain from) know nothing as a rule of the subtler qualities, the surprising insights, which close acquaintance discovers in not a few of them. Pasquell himself when I first met him struck me as mass-produced: good but unremarkable features, with the impeccable grooming which attests a visit to an expensive barber every second day; a neat, athletic frame upholstered in one of those suits which Savile Row designs to be totally inconspicuous—the faultless pelt of an English thoroughbred. He spoke, all on one note, with that minimum use of the lips which never fails to convulse Americans. One learnt without astonishment of the two bars to his D.S.O. It did surprise me, though, to be told privately by Vladimir that since his retirement from the Army the man had spent a small fortune, and limitless energy, in establishing a holiday home for old women from the slums of Birmingham.

'Yes,' Pasquell drawled to me, when I took him to the Garrick and slightly loosened his tongue with homoeopathic doses of Marquis de Montesquiou Armagnac, 'O'Kneale was the sort of headache you never quite got used to. Late back from leave, late on parade, idle on parade, improperly dressed, dirty rifle, dumb insolence, damned insubordination—that bastard would go through the whole dam' calendar and then start again at the beginning. "Anyone for Company Office this morning, Serjeant-Major?" "Nobody, sir, except the usual—008-O'Kneale, Absent Without Leave 48 hours." I got sick of the bloody sight of him. I mean, you could C.B. him, dock his pay, put him up to the C.O.—it all made no difference. All that fellow needed was a different sort of army, made specially to fit him. But the Old Man was right, you know. Born leader—O'Kneale—you could see that, even in those days. Should have been a bank-robber, he'd have been at the top in that profession. I tried the standard dodge—first time he was out of trouble for about a week I put a stripe on him. Just four days and it had to come off again. Still, in the end they got him to France with two stripes. Looked odd on a bloke you could hardly tell on parade from a Maltese bus-conductor, but there it was. The lads in his Section soon stopped grinning, they'd do just anything he told 'em—and some rummy things, mark you, he did tell 'em ... The aggravatin' thing was I *liked* the bastard. We all did. You couldn't help it—there was something about him.'

Still more interesting, to me, was the testimony of Serjeant-Major 'Ox-gut' Childs, a 'regimental' type if ever there was one. When—with Pasquell's industrious help—I tracked him down, Childs was employed by an Urban District Council in their Parks Department, but no one would have failed to recognize the Regular soldier in the eyes which critically looked you up and down, the pistol-sharp responses, the ramrod bearing. Only by degrees did he thaw (as such men will) when he and I shared a congenial evening at the Maid of Wivenhoe.

'Remember him? I tell you, Mr Hushisson, I used to *dream* of that crackpot! Well, to start with now, you couldn't get a uniform to fit him, not a banana shape like him. And if you could, nobody could ever have learned him how to put it on. Or to march with his head up, or to swing his arm like any other human being. The way he did his puttees—crike! —you'd think he was dolling up the pillars of a holy church for the harvest thanksgiving. On top of that, we none of us knew any way to frighten him. I took him at the weapon pits myself one morning, taught him the handling of the Mills grenade, clear as could be. "You pull out this here pin," I tell him (like as you might be teachin' a kid of ten), "count three and bung it at the nearest Jerry—bloody quick, before it blows your own napper to Kingdom-come." "What, like this, Mr Childs?" he says, withdrawing the safety pin and cuddling the bomb, like it was a baby he'd just given birth to. "Chuck it—*out* of the pit!" I yell at him, going flat down on my face for the sake of my own wife 'n' kids. Nex' thing, there's the most almighty crack I ever heard out of the war zone, and when I screw myself to take a squint, there is oo8-Oh-Kennel with his tunic in rags an' tatters and his breeches and his under-drawers blown clean off him—not even *decent*, he wasn't then. With the grin still stuck to his face like the paint on a tart's kisser. "Och, did I scare you, now?" he has the farting impudence to say to me. "It's my weakness in arithmetic that made the trouble—I forgot for just the time being," he says, "what you kindly told me as to counting three"...

'Oh-Kennel, he got to be a byword an' a mockery in the whole Battalion. We'd be sitting in the Serjeants' Mess, resting ourselves with a wet an' a quiet game of rummy, and all on a sudden you'd hear a bang go off what shook the whole outfit like a farting earthquake—it came so regular we got to pay no attention. "That's oo-bloody-8-Oh-Kennel," someone'd say, "been trying his luck again with something he's been and nicked from the ammunition," an' we'd just carry on with the game. Or you'd see a bloody great tent come crashing down, which a new batch of recruits was messing in—frighten the poor buggers half out of their civvy minds. "That's the one Oh-Kennel had a hand in pitching," someone'd say—right every time. You got to hope and pray they'd send you out double-quick to the bleedin' War—it wasn't safe to be in a training camp, not with oo8-Oh-Kennel as part of the training...

'Mind you, he was all right on the range. That was a queer gift the good Lord gave him (and only the good Lord knows why), a sort of knack for shooting. Something near the best marksman in the whole Battalion. But I mean to say,

331

what's the good of being a First Class Shot if you're on a charge once a week for havin' a filthy rifle...

'You know, Mr Hushisson, a bloke like that, you can't do nothing with him. The Colonel stop me one day, passing the Orderly Room. He says, "Childs," he says (man to man, as it might be), "what are we to do with this Oh-Kneel" (the way he says the bloke's moniker) "before he wrecks the whole bleeding Unit?" "Transfer him, sir," I says straight off. "Put him in the Chinese Labour Corps." "I'll think of it," the Old Man says. "But you know, Childs, we might make something of him in the end, you and me and Captain Pasquell together. A fighting man, that's what we might make of him, if we ever got to the bottom of what's on his mind." Funny he should talk like that. Colonel Brayde, that was. Not one of your civvies dolled up, but a proper officer...

'I'll tell you another funny thing—we sort-of liked him, oo8-Oh-Kennel. I mean, all of us did. Nothing but a perishin' bloody headache, he was—drove us all near barmy, me specially. But you couldn't hold a grudge against the bastard. It's only the truth I'm telling you, Mr Hushisson—there was something about him.'

A study of Von Arnstein's 1915 dispatches reveals that Winckler, commanding his reserve brigade, had orders to capture and hold Saint-Sauvain not later than the 19th June, that village being the pivot where Bessonneau's advance towards the Valne could be rendered ineffective. A well-informed article in the *United Services Quarterly* makes it clear that Bessonneau (as was to be expected from a soldier of his calibre) appreciated the crucial importance of Saint-Sauvain but simply lacked the forces adequate for its defence, needing every available battalion for his essential thrust between Nichy and Louvaire. Certain obscurities remain; but it seems that the British commander in the adjacent sector, Boyce-Harvers, himself hard-pressed, detached a depleted battalion of the Cardigans to hold Saint-Sauvain in response to Bessonneau's desperate appeal. It was the north-eastern quarter which 'C' Company of that scratch battalion was detailed to defend. 'C' Company was commanded by Captain Dorman Frankland, a Norfolk man.

Frankland, when I traced him in 1934, was Branch Manager of a bank in Wymondham; a diffident, soft-voiced, extremely likeable person.

'It was the first action of any significance I was involved in,' he told me, 'and I did it badly. A case of faulty appreciation. The maps I had to work on weren't very good—or else I wasn't clever at reading them. Of course I was still a hopeless amateur, all on my own, and I had precious little time for planning. There was a road coming in from Parmêle, and I was convinced the first lot of Boches would come that way —I suppose a professional wouldn't have been so sure. But that road had to be sealed off anyway, which wasn't a simple problem with all the outlying buildings—and damned few men for me to play with. There was another road which curled in from the east of it, a very narrow, rough one, built I suppose to link the farms on that side. According to the map it went to Les Roubes, in a roundabout way. It looked as if a lot of it would be under observation from the high ground north-west of Euzailles, where the French had outpost positions—or so we were given to understand—so I thought it unlikely the Boches would make any use of that one. All the same, I did post a half-platoon to watch it, with a serjeant in command and two junior N.C.O's—one of them was that fabulous oddity O'Kneale. I picked some farm buildings for them to occupy, which I thought would give them a decent range of observation and what looked like adequate cover—there were barns and things with walls about eighteen inches thick. Well, that was my second outsize bloomer—it was the wrong position altogether. For one thing, it was too far out. Any trouble—which there was, plenty—and that detachment was too far off for me to reinforce them in a hurry, even supposing I had the men handy...'

A pardonably disjointed account of the actual engagement

333

came to me from another man of singular charm, Chris Howell, a native of Midhurst, who when I discovered him was working as a Charge Nurse in a hospital not far from where I live now.

'There were three of us,' Howell said, 'who the Serjeant had posted in the loft over a great cow-house, me and Davies and another chap I can't remember—it gave a good view along the road and the fields to either side. Well, I say it gave a good view, but there was a ground mist that morning, the sort you can get almost any time of year on low ground with a stream running through. That's how it was at first light, when Davies woke me, not long after he'd taken over the look-out, giving me my turn for an hour's kip. "There's something I seen moving near the road," Davies said to me, "a cow or something or it could be a couple of Jerries." "You'd best get over to the farmhouse." I said to him, "and report to the Serjeant"—the farmhouse was where the Serjeant had put himself, with most of the other blokes. "I'll stay here and keep a dekko on whatever it is you might have seen." Well, he wasn't hardly gone when this thing he'd seen started moving again, the way it wouldn't be any sort of animal, so I made up my mind it *was* Jerries, and I up and let them have one round from my rifle, just for luck, as you might say. And lucky it was, in one kind of way, because half what I saw falls down flat and lies like a log, and the other half goes skipping back out of sight in the fog. Well, after that it was quiet for a bit, and I made up my mind they were just two Jerries had lost their way in the fog and that was the end of it. And then all of a sudden there was one hell of a bang and a rumpus—shook the floor I was standing on—and I went to the window on the other side and when the smoke cleared off I see the farmhouse with a great piece carved out of the corner of it. About the same time there was a bullet come cracking through the window I'd just been looking out of and then two more.

'Just then—it must have been—Davies come back, crawling on his hands and knees, and says we're all to go back to the

334

main building—the one with the chunk torn off it—and we all three did that, taking trouble not to show ourselves, that I can tell you for sure.

'A dainty old mess we found when we got there, that I can tell you. Three of our boys dead as mutton, two more sitting against the wall looking as if they wished they *was* dead, the Serjeant himself lying in a pool of blood letting out a noise like a baby does when it has a colic in the night. And there in the middle of it was that long-nosed Irish joker, Corporal O'Kneale, with a stream of blood running all down one side of his face but the same great grin on his mug he always had.

' "You've put the backs up of them Jerries," O'Kneale says to me. "They're a type what objects to being fired at. They've got a mortar with them, farther back, or some such machinery. We'll need to handle them careful, a nasty-tempered mob like that."

'Well now, I was a corporal myself then, the same as him. Come to that, I was a bit ahead of him, in the way of promotion. But O'Kneale had taken over from the Serjeant and there it was—I wasn't objecting. Well, speaking frankly to you, sir, I was sick and scared so my brain didn't seem to be acting, and there come a time when something tells you plain as porridge who's the bloke to give the orders.

'He'd got three men posted where they got a view all round, and down below in what must have been the parlour one time he'd set old Dafydd Evans by the doorway, stuck in cosy among a heap of rubble what had tumbled down, with a Lewis gun they'd wished on us to keep us happy and content—a nice position that was, even I could see, where the gun would sweep the whole yard as far as the road, and O'Kneale keep tabs on old Dafydd through a hole the Jerries had kindly made in the floor where we were. "Now nobody's to fire," O'Kneale says, "till I give the word. We'll stay quiet and peaceful for the time being, to keep the buggers guessing. And when they're nice and satisfied the War's all over we'll use the stuff we've got to muck 'em about a bit."

'Well, that, more or less, was just what we did—just keep

335

ourselves to ourselves, for half an hour it might have been, maybe less, maybe more. But we was busy, mind. O'Kneale himself, specially. He had some dope he give the Serjeant to quiet him down, and he was tearing up whatever he could lay his hands on to bandage up the boys who'd copped one. The stiff ones he lugged off down to the dairy place at the back—they were getting on the nerves of the other boys, me included, the way they sort-of stared at you with eyes that didn't work any more. And all the time he was keeping up a line of talk, the way the Irish do, the same as if it was a birthday party he was in charge of. "Breakfast at eight, boys," he says. "Not before, because we're a wee bit short on the rations. There'll be a charge," he says, "for all these dainty bandages—I'll tell the Quartermaster-serjeant to make a tally in your pay-books. Nobody to smoke, mind, and you, Dafydd," he says down through the hole, "you keep your lovely blue eyes skinned, an' don't you dare touch that farting trigger till I give the word. Parkin, you take over from Two-nine-Jones now. Are you all fresh and cosy?" he says. "Any complaints to the Management—in writing, mind. Orders for breakfast taken at half past seven, except that everything bar the haversack rations happens to be off the bill of fare today."

'Well, outside there's still this ruddy mist, and as far as we could tell nothing happening any more. Myself, I was thinking the Jerries might have changed their mind and gone some other way. Then Parkin reports he got a sight of something moving, close by the cow-house where Davies and me had been, and then some more blokes creeping up to have a careful look-see round a shed beside the road. Next thing a bullet come through the window and take a small piece out of O'Kneale's right leg, and then another, and a bloke called Jenk Morgan who'd been a pal of mine falls down flat on his face and don't move any more. "Hold your fire, boys," O'Kneale says again, keeping his voice down low. "No shooting now, till I give the O.K.—only see your rifles is clean and smart, all of you," he says, still grinning the way he always did, "in case the Captain come on over to inspect 'em. And apologies to one and all," he says, like a caffy waiter might, "if breakfast come on half an hour late today."

'Well, the way I reckon—looking back afterwards—that bunch of Jerries manoeuvring round the farm didn't rightly know what was happening. They'd have seen clear enough they'd made a nice dirty hole in the place—could be they guessed our lot had made the best of a bad job and gone off and left it empty. And if that's right, they must have got a bit of a surprise packet before they settled down to enjoy their nice morning. There must have been a dozen of them—I was on the look-out job myself then—making their way cautious up one side of the yard, when O'Kneale goes to the hole in the floor and calls down, very quiet, like the teacher might say to a boy who's been kept in school, "O.K., Dafydd, you can let 'em have a burst now, only make it careful." Next thing, there was a rackety-bang that felt like it made a hole right through my ear drums, and the next thing I see seven or eight Jerries rolling on the ground like a bunch of drunks, and then all but two of them lying quite still and like you might say peaceful.

'That wasn't the end of it, though, by no means. They were in the other buildings now—there must have been a tidy score of them, all told—and they didn't take long returning our fire. Evans gives another burst on the loft where Davies and me had been, and they come back at us with their rifles. Say what you like about Jerries, they'd learnt their shooting like they'd been on the special course at Hythe. I copped one myself then—two, come to that, one in this shoulder which still give me gyp in wet weather and one that bust this bone down here, too near the privates for my liking —and that put me out of the War for the time being. I don't remember much after that. Only one thing I do remember, that was O'Kneale picking up my rifle. "If you're not using this I'll take a loan of it," he says. "I promise," he says, "I'll give it a nice clean-up for you when we knock off for the day."

'No, all I remember is it seemed to go on for hours and hours. The Jerry bullets keep arriving, and one after the other one of our boys keep copping one. I could see O'Kneale was limping worse and worse as he goes about, and his face look like something you only see in a butcher's window, but he keeps on talking friendly all the time. "Here, Roberts, d'you mind taking Corp Howell's place—looks as if he's resting.... I want the Lewis on the other side now, that'll maybe fox 'em ... Two-nine-Jones, there's a piece of the yard that side isn't covered, just you go and find a place down below where you can keep an eye on it—you'll have to shoot the best you can with your wrong arm. When breakfast is up I'll send to let you know." And all the time he'd be limping to the side of one window and letting off a round or two, and then picking up another rifle and hobbling on and doing the same thing from another look-out. The way I remember, looking back, it was like a queer sort of theatre piece, put on for a lot of poor buggers who'd got to spend the rest of their time-everlasting in hell.'

From Frankland I had some account of how the affair ended.

'The sounds gave us a vague idea of what was going on,' Frankland said, 'and about seven o'clock a runner O'Kneale had sent got through with a message. But it wasn't till nearly eight that I felt I could take a gamble with my main defence by sending a reinforcement—under a very good man— Serjeant Witherby. That was a waste of effort, as it turned out. By the time Witherby got through to the farm the Boche had skedaddled. A forward reconnaissance platoon they must have been, and it's likely they decided we'd set up our main defence on that side.... From the time the firing started, O'Kneale had held that position for most of two hours, and for the best part of that time he'd had exactly four men besides himself still capable of firing. He'd been badly hit himself, but that he didn't seem to have noticed. Witherby —he was a Regular, and one of the silent sort, as a rule— Witherby told me it passed all belief, the way O'Kneale had

338

worked the show. "I mean to say, sir, a man like that—what looks like a giraffe in uniform and can't even keep his rifle clean—running the whole circus just about single-handed, as you might say. And him a bleeding amateur—if you won't misunderstand me, sir."

'I made time to go to the farm myself just afterwards, along with a stretcher party. And I'll tell you a queer thing. I found O'Kneale limping about the yard, staring at the German corpses, as if they were a piece of his own property he'd smashed up through a piece of carelessness. "O'Kneale," I said, "you've done a damned fine job. We're proud of you." But he didn't seem to hear me. "I suppose this was my doing"—that was all he said, without turning his eyes away from the bodies. And it looked to me as if he was crying behind his face, the way a woman would.'

It goes without saying—Frankland being the conscientious officer he was—that he sent back a full report of Kevin's performance. (A part of what he wrote appears in an appendix to Gwilym Evans's *Story of a North Welsh Regiment*.) Accounts which went from mouth to mouth made a certain stir, even at that fevered time; there was talk of a possible decoration. But decorations are chancy, and that one didn't happen.

Later on the C.O. of the Battalion, a Colonel Griffith, made an awkward journey to visit Kevin in the Transit Hospital at Maubergines.

'Well, O'Kneale,' Griffith said, blowing benevolent clouds of cigarette smoke over the bed, 'you and I have generally met each other over some small bit of trouble. This time I've come to congratulate you.'

'Well, sir, that's a real kindness,' Kevin answered genially. 'I had the news myself only this morning. Eight and a half pounds—you can't do much better than that, sir, can you now!'

339

Griffith said afterwards, to Frankland, 'I never could make head nor tail of that fellah.'

The leave which followed was, broadly, like a million other leaves: intervals which start in rapture, to be dimmed progressively by the extending shadow of another parting. You say to yourself, as the days pass at increasing speed, 'It may not happen, some miracle may intervene.' But the voice of reason continues to assert, ever more loudly, that it is bound to happen.

A little of that experience Helma was able—years later, and still with painful effort—to recount to me.

'As a father,' she said, 'Kevin was almost like a mad man. He could not bear that his child should ever be out of his sight, for many hours he would watch her even when she was asleep. When she cried he was distracted—he thought she must be in some terrible suffering, sometimes I had difficulty to stop him from going to bring a doctor. All the cleaning work he did himself while he was at home—he said it was not right that one who had suffered the pain of childbirth must do the cleaning also. I think it troubled him sometimes that he had not the bosoms for feeding the baby as well.'

But yes, it had to come, the parting. That hour was one which Helma never spoke of—nor should I have cared for her to do so. To uncover ancient scars is to add to the sum of pain in human living, with no purpose.

The first of Kevin's letters after his return to France told her that he had been transferred once more to a new unit. 'With these boys,' he wrote, 'I am having quite a peaceful time, so I can think of you and our Cathleen all day long.' A fortnight later came the incident at Plouvières.

Plouvières: loosely, one could describe that marginal action (too small to rate more than a footnote in any standard history of the autumn campaign) as a repetition in reverse of the one that occurred at Saint-Sauvain.

Retreating to a prepared position north of Noucis, Schacht-meyer's division had as rearguard a barely adequate force commanded by the reliable Oberst Bautz. Bautz, withdrawing from Plouvières 'in parade-ground order', left a machine-gun detachment to hold as long as possible the Auberge Trumel, overlooking the only feasible route towards Vilard-la-Poigne. Since Collison's brigade was starved of artillery, the Trumel detachment did, in fact, delay the British vanguard for more than thirty-six hours. Thereafter Captain Austerley, an able officer (not burdened with excessive sensibilities), was ordered to destroy the post: for this task he detailed as assault party the equivalent of two platoons under a subaltern's command, with a serjeant and three other N.C.O.s—all he could afford—of whom Kevin was one; the remainder of his company he kept under his own hand, to act in support.

The party set out from Plouvières in the hours of darkness, the plan being to attack at first light. Half an hour or so after its departure, Austerley, working with his colour-serjeant in the stable which served for the time as his Company Head-quarters, looked up to see—with no small astonishment—Corporal O'Kneale standing before him in correct battle order except that he lacked his rifle. He said,

'O'Kneale, what the hell are you doing? What's happened?'

'I've come back, sir,' Kevin said laconically. 'I decided to fall out.'

'What d'you mean, you "decided"? You're not asked to decide things. Where's your rifle?'

'It's gone, sir.'

'"Gone"? You mean you've lost it?'

'I chucked it away, sir. I've decided I'm done with this business. I'm against killing people—I've done enough of that already.'

'What d'you mean, you bloody fool!' Austerley said. 'What do you think war is for, except killing people! And the

341

quicker the better, to get the bloody thing over.'

'That's not the way I see it, sir.'

'I'm not asking how you see it. What you mean is you've lost your nerve—is that right? Putting it in plain English, you've been given a job and you're funking it.'

'No, sir. You can think what you like. Only I'm done with killing people—Germans or any other.'

Austerley said: 'O'Kneale, you will go immediately to the Company store across the road and draw another rifle—you'll have to wake up Denby and give him a signature. You will then report back to me—within five minutes from now —and you will give me a solemn statement that you've put this bloody nonsense out of your head. After that you will go at double-quick time and report back to Mr Lawson and carry on with your duty.'

'I'm sorry to have to displease you, sir,' Kevin answered, 'but my own mind's made up—my mind and my conscience. I'm done with it, for good and all. It's right, what you're saying—the War just means killing people. So I'm done with it altogether.'

Austerley spared himself some five seconds to review the situation, unique in his experience.

'Very well!' he said.

Early next morning Kevin was sent back under guard to Battalion Headquarters at Vaucelle. It is unnecessary to dilate on Austerley's feelings at having—when his company was seriously under strength—to spare men for that purpose.

The battalion was under the temporary command of one Major Staines, in normal life a lecturer in Civics at Durham University (and later at Cambridge). Of Staines it was said that he 'never quite fitted the army pattern', but he was a person of rare versatility (as well as outstanding courage). It is characteristic of the man that he first interviewed the mutinous N.C.O. in his own quarter, with no one else present —devoting perhaps twenty minutes to the enterprise, on a day when his time and mental resource were not otherwise disengaged. Still more remarkably, he had the prisoner sitting down for that interview. He said, among other things,

'Listen, O'Kneale: you loathe the business of killing. So do I. I hate it like hell. But the simple fact is that you can't win a war without killing people. And you and I have got to win this filthy war—which the other side started—because if we don't the whole of Europe, which includes our own homes, mind you, is going to be overrun and held down for as long ahead as we can see by a race of incurable bullies—the most ruthless tyrants the world has seen since the time of Genghis Khan.'

'You might be right or wrong, sir,' Kevin said, as if in a philosophers' causerie. 'But it isn't in me to go on killing boys who don't look much different from myself, when you come to see them close.'

'Now look,' Staines said, 'you're talking as if you had an option, the same as you get in civilian life. Well, you just haven't—you've parted with your options. You're a volunteer soldier, same as myself. But when you joined you entered into a solemn obligation to obey orders. You can't go back on that—it's too late. You've used the word "conscience". One thing "conscience" means, if it means anything at all, is doing what you've promised to do—you and me and the rest of us. You've had the Army Act read to you—the bits that apply to Active Service?'

'Oh yes, sir. Captain Pasquell—that was my first officer—he wouldn't have neglected anything like that.'

'And you understood it?'

'Why, yes, sir. The way Captain Pasquell set it out, it was all quite straightforward. He was a great hand at the business, Captain Pasquell.'

'May be! But did he make it clear what's meant by "Desertion"? Desertion while on Active Service, I mean.'

Kevin faintly smiled. 'The Captain took a lot of trouble explaining that.'

'Then you know—because you're not a fool—that if you refuse to see reason, if you refuse to carry out what you've solemnly promised to do, it's my business to put you before

343

a Field General Court Martial.'

Kevin nodded. 'I know that, sir.'

'And if they find you guilty—as they're bound to do—you know what happens then?'

'Why, then I get shot, sir, surely.'

'Just so. I'm glad you understand that.'

Staines got up and went to the window. For a few moments he stared across the ruinous street at a group of soldiers who were laughing and ragging each other just as if they were in Hoxton market in their ordinary clothes. Returning, he said,

'You're a married man, aren't you, O'Kneale?'

'Yes sir. With one child, sir—a little girl.'

'Have you thought at all what it's going to mean to your wife and child when the news gets through? Your wife a widow, having to struggle on alone. Your child growing up without a father, *and* finding out by degrees—as she's bound to, sooner or later—that her father died in the deepest disgrace.'

Kevin said, 'If you'll believe me, sir, I've given a fair amount of thinking to that side of it.'

'But thinking hasn't altered your determination to go the way you're going—to die disgracefully?'

'There's different sorts of disgrace, sir. I know my own mind on that matter.'

Staines then pronounced the words which Austerley had used a few hours before, but with (I surmise) a less clipped, less acrid intonation:

'Very well!' he said.

In recounting (years later, in his room at Magdalene) that irregular conversation Staines told me that he really knew from the start he was wasting his precious time.

'Two things,' he said, 'were absolutely clear to me from the word "go". First, that O'Kneale was completely sane— a chap who could reason out an ethical problem just as soberly as I could. And secondly that he was utterly fearless. So there it was! With a man who's afraid of nothing in

344

Heaven or earth—or, more accurately, nothing and nobody on earth—well, there's simply not a thing anyone can do.'

At the Court Martial he was defended by Conrad McPhail (then an obscure staff officer) with predictable resource. The psychiatric terminology in common use today was then largely unknown; but McPhail argued that the accused had suffered, and continued to suffer, from a mental disorder so cardinal that he could not be held responsible for his actions. He reminded the Court of the prisoner's outstanding and valorous action at Saint-Sauvain; that experience, he said (and he procured a medical witness of some renown to support him), had been catastrophic in its effect on the mind of a man who was, after all, a mild civilian, unhabituated to any kind of violence, only lately put into uniform ... But such a thesis could carry little weight with serving officers who themselves had, mostly, lived quiet domestic lives before encountering, without derangement, the experience of battle —of the days and hours preceding the ordeal of battle and those which follow it. Moreover, the prisoner himself did nothing to substantiate the image of his mental state which McPhail was propounding. As Hugo Staines remembers, he looked—however singular his profile—a man of impregnable sanity. In answer to every question he spoke with a quiet composure, as one patiently trying to follow the difficulties of people incapable of solving a moral problem so conclusively as he.

When the President said, 'The findings of this Court will be made known,' no one present can have doubted what those findings would be.

There was, however, an abnormally long delay in the staging of the final act; a delay occasioned, in Staines's view, by the devious industry of publicists. A garbled account of the Court Martial got through to a local paper in County Mayo, and the editor, a passionate adherent to the Irish Republican Brotherhood, made the most of it. In a leader written with remarkable finesse (if with something less than strict attention to honesty or logic) he contrived to suggest that Corporal O'Kneale, who had fought one engagement with outstanding coolness and gallantry, was being victimized as a lesson to other Irishmen in total subservience to the British. That effusion might have passed unnoticed by anyone who counted; but it came into the hands of a Fleet Street man whose pungent articles were the mental fare of millions—one highly skilled in his craft (and adept in making rings round Section 27 in the Defence of the Realm Act). *Leo Britannicus* (to use the best known of his pseudonyms) was never wasteful of inflammatory material: he gave the subject what would now be called the full treatment. The Mayo leader was quoted almost in full, exuberantly headlined; paragraph by paragraph its innuendoes were rebutted; persons in high office, unnamed but shrewdly indicated, were then rapped over the knuckles for pusillanimity in their general handling of the recalcitrant Irish. This turgescence brought the expected rebound from citizens who dared to hold sentiments at variance with those of *Leo Britannicus*. There was a harvest of emotional letters. The *affaire* O'Kneale became—even in those days of alarm and crisis—a topic for amateur polemics in clubs, pubs and places where men expostulate. For myself, I largely discount the speculations with which lay-historians adorned the affair in later years: that long coded telegrams about O'Kneale passed between Haig and Robertson, that Robertson exchanged irascible Minutes with Kitchener, that the final decision was referred to a higher level still. None the less I believe that the repercussions of the *Britannicus* tocsin were a source of large anxiety in Whitehall; for the English are for ever jittery when the words 'Ireland' and 'political implications' are discovered side by side. Except for prolonging certain private agonies the commotion made no difference. What had to happen happened.

By pure coincidence—of an ironic sort—the arrangements

were under the overall supervision of that Colonel Brayde
who had been Kevin's first C.O. It follows, for anyone who
knew Brayde, that the details were ordered with scrupulous
care. For the firing party men were hand-picked from units
distant from any the condemned man had served in; they
were reliable marksmen, of a temperament not subject
to what are called 'nerves'. The officer in charge of the execu-
tion was able to report immediately afterwards that their
performance of the duty had been 'satisfactory'.

It was done on a drizzling January morning in an orchard
on the outskirts of Dubeil. On the sunny day when my wife
and I visited that place the pear trees were in bloom. The
high stone wall on the north side was so smothered by peach
blossom that it would have been hard to find the small area
of pitting which bullets may have made. At one side a very
large yellow sow (a replica, perhaps, of that Elisabet who
had brought a day of glory to the little town of Obervelden)
was rootling among the refuse of the previous year's crop,
noisily surrounded by a swarm of piglings; elsewhere a few
geese and hens foraged about the field with an air of tireless
dedication. It was a pleasantly untidy scene, very French, with
the breeze carrying a whiff of old wine casks; sublimely
tranquil. But we did not linger.

I believe it was Colonel Brayde who arranged that a Liver-
pool-Irish priest, Father Bernard Hogan, then serving as
Chaplain with a battalion of the King's Own, should be
with Kevin during the final hours. (That, again, would be
typical of Brayde; attention to detail, and something I dare
to call 'imagination', is built into some hardshell soldiers of
his kind.) By Father Hogan's account the prisoner, even in
the final minutes, showed no fear.

'He was pale, you'll understand, like a chap in convales-
cence—but then you don't look for rosy cheeks in a man
who's been under guard for weeks. There was a sort of peace-
fulness about him, even before he and I had done our busi-

347

ness together ... It seems as if he wasn't much in touch any more with the things around him, except for the small crucifix I had on me, which he seemed to find no ordinary sort of satisfaction—if you will understand me—in fingering and caressing ... Perhaps it's a queer thing to say to you, but I thought when I was with him, This is a fellow I'd have liked to have as my own son.'

He had spent much of his time in the last week writing letters, in his small, neat, rather pretty hand. (I have sometimes wondered what a graphologist would make of it.) What must have been much the longest, and most costly, was of course to Helma. That one I have never seen; almost certainly it still exists, but if it were laid before me I could never bring myself to read it. I possess the one he sent to his mother, full of tender thanks for all her care of him, reminding her repeatedly that she had other sons and many grandchildren. *'The loss of one bairn is a thing you'll come not to trouble over as time goes on.'* To my own parents also he addressed a letter of beautiful gratitude; adding *'If you could find the time just now and then to look in and see how my poor wife is managing, then you will increase my thankfulness for all your other goodness to me.'*

There were shorter missives, some bizarre in conception. To a Corporal Scourie, who at one period had shared the job of guarding him, he wrote: *'You'll remember, Ian, you and I had a bet together, you betted me ten bob they'd find some reason in the end not to shoot me. Well, it's myself who's won, only I had not the presence of mind to cogitate that if I won the bet I wouldn't be there to take the money. Let that be no worry to you, we won't let a mere financial calculation stand between you and me. I'd like you, Ian, to have those bobs, and many more if I was in a state to supply them, as a small remembrance for all the decency you showed me.'* Then, too, in a letter of warm affection to Fr Killalee he enclosed a note to be forwarded to Fr Sestino; in this he asked, very humbly, for Sestino's forgiveness *'for the injury I did to you at the time when you and I were out of personal*

348

agreement with each other'.

Among the papers which I preserve most carefully is another letter of his which seems to reveal the man's mentality in an interesting way—showing how his thoughts travelled to a future which (as far as anyone could tell) he himself could take no part in. It is quaintly addressed 'To the husband of my little Cathleen on her Wedding Day.' *'It will be a queer surprise to you,'* he wrote, *'to have a letter from a man whose corpse has been below the ground for some years now, but I hope you will forgive the liberty I take in writing, on a matter which has vexed my mind a great deal. You will know that my Cathleen, who now belongs to you, will have had to manage her childhood without the assistance of a father, and even with the perfect Mother she has they say that for any child the lack of a father is something of a disadvantage. Also it will be hard for her to find, as she must have done by now, that her father died in a way that most would say was shameful.'* (Was that an echo from his interview with Major Staines?) *'So I take the liberty to ask you, as a favour to a man you never knew, that you will give her such kindness in every way you can think of as will make up to her a little for the loss and painfulness which she has suffered. They say it's no easy thing to be a good husband, and only God Himself knows if myself has failed in that entirely. But what I'm asking you is that you will contrive in some way to be a father to my Cathleen as well, all the years you spend together, to take the place of what she had to do without when she was small. If you will do that, the best you can, you will earn a gratitude from me such as won't go into any words of mine. And in so far as I shall be allowed I will always pray for both of you.'*

It can be argued that the writing of that letter was not altogether fruitless. In the event, Cathleen married before she was twenty. She chose for husband a consummate egotist (like herself half-Irish); one who, with his many puerile vanities, could never earn enough to provide the material comforts with which so rare a woman ought to be surrounded.

But he did take Kevin's message seriously: within his fragile capacities he has tried to fulfil the congenial obligation it imposes.

Yes, I swear to you, Kevin, by all that you and I know to be holy, that—*Deo favente*—I shall never fail you in the charge you have laid on me.

Blechingley
1968-70